What people are saying about

# The Guardians

*"Jack [Cavanaugh] brings the Morgan family into the present with a gripping, fast-paced story I couldn't put down."*
—LIN JOHNSON, MANAGING EDITOR OF *CHURCH LIBRARIES* AND DIRECTOR OF THE WRITE-TO-PUBLISH CONFERENCE

*"Once again, Jack Cavanaugh compels you to keep turning the pages in this high-interest story following Ethan Morgan through his dangerous and risky journey to preserve his family heritage, the Morgan family Bible. This story contains valuable lessons for all of us as we strive to preserve our faith and pass on the truths of God's Word to the next generation."*
—PAUL AND SHERYL RUSSELL, FOUNDERS OF CHRISTIAN YOUTH THEATER

*"My students will continue to read Cavanaugh ... stories full of history, intrigue, and spiritual challenge. His plots and his characters fully engage his readers.* The Guardians *is a reminder of stories read, symbols analyzed, and situations not being what one might have expected!"*
—MELINDA MILLER, HIGH SCHOOL ENGLISH TEACHER AND ENGLISH DEPARTMENT CHAIR

"I will simply say … read *this book!* In addition to recommending Jack Cavanaugh's books, I have purchased them to give to others knowing how inspiring, uplifting, and enjoyable they are. The Guardians *is no exception. If you're looking for a story packed with action, mystery, and suspense, you must pick up this book."*

—LARRY BUBB, INTERNATIONAL SPEAKER,
RECORDING ARTIST, HUMORIST, TV SHOW HOST

*"Jack Cavanaugh is a master of narrative momentum. Spread over two continents, his characters become embroiled in murder, revenge, love, family legacies, and self-identity challenges. You definitely won't be bored!"*

—DENNIS E. HENSLEY, PhD, AUTHOR OF
HOW TO WRITE WHAT YOU LOVE AND MAKE A LIVING AT IT

*"I love a well-told story, and Jack Cavanaugh is a master storyteller. In his new book,* The Guardians, *he grabbed my attention at the very beginning with a mysterious murder and held it until the very last page. Somewhere in the middle, however, he also managed to remind me of the things that are of lasting value."*

—DR. RIK DANIELSEN, PASTOR AND AUTHOR

# THE GUARDIANS

# THE GUARDIANS

## JACK CAVANAUGH

David C. Cook

*transforming lives together*

THE GUARDIANS
Published by David C. Cook
4050 Lee Vance View
Colorado Springs, CO 80918 U.S.A.

David C. Cook Distribution Canada
55 Woodslee Avenue, Paris, Ontario, Canada N3L 3E5

David C. Cook U.K., Kingsway Communications
Eastbourne, East Sussex BN23 6NT, England

David C. Cook and the graphic circle C logo
are registered trademarks of Cook Communications Ministries.

This story is a work of fiction. All characters and events are the product of the
author's imagination. Any resemblance to any person, living or dead, is coincidental.

All Scripture quotations are taken from the *Holy Bible, New International
Version*®. *NIV*®. Copyright © 1973, 1978, 1984 by International Bible
Society. Used by permission of Zondervan. All rights reserved; and the
King James Version of the Bible. (Public Domain.)

LCCN 2007940814
ISBN 978-1-58919-100-6

© 2008 Jack Cavanaugh

The Team: Jeff Dunn, Steve Parolini, Theresa With, Jack Campbell, and Karen Athen
Cover Design: The DesignWorks Group, Tim Green
Cover Photo: ©PictureQuest

Printed in the United States of America
First Edition 2008

1 2 3 4 5 6 7 8 9 10

*To my father, William J. Cavanaugh,*
*and my uncle, James D. Cavanaugh*

*You taught us what it means to be brothers.*

# ONE

Death had no good reason being out on a night like this.

It was September warm. The Santa Ana wind had scrubbed the sky clean. The harvest moon cast a soft light. It was a perfect evening for a carefree stroll. Not a killing night at all.

From the backseat of a patrol car, through the wire mesh screen, Detective Ethan Morgan saw two things that didn't belong together—his house and a crime scene.

The media vultures were circling while his neighbors clustered in nervous pods on the sidewalk, pointing and whispering.

Ethan closed his eyes and took a deep breath, praying for the strength to face what awaited him. In his hand he clutched the program of an elementary school production.

### THE WORLD PREMIERE

OF

*An American Family Portrait*

A PLAY ADAPTED FROM THE GRAPHIC NOVELS OF

ANDREW MORGAN

He found it difficult to believe that just a short time ago he'd been sitting in a school auditorium bored out of his mind.

---

"Trust me. You're going to survive the night."

Ethan Morgan's knee was pumping up and down like a piston. Seated next to him, Meredith placed a hand on his knee to quiet it. He took a deep breath and told himself to calm down.

He checked his watch.

"I'm not going up there. I'm not going onstage," he insisted. "Sky promised me I wouldn't have to go onstage. Even if he doesn't get back in time, I'm not going onstage."

"Ethan, will you relax? He'll be here."

The houselights went down.

The audience hushed.

"All I'm saying," Ethan whispered, "is that Sky promised me I wouldn't have to do or say anything tonight. All I had to do was show up."

His leg started bouncing again.

A spotlight hit the crimson curtain, center stage.

Like a traveler stepping through a portal from the world of make-believe into the world of reality, a man slipped through the curtain. He was rail thin with baggy brown trousers, a long-sleeved pale yellow shirt, and an argyle sweater-vest. His reddish brown mustache twitched side to side as he cleared his throat.

A smattering of applause greeted him.

"That's Mr. Pandurski," Meredith whispered. "He's the sixth-grade teacher who approached Andrew about doing the play."

Ethan's eyes narrowed on the wretch responsible for this night of torture.

Mr. Pandurski adjusted his wire-rimmed glasses. The stage lights caught them at an angle so that Pandurski appeared to have blank Little Orphan Annie comic-strip eyes.

"Welcome to William Jennings Bryan Elementary School," Pandurski said with exaggerated enunciation. "Tonight, we take great privilege in presenting to you the world premiere of *An American Family Portrait*, a play adapted from the graphic novels of Andrew Morgan."

The audience applauded politely.

Meredith leaned against Ethan. "How does it feel to have a play written about your family history?"

"Uncomfortable."

Mr. Pandurski continued. "A little later in the show I'll introduce our guests of honor. It is our privilege to have with us tonight the author himself, Andrew Morgan; his lovely wife, Meredith; and his brother—his identical twin brother—Ethan Morgan, who is a detective with the San Diego Police Department."

Ethan groaned. This was shaping up to be the worst night of his life. "They can't drag me up there," he hissed.

Meredith's brow furrowed into a scowl. "Just hush. If you had brought the Bible in the first place, Andrew would be here now."

"I didn't forget it on purpose."

Mr. Pandurski clapped his hands and rubbed them together deliciously. "And now, sit back and enjoy the William Jennings Bryan not-ready-for-prime-time players as they perform *An American Family Portrait.*"

With a dramatic flourish he backed off the stage.

"Let the drama begin!"

The curtain parted.

The lights came up.

A black figure slipped silently from bush to bush. He paused to get his bearings. Everything was exactly as it had been described. The alley. The security light on the telephone pole. The fence. The layout of the backyard. The white clapboard house.

He had everything he needed to complete the job, including a semiautomatic with its registration number wiped clean. The only thing they hadn't provided was motive. Corby didn't need that. He had plenty of motive.

The overhanging eaves on the south side of the house were sufficient to conceal him. From the pouch of a shoulder bag he pulled a flat metal blade and jimmied the screen, then the window.

A rush of warm interior air spilled out. It smelled of fried potatoes.

He felt a wicked pleasure in knowing that a short time ago the cop had shoveled fried potatoes into his maw. Sort of like a prisoner's last meal before execution.

Corby surveyed the surrounding neighborhood for signs of anybody walking their dog or jogging by or taking an untimely peek out a window. Confident nobody had seen him, he hitched up his shoulder bag and climbed inside, his heavy work boots stepping onto a white linoleum kitchen floor.

Inside, he stood with his back to the wall, his right hand resting on the butt of the gun. He listened for sounds coming from the interior of the house. A man committing murder couldn't be too careful.

Satisfied he was alone, he closed the window.

A small stack of mail weighted down by a razor-blade letter opener, compliments of Sweet's Towing and Auto Repair, lay on the counter to his right.

The top letter was a bill. San Diego Gas and Electric. Corby examined the addressee.

        Ethan Morgan
        127 Copely Ave.
        San Diego, CA 92116

Corby grinned. He was in the right house and everything was going according to plan.

He crossed the kitchen floor. He spotted a frying pan, a single plate with ketchup on it, a fork, and a coffee mug stacked in the sink.

A doorway to his right opened to a dining area and beyond that the living room and front door. A hallway led to two bedrooms.

They'd told him Morgan lived alone. Corby checked for himself and found the house empty.

There was something about walking through another man's house when he wasn't there that gave Corby the willies. He would be glad to get out of there as soon as Morgan was dead.

The cop's lair was an old house with small rooms. The furniture had been purchased for comfort, not for entertaining. A worn recliner was situated a few feet in front of the television. Next to it was a small table with a lamp, a drink coaster, and a viewing guide folded open to last night's program list.

An overstuffed cloth sofa served as a room divider. A stack of newspapers and two stacks of magazines on the sofa indicated the cop hadn't had company for a while.

One piece of furniture in the living room didn't fit. From a distance, it appeared to be an old-fashioned accountant's desk, the kind a bespectacled keeper of ledgers would labor over while sitting on a high stool. Only the wood was too fine and polished for a desk, and the tilted flat surface on top wasn't wood, but glass.

Corby wasn't confused by its appearance. He knew exactly what it was, a museum-quality display case. He also knew exactly what the case had been built to display.

He peered inside.

"That's not right ..." he muttered.

It was the first piece of information they'd given him that was wrong.

"It's supposed to be empty."

But the case wasn't empty. Inside was an old Bible, laying open to Psalms, with elaborately drawn colorful vines cascading down the margins.

Corby stroked his chin, wondering what the presence of the Bible meant. He tried opening the case. It was locked.

For a long minute he stared at his reflection in the glass with the Bible in the background. He'd been told Morgan would have the Bible with him when he returned. As it was, all Corby had to do was have the cop unlock the case before he killed him. The result would be the same. Morgan would be dead, and Corby would have the Bible.

Satisfied that there was nothing to worry about, he positioned the recliner so that it was facing the front door and settled into it with the semiautomatic on his lap. From here, through sheer curtains, he could see headlights turning into the driveway and ghostlike images of anyone walking up to the front door.

A moment later, he was out of the chair and in the kitchen. He returned with a bag of potato chips, a package of chocolate cupcakes, and a soda.

Just as he was ready to settle again, a framed picture caught his eye. It was of a slim, attractive redhead standing between a pair of human bookends. Two identical males.

"Well, whattya know," Corby said. "There's two of 'em."

---

The setting for the first scene of act one was a boy's bedroom divided into equal halves with identical twin beds, nightstands, and lamps. However, that's where the similarities ended.

The bed on the left side of the stage had a San Diego Chargers bedspread with a huge lightning bolt. The walls surrounding it had posters of football players, mostly quarterbacks—Dan Fouts, John Elway, Dan Marino, and Joe Montana connecting with his favorite receiver, Jerry Rice.

The bed on the right had a large S-logo and the walls were plastered with posters of superheroes—Batman, Superman, Spider-Man, and the Teenage Mutant Ninja Turtles: Michelangelo, Leonardo, Raphael, and Donatello.

A ten-year-old boy sat on the lightning bolt bedspread tying his tennis shoes. A football rested against him.

The boy's mirror image entered the room from the superhero side of the stage carrying a white and pink plastic container. He moved to his mark, center stage.

"What do you want, super wimp?" the boy playing Ethan Morgan asked.

"I want to be the oldest," said the boy playing Andrew.

"Can't. I beat you by two minutes." Hoping off the bed, he grabbed the football. "Some things you just can't change."

"But you don't want to be the oldest."

"Who said?"

"You did. In Sunday school, remember? The teacher said that the firstborn son had special privileges and responsibilities."

"Tell you what," boy Ethan said. "I'll split it with you fifty-fifty. I'll take all the privileges. You take all the responsibilities."

The audience laughed.

"It doesn't work like that!" boy Andrew protested. "Your name is going to be written in the front of the Bible just because you were born first."

"Yeah? So what?"

"So, that means you gotta act all good and spiritual."

Boy Ethan sneered. "Does not."

"Does too, and you know it."

From the expression on boy Ethan's face, he did know it, and he didn't like it.

"Once your name's in the Bible," boy Andrew pressed, "you're responsible for the future of the Morgans. That's the way it's always been."

"Not any more," boy Ethan insisted.

"So let me do it."

"Do what?"

"Be the firstborn son."

Boy Ethan scoffed. "It's kinda late to change that."

"No, it isn't. Esau and Jacob were twins. Esau was the oldest, but he didn't want to be, so he sold being oldest to Jacob for a mess of cottage cheese."

Boy Andrew held out the white and pink container.

"All you have to do is eat the cottage cheese, and I'll be the oldest."

Boy Ethan took a good look at the container. "Yech! I hate cottage cheese."

Just then Mother walked onstage in a freshly ironed print dress.

"What are you boys doing?" she asked.

"I'm going to be the oldest," boy Andrew said excitedly.

"Oh?" said Mother, perplexed.

"Just like in the Bible. I'm buying it from Ethan for a mess of cottage cheese!"

Amusement registered on Mother's face. She hid a laugh. "I'm afraid you misunderstood, dear," she said. "You see, in the Bible, Esau sold his birthright to Jacob for a mess of pottage, not cottage cheese."

The audience laughed again.

"Told you we couldn't do it, dimwit," boy Ethan said.

"Ethan! That wasn't very nice! You apologize to your brother!"

"I'm sorry," boy Ethan apologized. "I'm sorry you're such a dimwit!"

The audience howled.

On the front row Ethan whispered to Meredith. "It didn't really happen that way."

"Shush and watch!" Meredith replied.

On stage Mother corralled a reluctant Ethan and Andrew together. Then Father walked in.

"I think it's time to tell the boys about their spiritual heritage," Mother said.

Boy Ethan groaned. "But the guys are waiting for me! We're gonna play football!"

In the audience Ethan whispered, "Now that part's true!"

"Shush!"

Father—who was much thinner and better looking than the real father—said, "It's an exciting tale, Ethan, of spies and Indians and pirates ..."

"Pirates!" boy Andrew exclaimed.

With the boys sitting at his feet and Mother sitting at his side, Father began to narrate the tale.

"The story begins at Windsor Castle," he said in a storyteller's voice, "the day Drew Morgan met Bishop Laud. For it was on that day Drew's life began its downward direction ..."

The stage lights dimmed on the family scene. A spotlight hit Mr. Pandurski standing on the other side.

"And so beings *An American Family Portrait*," he said, "a tale of a most remarkable family and …" He held up an oversized Bible prop. "… a most remarkable book—the Morgan family Bible."

———————

Andrew Morgan left the car door open.

In and out. That was the plan. Grab the Bible and get back to the school.

He considered leaving the engine running but thought better of it. His brother would never hear the end of it from his cop buddies if a car was stolen from his driveway with the keys in the ignition.

Slipping his keys into his pocket and starting to walk briskly, Andrew worked his brother's key ring until he located the key for the front door and the key for the display case.

Then he broke into a half run up the walkway, checking his watch. He'd checked his watch less than a minute ago when he pulled into the driveway. Just nerves, he guessed. It's not every night somebody puts on a play based on your family.

Unlike Ethan, the play excited him.

Ethan.

Although he'd defended his brother to Meredith, Andrew was certain Ethan had conveniently forgotten to bring the Bible with him just to have an excuse to leave.

If Andrew had allowed his brother to return home for the Bible, Ethan would have taken most of the show to do it. He would have gotten back in time to see part of the last act. Andrew had watched several practices and the dress rehearsal, so he wasn't missing anything. He wanted Ethan to see the play.

The shuffle of his feet echoed in the entryway as he inserted the house key into the deadbolt lock.

He pushed opened the door.

Startled, he said, "Who are you?"

# TWO

The stage flat had been painted to resemble the stones of an interior wall of Windsor Castle. An impressive array of medieval suits of armor lined the walls. One suit of armor stood out from the others.

According to the story, it was the only suit of armor that was actually inhabited by a person. However, given an elementary school drama budget, it was the only suit of armor that could have been inhabited by a person. The others were cardboard cutouts.

A bishop with a distinctive paunch led his whining servant to the door and made a pretense of exiting the room. He opened the door, then closed it, giving the impression he'd left. In reality, he tiptoed closer to the occupied armor.

The knight, thinking he was alone, leaned forward slightly, then took a cautious step away from the wall.

The bishop sprang forward. "Halt, sir knight!" he shouted.

Startled, the knight lost his balance and with flailing arms stumbled backward into the row of standing armor, which fell in dominolike succession.

The audience loved it.

"Do you really think it happened like that?" Ethan whispered to Meredith.

Meredith watched with amusement as the bishop helped the fallen knight to his feet.

"Life was so much simpler back then," Ethan continued. "Not like it is today."

"I'm not sure your ancestors would agree with you," Meredith replied.

"No, Sky's right. This is the stuff of comic books."

Meredith shook her head. "I disagree. The thing that attracts me to your family's story is that there's a ring of truth to it."

Ethan didn't budge. "I don't see it. There's no adventure to life anymore."

───────────────

A featureless shadow sat in the recliner, pointing a gun straight at Andrew.

Andrew stood motionless in the doorway, his brother's keys still in his hand.

"What do you want?" he demanded. A tremor in his voice weakened the question.

"Forget something, did you?" the intruder asked. No tremor in *his* voice. He sounded cocky. And why wouldn't he be? He was the one with the gun.

A hundred thoughts flitted around in Andrew's mind like moths testing the heat of a lightbulb. How many times had he drawn situations similar to this where his heroes came face-to-face with their mortality? The stories were never this intense though. Probably because the artist knew that in the next panel he'd draw his hero diving to safety while bullets zinged harmlessly past him.

Andrew inched backward. If he bolted, he could probably avoid one bullet, maybe two. But what then? He could never clear the yard or the walkway in time to escape. He almost certainly would take a bullet in the back.

The intruder rose from the chair. He was surprisingly small.

"Close the door," he said.

*Decision time. Run? Dive? Or do what he says? What I wouldn't give for a superpower right now.*

Taking a step into the house, Andrew swung the door closed, leaving it ajar just in case the chance to run presented itself.

"Look," he said. "So far, no harm's done. If you leave now, we can pretend this never happened."

The intruder took a step toward Andrew. His shadowy form took on features. A rough, pockmarked complexion. A scar over his left eye that severed his eyebrow in two.

"Oh that's rich," the intruder scoffed. "No harm, no foul. Is that it?"

"Something like that," Andrew said.

Another step closer and the gun picked up detail. Andrew had drawn enough guns to recognize it as a semiautomatic.

The intruder shook his head and cursed. "You don't recognize me, do you?"

Without turning around or lowering the gun, the intruder retreated to the chair and pulled something from his bag, which he flung at Andrew.

A midnight blue T-shirt flew at Andrew like a specter, hitting him in the chest. Andrew caught it and unfolded it. The print on the front of the shirt was that of the Nevada Outlaws, a professional football team.

Ethan would have understood instantly. It took a moment for Andrew to get the message. When he did, his heart sank. He was in greater danger than he'd first thought.

"The shooting in the parking lot," he said.

With surprising speed the intruder closed the gap between them and jammed the gun against Andrew's forehead. "That was my brother you killed!" he raged.

The intruder thought he was Ethan.

While the realization came as no surprise, it presented Andrew with a dilemma. Reveal his true identity or keep it a secret?

"Roger Corby," Andrew said.

"My brother!" Corby shouted.

*Should I tell him?*

If he told him, what would Corby do? What would stop him from killing him, and then killing Ethan when he came looking for him? What if Ethan brought Meredith?

Andrew decided to pretend he was Ethan.

"Your brother tried to run me down," Andrew said, assuming the role of his policeman brother.

"My brother was unarmed!" Corby shouted.

"He tried to run me over with a truck!" Andrew countered. "He was on a rampage in a crowded parking lot. What else was I going to do? He gave me no choice. I had to stop him before anyone got hurt...."

"Yeah? But you didn't, did you?" Corby sneered. "Because of you that kid died."

Andrew felt his brother's pain. He remembered how depressed Ethan had felt after the shooting. While he'd saved countless lives that day, one teenage boy who had gone to see a football game went to the morgue instead.

"Your brother gave me no choice," Andrew said, echoing the words and the tone his brother used when describing the incident. "I did what I had to do."

"And now I gotta do what I gotta do," Corby said. He walked over to the display case. "Open it."

Perplexed, Andrew asked, "What do you want with a Bible?"

---

Ethan angled the face of his watch to the stage lights, then turned and scanned the back of the room for his brother.

"He's probably eating all your chocolate cupcakes," Meredith said with a smirk.

"Andrew's not stupid. He knows if he touches my cupcakes I'll hunt him down like a dog."

On stage a generation had passed. The Morgans and their family Bible had survived the treachery and persecution of Bishop Laud, a tempestuous Atlantic crossing, and disease and starvation in the New World.

A new scene appeared. At one end of a cornfield stood a wooden tower with an open platform where a pretty Indian maiden sat guarding the field from crows.

Unseen by her, a male colonist sneaked into the cornfield. He stared at the maiden. His infatuation was obvious.

While maneuvering to get a better view of her, he rustled a stalk. The maiden instantly sprang to her feet and let loose a salvo of well-aimed rocks.

"Ow! Ow! Stop! It's me, Philip!" the colonist cried.

Meredith leaned against Ethan. "Generations come and generations go," she said, "but Morgan men remain the same."

"You have never and will never see me wearing a goofy expression like that," Ethan protested.

"Put a Morgan man in breeches, a uniform, or a suit and tie, and the story's the same. They're suckers for wide, innocent eyes and a sharp tongue."

"I don't know about the innocent eyes," Ethan said, "but Sky certainly married a sharp tongue."

---

Corby waved the gun casually. "We can do this the easy way or the hard way," he said. "Toss me the key, or I kill you and fish it out of your pocket."

Ethan's key ring sailed between them. Corby snatched it out of the air.

He didn't have to ask which key unlocked the case. An unusual lock requires an unusual matching key.

The glass top swung open on gold hinges.

"Put the T-shirt on," Corby said.

"Why?"

"Just do it. Put it on under your dress shirt."

Andrew didn't move. Corby stared at him until he began unbuttoning his shirt.

"It's not worth as much as you think," Andrew said as Corby prepared to extract the Bible. "It's damaged."

The Bible proved heavier and more unwieldy than Corby anticipated. Lifting it out of the case would require two hands. He set the gun aside without regard to Andrew who was too far away to pose a threat.

"Turn it over," Andrew said. "You'll see I'm telling you the truth."

Corby examined the bottom of the Bible. "Looks like someone shot it," he said.

A sizeable gash penetrated the back cover and several hundred pages into the text.

"Flak over Nazi Germany," Andrew said. "One of my ancestors was a B-17 pilot. That Bible saved his life."

Corby seemed fascinated with the gash. "Too bad it won't do the same for you," he said matter-of-factly. "So how much is it worth?"

Pulling off his dress shirt, Andrew worked his arms into the sleeves of the T-shirt. "That Bible's been in my family for four hundred years," he said.

"How much?" Corby barked.

Andrew shoved his head through the neck hole of the shirt and pulled it over his chest and belly.

*The things I do for my brother,* he thought.

"There are fewer than two hundred original printings of the 1611 King James Bible," he told Corby. "Five years ago one sold at a Sotheby's auction for $400,000."

"That's almost a half a million dollars!" Corby shouted.

"No! You haven't been listening to me. That copy is damaged and worn. It won't bring nearly that much."

Corby wasn't listening. He gazed at the book in his hands with avaricious eyes.

Andrew tried putting the pieces together. Corby knew that Ethan would be out of the house. His comment about forgetting something indicated he didn't expect Ethan to return so soon. Was his original plan to break into the case and steal the Bible? That didn't explain the T-shirt and all the talk of revenge over his brother's death. And he didn't know the value of the Bible.

"I doubt you could get fifty dollars for it at a pawnshop," Andrew said. "To get the kind of money you're thinking of, it would have to be auctioned by a reputable dealer. No reputable dealer is going to touch it once it's reported stolen."

Corby was nodding his head as though he'd come to a conclusion.

"Tell you what I'll do," Andrew said, buttoning his dress shirt. "I'll give you half a million dollars to put the Bible back in the case and walk out of here."

Corby scoffed. "What kinda fool do you take me for? Cops don't have that kinda money."

"I can get it. My brother's rich."

Corby thought about the proposition for a moment. He shook his head. "Nice try, Morgan. Now finish buttoning your shirt so I can kill you."

Meredith flipped shut her cell phone.

"He turned it off," she said. "He didn't want it ringing during the performance."

Ethan stood in a corner of the open patio, partially concealed by a tree in a planter, clutching a half-empty cup of punch.

It was intermission. People mingled under the stars on a September evening, drinking punch, eating cookies, and frequenting tables that promoted the school's art department and displayed an array of Andrew Morgan's graphic novels. The eight-book set of his American Family Portrait series was featured prominently.

Meredith looked worried.

From behind her a small Filipino woman, barely five feet tall, approached. She was wringing her hands. Ethan couldn't remember the last time he saw anyone actually wringing her hands.

"Mrs. Morgan," the woman said, pleadingly, "your husband promised he would—"

She spotted Ethan.

"Oh, there you are! Mr. Morgan, you promised to sign your comic books at the book table, remember? As you can see there's quite a line."

"Graphic novels," Ethan corrected her.

"Excuse me?"

"They're graphic novels. Not comic books."

The woman flushed. "Very well … but as you can see …"

"You have the wrong Morgan," Ethan said. "I'm the cop."

"Oh."

"You want Sky."

"Sky?"

"That's Ethan's nickname for Andrew," Meredith interjected. "Unfortunately, Mrs. Dubai, my husband isn't here. He went to get the Morgan family Bible and hasn't returned yet."

"Oh my," Mrs. Dubai said, wringing her hands harder. "He promised to sign his com—graphic novels."

"I'm sure he'll be here any—"

"It's my fault," Ethan inserted.

Mrs. Dubai blinked her eyes at him.

"I was supposed to bring it. The Bible. It was my responsibility. I'm the oldest. The one who hates cottage cheese."

"I see."

"So blame me," Ethan said.

"Well, I'm sure you didn't mean to forget it."

"Yeah. I did."

"Oh my."

This time Meredith physically stepped between Mrs. Dubai and Ethan. "Just tell everyone that Andrew will be glad to sign their books after the performance. He'll stay for however long it takes. Everyone who wants one will get a signature, Mrs. Dubai."

"I just had a thought …" Mrs. Dubai said.

Her head appeared from behind Meredith as she addressed Ethan.

"… could his brother sign books in his absence? You look exactly alike. Who would know?"

"I would know!" Ethan snapped. "Besides, that's forgery! I could run you in just for—"

Her head darted back behind Meredith.

Ethan's voice had carried across the patio. Clusters of people were staring at them.

"Mrs. Morgan, I didn't mean to suggest ..."

"Of course not, Mrs. Dubai. Just tell everyone Andrew will be back soon."

Meredith whirled around. "Ethan! That was uncalled for!"

"What? It's fraud," Ethan protested. "What if there's a collector in the crowd? We could all be sued. She was trying to enlist me in a conspiracy to commit an illegal act. I have half a mind to slap cuffs on her."

He was having fun with this; the first fun he'd had all night. Meredith didn't appreciate his levity. Her mind was on Andrew.

Ethan looked around for a place to put his punch cup. When he couldn't see one, he set it in the tree planter.

"I'll go see what's keeping him," he said.

He started to leave. Meredith grabbed his arm.

"You stay. I'll go."

Ethan started to object, but she cut him off. She was already pulling keys from her purse.

"You and Andrew are the celebrities tonight. At least one of you should be here."

"I'm not a celebrity," Ethan objected. "I don't want to be a celebrity."

"Tonight you are," Meredith insisted. She had that motherly tone, the kind they use when they're forcing you to eat your peas. "I'll be back shortly."

"That's what Sky said," Ethan said.

He watched her leave.

"I'll stay," he muttered. "But I don't have to like it. And I'm not going up on that stage."

A three-foot-tall actor wearing a suit of armor made of paper tubes and construction paper waddled across the patio ringing a hand bell. People pointed, laughed at how cute he was, and began migrating back to the auditorium.

Ethan made his way to the front row, noting the stares, whispers, and smiling nods of the audience. He never felt this uncomfortable even at a job-performance review.

The house lights dimmed.

The audience hushed.

Ethan folded his arms.

Mr. Pandurski split the curtains as he had at the opening, his mustache working back and forth as though it was brushing his teeth.

"Before we start the second act of *An American Family Portrait*," Mr. Pandurski enunciated, "as I mentioned at the beginning of the show ..."

"Oh no ..." Ethan muttered.

"... we are privileged to have with us tonight ..."

"Please, no ... please, please, please, no ..."

"... two Morgan brothers who are direct descendants of the very people whose inspiring story you are watching tonight."

Ethan wasn't the kind of man who believed in miracles, but that didn't stop him from praying for one. He looked desperately to the back of the room, then to the side doors, then craned his neck to see into the stage wings, hoping, praying, that Sky had returned in the nick of time.

"While I understand we have only one brother with us at the

moment—the other brother is preparing an even bigger surprise for us after the show—let's give a big round of applause for Mr. Ethan Morgan!"

Ethan slumped in his seat.

They were applauding him. Why were they applauding him? And they weren't stopping. Why weren't they stopping?

Mr. Pandurski slid along the front of the stage until he was directly in front of Ethan. He motioned with open hand at Ethan.

The applause increased.

Ethan shook his head at Mr. Pandurski. *Don't do that. Please, don't do that,* he pleaded silently.

A spotlight hit him, and Ethan could see a silhouette of his head and shoulders against the base of the stage.

The applause continued unmercifully.

Mr. Pandurski urged him to stand.

It was all Ethan could do to keep himself from pulling out his service revolver and ordering Mr. Pandurski to back off.

---

Andrew lay prone on the floor, his cheek pressed against his brother's living-room carpet. The acrid odor of gunpowder hovered over him like a departing soul. Numb from the shock of having four bullets pumped into his chest, he thought it humorous.

*Overkill. Two bullets would have done the job.*

He felt tired ... so very tired.

Beneath him the carpet felt wet and warm.

He could hear his killer moving about the room but couldn't see him, couldn't stop him.

Breathing was becoming increasingly difficult.

He thought of Meredith. Tears came to his eyes. He loved her more than he'd ever loved anyone. He loved her even knowing she didn't love him, that she had never loved him.

Ethan. This was going to be hard on him. He was going to blame himself.

*Be strong, Ethan. It's not your fault. It's good that it was me and not you.*

Andrew winced as an invisible fist seized his heart with a death grip.

*I wish I could … I wish I could … tell you.*

Andrew moaned a breathy, dying moan.

An idea came to him. But did he have time?

He rocked his hips slightly to one side and reached for the cell phone attached to his belt. He managed to get his hand on it. It slipped out of his hand. He tried again. It slipped again. The holster gripped the phone like a tightened vise.

How many times had he played quick-draw, unholstering the phone like a six-shooter, flipping it open and answering with one continuous motion?

But now … now … the simple task seemed impossible, his fingers slippery … slippery with his own blood, his strength waning with each shallow breath.

"I'm … going to do this … if it's the last … thing … I … do," he muttered, pleased with the humor. Humor meant his brain was still functioning.

The phone came free of its holster.

A haze, like a white fog, clouded his vision as he lifted the phone close to his eyes. He fought to focus, summoning the last of his strength to complete this final task.

It took two hands for him to open the cell phone, then one hand to hold it while the other pressed the buttons.

4-3-1.

The effort nearly exhausted him. He paused to rest, then scolded himself for it. There was no resting. Resting meant dying.

Now he couldn't remember the number sequence. What was it? Think. Think! 4-3-1 … what?

1-6.

Yes! Then what?

He was running out of everything—strength and time and life. Air no longer filled his windpipe. Liquid did.

He pushed 1 again. His finger slid across the keypad leaving a red trail. It found 7. He pushed it.

"Hey! What's this?" a voice shouted from above him.

A black boot kicked the phone out of Andrew's hand.

Andrew watched it spin and skid across the carpet.

It didn't matter. He did it. He only hoped Ethan would get the message.

He could no longer focus his eyes. Darkness closed in on him, narrowing his vision like the white gray image on an old 1950s television screen shrinking to a single dot in the center.

He stared at the wooden table leg next to Ethan's recliner as his vision faded, then blinked out.

Memories were the only things remaining alive. He clung to an image of Meredith. A happy one. She was smiling coyly at him, back in the days when he mistakenly thought she loved him.

And then it, too, cut out.

# THREE

Ethan Morgan slumped in his front-row seat, grateful to be out of the spotlight. He swore to himself that he would get even with Sky if it was the last thing he did.

The second half of the play began with twin brothers arguing, the only set of twins in the Morgan line until Ethan and Andrew.

In a dank prison cell during the Revolutionary War, Jacob Morgan, a colonial patriot, had been captured as a spy and was to be hanged. Esau, his twin, had just drugged his brother and was switching his brother's shoes so that they were on the wrong feet in an elaborate ruse to fool the guards into thinking the prisoner was attempting escape. If all went as planned, Esau—a British sympathizer—would hang in his brother's stead.

Stifled sniffs popped here and there behind him as the audience got caught up in the scene of one Morgan offering his life for his brother.

For Ethan, it was just another scene of glorified drama.

*Meredith is wrong. Reality isn't glamorous.*

———————

Something wasn't right.

Meredith steered her car to the curb in front of Ethan's house and turned off the engine.

She noticed Andrew's car door gaped open in the driveway.

The door to the house stood ajar.

It was dark inside.

Even before she reached the front door, she was calling her husband's name.

"Andrew?"

No answer.

Slowly she pushed open the door.

"Andrew?"

The living room was dark. Her gaze immediately went to the display case on the far side of the room. It was open. She could see the Bible was gone.

"Andrew," she said again, stepping farther inside.

As she rounded the end table beside the sofa, she saw a pair of shoes on the floor, soles toward heaven. She saw ankles. Legs. Blood.

"Andrew!"

Her purse slipped from her fingers and landed with a thud. She fell to her knees, her husband's blood soaking her stockings and the hem of her skirt.

Andrew lay motionless, his eyes and mouth open.

Meredith sobbed. "Andrew ..."

She put a hand on his back and felt no life in him. His cell phone lay open on the floor a few feet away.

At that moment Meredith realized whoever had done this to Andrew might still be in the house. The realization came a second too late.

Out of the corner of her eye she saw a pair of black work boots. She swung around to face him, staying low, like a jungle cat protecting her own.

A smallish man with a bad complexion and an amused grin stared down at her. In one hand he held a gun. In the other hand he clenched the Morgan Bible.

"You're the broad in the picture," the killer said, pointing to the frame with the gun.

"Who are you?" Meredith cried. "Why have you done this ... this ...?"

Her mind refused to take it in.

"This is your unlucky day, lady," the killer said. "Two more minutes and I would have been gone and you would have lived to see another day."

*Keep him talking*, Meredith told herself. *Talking isn't killing.*

She inched backward.

"What's he to you?" the killer asked. "Are you his sister or something?"

"I'm his wife."

"Wife! You're his wife?"

Meredith kept inching.

"How could they have missed you? Baby, you're too good-looking to be the wife of a cop."

Inching. Inching.

"I wish you were here earlier. It would have been sweet to waste you with him watching, so the last thing he saw was his old lady getting whacked. Oh well. It's all good. He's dead. You're dead."

He raised the gun.

Meredith leaped to the end of the sofa, making her way to the door. He countered her move. She'd hoped he would. To do so he had to pass by the opposite end of the sofa. When he did, she shoved the sofa with every ounce of strength in her.

The sofa slammed against the end table which plowed into his kneecaps. With an animal-like howl, he stumbled backward, tripping, losing his balance, and landing on his tailbone.

Meredith bolted for the front door. She thought she was going to make it.

But he was quick. Too quick. At the threshold the killer grabbed a fistful of her hair and yanked her back inside. He threw her against the sofa.

Her back cracked as she hit, knocking the wind from her. She tumbled across the sofa's cushions, scattering magazines and newspapers, and rolled over her dead husband before landing atop her purse beside him.

Walking stiffly, the gunman rounded the sofa, pointing the gun at her head.

Meredith looked up. The gun was inches from her face. She bowed her head, unable to look.

"Just leave," she sobbed. "Just leave."

As she pleaded, she wormed her hand beneath her and into her purse.

"That was a stupid thing to do, lady," the killer said, his chest heaving as he fought back the pain. "I was just gonna waste you, you know? Short and sweet. But now I'm gonna hurt you. Then I'm gonna mess you up. I'm gonna mess you up so bad your momma wouldn't recognize you."

"Please," Meredith whimpered. "Don't ... please ..."

Her hand dug deeper in the purse. Searching ... searching ... searching...."

He took a step closer to her.

Meredith knew she had only moments to live. Any second now she expected to hear the report of a gun and feel hot bullets ripping into her.

"Please don't ... please don't ..."

Her hand found what it was searching for. A canister.

She raised her head.

The gun was an inch from her nose.

She looked past it into the eyes of the killer.

"Please ..." she pleaded.

The canister was out of the purse.

It was just like one of those old Westerns. Who was faster? Who would outdraw whom?

A stream of liquid fire hit the killer in the face.

He howled in pain. Staggered backward. The Bible dropped to the floor as his hands flew to his face. In his pain, he'd forgotten he had a gun in one hand. He clonked himself in the forehead with it.

He was reeling now.

Meredith was on her feet. Closing. Her finger pressing the canister button, keeping the stream going until it was empty. Tossing it aside, she grabbed the lamp from the end table, yanked the cord from the wall socket, and began using the lamp as club, whacking the killer repeatedly.

He stumbled backward. She advanced with increasing fury.

The killer flailed wildly, hitting only air.

Meredith didn't stop when the lampshade flew off. She didn't stop when the lamp broke in two. The two pieces held together by the electrical cord inside became nunchakus, which she used to continue her wild barrage of blows.

He hit the wall.

She planted her feet and continued wailing on him.

Then, he got in a lucky blow. A backhand, the one with the gun, slammed against the side of Meredith's head and knocked her senseless.

She flew backward, hitting the sofa with such force her back bowed. This time instead of tumbling over it, it threw her forward. She hit the floor hard, facedown.

Stunned. Defenseless.

Raging, the killer bumped into one wall after another like a madman, unable to keep his eyes open for more than a half second.

He had just enough presence of mind to snatch up the Bible and stagger out the front door.

Meredith remained sprawled on the floor for a couple of minutes before she was able to work her way onto her hands and knees, crawl around the couch, and fish her cell phone from her purse. She sat on the floor phone in hand, more than stunned, more than winded. The fall onto the floor had done some damage. She could feel it.

Taking a breath, she fought back first pain, then panic.

Her thumb paused over the buttons on the phone.

On her speed dial list was ICE Ethan.

ICE.

In case of emergency.

She hesitated. Call Ethan or dial 911? It was pretty much the same, wasn't it? But hadn't Ethan turned his phone off for the performance?

Andrew's head was inches from her knee. She touched his hair with her free hand.

She dialed the phone.

"It's me," she said. "Andrew's ... Andrew's dead ... I'm hurt, but all right ..." She stifled a sob with the back of her hand. "The killer ... he got the Bible.... I don't know, I ... I don't know ... I can't think right now ... no, I don't think so ... yeah ... I'm calling now...."

Meredith hung up and dialed 911.

---

Everyone was standing and applauding. Ethan stood with them, clapping politely while wishing everyone would just go home.

Two girls in frilly dresses appeared onstage, smiling like miniature beauty contestants. One held a pink carnation boutonniere. On the tip of her toes she danced across the stage until she was directly in front of Ethan.

He moaned. Would this nightmare ever end?

Suddenly, Ethan realized he wasn't alone. A woman appeared from nowhere, took the carnation from the little ballet dancer, and pinned it to Ethan's lapel. The woman smelled heavily of breath mints.

Mr. Pandurski appeared. Mr. Bad News himself. Not only was the nightmare not going to end, it was getting worse.

"Britanny … Rachel …" Pandurski said, "why don't you escort our guest onstage."

Ethan's heart lurched into his throat. He shook his head, declining. Vigorously declining.

"Really … thank you … no …" Ethan said to Mr. Pandurski, to the girls, and to the lady who smelled of breath mints.

Pandurski addressed the audience. "I think Mr. Morgan needs a little encouragement."

The applause grew louder.

Ethan took a good hard look at the man standing on the stage, memorizing every detail of his smiling, mustached face, because if ever he saw that face on the street, he was going to pull him over and find some reason—fabricate it if necessary—to run him in. And on that day, Ethan would take great delight in introducing Mr. Pandurski to *his* world.

The tutu-clad girls took Ethan by the hands and pulled him to the steps that led onstage. They might as well have led to a scaffold.

The spotlight dogged him from seat to stage making it difficult to see the steps. He stumbled on the last step and almost fell onto little Britanny or Rachel, one of them anyway. Only at the last second did he catch his balance and keep from flattening a future Miss America.

The girls led Ethan to center stage.

"Ladies and Gentlemen," Mr. Pandurski announced. "You have been watching a reenactment of scenes from the Morgan family history. It is my pleasure to introduce to you the real McCoy! Mr. Ethan Morgan!"

Ethan stood helplessly onstage, his hands dangling conspicuously at his sides like two hams on string. His feet were concrete blocks. With the spotlight in his face he couldn't see the people who were applauding him. He had but a single thought: Get off this stage.

The entire cast of *An American Family Portrait* came from backstage and surrounded him. The applause got louder. Ethan wished they'd just go home.

But as much as Ethan hated being onstage, Pandurski loved it.

"Ladies and Gentlemen," Mr. Pandurski said. "At this time it had been our plan to conclude the evening with a rare and very special appearance of the real hero of tonight's show, the authentic Morgan family Bible."

A collective gasp rose from the audience. You would have thought Pandurski had just announced a surprise appearance by Billy Graham, or the president, or Johnny Depp.

"Unfortunately …"

Mr. Pandurski stretched the word for emphasis.

"… it seems that while the Morgan Bible has survived a treacherous Atlantic sea voyage, been hidden by native American Indians, crossed lines during the Revolutionary War, and survived not only the Civil War, but a westward migration across the continent, World War I, World War II, and the Vietnam conflict … in short, while it has survived four hundred years of American history … it has not yet made the five-mile trip from Normal Heights to here."

The audience laughed.

"City traffic," Ethan said, and then wished he hadn't.

"So while we will *squelch* our personal disappointment … in the spirit of the evening, we would like to present to Mr. Ethan Morgan, a replacement for the Morgan Bible until such time as he can locate the missing original."

A small boy walked onstage carrying the prop Bible from the production. He handed it to Ethan.

The prop Bible was surprisingly heavy. Upon inspection, Ethan saw why. It was made out of a laundry detergent box ... and the detergent was still in it. A few white and blue granules fell onto his shoes.

Ethan thanked the boy and the clapping children surrounding him with as much kindness as he could muster.

"It's not lost," he insisted. "Our family Bible. It's not lost. It's just ... for some reason, Andrew was delayed."

From the wings, a woman stage-whispered something about another surprise. Ethan grimaced.

The houselights came up, and through the haze of the stage lights, Ethan saw the back doors to the auditorium open. It would be just like Sky to show up now and prolong his agony.

But it wasn't his brother. It was two uniformed police officers. Ethan recognized both of them.

They talked to an usher who pointed at Ethan onstage.

The officers spotted him. Their expressions told Ethan that they weren't here to see the play.

"Excuse me," he said.

Mr. Pandurski blocked his retreat from the stage. "Wait ... we haven't ..."

"We're done here," Ethan snapped, pushing past him.

He made his way through actors and crew and stage mothers and a kid dressed in some kind of bird costume holding a pillowcase.

Ethan charged down the steps to the front of the auditorium, then up the aisle. The police officers intercepted him halfway.

"What's up?" Ethan asked.

Neither one of them could look him in the eye.

That's when Ethan knew his brother was dead.

# FOUR

A metal screen separated Ethan from Officers Mitchell and Cisneros as they drove him home in the back of their patrol car. Orders, they told him. At first Ethan refused. He could drive himself. Then he remembered he didn't have his keys. Andrew had taken them.

The plastic on the backseat of the patrol car was dirty, sticky, and smelled of vomit. The screen was worse though. For all of Ethan's professional life, the screen had been a barrier separating men at work from criminals and victims. He was sitting in the victim's seat.

Victim. He didn't wear the word well. Victims were magnets that attracted sympathy and attention, emotions that made Ethan uncomfortable. Victims were too often prey, dupes, poor devils who didn't see it coming or who were too weak to defend themselves.

Repositioning himself, Ethan put his hand in something sticky. He tried to wipe it off with his handkerchief.

Since leaving the elementary school parking lot, neither Mitchell nor Cisneros had spoken a word. Not to him. Not to each other. The silence was broken every few minutes by the feminine voice of the Mid-City dispatcher:

> *415/314 coming in. Intersection of Texas and Meade in regards to a homeless male camping out on the sidewalk in front of Valley Liquor and threatening customers.*

> *811 John/814 John ... 415DV holding at Las Palmas Apartments, 2504 Polk Avenue. Physical 415 between husband and wife. Manager calling in. No further information.*

> *All units. Information on reckless driver. 3000 block of University Avenue. Last seen heading eastbound. Three teenagers in a light blue Mitsubishi Eclipse, license plate unknown, weaving in and out of traffic, cutting people off, making rude gestures.*

> *826 King. If you can start for a narcotics call, corner of Park and Meade. Two white males in their twenties wearing all dark clothing, dealing unknown narcotics. No further description.*

Routine calls for Mid-City. With each call the assigned unit responded accordingly.

Earlier it wasn't so routine when Ethan's house number and street had aired.

*Shots fired. Possible homicide.*

"Andrew ..." Ethan spoke his brother's name without realizing it.

He caught Mitchell staring at him in the rearview mirror. His eyes begging to ask a question.

*What does it feel like to have your twin brother murdered?*

It was all Ethan could do to keep from slamming the screen with the flat of his hand and telling Mitchell to mind his own business. The rage Ethan felt scared him.

He turned his head and stared out the smeared window. Smeared with what? Sweat? Spit?

At an intersection a late-model Volvo pulled up beside them. Inside, a middle-aged man and his wife stared at him, too civilized to point and laugh like some people did. Ethan could see what they were thinking.

*What kind of a monster are you?*

The faces of two boys gawked at him from the backseat.

*Do your homework, boys, say your prayers, and stay out of trouble. Otherwise some day you'll end up like that man in the back of a police car.*

Ethan turned away.

Why was it taking so long to get to his house?

Another mile and the cruiser turned left onto Oregon Street, then right on Copley Avenue. They approached his house from the west.

The evening was September warm. A Santa Ana wind had scrubbed the sky clean. The harvest moon cast a soft light. It was a perfect evening for a carefree stroll. Not a killing night at all.

From the backseat of a patrol car, through the wire mesh screen,

Ethan Morgan saw two things that didn't belong together—his house and a crime scene.

Normally by this time Ethan would have been shrugging off the day, unwinding, mentally taking inventory of the refrigerator's contents and the television-program schedule. The sight of police cruisers and television vans parked head-to-head in the middle of the street changed all that. Ethan could feel his defenses rising, an invisible armor, a detachment to protect himself from the horrors he was about to see.

The cluster of gawking bystanders across the street spoke in hushed voices. They didn't want to wake whatever monster had attacked the house.

Television crews plastered the outside of Ethan's house with a garishly unnatural light. Jittery black shadows danced on his garage door.

Yellow tape marked the boundaries of the crime scene. It stretched from a bush on the corner of Ethan's lot, around Meredith's car, hugging the back of Andrew's car, and tied off at the garage-door handle. The driver-side door of Andrew's car stood open as though it expected him to return at any moment.

The door to the house was also open. Ethan had closed and locked it when he left.

Through the sheer curtains of the front window ghostly images of police and homicide officers paraded back and forth. A photographer provided lightning flashes.

The patrol car pulled to a stop. Ethan couldn't get out of the backseat fast enough. He reached for the door handle and found none. Such a basic fact. It angered him that he'd forgotten it. He looked like any other victim struggling to get out the back of a police cruiser. Ethan fidgeted impatiently as Cisneros opened the door from the outside.

"Wait here," Cisneros told him.

But Ethan wasn't listening. Neither was he waiting. He ducked under the crime scene tape and was promptly intercepted by a uniformed police officer. The man easily had a fifty-pound advantage over him. Ethan didn't recognize him.

"I'm sorry, Detective Morgan," the officer said. "You can't go in."

"Just watch me."

Ethan tried to step around the officer. He was blocked.

"Lieutenant's orders," the officer apologized.

The man in blue had missed his calling. He should have been a lineman for the San Diego Chargers.

"Look, officer ..."

"Rappaport."

"... that's my brother in there and unless you're prepared to wrestle me to the ground I am going in."

Officers Mitchell and Cisneros joined ranks with Rappaport, one on each side.

"Sorry, Morgan," Mitchell said. "Orders."

Of the four men—five if you gave Rappaport his due and counted him twice—Ethan was the smallest. But sometimes size doesn't matter, and this was one of those times. Nobody was going to stop him from getting into his own house.

What was that old proverb? The bigger they are, the harder they fall. Ethan went for the big guy. A forearm to the chest.

Ethan bounced off him.

Rappaport obviously had never heard the proverb. Both Mitchell and Cisneros jumped to Rappaport's aid though he clearly didn't need it.

"Give us a break, Morgan," Mitchell cried, grabbing Ethan by the arm. "We're only doing our jobs."

A change of tactic was needed.

Ethan could see the back of his lieutenant standing in the living room. Savala was a big man, horseshoe bald, his pate shiny in the bright interior light. In the other direction several reporters were watching Ethan's confrontation from the street.

"I want to talk to Lieutenant Savala," Ethan said, yanking his arm free.

"No can do," Mitchell said. "The lieutenant is the one who told us to keep you out."

Mitchell didn't seem to get it. Ethan wasn't asking.

"I want to talk to Lieutenant Savala," Ethan shouted.

Now Mitchell understood. He glanced nervously at the reporters.

"Come on, Morgan," he hissed, "don't do this."

Ethan shouted all the louder. "What do you mean you won't let me see my brother?"

Reporters were bunching as close to the confrontation as they could without violating the crime scene. Cameras followed in their wake, taking aim at Ethan.

"I have rights! You can't keep me out of my own house," Ethan shouted. "All I want is to see my brother."

Actually, the police could keep Ethan out of his house, and he knew it. So did the press. But the accusation that a person was being denied his rights was like throwing a bone to a dog. The press would run with it. And as the ranking officer on the scene, Lieutenant Savala would have to field the question that would air on the eleven o'clock news.

The commotion and camera lights on four of his men had attracted Savala's attention. He parted the sheer curtains to get a better look and said something that couldn't be heard. Even before the curtains fell back into place the lieutenant was crossing the lawn.

Ethan began pleading his case before Savala reached them.

Mitchell shrugged an apology to his superior. With a scowl Savala dismissed the three officers. He took Ethan by the arm and led him away from the reporters and cameras.

"What do you think you're doing?" Savala demanded.

"I want in my house," Ethan said unapologetically. "That's my brother and sister-in-law in there. I want to see them."

"Your sister-in-law was taken to the hospital."

"How bad?"

"She was roughed up. Thrown over the sofa. She was complaining of abdominal pains. I'll have Mitchell take you to the hospital."

"First I want to see the crime scene. I want to see my brother."

"Morgan, be reasonable. You know I can't let you in there."

"What do you think I'm going to do? Get in the way? Destroy evidence? I'm a homicide detective for crying out loud. I know my way around a crime scene."

"That's exactly why I can't let you in. The defense would have a field day. Who better to tamper with evidence than a distraught family member who also happens to be a homicide detective? I can't allow it."

He had a good point. Ethan knew Savala to be a good man and a good cop, a family man with a solid marriage and two teenage daughters.

"Savala," Ethan pleaded, "If it was your brother in there, what would you do?"

Savala looked at him hard. "Don't touch anything."

At the porch Ethan asked, "Am I a suspect?"

"No. We know where you were. You have an auditorium full of alibis."

The two men stretched on paper covers over their shoes.

Savala began briefing him. "According to the first officers on the scene," he said, "Meredith was talking to someone on her cell phone when they arrived."

"The dispatcher?"

Savala shook his head. "They said she sounded like she was conducting business. When she saw them she hung up."

"Conducting business? What did she say?"

"All they were able to make out was, '… at least we can be grateful for that.'"

"I'll ask her when I see her," Ethan said.

He stepped through the front door into the heart of the crime scene. The place didn't look like his living room. With all the lights and people it looked like a studio representation of his living room staged for a police drama, all except for the body lying facedown on the rug. It looked real enough. Andrew's hands were bagged in paper to preserve evidence.

Ethan's knees grew weak. Seeing his brother prepped as evidence hit him harder than he thought it would. He had to steady himself against the door.

"Maybe this wasn't such a good idea," Savala said.

"I'll be all right," Ethan insisted with an assurance he didn't feel. He didn't want to give the lieutenant an excuse to take him out of the house.

An officer whispered something in Savala's ear. The lieutenant nodded. Turning to Ethan he said, "There is something I have to attend to."

"I'll be all right," Ethan said.

Savala looked at him warily.

"I'll behave myself. I promise."

As the lieutenant disappeared into the back of the house, Ethan fortified his practiced detachment. He told himself he would get through this.

He surveyed the scene through the eyes of a detective like he would any other crime scene. The body on the floor was the center of activity around which detectives and technicians orbited. They collected evidence, dusted for fingerprints, and photographed everything from every conceivable angle.

Not only did Ethan know what they were doing, he knew why they were doing it. He'd done it himself a hundred times and was itching to pitch in, to do something, anything. But Ethan knew if he touched anything Savala would have his head.

He rounded the sofa and stood over his brother's body, careful not to step in the blood. He knelt down beside it.

The room hushed. Ethan looked up. Everyone was standing statue still, staring at him.

They were wondering how weird it must be to look down at yourself lying dead on the floor. But they didn't know. It wasn't like that. It wasn't like that at all.

Never had Ethan looked at his twin brother to see himself looking back. Andrew was not his reflection. He could no more look at Andrew and see himself than he could mistake Andrew's side of the bedroom for his own. The difference between them was greater than physical appearance.

Andrew was the dreamer, the happy one, the popular one, the talented one, the one who attracted beautiful women like Meredith: He was the successful one. While Andrew was becoming nationally known and wealthy, Ethan was dodging creditors.

Unlike some twins there was no competition between them. Ethan didn't envy his brother's success. Success suited Andrew; it didn't suit him. Ethan was content to be the brooder, the moody one, the skeptic, the loner. His personality fit his profession and his lifestyle.

Activity in the room wound up again and soon it was at full speed giving Ethan and Andrew a measure of privacy.

Memories began chipping away at Ethan's defenses. He tried to examine the body in the same way he would any other gunshot victim, but flashes of the past kept reminding him that this was his brother.

He remembered how excited Andrew had been when he was eight years old and one of his drawings won an award and was printed in the newspaper.

He remembered his brother's voice in the dark of the night as kids when they were supposed to be asleep. That's when they were closest. When it was just the two of them alone in their bedroom at night.

He remembered Andrew sporting a lopsided grin and holding a ring in a green velvet box on the day he asked Meredith to be his wife.

And he remembered the look of chagrin on Andrew's face earlier this evening when he told him he'd forgotten to bring the Bible. Andrew wasn't fooled. He recognized the shoddy lie that Ethan had crafted as an excuse to escape the evening.

The body on the floor should have been Ethan. His childish scheme had cost Andrew his life.

"I'm sorry," Ethan whispered.

The words worked like a corkscrew opening a mix of emotions that until now Ethan had managed to bottle up. Sorrow, anger, and regret fizzed to the surface. Tears filled his eyes. A lump lodged in his throat. But revenge proved to be the strongest feeling. It surged through Ethan with an intensity that made his hands shake.

He bent low, close to Andrew's ear. He whispered so that no one else could hear him.

"I'll find who did this," Ethan swore. "If it's the last thing I do, I will find who did this." He emphasized each word because each word was a separate promise. The sentence was promise piled upon promise.

Ethan reached toward his dead brother with a trembling hand to seal the promise with a touch. He was losing the battle with his tears. His lip quivered.

The arrival of the medical examiner put a cap on Ethan's emotions just as they were threatening to get out of control.

From the medical examiner's double take it was apparent nobody had told him that Ethan's brother was a twin. He recovered nicely. The same could not be said for his apprentice investigator, a young man Ethan knew only as Newkirk.

"Whoa! Now that's spooky!" Newkirk exclaimed, his eyes darting back and forth from Ethan to Andrew. "Just like in the movies, you know, when a guy dies and his spirit rises out of his body and he's looking down on himself and he can't believe that it's actually him …"

"If you don't shut up," the medical examiner said, "there are going to be two dead bodies in this room."

Dr. Isaac Tekle pulled on a pair of rubber gloves. The medical examiner was in his late fifties with thick white hair and sparkling eyes that reminded Ethan of Santa Claus. The police community respected Tekle as a methodical professional. Though he oversaw an entire department, it wasn't uncommon to see him at a crime scene, especially one where his team might come under scrutiny, such as the death of a family member of a police detective.

"My heartfelt condolences," Tekle said to Ethan. He laid a comforting hand on Ethan's shoulder. "And my apologies for my insensitive assistant."

Newkirk was smart enough to keep his mouth shut. He went to work opening equipment boxes.

Tekle hovered over the body for several minutes, observing it and the surrounding area.

He looked up at Ethan. "I'm going to turn him over now," he said.

He was giving Ethan a chance to excuse himself.

"I'll stay," Ethan said.

With gentle hands the medical examiner rolled Andrew onto his back. Every inch of Andrew's shirt was red with blood.

Ethan's jaw clenched. It wasn't the blood that got him. He'd seen enough blood on this job to paint a barn. It was Andrew's sightless eyes. Ethan had thought of his brother's eyes as thirsty eyes, always drinking in everything. Colors. Mannerisms. Faces. Gestures.

Dr. Tekle examined the entry points of the four bullet wounds. Then he unbuttoned Andrew's dress shirt.

"An Outlaws fan I see," Tekle said.

Dr. Tekle moved aside so Ethan could see. What he saw didn't make sense.

"That's not right," he said. "Andrew didn't like football. That's not his shirt."

"You can be certain about what your brother was wearing?" Tekle asked.

"I know Andrew. He wouldn't be caught dead wearing an Outlaws T-shirt."

It was an expression. Ethan didn't realize what he said until he'd said it.

To their credit, everyone within hearing distance pretended they hadn't heard him, including Newkirk.

"Ethan, got a sec?"

Sgt. Edouard Weisberg came up behind him.

"I have a few questions for you."

Weisberg pulled Ethan aside. The leader of homicide Team I, Weisberg was a middle-aged man with a thin nose and eyes that were set too close together. Ethan didn't much care for him. Weisberg didn't earn promotions through hard work; he weaseled his way into them. His idea of leadership was that the number one responsibility of his subordinates was to make him look good.

Weisberg had been Ethan's first sergeant when he made detective. They had butted heads on several occasions, and when a position came open on homicide Team IV, Weisberg got Ethan transferred. Ethan was glad to go.

"Do you recognize that?" Weisberg asked, pointing to an open cell phone on the floor. "Is it your brother's?"

Ethan knelt down to take a good look at it. It was an expensive model. The screen was dark.

"I think it's Andrew's cell phone," he said. "But I can't be certain."

"Finch pulled this number off of it. Do you recognize it?" Weisberg showed Ethan a pad that displayed the number 431-1617.

Ethan shook his head. "431. That's not a local number."

"How do you know that?"

For a detective sometimes Weisberg was a little slow on the uptake.

"Have you tried calling it?" Ethan asked.

As he was speaking Ethan pulled his cell phone out of his pocket and dialed the number.

"What are you doing? Stop. Don't …"

Ethan figured Weisberg had not yet called the number, and he knew the sergeant would object to his dialing it. That's why he did it.

He got a phone company recording.

*We're sorry. Your call cannot be completed as dialed.*

He held out the phone so Weisberg could hear it.

"Is that the last number my brother called?" Ethan asked.

"Dialed. Didn't call. The number was still on the screen waiting to be sent."

Ethan weighed this bit of information. Another mystery. They were beginning to pile up. First Meredith's phone call, then the Outlaws T-shirt, and now this.

A typical crime scene is a composite of little mysteries. Ethan understood this. Each little mystery when solved became a puzzle piece to the larger picture. But in this case the picture was of his brother's murder and these little mysteries were irritating him more than usual.

Weisberg jotted down what Ethan had learned about the phone number, then said, "Come over here."

Skirting the area where the medical examiner continued to examine Andrew's body, Weisberg led Ethan toward the dining area.

Ethan stopped beside his recliner.

"I didn't leave those of there," he said, indicating the potato chip bag, cupcake wrapper, and empty soda can on the side table. "And that picture frame. It's been moved."

"Are you sure?" Weisberg asked, poking the wrapper with his pen.

"I haven't had anything to eat since lunch."

"Maybe your brother fixed himself a snack."

"No. He was in a hurry to get back to the school before intermission."

Weisberg wrote this down on his pad. "Pretty brazen," he muttered as he scribbled. "A thief breaks into the house, murders someone, then sits down and has himself a snack."

"He may have been lying in wait."

Weisberg's head came up. "For you? Or are you saying your brother was targeted? But then, how did the killer know he would be here?"

"Mistaken identity." Ethan said. "The killer thought Andrew was me. Not even Andrew knew he was going to be here tonight."

Weisberg wrote that down.

"What was in here?"

He pointed to the display case. It was open. Empty. Ethan's key ring dangled from the display key that was still in the lock.

The sight of the empty case and his key ring was a double punch to Ethan's gut.

"A family Bible," Ethan managed to say.

Weisberg's eyebrows rose. "You never struck me as the religious type, Morgan."

"It's a family heirloom."

"Valuable?"

Ethan glanced at his brother on the floor. Dr. Tekle had finished his initial investigation. He was stripping off his rubber gloves and dictating something to Newkirk.

"The last time Andrew had the Bible appraised, it was valued at $500,000."

Weisberg whistled. To the room he announced, "We just found our motive, boys and girls. A missing Bible worth half a million dollars." To Ethan he asked, "How many people know about this Bible?"

"That's hard to say."

"Why is it hard to say?"

"It's sort of famous. Andrew wrote a series of novels about it. And before that there was a Hollywood film, but it never got out of production."

"Film, huh? Who was playing you? Wait ... let me guess ... who's that heartthrob? The one all the junior high girls go gaga for ... oh yeah, Johnny Depp."

Ethan offered a wry smile in response. "The movie was about my ancestors. My family and that Bible go back four hundred years."

Weisberg looked unimpressed. Without touching the display case he took a closer look at it. "A four-hundred-year-old book worth half a million dollars. If I had something like that, I wouldn't leave it lying around my house."

Ethan suppressed a retort. Weisberg's comment was a temptation cops couldn't resist, tossing out "you got what you deserve" comments, letting people know after the fact what they should have done to prevent the crime. Ethan himself had done this a hundred times. He didn't appreciate being on the receiving end.

"Where was the point of entry?" he asked.

Weisberg walked him into the kitchen where Det. Brian Hinkey was dusting the windowsill for prints. Ethan cringed at the sight of this man in his house.

With short, tight curly red hair and a complexion that couldn't be described without using the word freckles, Hinkey was fingernails on a chalkboard incarnate, an instant and constant irritant. Ethan was certain the man lay awake nights devising new ways to get under people's skin.

Of all the people that could be dusting for prints, why did it have to be Hinkey? On Ethan's first day as a detective he got a preview of Hinkey in action.

They were investigating the murder of a young woman, a San Diego State coed who lived in an apartment adjacent to Balboa Park. She had come home after jogging one morning to find an intruder in her apartment, an old boyfriend as it turned out.

It wasn't immediately clear how the murderer had gained entry. One theory was that he had a key. The mother of the victim, who was also the owner of the apartment, was most insistent that her daughter would not have given a key to her ex-boyfriend. In fact, she had moved into this apartment to get away from him.

When no fingerprint leads were found on the ground-floor windows, the mother insisted Hinkey dust the second-story windows. Hinkey told her it was a waste of time. The windows were inaccessible. The mother insisted and eventually complained to Weisberg who ordered Hinkey to dust the upstairs windows.

Angry that she had gone over his head, Hinkey dusted every upstairs windowsill and every inch of every frame around every window in the house. Then, he dusted every door, every cabinet, every piece of furniture, every picture, and every knickknack. It was payback for the woman telling him how to do his job.

Most people assume that the worst part of cleaning a crime scene would be the blood. It's not. The worst is fingerprint dust. It's messy, sooty, gritty, and next to impossible to clean or to work with. Just like Brian Hinkey.

It didn't matter at all to him that he found the ex-boyfriend's fingerprints on an upstairs windowsill that, as it turned out, was accessible after all.

"Any luck?" Weisberg asked Hinkey as he dusted Ethan's kitchen windowsill.

Hinkey glanced at Ethan before answering. "The guy must have worn gloves. There are gouge marks where he forced the window, but no prints."

"Try the kitchen cabinet and the refrigerator," Ethan said.

"Waste of time," Hinkey replied.

"We know he got food and drink," Ethan said. "He may have taken the gloves off. There are wrappers and an empty soda can in the living room that should be dusted."

"I'm telling you it's a waste of time. You want the trash dusted? Do it yourself."

Hinkey knew full well Ethan wasn't allowed to touch anything.

"Just do it!" Ethan barked.

Hinkey stood up and squared his shoulders to Ethan.

Weisberg stepped between them. To Hinkey he said, "Dust the cabinet, refrigerator, wrapper, and soda can."

Grumbling, Hinkey shot a murderous glance at Ethan. He gathered up the kit and went to the far side of the kitchen and began dusting a cabinet door, starting at the top.

"What are you doing?" Ethan cried.

"What I was ordered to do."

"I keep the cupcakes over here."

"The guy who broke in didn't know that. He may have searched these cabinets before finding what he was looking for."

"But we know he opened this cabinet," Ethan said.

Hinkey ignored him and kept dusting.

Ethan knew what he was doing. Payback for telling him how to do his job. Ethan started toward him. Weisberg stopped him with a hand to his chest.

The sergeant glanced over his shoulder, worried that Lieutenant Savala was witnessing this. The lieutenant was not to be seen. Turning his attention to Hinkey he hissed, "For once in your life stop acting like a chowderhead. Just do your job!"

Hinkey started to say something, then in a rare moment of self-control, stopped. Gathering up his kit, he moved to the cupcake cabinet.

"Make sure he does the framed photo in the living room," Ethan whispered to Weisberg.

"I'm perfectly capable of doing my job, Morgan," Weisberg snapped.

Hinkey overheard. "The photo with that good-looking redhead? She's one hot babe."

"Shut your trap, Hinkey," Weisberg said before Ethan had a chance.

Hinkey persisted. "The three of you look cozy in that photo. Hard to tell which one's her husband. Was she able to tell the two of you apart?"

Ethan balled his fists. He turned his back on Hinkey and began walking out of the kitchen before he did something he'd regret. Hinkey never knew when to quit.

"Hey, Morgan, did you ever go over there late at night and pull one over on her? You know, pretend to be your brother?"

Ethan didn't remember turning around. He didn't even recall throwing himself at Hinkey. But he did remember landing a punch on Hinkey's jaw, and knocking the powder jar out of Hinkey's hand, and watching Hinkey fall hard to the floor with the powder spilling on top of him.

Out of reflex Hinkey closed his eyes when he saw the powder coming. When he opened them again his eyes were white, but the rest of his face was black, like an old vaudeville actor.

That's when Lieutenant Savala walked into the kitchen.

It took several officers to pull Ethan off Hinkey. When they did, Lieutenant Savala had Ethan escorted out of the house. Officers forced him into the back of the patrol car with orders that he be delivered to Mercy Hospital.

# FIVE

The ride to the hospital was mercifully a mere three miles from his house. Ethan was stuck in the back of the patrol car for less than ten minutes.

Mitchell and Cisneros delivered him to within a dozen steps of the front doors. Cisneros opened the back door for him without comment. Both officers gave a final "poor Ethan" glance before driving away.

While Ethan stood in the circular unloading zone with the soapbox Bible replica under his arm, his eyes took in the building's modern facade with its sharp angles, reflective windows, and stylish landscaping. The hospital looked elegant from this side. Ethan was more familiar with the whitewashed, no-frills emergency-room entrance in the back.

Twin electric doors slid open, anticipating his approach. Ethan hated hospitals. They could camouflage human frailty with warm colors, indoor foliage, smiles, and a false sense of order and decorum, but the truth was that death always had the final say.

A vaulted glass ceiling stretched over him the length of an atrium leading to a suspended twenty-foot wooden cross against the far wall. The hour was late, so he had the lobby to himself. The information desk was unmanned. Ethan kept walking until he located the admissions counter.

"I'm here to see Meredith Morgan," he told a heavyset nurse. "She just arrived, so she might not be in the system yet."

The nurse, who looked to be in her twenties, scrutinized the box under his arm. It had left a trail of laundry detergent across the lobby.

"Oh, sorry," Ethan said. He stopped the flow of granules by placing a finger over the tattered corner. "It's a prop for an elementary school play."

"Husband?" the nurse asked as she entered Meredith's name into the computer.

"Brother-in-law."

"I'm sorry, sir. Visiting hours are over."

"Her husband was killed tonight."

He couldn't tell if she put it together, that the death of his sister-in-law's husband meant his brother had been killed. But woman showed no emotion at all. No shock. No sympathy. She simply tapped the keyboard dutifully. Ethan figured even as young as she was, she'd probably seen it all. Human tragedy failed to shock her.

He reached for his badge just in case he needed it. One way or the other, he was going to see Meredith tonight, regardless of the time.

"Room 426. Elevators are under the cross."

Ethan chuckled. *Of course they are*, he thought. Placing the elevators under a cross gave "Going up?" and "Going down?" a whole new meaning.

He crossed the expansive lobby, very much aware that he was alone. He felt as though the world had served notice. Andrew was dead. From now on, he was on his own.

He pressed the UP button and the doors opened instantly.

Exiting on the fourth floor, he paused to get his bearings, then turned to his right. A short hallway led him to the center of the wing and the nurses' station, which was not only the hub of activity but the geographical center. Patients' rooms circled it on the perimeter.

Four nurses were busy behind the desk, all of them with their heads down, reading or writing on charts, or placing medications in little paper cups. Either they were unaware of his presence or they were ignoring him.

It didn't matter. Ethan could find the room on his own.

Room 426 was a corner room with a single bed. The overhead lights were turned off. All was quiet. Meredith lay peacefully on her back, her arms at her sides with the bedclothes folded neatly across her abdomen. Her eyes were closed.

She looked exactly like the hospital's publicity department wanted her to look, not at all like a woman who had just seen her dead husband, and who herself had survived hand-to-hand combat with the killer.

She looked drained and much older than she had just a few hours ago at the play.

The head of her bed fit into a metal alcove with horizontal neon lights on each side. The alcove was the electrical nerve center for the room with all manner of gauges and sockets, some Ethan recognized, some he could only guess as to their function. A packet of clear liquid hung on a hanger and fed into Meredith's arm through a plastic tube.

Ethan set the Bible replica down on a chair and stood beside the bed, looking down at her. He was relieved she was asleep. It was better this way. Asleep, the pain of the night's events would not torment her. Besides, he didn't know what he would say to her.

Her eyes fluttered open. They focused. Awareness took hold of her with him standing beside the bed. Of what had happened.

"Oh, Ethan ..." she cried.

She raised a hand to him and he took it, cupping it with both hands. She pulled the hands to her lips and sobbed against them. Ethan could feel the heat of her breath and her tears.

She tried to speak. Her words were garbled by sobs but clear enough to wrench Ethan's heart.

"It was horrible," she cried. "A nightmare. He was just lying there. So still ... so ... so still. There was so much ... so much blood. And there was nothing I could do! Oh, Ethan! There was nothing I could do!"

Ethan felt helpless. Words were beyond inadequate, masqueraders of comfort.

This was why Ethan hated hospitals. In every room, in every bed, people were in pain, and he couldn't say anything to help them. All he could do was stand and watch.

So he stood, holding Meredith's hand as he watched her cry. He said nothing. But he hurt. He hurt for Meredith. He mourned for Sky.

After a time, Meredith's supply of tears ran low. She looked up at him. "How are you doing?" she asked.

"Don't ask that," Ethan begged. "I should be asking you. They said you were roughed up pretty good."

A fresh wave of emotion crested, a wave of considerable size if her effort to hold it back was any indication. She pursed her lips tight. A new pain filled her eyes.

"He hurt me," she sobbed. "He hurt me and … and … I lost the baby."

The news crashed down on Ethan, sweeping him off his emotional feet, pulling him under.

His mind flashed back to the elementary school stage, to the kid wearing a bird costume and holding a pillowcase; then to the stage mother stage-whispering from the wings, "What about the other surprise?"

It all made sense now.

The kid was supposed to be a stork.

"Did Andrew know?" Ethan asked.

Meredith shook her head. "I wanted to surprise you both at the same time … to see the expressions on your faces."

When Ethan first walked through the hospital doors, he didn't think his heart could sink any lower. He was wrong. At this moment he explored depths he never thought possible.

Sky … a father.

Ethan knew of no man better suited to be a father. Sky would have loved the stuffing out of his children. He would have played with them, laughed with them, instructed them, and taught them to be proud of their Morgan ancestry. Ethan had always told Sky that if the Morgan family was to continue, it would be up to him.

"A boy?"

Meredith nodded.

What kind of justice was there in a world where a man and his unborn child were both killed on the same night?

"I'm going to find the man who did this," Ethan swore. "I promise you, Meredith. I will find the man who did this and bring him to justice."

The vow, charged with anger, hung heavy in the air like summer lightning. Ethan had said it to comfort her. It did just the opposite.

"Did you see Andrew?" she asked in a hushed voice.

"I just came from the house."

Her eyes lost focus. For a moment she was back at the house, reliving the horror.

Ethan touched her arm. Brought her back.

"I'll get the man who killed him, Meredith. I promise."

"Who, Ethan? Who would do something like this? Who would want to kill Andrew?"

"It's possible he surprised a burglar."

"Is that what you think?"

"I don't know. Some things don't add up."

"What do you mean?"

Ethan had promised himself he wouldn't ask Meredith any questions tonight, but her desire to make sense of the night seemed to take her mind off the pain.

He said, "Did Sky own a Nevada Outlaws football T-shirt?"

"Andrew didn't like football. You know that."

"I know. Maybe he wore the T-shirt as a joke?"

"He was wearing a football T-shirt?"

"The medical examiner found one under his dress shirt."

"Under his dress shirt?" Meredith cried. "That doesn't make sense. It would show through."

Ethan hadn't thought of that. When he saw the shirt it was saturated with blood and plastered against his brother's chest.

"You're right," he said. "You would have noticed it, wouldn't you?"

Meredith shook her head. "I hardly saw him today. Andrew spent most of the day at the school. I drove there in my car. What about you? You saw him tonight. Was he wearing the T-shirt then?"

Ethan did his best to call up an image of his brother's shirt earlier that evening, but couldn't.

"I was so ticked off at having to be there, I didn't notice anything," he said. "I couldn't tell you what color pants he was wearing."

Meredith put her hand on his. "You're being too hard on yourself," she said. Then added, "He was wearing his khaki Dockers."

Ethan turned away so she couldn't see the disgust on his face. Everything tonight was his fault. It was his fault Andrew found himself on the deadly end of a killer's gun. And it was his childish pouting that kept him from being observant. He was trained to be observant, for crying out loud.

"What's that?" Meredith asked. She pointed to something behind him.

Ethan followed the direction of her finger to the replica of the Bible.

"When Sky didn't show up with the Bible," he said, "they joked that after centuries of safekeeping, Sky and I managed to lose it. They presented the stage prop to me as a joke. Said we could keep it until we found the real Bible."

Ethan didn't think it was funny, but the gesture made Meredith smile. The smile quickly faded.

"You saw the killer take the Bible, didn't you?" Ethan asked.

Meredith nodded.

"I'll get it back."

She squeezed his hand. "Promise me you won't take any unnecessary risks. It's just a book, Ethan. It's not worth your life too."

Ethan studied her. That didn't sound like Meredith. She was just as proud and protective of the Morgan family Bible and the heritage it represented as Sky, if not more so. But then, a night of killing has a way of changing a person's priorities.

A nurse carrying a tray holding a small paper cup interrupted them. "You're not supposed to be here," she snapped. "I'm going to have to ask you to leave."

By the way she spoke and moved, this was her kingdom and she wanted it clearly understood that she was the undisputed queen.

Meredith came to Ethan's defense. "This is my husband's brother," she said.

The nurse poured her patient a glass of water from a plastic pitcher and handed the glass and a pill to Meredith. She stood there until Meredith downed the medication.

While the nurse's attitude toward Ethan softened, she held her ground. "My condolences, Mr. Morgan," she said, "but Mrs. Morgan needs her rest."

Ethan picked up the Bible replica, making sure to place his finger over the hole in the corner.

"Have you called your parents yet?" Meredith said to his back.

"I figured I'd do that from the hotel."

"Hotel?"

"My house is a crime scene. I can't stay there tonight."

"Use our house."

The plural pronoun momentarily knocked the breath out of the conversation.

Ethan recovered first. He said, "Thanks, but I don't think I'm up to that. Not tonight anyway."

Meredith understood.

When he reached the door, Ethan turned back. "When the police first arrived at the house, they said you were talking to someone on the phone."

The question flustered Meredith.

"Oh … um … my mother. I called my mother. I was just sitting there, waiting, you know … for the police … and … well, it was sort of unnerving, and so I … I called my mother. She told me to dial 911 then call her back. I didn't want to be alone."

Meredith looked down as she spoke, her eyes darting side to side. She was lying. As a policeman Ethan had been lied to often enough to recognize the characteristics.

Why was Meredith lying?

The nurse stood within inches of Ethan. She looked up at him and said, "You go now. Come back tomorrow."

He turned to leave.

"Ethan?"

When he turned back, the nurse bumped into him and scowled.

Ethan met Meredith's gaze halfway. It appeared she didn't want the night to end with a lie but couldn't think of what else to say. They exchanged silent condolences.

"I'll see you tomorrow," he said.

Ethan was in the lobby before he realized he had no car in the parking lot. He pulled out his cell phone and his thumb went instinctively to his brother's speed dial button. He paused.

He considered calling the department, but he'd had enough of patrol-car backseats and sympathetic glances for one night.

He dialed information and got the number of a cab company. The cab operator asked him where he was and where he wanted to go. Ethan had run out of answers. He had no idea where to go from here.

---

Ethan sat on the edge of his hotel-room bed. The cab driver had said he put his mother and obnoxious stepfather up in this hotel whenever they visited from Louisville. He said it was worth the money not to have to watch game shows at night with his stepfather.

The Bible replica sat on the dresser. A small pile of laundry granules had spilled onto the simulated wood surface. Other than his cell phone, this box was the only thing Ethan had when he checked in. He had no luggage. No pajamas. No toothbrush or toiletries of any kind.

He sat slump shouldered, his thumb resting on the button that would connect him with his parents in Las Vegas. Only once in his career as a police officer had he told parents their child had died. A car accident victim. The kid was a passenger; his buddy was the driver. It was late. They were speeding.

The parents knew it was bad news the moment they saw two uniforms standing on their porch at two o'clock in the morning. They came across as good people. Good parents. Ethan remembered thinking they didn't deserve news like this.

The feeling revisited him now. His father, a Vietnam veteran, was no stranger to life's cruelties and death. His mother had lost a brother in a motorcycle accident, and her first child in the early stages of pregnancy. But no matter how many hardships life had dished out to them, this news was going to hit them hard.

He pushed the button. The other end of the line rang.

Ethan had practiced several sentences hoping to find one that would deliver the news with velvet gloves. But there was no easy way to tell your father and mother that their son—the good one—had been murdered.

The phone continued to ring.

Ethan panicked. What if his mother answered? He couldn't tell her. It would be hard enough breaking the news to his father, he couldn't tell his mother. He just couldn't. But if she answered, he couldn't ask her to hand the phone to his father. She'd know something was wrong. And what if his father wasn't home? He couldn't tell her he'd call back later, not with this kind of news. He'd have to tell her.

The phone continued ringing. Ethan almost hung up.

"Hello?"

Ethan closed his eyes in relief.

"Hello, Dad."

"Ethan?"

By sight his father had no trouble telling the boys apart. On the phone they sounded alike. But that was no longer a problem, was it? He had only one son now.

"Yeah. It's me."

"We've been expecting your call," his father said.

Ethan straightened up. Had someone already phoned them? Who could have possibly … wait … no, they didn't know. His father's voice was all wrong.

"Tonight's the big premiere, isn't it?" his father asked.

"Oh that. Yeah."

"Well? How'd it go? What was it like watching your family history portrayed on stage by kids?"

"Um … it was great. Listen, Dad. I'm glad you answered the phone and not Mom."

The end of the line went dead silent.

Ethan cleared his throat. "Dad, I'm … I'm afraid I have some bad news."

"Dear God … is it … is it Andrew?"

"Yeah, Dad. It's Andrew."

───────────────

Lying on a strange bed on his back in the dark, Ethan stared at the ceiling. Sleep would not visit him. It didn't like death any more than he did.

"Well, Sky … where do we go from here?"

He waited for an answer. The question wasn't rhetorical.

After talking to his parents for over an hour, Ethan wandered down to the front desk and picked up an emergency toiletry kit and then bought a soda from a vending machine next to the ice maker at the end of the hallway. He turned on the television and flipped through the channels, avoiding the news. Reporters seldom got a crime story right and tonight it was personal; it would only anger him more. He watched a couple of sitcom reruns and the last round of a woman's championship billiards tournament in Atlantic City.

He was afraid to turn off the lights and go to bed. Darkness and loneliness were twin demons who were strongest when working in tandem.

But leaving the light on until morning seemed childish, so around 4:00 a.m. he flipped the switch and it was dark. To his surprise, he wasn't alone.

Ethan couldn't explain it, but he felt a familiar presence. It was like when he and Sky were kids and shared a bedroom. It was so real that Ethan would not have been startled to hear the rustle of bed sheets or the creak of mattress springs coming from the other side of the room.

"Just like old times, huh?" Ethan said, smiling in the dark.

Andrew agreed. Not with words. Ethan sensed his agreement. Was that really so strange?

All their lives people told Ethan and Andrew spooky stories of identical twins who knew each other's thoughts, finished each other's sentences, felt each other's feelings, sometimes across great distances. Stories of twins feeling their counterpart die though half a world separated them, or of twins dying at the same instant.

In life Ethan and Andrew experienced none of those twin oddities. They couldn't have been further apart. Death had changed all that. They were closer now. So close that Ethan could feel his brother inside of him. They shared one heart, one mind.

"I'm scared, Sky," Ethan said. "It's all on me now, isn't it?"

Andrew agreed. *If anybody can do it, you can.*

"That's easy for you to say," Ethan said.

He began to weep.

Wiping tears from his cheeks, he said, "I haven't cried since I was thirteen years old."

*When you failed to qualify for the swim team.*

Ethan grinned. "You remember."

*It's nothing to be ashamed of. In one night you have lost your twin brother, an unborn nephew, and the Morgan family's four-hundred-year-old Bible. Weep tonight. Tomorrow we will begin to set things right.*

With his brother's permission, Ethan wept.

# SIX

Ethan's eyes stung and his eyelids felt weighted from lack of sleep. He walked to the bathroom in a fog. Yet, as ragged as he felt, his spirit was light. Happy. It had been years since he'd had a heart-to-heart talk with his brother.

He washed his face, brushed his teeth, and combed his hair with the cheap complimentary hotel toiletries. Dressed in yesterday's clothes, he ordered the morning special—two eggs any style, two sausage patties, toast, and coffee—at the hotel's coffee shop.

Normally he scanned the newspaper headlines while eating breakfast. Today he mulled over the new world in which he'd found himself, the one into which he'd been cast against his will, the one in which he was an only child, the one in which he alone was responsible for a family heritage without the centuries-old family Bible that recorded it.

Mostly he felt the need to reassert some sense of control over his life. He had been reeling like a boxer against the ropes ever since he first heard the news about Sky. With the start of a new day, a new round began. He was off the ropes and itching to land a few punches of his own by finding his brother's murderer.

Instead of a bell signifying the start of round two, Ethan heard a ring tone. It was Lieutenant Savala. The detectives had released his house. A uniformed officer would meet Ethan and hand over the keys. Savala told him to take a couple of days off.

Only four bites into his meal, Ethan wiped his mouth with a napkin, tossed it on top of the plate, and asked Savala to have the uniform pick him up at the hotel.

Before hanging up, he told his lieutenant he wanted to be in on tomorrow's Team I briefing. Savala didn't think that was a good idea. But Ethan persisted, and after promising that he would behave himself, Savala said he would contact Weisberg and see what he could do.

Ethan paid his bill. Round two had begun.

---

Ethan spent the day reclaiming his house, changing it from a crime scene back into a home. He began by ripping out the bloodstained carpeting. He considered hiring out the job, but with energy to burn, the act of ripping up carpeting proved to be therapeutic. Next, he attacked every black smudge Hinkey left behind. Ethan stopped counting after a hundred smudges. With a combination of industrial-strength solvent, elbow grease, and curses, he managed to erase most of the fingerprint dust from the walls, sills, and cabinets.

At one o'clock he grabbed a Spartan lunch of cheese, celery sticks, and a bottle of water. His muscles aching from the rug extraction, Ethan scrubbed himself hard in the shower, put on fresh clothes, and went to the hospital. What he had to do next would be harder than cleaning the house. He had to figure out what his relationship to Meredith would be without Sky.

It didn't start off well when Ethan arrived at Meredith's hospital room. She looked up from a magazine. With a sharp intake of breath, she startled as though she had just seen her husband resurrected from the dead.

She dissolved in tears.

"Meredith … I'm sorry," Ethan said. "I should have called."

She waved a tissue dismissively.

"Really … I should have …"

"You have nothing to apologize for," she insisted.

Meredith and Sky had always been close. Ethan wondered if there would ever be a time when she would look at him and not see her dead husband.

He learned that the doctors were keeping her one more day for observation. They'd prescribed antidepressants and counseling sessions with hospital staff. Chaplains visited her room regularly, as well as her own minister and friends from the church where she and Andrew were members.

Ethan learned that Meredith's mother was flying out from Ohio and would stay until after the funeral. While he was glad for Meredith, her mother's presence would put a strain on further conversations. Olivia Cooper had never liked Ethan, though she seemed to like Andrew well enough. But whenever she was around, her attitude toward Ethan ranged from cool to chilly.

After leaving the hospital, for the rest of the afternoon and well into the night, Ethan cleaned every inch of his house as though by scrubbing he could exorcise the evil that had visited it. But he couldn't scrub his memory.

That night when he set up a TV tray in the living room to watch the baseball playoffs, those memories haunted him. Every time he looked down he saw Sky lying dead on the floor at his feet. He tried to forcibly shove the images from his head. He would have had more luck manhandling a cloud.

Ethan watched the game at a local sports bar.

---

Ethan went to work on the second day after his brother's killing. The San Diego Police Department headquarters occupied an entire city block at 14th and Broadway on the east side of downtown, less than a mile from Interstate 5.

The building was blocklike and utilitarian, seven stories high. Even though it was a necessary upgrade, when the structure was built in 1987, it drew considerable criticism because of the sterile gray and blue exterior. It was a far cry from the romantic Spanish architecture of the previous building on Market Street, which had been erected on Dead Man's Point, so named for the sailors and marines who had been buried there during the charting and surveying of San Diego Bay. The old headquarters was turned into a national landmark.

Ethan drove through the front parking lot to the employees' underground lot and held up his key card to the scanner. An elevator took him to the fourth floor, which homicide shared with communications.

It was customary for homicide teams to meet regularly and exchange information. This way everyone knew what everyone else knew. Savala had managed to talk Weisberg into letting Ethan attend Team I's meeting. He reminded Ethan that he was to say nothing to Detective Hinkey. Ethan accepted the condition. He would have agreed to wear a Santa Claus outfit and high heels to get into this meeting.

Each homicide team shared a fifteen-foot square cubicle that was large enough for desks, a couple of file cabinets, and a few extra chairs for visitors. Each desk was equipped with a computer and a telephone. The desks faced the walls. Team members sat with their backs to the center of the cubicle.

Ethan arrived just as the meeting was starting. He made eye contact with Weisberg, out of respect for being allowed onto Team I's turf, grabbed an empty chair, and sat down without greeting anyone else. Weisberg gave him a cautionary glance.

"What's he doing here?" Hinkey complained.

Hinkey looked sick, as though he had lost a lot of weight. His eyes appeared sunken. Every line on his face was accentuated. All of this was because fingerprint dust had settled into the recesses of his face and wouldn't wash off.

Ethan suppressed a laugh but couldn't keep a grin from forming. The grin was enough provocation for Hinkey.

Hinkey came at him. Weisberg ordered him to sit down. From the chuckles in the cubicle, the other officers must have thought Hinkey looked as ridiculous as Ethan did.

"What do we have on the Morgan case?" Weisberg said, getting the meeting started. "Osorio, you go first."

Ivy Osorio was a dark-complexioned brunette who, when she smiled, showed equal amounts teeth and gums, a trait which made her very self-conscious about her smile. Ethan didn't know much about her other than the fact that occasionally she pressed too hard to prove that she could be just as much a man as any of the guys. He had heard she had a vindictive streak that wouldn't quit, but he had never known her to be anything less than professional.

Osorio read from a yellow pad. "The phone number on the cell phone doesn't connect to anything," she said. "The 431 exchange doesn't exist. Tyler, Texas, is 430. Odessa, Texas, is 432. There is no 431."

"He could've misdialed," Weisberg said. "Understandable given the circumstances."

"I considered that," Osorio replied. "But which number or numbers did he misdial? The 4? The 3? Or the 1? Did he misdial two of them? Or possibly all three?" She turned her yellow pad so that all could see it. Two columns of three digit numbers ran the length of the page. "I played around with possible combinations, trying to match them to the numbers in the cell-phone memory. No luck."

Weisberg turned to Ethan. "Do you know if your brother had any contacts in Tyler or Odessa?"

"Not that I'm aware of," Ethan replied. "But that's not to say he didn't. He did business with people all over the country. You'll need to ask Meredith."

As soon as he said that he wished he hadn't. Of course they would ask Meredith. They knew how to do their jobs.

Wincing, Ethan raised a hand of apology and said, "Sorry."

Everyone seemed to understand and accept his apology. Everyone except Hinkey.

Weisberg moved on. "Finch, what did you get from ballistics?"

Det. Bobby Finch cleared his throat to speak. He had a striking resemblance to the cartoon character Charlie Brown, with a round face and prominent ears. His passion was pitching horseshoes. Anyone who had attended a department picnic had at least one horseshoe story about him.

Finch delivered his report to the floor, consciously avoiding Ethan's eyes. "Four .45-caliber bullets were fired at close range. According to the medical examiner, they missed the heart and vital arteries. He bled to death. Had he received medical assistance in time, he could have been saved."

The cubical fell silent. Police work often involves a race against time. This was one race they'd lost. It didn't sit well with any of them.

"Wallach," Weisberg said, "did you find out anything from the neighbors?"

Bill Wallach was the oldest member of the team, which was visibly evident from the gray hair at his temples. He hated internal politics and had no ambition for advancement. He liked being a homicide detective. He was thorough and professional.

"Nobody heard anything or saw anything unusual," Wallach reported, "until the units arrived."

"That's impossible!" Ethan cried. "Did all of them have their heads stuck in the refrigerator? It was a warm evening. Windows were open. How could they not hear the shots?"

Wallach took exception to the implication he had not done his job. He defended his report.

"The neighbors on either side of the house were away from home at the time of the shooting," he said. "Two houses down, the Blackburns thought they might have heard shots, but they are both hard of hearing, and the television was loud, and the time they thought they heard shots does not coincide with the time we know the killer to be in the house."

With each report Ethan's mood deteriorated. It was still early in the investigation, but so far none of the evidence looked promising.

"Hinkey," Weisberg said. "You're up."

Hinkey cocked his head and grinned at Ethan with a punk's smirk.

"Just as I suspected," he said, "there were no fingerprints. Not on the kitchen windowsill. Not on the cabinets. Not on the wrappers or soda can. Nowhere. The killer wore gloves." Glaring at Ethan, he concluded. "And believe me, I was thorough."

He cackled at his own jab.

Ethan clenched his jaw to keep from saying anything. He didn't want to give Hinkey the satisfaction.

Finch caught Hinkey's attention. "Hey, Brian, you have a little something right there." He indicated a spot on his own face with his little finger.

Hinkey touched the identical spot on his face and attempted to rub whatever it was off.

"Sorry, my mistake," Finch said. "Must be that new makeup you're wearing."

His comment drew laughs from the other detectives and a curse from Hinkey.

"What about the Outlaw T-shirt?" Ethan asked.

Weisberg was ready for him. "I spoke to your brother's wife and she could neither confirm nor deny that he owned an Outlaws T-shirt."

"He didn't," Ethan insisted. "And even if he did, he wouldn't have worn it that night. He was wearing a dress shirt."

"A lot of guys wear T-shirts under their dress shirts," Hinkey said.

"Not one with printing on it," Wallach offered. "Not if they have any taste. And everything we've learned about the victim indicates he was a classy guy."

"My brother wouldn't wear a sports T-shirt under a dress shirt," Ethan insisted.

"And yet, he did," Hinkey quipped.

"You saw your brother earlier that night," Weisberg said to Ethan. "Can you say for certain he wasn't wearing the shirt then?"

"I can't remember," Ethan confessed.

It grated on him to admit the truth.

"Just for the sake of argument, what if it wasn't my brother's T-shirt?" he said. "Why would someone force him to put the T-shirt on and then shoot him?"

"Where is the evidence that anyone forced him to wear the shirt?" Hinkey taunted.

"I know my brother. That's evidence enough."

Weisberg didn't agree. "It's a hunch based on the assumption that the break-in and killing had something to do with the Corby incident in Las Vegas, isn't it?"

"Corby incident?" Osorio asked.

"Another lifetime ago," Ethan said dismissively, eager to hear what Weisberg had to say.

Weisberg followed his lead. "Las Vegas PD confirmed that Corby had a brother," he said, "and at my request they checked him out. Sorry, Ethan. He has a solid alibi."

"Don't tell me it's his mother," Ethan said. "She would say anything to cover for her boys. During the trial she told the news media she was the one driving the truck."

"This time it's not the mother," Weisberg said. "Corby has a time card and a supervisor who vouch for the fact that he worked a full shift that day. He couldn't have made it to San Diego in time to kill your brother."

"Iron Fist Shredding?" Finch asked.

"I think that was the name of it," Weisberg said. "Why?"

Finch reached for a book on his desk. He held it up. "It's not relevant to the case," he said. "It's just that it's one of F. Malory Simon's companies."

The book Finch was holding could be seen on any number of desks in the department. A contingent of police personnel had been registered for a conference in Las Vegas in which the book's author was the key speaker.

Multimillionaire F. Malory Simon made his fortune in the burgeoning document-shredding business. Once every two years he conducted a leadership and motivational seminar based on his best-selling book, *Simon Says: Take Three Giant Steps to Success.* It was the hottest seminar in America. People from all over the world attended.

"Anyway," Weisberg said, directing them back to the business at hand, "Corby is a dead end. Which brings us to motive. Osorio, did you get the word out to the pawnshops about the Bible?"

"Affirmative," Osorio replied. "We've called all the local shops and are following up with these flyers."

She handed out green single-sheet pages with the description of the Morgan family Bible and instructions to notify the police immediately should anyone attempt to pawn it.

"Patrol units are distributing these to local shops," she said. "In addition, we are posting the information on the Internet and informing antique and rare-book dealers to be on the lookout for the Bible."

Weisberg nodded. He seemed satisfied the case was progressing as well as it could. Ethan didn't share his satisfaction.

"Does anybody have anything else on the Morgan case?" Weisberg asked, shuffling file folders to the next case.

No one spoke up.

Weisberg dismissed Ethan. "I'll keep you informed," he said.

Ethan stood. Nobody looked at him. Not even Hinkey.

Before leaving, he asked, "What is Corby's first name?"

"What difference does it make?" Weisberg asked.

"No difference. Just curious."

Weisberg squinted as though by doing so he might reveal any ulterior motives that were lurking behind Ethan's eyes. Apparently he saw none, because he said, "Richard. Richard Corby."

Ethan made his way through the maze of fourth-floor partitions to the Team IV cubicle in the northeast corner of the building. Of all the unexplained mysteries surrounding his brother's murder, the one that gnawed at him the most was the Outlaws T-shirt. Sky and the Nevada Outlaws were a pairing so unnatural it couldn't be dismissed.

Of course, that in and of itself might be the key. Sky might have taken a dare or lost a bet. It could have been some sort of joke or prank. Meredith had arranged for some kid to wear a stork costume as a surprise. Had Sky arranged for some sort of surprise of his own? It didn't seem likely. Sky knew how painful the Las Vegas incident had been to Ethan. If it was a joke, it wasn't a good one.

But if he hadn't worn the shirt willingly, that meant he'd been forced to wear it. Forced at gunpoint? Payback for Las Vegas? That was a possibility, especially if the killer knew that Sky was his brother.

*Revenge if the killer thought it was me,* Ethan concluded.

Richard Corby had something to do with it, if not directly, then indirectly. Weisberg was wrong. And if he wasn't going to pursue the Corby lead, Ethan would.

Back at his desk Ethan booted up his computer. Occupied at their own desks, none of the other detectives looked up to acknowledge him. The working case file on Ethan's desk was of a woman who had stolen drugs from her employer, a pharmaceutical company, which she used to poison her husband. Ethan shoved the file aside and called up a Las Vegas directory onto his computer screen. Within a few moments he had Richard Corby's home address.

The Corby incident in Las Vegas was a matter of public record. While Ethan had been exonerated in the shooting, the fact remained that two people were dead. One he shot. The other, he couldn't save.

When his parents took early retirement and moved to Las Vegas, Ethan moved with them. Zachary "Buck" Morgan had made a comfortable living as the owner of his own electrical business. He got lucky with some early investments, having bought Qualcomm stock for no reason other than they were a local company. When Qualcomm stock skyrocketed, Buck retired, figuring there was more to life than stringing electrical wire. He sold his business and moved to Desert Palms retirement village where he took leisurely morning walks, made wooden three-legged footstools, and played solitaire on the computer.

The bright lights of the casinos held no attraction for him. Buck chose Las Vegas for its desert location and size. He thought a city with a population of half a million people and a thriving tourist industry should be able to bring in sufficient revenue to keep the lights on, the water flowing, and support an airport large enough to fly him to San Diego to visit his grandchildren if his boys ever got around to making any.

Fresh out of the police academy, Ethan moved to Las Vegas. He was eager for new challenges and a change of scenery. He had been on the force ten years when he shot and killed Roger Corby.

The Nevada Outlaws, an NFL expansion team, routinely hired Las Vegas police officers as security. True to their colorful city, Outlaws fans were known for their outlandish costumes and intimidating behavior. One New York sportswriter said of them, "What would you expect? These are people whose brains bake in the desert sun six months out of the year. They are as crazy as inbred cousins, as welcome as skunks at a cocktail party, and as friendly as a room full of rattlesnakes." The Outlaws led the league in personal fouls, fines, brawls in the stands, and arrests—both fan and player.

It was mid-October. Outlaws fans had been looking forward to the game against the Washington Redskins since the playoffs the previous year when a final-second Hail Mary touchdown pass sent the Redskins to the Super Bowl and the Outlaws home. Replays of the down showed that the clock had expired before the ball was snapped. The referees missed the call and Outlaws fans had all summer to stew over the injustice.

Ethan was patrolling the parking lot on foot. The security job brought in extra money, which he was putting aside for a new Mustang

GT Convertible; four on the floor, none of this automatic-transmission nonsense; leather seats; red with silver racing stripes.

Normally pregame patrol was limited to solving disputes over parking spaces, telling fans to turn down their car stereos, refusing offers of beer and barbeque, and arresting the occasional drunk. But this was the Redskins game and payback was on everyone's mind.

Ethan and his partner—a rookie from Oregon who was patrolling his first Outlaws game—began hearing rumors that some Redskins fans were being held against their will in section G4. They went to investigate.

They found a crowd about ten deep around a black pickup truck, the kind with oversized tires so tall a step stool is needed to climb into the cab. A man wearing nothing but boxer shorts and cowboy chaps waved a large Outlaws team flag and screamed like a banshee atop the truck's cab.

In the back of the truck, bound and gagged and on their knees, were five men wearing Washington Redskins shirts and caps.

Ethan called for backup.

Nobody appeared to be in immediate danger, but the situation was volatile. For the moment, the captured Redskins fans were more angry than frightened. Also, for the moment, the crowd, which Ethan estimated to be close to a hundred inebriated Outlaws fans, seemed content to heckle them. All that was needed was a spark—a word, a suggestion—and the whole thing could blow up.

Ethan's rookie partner drew his nightstick like he was Sir Lancelot drawing a sword. It was a defensive act. He was scared.

Ethan told him to relax. They weren't going in just yet. He wanted to identify the instigators.

There seemed to be four, counting the screaming flag waver. Two dressed in black cowboy hats and bandannas huddled shoulder to shoulder at the tailgate looking pleased with themselves for all the attention the crowd was giving them. A third man, a bodybuilder from the size and shape of his bare chest, wore a black bandanna as a scarf and a pair of worn jeans so tight they appeared to be painted on.

Ethan learned later that the bare-chested man was Roger Corby, a professional wrestler known in the ring as Deathblow.

In full entertainment mode, Corby paced back and forth in front of his captives pausing occasionally to flex his muscles and growl at them, much to the delight of the crowd.

When the pacing stopped, he turned to the crowd and shouted, "Scalp the Redskins!"

The crowd went crazy. A chant started.

*"Scalp the Redskins!"*

*"Scalp the Redskins!"*

*"Scalp the Redskins!"*

Corby leaped into the bed of the truck with his captives, urging the crowd on. The captives were scared now. One of them was crying.

Ethan checked for backup. All he could see were more Outlaw fans running toward the truck to see what all the ruckus was about.

"We're going in," Ethan said to the rookie. "To talk. Just to talk. Understand? We need to defuse the situation."

The rookie nodded nervously. "Can I …"

He held up his nightstick. It was shaking. Ethan was afraid if he told him to put it away, if things got tense, the kid might go for his gun. The nightstick kept his hand occupied.

"Keep it lowered and hidden behind your leg," Ethan said. "Don't raise it unless you absolutely have to."

The rookie agreed.

His hand became a ship's bow as Ethan plowed his way through the crowd with the rookie in tow.

Their approach caught Corby's attention. He turned to face them. Standing behind his captives he looked down at Ethan from on high as though he were a god of Olympus.

"Looks like you bagged yourself some Redskins," Ethan shouted, keeping his tone jovial.

Corby's buddies closed in on them grinning like a couple of drunken hyenas.

"We aim to rustle up ourselves a few more before the day's over," Corby boasted.

The hogtied Redskins pleaded to Ethan with their eyes.

"Maybe on the football field," Ethan said to Corby. "But out here I'm afraid the game's over, boys. Untie these men and let them go."

"Ain't gonna happen," Corby said, folding his arms as if a show of muscles settled the matter.

Corby's buddies crowded Ethan's partner who was gripping and regripping his nightstick. The banshee on top of the cab continued screaming and waving the flag, his eyes charged with drugs.

Ethan held Corby's gaze. The wrestler had him by at least thirty pounds. His chest, arms, and thighs were massive. Ethan was content to keep it a contest of wills until backup arrived. As long as Corby was focused on him the captives were in no danger. He only hoped his partner could keep it together for that long. He wanted to see how the rookie was doing, but he dared not break eye contact with Corby.

"You don't want to hurt them," Ethan said, keeping Corby engaged.

"Yeah? Shows how little you know."

"No," Ethan insisted. "You don't want to hurt them, because if you do, you'll miss the game."

The Nevada sun was hot for October, adding to the already sizzling crowd that was feeding off the tension of the confrontation. The chant picked up again for Redskin scalps. The banshee wailed incessantly. Corby was growing bolder, encouraged by the crowd's support.

All of a sudden Ethan had a new problem. Out of the corner of his eye he saw that one of Corby's men had managed to snatch the rookie's nightstick. Showing a mouthful of blackened teeth, he held it over his head like a prize.

The rookie's hand went to his gun.

Ethan grabbed the rookie's wrist. The last thing he needed was a scared rookie pointing a gun into a crowd.

The man with the nightstick saw the rookie's hand go for the gun. He gripped the nightstick like it was a baseball bat and swung for the fences. The crack against the rookie's head was loud enough to silence the immediate crowd. The rookie dropped to the ground like a sack of bones.

What happened next took only a few seconds.

With Ethan's hand still on the unconscious rookie's wrist, his partner almost pulled him to the ground on top of him while the man with the nightstick raised it for another blow, this one aimed at Ethan's head. The nightstick raised to its highest point and hovered there for an instant before coming down at the same time that Corby, looking like Hercules descending from Olympus, launched himself from the bed of the truck toward Ethan, his mass blocking out the sun. Releasing the rookie, Ethan grabbed the nightstick away from the man, stepped to one side, and continued the swing, catching an enraged Corby square on the jaw, knocking him out. Ethan could have sworn the earth trembled when the wrestler hit the ground. His instinct and training kicked in. He wasted no time scrambling to place a knee in Corby's back and cuffing him just as a half-dozen security officers arrived.

With their hero down for the count, the fight had gone out of the two hyenas, and they were arrested easily enough. The drugged banshee was a different story. When backup arrived, it took several Taser hits to bring him down. Once the Redskin fans were untied, the crowd dispersed, their attention turning to the football game and kickoff.

The next day Ethan got his fair share of ribbing at headquarters when a newspaper article declared him a legitimate contender for the world wrestling federation crown for having taken down Deathblow in the first round.

Sky sent Ethan a drawing of him in his uniform with an oversized shiny badge, standing on the back of the fallen wrestler, holding a wrestling federation championship belt over his head.

Ethan's partner spent a few days in the hospital with a concussion and was released in time to attend a ceremony where Ethan was presented with a citation for his handling of the situation.

Ethan thought that would be the end of it. But it wasn't.

Two weeks later the Outlaws hosted the Oakland Raiders in what many columnists referred to as a Fan Freak Fest, with supporters from both teams sporting costumes designed to intimidate. To make matters worse, it was Halloween.

As Ethan strolled through the parking lot, he felt as though he was walking the gauntlet in a house of horrors. Acre after macadam acre black and tan clashed with black and silver. Two hours before kickoff they'd already made fifty arrests for drunk and disorderly conduct. Ethan had broken up two fights, one between men and one between women. It was his first Outlaw/Raider game, and he vowed it would be his last. They didn't pay him enough to do this again.

For the moment he was alone. His partner had lagged behind to give a Wisconsin man with a cheese head (Ethan didn't want to know how he happened to wander into Outlaw country) directions to Circus Circus on the Strip.

The smell of carne asada sizzling on a grill distracted Ethan. A plump man with an oversized orange foam Outlaws cowboy hat and a fringed leather vest lifted strips of seasoned meat from the barbeque for his two teenage boys who held plates blanketed with flour tortillas. Containers of shredded cheese, guacamole, and salsa sat on a folding table next to them.

Ethan's stomach rumbled. Growing up in San Diego, he'd developed a taste for Mexican food. More than a taste, really. It was a weakness.

A second rumble followed the first, only this one was deeper and more mechanical. Ethan turned to see a black pickup truck with oversized tires. Rage sat behind the wheel wearing the face of Roger Corby. His eyes weren't right, more animal than human, and they were tracking Ethan.

The truck inched through the parking lot between rows of tailgaters like a big cat moving through tall grass stalking its prey.

Ethan's chest constricted, not out of fear for himself, but out of fear for all the people around him. His eyes darted, taking in his options.

They were near the edge of the crowd. Ten or twelve parking stalls behind him and the lot opened up where two boys were throwing a Frisbee. He had to lure Corby out into the open, away from the tailgaters.

Ethan stepped into the middle of the roadway and faced Corby, like two gunfighters meeting at high noon; only today it was man versus truck driven by a crazed professional wrestler.

The man with the orange foam cowboy hat looked up with tongs in hand, a strip of cooked meat dangling. Then he looked at the truck.

"God have mercy," he said.

He dropped the meat. It fell between the grill's rungs and into the fire.

The truck rumbled, then roared and roared again as Corby raced the engine.

Ethan spoke into his radio. "Officer needs help." He transmitted the parking lot section number, a description of the truck, and its license plate.

He holstered his radio. Turning his back on Corby, he strolled casually down the middle of the roadway. The number of tailgaters between him and the open parking lot served as a visual countdown.

Five.

The fifth tailgate party from the end consisted of two guys sitting in low beach chairs behind a white Toyota truck eating fast-food hamburgers and super-sized fries and drinks.

Four.

A trio of middle-aged men leaned against a green Lexus, giving each other high fives as they regaled themselves with verbal replays of previous games.

Three.

Ethan's time ran out. He didn't get a good look at the tailgaters in the third-to-the-last parking space.

Behind him the truck engine screamed. Tires screeched. Ethan turned to see plumes of white smoke as the truck leaped forward with sudden speed, enough to lift the front tires off the pavement.

Corby lost control of the vehicle.

To Ethan's horror, it swerved toward the man grilling carne asada. The barbeque, the grill, and red coals exploded off the truck's front bumper. The man with the orange foam hat managed to dive out of the path of the truck. One of his sons wasn't so lucky. The boy looked like a rag doll tossed into the air.

Ethan yelled his frustration.

Corby regained control of the truck.

At this point in the movies everything slows down. Not so now. Everything happened with surprising speed. For all its bulkiness, the truck covered the distance between them like a cheetah.

On either side of him the tailgaters stared with wide eyes and open mouths at the rampaging black truck, making no effort to get out of its way. Why should they? This was Las Vegas where everything was a show and they had front-row seats. Desensitized by movies and stunts, they were unable to comprehend that they were in mortal danger.

Ethan shouted at them to get back.

They did just the opposite. They crowded closer to get a better look. Behind them, others came running, not wanting to miss the show.

This was no time for crowd control. Ethan turned and ran toward the open lot, shouting at the Frisbee-throwing boys to clear out. He could hear the roar of the truck closing behind him.

He knew his only hope was to time a dive out of the path of the oncoming man shredder.

*This is ridiculous*, he thought. *The stuff of stunt men.*

If he dove too soon, Corby would adjust and steer into him. If he dove too late ... well, it would be too late.

With macadam to the left of him and macadam to right of him, there was no good place to dive. Ethan hated diving. In high school he lost his position as shortstop because he wouldn't dive for the line drives. He played second string on the football team because he wouldn't sacrifice his body for an extra yard.

It wasn't for lack of motivation. The ground just had it in for him. Whenever he dove, the ground would knock the wind out of him. How did the coaches expect him to throw for an out or dive for a yard if he couldn't breathe?

The truck was upon him.

Ethan jumped to his right.

He nearly waited a nanosecond too long. While he was in the air, the headlight clipped his heel and sent him spinning. The ground leaped up at him. He hit hard and skidded. Then he rolled and finally came to a stop on his back, looking up at a sky filled with air; yet, despite his gasping, he could coax none of it into his lungs.

He pulled with all his might and got a teaspoon of breath. Another pull and another teaspoon. He managed to prop himself up on an elbow.

In the distance, the truck fishtailed, nearly hitting one of the Frisbee boys. The engine roared. The tires smoked.

Corby was coming back to finish the job.

Ethan struggled to his knees. He looked behind him. To his horror people were running to watch the drama unfold. What were they thinking? They were lining up like so many bowling pins.

Ethan struggled to his feet.

The truck did a little sumo-wrestler waddle until the tires bit the pavement and it lurched toward him.

Ethan drew his service revolver and aimed it at the truck.

"Back off, Corby!" he yelled. "Back off! Back off!"

He knew Corby couldn't hear him. The whine of the engine was too loud. His rage plugged his ears. Still, Ethan shouted.

Then he stopped shouting and he fired.

He had no hope of stopping the truck. By the time it came into range, physics were in play. To stop it he would have to alter the laws of the universe. But he had to try.

He fired until his gun was empty.

The driver's side of the truck's windshield spiderwebbed with the first bullet, shattered with the second, obscuring the driver. But Ethan knew he'd hit Corby when the shattered windshield turned red.

Then, Ethan got lucky. He never knew for certain whether he hit the front tire, or whether Corby jerked the wheel, but the truck swerved suddenly and tumbled across open lot, finally coming to a rest on its side, missing the crowd completely.

The audience clapped and cheered.

If it was up to Ethan, he would have arrested every single one of them.

Following the incident Ethan was put on administrative duty, standard procedure while the shooting was investigated. That didn't mean he liked it any less. He felt as though he was being put on trial. In due time the review board determined it was a good shoot, and the department heads not only exonerated Ethan for his actions, they presented him with another citation.

For Ethan it was a somber ceremony, attended by the man in the orange foam cowboy hat and his surviving son.

Maybe Ethan had saved countless lives that day. But all he could think about was the one life he'd failed to save.

Six months after the awards ceremony, Ethan moved back to San Diego.

———————

"Morgan, you're back," Sergeant Majeski said, entering Team IV's cubical.

Ethan clicked the Home icon on his computer. The San Diego City Web site home page popped up. He thrust the piece of paper with Richard Corby's address into his pocket and found that his chest had swelled with anger and his breathing was labored, like it did whenever he woke from dreams of black trucks and death.

Majeski pulled the morning newspaper from under his arm and tossed it onto his desk. He removed his suit coat and draped it over the back of his chair.

The leader of homicide Team IV, Majeski was a thin man with no hips. His belt always looked cinched and even then Ethan wondered what was keeping the man's pants from falling down. He had a full head of sandy reddish hair, which he had trimmed every Saturday. He was a cop's cop. Loyal to the city. Loyal to the force. But mostly, loyal to his men.

"Let's get this show on the road," Majeski said.

The three other detectives of Team IV—Joe Kang, Joan Durso, and

Oscar Gomez—swiveled in their chairs until they were facing the center of the room. They each welcomed Ethan back and offered their condolences.

Ethan was more embarrassed than consoled, but he knew they meant well, and he thanked them. He felt at ease with this team. They worked well together, respected each other's space and work, and generally got along. They had none of the pettiness and bickering and politics that plagued Team I.

Ethan concentrated on making the mental adjustment from personal issues to his job. However, that process was quickly deterred when he saw a picture of Sky grinning at him from atop Majeski's desk.

This was the second day the *San Diego Union* had run a story on his brother's murder. The morning following the murder, the story of the break-in and killing made the front page. Today's follow-up story was also front-page news, but below the fold. Next to Sky's publicity picture was a panel from one of his graphic novels.

"Sorry," Majeski said, turning the paper over. "I didn't mean to do that."

Ethan knew Majeski well enough to take him at his word. "No problem," he said.

"Really, Ethan, I—"

"Hey ..." Ethan cut him off. "Like I said. No problem."

A different picture grabbed his attention, this one taking up most of the page above the fold. Ethan snatched up the paper to get a better look.

"When did this happen?" he asked.

"Are you kidding?" Joan cried. "It's been all over the news."

"The security alert at the airports has been heightened," Joe added. "A radical Muslim group has claimed credit for it."

The full-color picture showed the ruins of Notre Dame Cathedral in Reims, France. The flying buttresses, no longer attached to the building, looked like ribs of a carcass. The famed rose window was gone. The only thing remaining was the bottom half of the supporting structure. An insert picture showed one of the two great bells, "Charlotte," reported to weigh eleven tons, lying on its side in the rubble.

The text beneath the picture reported that the cathedral was over seven hundred years old, having been completed in the thirteenth century. Only one of its two 267-feet-high towers was left standing.

"This is exactly what's wrong with the world today," said Ethan.

"How do you mean?" Majeski said.

"We're no longer a race of builders. We're destroyers."

"That's a little harsh, isn't it? The people who did this are terrorists."

"The only difference between them and everyone else is that they make a spectacle of it. I'm serious. Look around. We've discovered it's not only easier to tear things down than it is to build them, there's a certain satisfaction to it." He pointed to the front page of the paper as an example. "Why take centuries to build a grand edifice when you can make the front page of the paper by bombing it? If you're a politician, why labor to build a coalition for change when you get more publicity by criticizing and attacking those who are trying to effect change? Why spend countless hours learning to perform when you can get easy laughs heckling a performer? Why save and invest when it's easier to steal from or sue those who have money? Even the games our children are playing award points for destroying property and lives."

Ethan flipped the newspaper over so that Andrew's picture was face up.

"My brother believed in heroes. But if you ask me, the day of the hero is dead. We're living in the day of the destroyer, an era when violence is glorified."

Nobody challenged him. On a normal day they probably would have, but not two days after his hero brother was tragically killed. He knew they were thinking it was grief talking, but it wasn't. He'd seen too many destroyers in every walk of life. His philosophy was born of observation.

"Well, on that happy note," Majeski said, taking a seat among the circle of detectives, "let's solve some crimes, shall we? Kang. Get us up-to-date on the Robbins murder."

# SEVEN

"Do you not know?
Have you not heard?
The Lord is the everlasting God,
the Creator of the ends of the earth.
He will not grow tired or weary,
and his understanding no one can fathom.
He gives strength to the weary
and increases the power of the weak.
Even youths grow tired and weary,
and young men stumble and fall;
but those who hope in the Lord
will renew their strength.
They will soar on wings like eagles;
they will run and not grow weary,
they will walk and not be faint."

His open palms serving as a pulpit, the minister read from the Bible, the book of Isaiah. Ethan stood a few feet from his brother's coffin, next to Meredith. In the row behind him were his parents and Meredith's mother.

Local dignitaries were present, so were representatives from Andrew's publishers. Hundreds of people from his church and the community had come to pay their respects, including Mr. Pandurski from William Jennings Bryan Elementary School.

Even characters from his novels, printed on oversized posters and displayed on art stands, attended the funeral. Drew Morgan, the original owner of the family Bible, attended in caricature.

Ethan took it all in from behind dark sunglasses, careful to keep his emotions in check. It was a perfect day for a send-off. The sun warm, the sky cloudless blue. A refreshing breeze off the ocean combined in chorus with trees, seasonal flowers, lakes, garden areas, and 117 acres of green grass reminded the mourners that life exists in the presence of death.

Rev. Scott Grogan, Andrew's minister and personal friend, was a genial guy, middle-aged with a receding hairline.

"Through the prophet, God offers us hope in time of suffering," Grogan preached. "He describes life at three levels. There are days when life is sweet—when it couldn't be any better—when we feel like we are soaring on the wings of eagles.

"Other days are filled with activity, work, family responsibilities; the schedule is full, but with youthfulness and vitality we find the strength to get everything done and to do this day after day, as if we are running and not growing weary.

"But there is a third type of day, when it is enough just to get through it, when it is enough to be able to put one foot in front of the other, when all we ask is for the strength to walk without fainting. This is one of those days. For our sorrow is great, and it weighs us down.

"But those who hope in the Lord will renew their strength … they will walk and not faint … and it will be enough. O God, it will be enough."

Meredith wept softy beside Ethan.

———————

"Nothing personal," Mr. Pandurski said, "but you give me the willies every time I see you."

If there was one thing Ethan hated more than funerals it was the reception following funerals. He stood in Andrew's living room holding a plastic cup of punch.

The front door stayed open as people came and went, offering condolences and bringing food. A large and loud group had formed in a corner around Buck and Connie Morgan. Some were friends from before the boys were born.

Another group formed around Rev. Grogan. Replace his cup of punch with a microphone and you'd think he was a stand-up comic.

Those who didn't fit in either of the large groups buzzed around Ethan like flies. Pandurski buzzed the loudest.

"I was sitting in that easy chair by the window," Pandurski said, his bottlebrush mustache sweeping the words that came out of his mouth, "and every time I looked up from my plate of cookies, I nearly had a heart attack. I wanted to shout, 'Hallelujah! Andrew's raised from the grave!'"

He laughed at his own story.

Nudging Ethan, he said, "I mean, after all, didn't we just bury you?"

"Excuse me," Ethan said, hefting his punch cup, "I need some ice."

Ethan bypassed the bowl of ice on the buffet table and went to the kitchen.

He took his time in front of the open refrigerator selecting three ice cubes. When he closed the door, Meredith's mother appeared.

"What did you think of the service?" she said.

Olivia Cooper was a formidable presence in any setting. Her eyes direct, her voice husky. Her face was set between parentheses of short red hair. She wore a black suit with a coat to camouflage a substantial frame. A gold circle pendant hung on a chain around her neck.

Ethan fell back on a well-worn funeral cliché. "I think Andrew would have liked it," he said.

"I asked what *you* thought of it." She folded her arms to indicate she wasn't going anywhere anytime soon.

"I thought Rev. Grogan did a nice job."

Ethan rattled the cubes in his plastic cup to indicate he had unfinished punch-pouring business.

Olivia said, "Did you notice how Rev. Grogan mentioned that the Morgans and the Coopers were influential in founding the Heritage Churches of America?"

"I noticed."

"It was almost as though he was speaking to you directly."

"Really? That's not the way I heard it." He strained to keep his tone civil.

"You don't think much of it, do you?"

"Of what, Olivia?"

"Your family legacy."

She was setting him up. That much was obvious. But what could he do? Deny his family's heritage just to get away from Olivia Cooper?

"Of course I value it."

"Then you have prospects? You're not getting any younger. It's time you produced an heir."

Ethan forced a smile. "Everything in its time, Olivia. First a punch refill, then I'll find a wife."

"You think this is funny."

"Talking to my brother's mother-in-law about my romantic prospects on the day of his funeral? What's funny about that?"

"Do you know what your problem is, Ethan?" she said.

He didn't answer her. She told him anyway.

"You live life as though it were a ship. That way you have a manageable world with a handful of shipmates passing the time, arguing over shipboard politics. And as long as everyone knows their place and performs their assigned duties, you can float in your boat and life is good. You ignore the fact that there is a larger world beyond your little ship and crew, larger ships and pirates and kings and governments, forces that are greater than you, forces that can scuttle your ship on a whim. You ignore them at your own peril, Ethan. And someday, if you're not prepared, they'll blow you out of the water, and there will be nothing left of you and your little ship."

---

Punch was on his mind when he left the kitchen, not the kind you drink, the kind that puts holes in walls. Ethan wanted to hit something.

He was in no mood for chitchat or to have people tell him he looked like the ghost of his late brother.

But he couldn't leave. His parents had come with him.

Ethan made his way to Andrew's office at the back of the house. The door was closed. There was no lock on it, so he let himself in.

Meredith sat at Andrew's drawing desk. She was absentmindedly slapping her leg with a straightedge ruler.

"Sorry, I didn't know you were here," he said.

She shrugged. "I had to get away for a while."

"I'll leave."

Ethan backed out of the room.

"No. Stay," Meredith said.

"But you want to be ..."

"Now that I am, I find I don't," she replied. "Please ..." She offered him an identical wooden stool to the one she was sitting on.

Ethan pulled it beneath him and sat. Andrew's drawing desk was a hodgepodge of sketches and panels in various stages of completion, along with stacks of story scripts and sticky notes stuck everywhere with reminders penned in professional lettering.

Fingering one of the sticky notes, Ethan marveled at the handwriting. "Half the time mine is illegible," he said. "I write myself notes I can't read."

Meredith chuckled softly. She appeared pensive, uncharacteristic for her, but understandable given the events of the day.

"How are you feeling?" Ethan asked softly.

She read his face and knew what he was asking. Placing a hand on her stomach, she said, "It's going to take awhile."

He considered telling her about his run-in with her mother in the kitchen, but the incident was minor compared to her pain, so he didn't bring it up.

"I know you haven't had much time to think about it," he said, "but what's going to happen with Andrew's business?"

She cocked her head and looked sadly at the drawings on the walls and the racks of graphic novels and stacks of comic books. "Someone wanted to buy Andrew out about a year ago," she said.

"He never told me that."

"At the time it was a no-brainer. Andrew loved working. He couldn't imagine ever retiring, no matter how successful his books became. So I guess I've known all along I'd sell it after he was dead. I just didn't think it would be this soon."

"Who wanted to buy it?"

Meredith squeezed her eyes shut as she searched her memory for the name. "Um ... a corporation in Dallas ... Shiva Enterprises, I think."

"I've never heard of them. A comic-book firm?"

"I don't know anything about them. Andrew said their offer was above market value. I'm sure he kept their business card."

"When the time comes ... if you need any help ..."

"Thank you, Ethan. Right now, I don't know what I'm going to do. Stay here. Move back to Point Providence."

"You'd consider going back to Ohio? Why?"

Meredith shrugged. "My mother."

Ethan thought that was a reason *not* to go back to Ohio, but he didn't tell Meredith that.

"Oh! I want you to see something," Meredith said, sliding off the stool.

She went to another drawing desk, a smaller one, Andrew's first desk, and collected a few pages and cardboard panels, sorting them.

"I found these last night when I was going through some of Andrew's things for the funeral displays. I didn't even know Andrew was working on it."

She held up a panel.

Ethan laughed. "That rascal!"

In dynamic lettering the title at the top of the page of cartoon panels read "The Adventures of Sky Walker."

Together they turned the pages, reading the first story. It was a typical comic-book-hero story about an ordinary young man on the cusp of adulthood who, while stuck in a humdrum existence, dreamed of adventure and romance.

Page after page Ethan found himself smiling at obvious references to his and Andrew's childhood, little incidents, comments, phrases that only he and Andrew would know were drawn from actual experience. He stopped smiling when Sky Walker enlisted in the police academy and began having experiences that mirrored Ethan's life.

"What's wrong?" Meredith asked when she noticed the change in his mood.

"This is about me," Ethan said.

"There are some parallels, aren't there?"

"Not parallels. This is me." He thumped the pages for emphasis. "With one major difference."

"What's that?"

"I'm not a hero."

"Andrew thought you were," Meredith said.

Ethan turned his back to the desk. "He was wrong."

He crossed the room while Meredith continued reading. This was exactly where he and Andrew parted company. Andrew believed in heroes and superheroes. Ethan, on the other hand, had grown up.

In his line of work heroes got themselves killed. There was nothing heroic about rousting a homeless man from in front of a business, or ticketing drivers whose frustration had boiled over, or trying to keep prostitutes and johns away from each other. It wasn't heroism; it was civic babysitting.

And despite whatever everyone else said, it wasn't heroic to shoot to death the driver of a black truck. Pulling the trigger was the act of a desperate man, not a hero. If it was so heroic, why did he still have nightmares about it years later?

"Ethan? I want you to see something."

She held up several photocopied pages clipped together. They were of old books.

"Look at the author's name," she said.

Ethan read it aloud. "Sarah Morgan Cooper."

Meredith read the text clipped to one page. "Along with Mary J. Holmes and Horatio Alger, Mrs. Cooper wrote popular stories with a spiritual element. The most popular of her works, the adventures of Truly Noble and Charity Increase, were based on moral premises taken from the Bible. In Mrs. Cooper's fictional world faithfulness and industry always won the day. Her hero, a sixteen-year-old orphan, never used violence except as a last resort. He always learned a moral lesson at the end of the novel, and he always, always won the heart and admiration of the lovely Charity Increase."

She lifted the page.

"This is in Andrew's handwriting. 'What about a series of stories that does what Sarah Morgan Cooper did in the nineteenth century. Same concept, but brought up-to-date?'"

"Can't be done," Ethan said. "Kids don't want heroes anymore. They want tough guys with big guns who blast people away and cut a wide path of destruction, climbing upon piles of bodies like it's the ladder of success. And for what? Revenge. Or to obtain ultimate power or wealth."

"Maybe Andrew wanted to show them a better way," Meredith said. "And I think you're wrong about this story being about you."

"Policeman hero? It's obvious."

"Then, why did he use the name Sky Walker? That's the name you gave him."

Ethan had to think about that for a moment.

"You know what I think?" Meredith said. "I think Sky Walker is both of you. You and Andrew together in one person. His spirit, your strength."

Ethan looked at the panels again with this thought. She was right. The twins had become one for this story. The concept intrigued him. He continued reading.

Sky Walker was a rookie police officer, his first night on the streets. He and his partner were on a call to a rough section of the city where three known gang members taunted and threatened a couple out for a walk. Sky and his partner climbed out of the car.

The story was based on Ethan's first night on duty as a patrolman. The memory of the fear he felt that night quickened his breathing and heart rate.

Officer Sky Walker felt scared too. As he approached the gang members, the panel showed a thin paperback book partially sticking out of his back pocket, the author's name at the top: Sarah Morgan Cooper. In the balloon caption Sky asked himself, "What would Truly Noble do?"

"Ethan?"

"Yeah."

"Are there any leads on finding the Morgan Bible?"

He looked up. "A few. I'll get it back. I promise."

Meredith wasn't looking at him. She picked at a fingernail and spoke softly. "Promise me you'll be careful," she said. "It's just a book. Not worth getting hurt over."

This was the second time she'd told him the Morgan Bible wasn't worth injury, and the second time the comment perplexed Ethan. Before Andrew's death she had expressed strong feelings about the Morgan Bible, elevating it to the level of a family Holy Grail.

"I don't want to lose you, too," she said.

Ethan had never seen her so vulnerable. She was shaking. Death and violence had that effect on people. He approached her.

She didn't back away.

He opened his arms in invitation.

She stepped into them.

Holding her, he said, "I'll be careful. But it's something I have to do. You understand that, don't you?"

Ethan knew how inappropriate this looked, alone with his brother's wife, holding her in the dead man's office on the day of his funeral. His eyes darted repeatedly to the closed door.

"I'd better get out there," Meredith said, stepping back.

"Yeah."

Without looking at him, she left the room.

Ethan closed his eyes, scolding himself. Not for what he did. They were family. They were hurting. In time of grief families comfort one another.

But Ethan felt more than that, and what he felt surprised and disgusted him.

# EIGHT

A last-minute change of plans sent Ethan scrambling. He was supposed to drive his parents back to Las Vegas following the funeral. Lieutenant Savala had approved his request for personal leave. Ethan figured while he was in Las Vegas he could track down Richard Corby to see if his alibi would hold up under questioning.

But then his parents decided to go with friends to Phoenix for a couple of weeks. Spur-of-the-moment vacation plans were one of the perks of retirement, his father told him. Ethan had to come up with another way to get to Las Vegas.

The alternative presented itself when he saw Majeski's copy of F. Malory Simon's book on the front seat of his car. Ethan put in a request to attend the seminar. Lieutenant Savala turned him down.

"You had your chance," Savala told him. "The deadline for signing up for the seminar was two months ago. And if I remember correctly, when I asked if you wanted to go, you said something to the effect, 'The last thing I want to do is attend some motivational seminar to hear a millionaire brag about how he made his millions.'"

Then, the day before the conference Brian Hinkey came down sick. Toxic poisoning from the fingerprint dust according to rumor. Just the opening Ethan needed.

Savala agreed to let him attend in Hinkey's place provided he read *Simon Says* in its entirety before they loaded into the vans. Ethan had twenty-four hours.

"Did you read it?" Savala asked him as they were loading luggage into the back of the van.

"Of course I did," Ethan replied.

"Let me see it."

Ethan dug into his bag. "I didn't underline or anything. I just read it."

"I still want to see it."

"You can tell someone's read a book just by looking at it?"

"I can tell. Let me see it."

Ethan handed Savala his copy of the book. Its corners were dented badly, and when the lieutenant flipped through the pages he found that some of them had been torn out.

"This looks like it's been in a tornado."

"There were some parts I didn't like," Ethan explained.

"So you threw it against the wall?"

"Sometimes a page at a time. After I crumpled it."

"If you hate the book so much, why do you want to go to the seminar?"

Ethan shrugged. "Might be fun."

For the next eight hours Ethan sat in the back of a ten-passenger van watching grown police officers act like they were a bunch of sixth graders going to camp.

When the van pulled up in front of the Las Vegas Hilton Hotel, Ethan was the last to climb out.

"You'll be rooming with me," Savala said as they unloaded the luggage.

"Did you draw the short straw?" Ethan asked.

"In a manner of speaking, yes. I was supposed to room with Hinkey. Nobody else wanted him."

"I saved you from two days in the same room with Hinkey?" Ethan cried. "You owe me. Big time."

"Don't press your luck. Hinkey's not here because he's sick."

"Seems to me, I had a hand in that, too."

Savala grinned at the memory. "All right. I owe you one."

The path to the front desk of the Hilton was paved with white tiles and black diamonds. Barry Manilow posters lined the length of the lobby. Some of the guys were talking about hitting the casinos.

"You know the agreement," Savala said. "Not until after the seminar."

A chorus of objections came whining that other lieutenants were letting their guys go to the casinos.

"Other lieutenants are not me."

"What about the video arcade?" one of them asked.

Savala had no objection to that as long as the payoffs were only in points and not coins. Half decided to head to the arcade while the other half went to Star Trek: The Experience.

"What about you?" Savala asked Ethan while they waited for an elevator.

"I'll probably make an early night of it," Ethan replied.

Savala raised an eyebrow, but said nothing.

Just as the elevator doors opened, four women dressed identically in black dresses joined them. The women were heavily accessorized with fake diamonds—necklaces, bracelets, earrings, some were even glued to their eyelashes.

One produced a pitch pipe.

"Do you mind?" she asked.

"Knock yourself out," Savala said.

Once they had their pitch, the women sang "Diamonds Are a Girl's Best Friend" in four-part harmony. Ethan thought they sang surprisingly well for four middle-aged women who, despite their dress, looked like they hailed from the Midwest.

"Do you ladies perform here in Vegas?" Savala asked.

His question set off a quartet of giggles.

The woman with the pitch pipe said, "We're here to compete in the Sweet Adelines International Competition."

Savala was delighted. "I saw the Sweet Adelines on the list of conventions! I thought it was some kind of confectionary company." He remembered what else he'd read and his face lit up even more. "There are nine thousand of you! I thought we had a big group, but you are almost double our size!"

Ethan's head swam at the thought of nine thousand diamond-studded women singing in elevators all over Las Vegas.

"Maybe you can help us with a decision," pitch-pipe lady said. "What do you think, girls?"

They seemed to know what she was talking about.

Turning back to Savala, she said, "May we prevail upon you for a moment? We can't decide which song to sing. Would you mind listening to one more song and telling us which one you prefer?"

"I'm no music critic," Savala said. "But I know what I like."

"That's all we ask."

Savala decided for both him and Ethan. So, on the fourteenth floor of the Hilton while Savala held the elevator, the four women sang an arrangement of a song Ethan had never heard before, but from the recurring phrase he figured the title had something to do with red-hot mommas.

As the ladies sang, Lieutenant Savala's eyes danced, and he grinned so hard Ethan thought his head might split in two. He clapped when they finished and, without consulting with his cojudge, announced that he thought the red-hot-mommas song was the better of the two.

The ladies thanked him. But as the elevator doors closed, Ethan heard one of the women arguing that they were already in their diamonds dresses.

After settling into their room, Ethan and Savala joined some of the other officers downstairs for dinner after which Ethan excused himself and went back up to the room, grateful that the elevator ride was free of Sweet Adelines.

Standing in the silence, he looked out the window at the view of Las Vegas Boulevard. From here he could see the Riviera Hotel and Casino, the Sahara Hotel and Casino, Circus Circus, the New Frontier, and Treasure Island. The monorail floated silently below him, linking the hotels and convention center.

Though he'd lived in Las Vegas for several years, Ethan had ventured onto the Strip only when family or friends came to visit, and occasionally during work, though most of his duty was spent in the northern part of the city, the suburbs.

He pulled closed the curtains, shutting out the bright lights and games. Lying down on one of two double beds, he thought about how he'd approach Richard Corby tomorrow and what he would say. And how he'd respond if Corby recognized him as the cop who shot and killed his brother.

In the darkness of the room, he talked things over with Andrew.

---

Ethan estimated the room held at least five thousand seats, and every one was occupied. The officers from San Diego sat about a third of the way back from the stage.

The first session was scheduled to begin at 9:00 a.m. But like so many rooms in Las Vegas, this one had no windows, and you couldn't tell if it was night or day without looking at your watch.

Lights dimmed. The stage was bare except for a lectern in the center. The absence of lighting hushed the audience. A deep rumble came from the speakers. It circled the room, taking advantage of a state-of-the-art surround-sound system. The sound escalated in pitch and intensity.

Then, nothing again.

From the front a laser beam shot over the audience in a single burst. The back wall retaliated, sending a second burst toward the front. Laser ping-ponged back and forth, then split impressively in an array that formed a pulsing net overhead.

Music swelled, reminiscent of the *2001: A Space Odyssey* theme.

The laser net gave way to a spotlight that shot down the center aisle hitting a man standing in the back. He was dressed in jeans, a forest green patterned shirt, and a dark blue blazer. In each hand he held a wooden bucket by the handle.

To the applause of thousands, F. Malory Simon strode purposefully up the center aisle, the spotlight marking his path. Two giant viewing screens in the front of the room tracked his progress.

He set the wooden buckets on the stage, then swung around dramatically to face the audience. His upper body filled both video screens, showing a lean face, a shaved head, and slate gray eyes that projected strength and confidence.

"Wooden buckets," he said. "You would be hard-pressed to find them in stores today, even harder-pressed to find a company that makes them. Yet, a hundred years ago, wooden buckets were a thriving business. But now those companies are gone. Out of business. Why?"

He let the question hang over the audience for a time before answering his own question.

"They went out of business because they thought they were in the wooden-bucket business, and they were wrong. They were in the water-delivery business."

He raised a rigid finger.

"Lesson number one. Know what business you're in, because if you don't know what business you're in, soon you will be out of business."

Men and women all around Ethan scrambled for their notebooks to write that down.

"Let me introduce you to a friend of mine," Simon said.

Once again the spotlight raced the length of the center aisle and struck a figure in the back of the room. This time it fell upon a man wearing a professional-football uniform and carrying a football.

An announcer's voice came over the sound system. "Ladies and Gentlemen, Bo Bradley, quarterback for the Nevada Outlaws!"

The room erupted with cheers as Bradley broke into a victory trot up the center aisle. The screens displayed a rapid succession of video highlights—Bradley completing passes, Bradley scoring touchdowns.

Savala, clapping as lustily as anyone, leaned toward Ethan. "Simon is the owner of the Outlaws," he shouted over the noise.

Ethan nodded. "I know. I used to live here."

When Bradley was a few feet from Simon, he tossed the owner the football. The two men shook hands. Bradley removed his helmet and faced the audience. His face was youthful, his smile charismatic.

Simon's voice came over the system. "We will hold a press conference later this morning, so you are the first to hear that we have just extended Bo Bradley's contract for five years to the tune of $100 million!"

Cheers erupted even louder.

"I hire winners!" Simon shouted over the cheers.

The two millionaires basked in the applause. When it died down, the seminar continued.

Simon said, "Bo, tell me ... what business are you in? Are you in the quarterbacking business?"

"No, sir," Bo replied with a toothy grin.

"Are you in the professional-football business?"

"No, sir."

"Then, tell me, Bo. What business are you in?"

"I'm in the entertainment business," Bo said.

Simon grinned. "Smart boy."

The rehearsed act continued for a while, during which time the attendees learned that Bo Bradley had a press agent, a publicity agent, and a Hollywood agent as well as a sports agent. When he wasn't honing his football skills, Bradley was taking acting lessons and filming commercials.

At the end of the skit, Bo Bradley "went long" down the center aisle and Simon threw an impressive pass to him, much to the delight of the audience.

"Those of you who have read my book know that I made my first million in the secrets business. Many people mistakenly believe I'm in the shredding business, but I know better. That's why I have the largest business of its kind in the world. Businesses pay me to keep people from learning their secrets. I don't just shred documents and data devices, I destroy information. My clients sleep easier at night knowing that their information is no longer accessible. In an age where information is power, my services are invaluable.

"And how did I rise to this position of power and wealth? Was it handed to me? No. Did my father teach me the secrets of success? Let me tell you about my father. He was a middle-class, churchgoing man who led a life of mediocrity. He was a little man who thought himself clever, rejoicing over petty victories. Every Saturday night my father would sit at the kitchen table inserting nickels into rolls of quarters that he would hand to unsuspecting bank tellers for the full value of the roll. My father's exalted motto was, "You snooze, you loose." I can tell you story after story of my father cutting into long lines, short-changing cashiers, and stealing coupons off packages he didn't buy. He took pride in his antics.

"To my dismay, when I was in high school, I realized I was just like him. So how does a man break away from a lifetime of lessons? How does a man stop a cycle of small-mindedness? It takes a decisive act, a violent stroke. You have to cut deep. If you don't, the old ways will surface again and again. You have to destroy the ties to your past. Cut the root and the flower dies. There's no other way."

Simon paused for emphasis.

"Cut the root and the flower dies," he repeated.

Thousands of pens all around the room went to work.

"I clearly remember the day I knew I was no longer shackled by my past. A man came up to me and said, 'Aren't you Larry Simon's son?' And I told him, 'No. I am the son of success.'"

Applause broke out across the room. Simon waited for it to play out.

"This is my family heritage. This is my bloodline. If you were to look at my genealogical chart, under father it would say, Courage. Under mother it would say, Perseverance. These are my true parents. I am the offspring of courage and perseverance. I am the son of success!"

The crowd offered a standing ovation.

---

Following the morning session, one of Simon's business partners, Gil Getz, led a workshop titled "Three Keys on Every Great Leader's Keychain." The seminar notebook had a listening sheet with three blank spaces labeled "Keys" to fill in, along with Gil's personal slogan, "Gil always Getz what he wants." All three keys in Ethan's notebook remained blank.

When they broke for lunch, Ethan hung back. Savala bumped into an old buddy on the Santa Barbara police force. One by one the other San Diego conferees paired up and disappeared in different directions. Ethan went up to his room and got his gun.

He bypassed the concierge and ordered a cab using his cell phone, then turned it off. If anybody happened to miss him, he didn't want to make it easy for them to find him.

He directed the cabbie to turn left at Sahara Avenue, then north onto Interstate 15. "Exit at Range Road, near the Motor Speedway," he said.

"You sound like you know where you're going," the cabbie replied, his gaze lingering on the rearview mirror. "You live here?"

"In a previous life," Ethan replied.

At Range Road he instructed the cabbie to drive once through the mobile-home park while he sat back and made mental notes of the layout.

The park was small, only three parallel streets and approximately twenty-two mobile homes. Most of them were older, single-wide units, the kind that were called trailers when he was younger. The park rested on the side of a hill crowned with a pale-green water tower, the canister type. Corby's address was halfway down the middle street. From the amount of rust, it appeared to be the oldest unit in the park. Three metal steps led to a side door. Aluminum foil covered the front windows. The place was shut up tight.

Ethan got out of the cab beneath the Starlight Mobile Home Park sign on Range Road and dismissed the driver. Entering the park on foot, he circled around on an adjacent street and approached Corby's unit from high ground.

His coat pulled back slightly for quick access to his gun, he knocked on the trailer's metal door. No answer. He knocked again, this time calling Corby's name. Still no answer.

He circled the residence. Everything was locked up, and there was no vehicle. According to the investigative report, Corby's alibi was that he was at a day job. Ethan didn't believe the alibi.

However, one of Corby's neighbors confirmed that he had a job. At least he confirmed Corby left regularly at eight o'clock in the morning and returned at five o'clock. The times were firm. Corby drove a motorcycle that was loud enough to wake the dead according to one neighbor.

Ethan thanked him and, hiking back up the hill, found a hole in the chain-link fence that separated the park from the water tower. He camped out under a cluster of palm trees. From here he could keep an eye on Corby's trailer.

With about four hours to kill he dismissed the thought of returning to the hotel. Corby was his priority. Ethan would wait.

He didn't have to wait long. The distant roar of a Harley-Davidson announced Corby's approach. He wheeled the bike between trailers, revving the engine a couple of times within feet of his neighbor's bedroom window before shutting it down.

Corby unstrapped a bag of groceries from the motorcycle. He resembled his wrestler brother, only smaller.

Ethan waited for him to enter the trailer before leaving his post under the palm trees. Shielding himself with the row of mobile homes for as long as possible, he approached Corby's trailer.

Corby had left the door open. Through a tattered and torn screen door, Ethan could see Corby's back as he stood at the kitchen counter unloading his groceries. Stepping to one side so Corby couldn't see him, he knocked and called Corby's name.

Ethan didn't draw his gun. He wasn't here to arrest Corby, merely to question him.

The sound of movement inside the trailer stopped. Corby didn't come to the door.

"Yeah? Who's there?" he said, cautiously.

Ethan didn't reply. He waited.

Corby stuck his head out the door.

When he saw Ethan, his double take was classic. Surprise twisted by horror.

"What's the matter, Corby?" Ethan asked. "Seen a ghost?"

You had to give Corby credit. He recovered quickly.

"Morgan," he said. "You've got a lot of nerve coming here after what you did to my brother. Give me one good reason why I shouldn't call the cops."

"Because they're all buddies of mine," Ethan said, flashing his badge.

"That ain't good here and you know it." Corby turned his back and went inside. "I got nothing to say to you."

Ethan followed him in.

"Hey! I didn't say you could come in!" Corby objected.

"I have some questions for you."

Corby pulled a six-pack out of the grocery sack, set it on the counter and said, "Well, I got no answers. But I do have beer. Want one?"

Before Ethan could react, Corby clobbered him on the side of his head with a beer bottle. The blow knocked Ethan back against the metal doorframe; the edge cut into his spine and nearly cleaved the back of his skull.

Corby was fast. He followed close behind the blow, grabbed Ethan by the shirt and flung him to the floor in the kitchen area. He pulled a handgun from a drawer and pointed it at Ethan's head.

"You armed?" Corby asked. "Come on, let me have it."

Looking through the pain, Corby appeared blurry. But Ethan's vision wasn't so bad he couldn't see the murderous look in his eyes. He reached for his weapon.

"Slide it to me."

The gun slid across the dirty tiles until Corby stopped it with his foot. Once he had the weapon in his hand, he relaxed a little.

Corby chuckled. "This is so cool. It's like gettin' to kill you twice."

Ethan felt like a fool. He knew better than to allow himself to be caught in close quarters.

Corby grinned like a kid at Christmas. "So tell me, Mr. Policeman. How did it feel to see your brother gunned down for no reason?"

"I shot a man who was out of control and a danger to others. You shot a man in cold blood. My brother did nothing to deserve what you did to him."

"Being your brother was crime enough. Besides, he never said anything. I thought he was you, and he went along with it. Now why would he do that?"

"It's something you'd never understand," Ethan said.

Corby shrugged. "Worked out fine for me. I hurt you. And now I'm gonna kill you."

"No you're not. Everyone in this park would hear the shot. You're not stupid enough to shoot me. Not here."

Corby *was* stupid enough to shoot him here. Ethan was just trying to buy time and give himself a chance to turn the tables.

Before Corby could make a decision, an unmarked white panel truck skidded to a quick stop just outside the trailer. The side door slid open and a man wearing dark sunglasses and a suit jumped out. He was reaching inside his coat.

Plainclothes policemen? That was Ethan's first thought. Corby saw them too and became agitated.

The screen door flew open.

Corby had his hands up. "Don't shoot! Don't shoot! Don't shoot!"

Ethan managed to get to his feet. His movement caught the attention of the man in the doorway.

The man aimed a gun at him. It was not police issue. It had a silencer.

A bullet slammed into Ethan's chest, a second one hit him in the left shoulder, spinning him around. The force of the impact threw him against a built-in oven. He clawed at the door handles as he slid to the ground.

Ethan didn't remember hitting the floor. His eyes shut; he smelled dirt and old wax. A moan welled up inside him. He suppressed it. A sound, a movement would invite another bullet.

Corby pleaded frantically for his life.

"You know what I came for," the suit said.

All of a sudden Richard Corby was Mr. Hospitality. "Of course! It's right here. Let me get it. I'll only be a second. Just don't shoot."

Through slits of barely opened eyes Ethan saw a gray suit filling the doorway, a gun with an exaggerated barrel in his hand. Corby had set his gun on the counter. He was throwing seat cushions from a bench seat at the front of the trailer. He lifted a wooden panel.

The suit sensed danger. He stepped toward Corby.

"Easy … easy …" Corby pleaded. "It's down here. Look …"

Reaching inside the bench seat, Corby used both hands to lift out an oversized book. The Morgan family Bible.

He offered it to the suit.

"I was going to deliver it to him, I was! It was just a misunderstanding. I wanted him to know it was worth half a million dollars. I was just telling him. I wasn't …"

Gray suit pumped three quick bullets into Corby who flew backward onto the bench before rolling over onto the floor. The suit snatched up the Bible with one hand. Before leaving, he shot a quick glance at Ethan. Believing Ethan was dead, he stepped out of the trailer and slammed the door closed, shutting Ethan in with his brother's dead killer.

Ethan allowed himself a moan, then wished he hadn't. The vibration set off a blaze of pain in his chest. For a time he just breathed, but that hurt too.

Getting up wasn't his only problem. He smelled smoke. Within seconds it was billowing across the ceiling. Flames appeared on both sides of the trailer, licking the walls.

Ethan pulled his hands into position at his sides to push himself up. But that wasn't going to happen. His first attempt to push with his left arm was nearly his last. He almost blacked out from the pain. The best he could do was to push with his right hand and turn himself onto his back.

The ceiling of smoke kept getting lower and lower. Ethan choked. Coughed. It felt like Corby's wrestler brother was jumping on his chest.

He could feel the heat of the flames. His coughing became worse and the repeated blows of pain to his chest were more than he could stand. His consciousness was waning. It was getting harder to see. Not from the smoke. His eyes were failing, as was the rest of his body.

The last thing he remembered was Meredith telling him to be careful, that the Bible wasn't worth another life.

Ethan knew he wasn't dead when he smelled peanut butter. Peanut butter and crackers.

"Savala," he croaked, his mouth and throat dry as desert sand. "Can't you let a man die in peace? You're getting crumbs all over my corpse."

He hadn't opened his eyes yet. There was a scraping of chair legs against the floor. Ethan's first glimpse of Savala was of the man peering down at him, wiping cracker crumbs from his chin.

"Is that the gratitude I get for passing up a top sirloin dinner and a Las Vegas show to sit here at your bedside?" he said.

Ethan didn't try to move. He was content to have his eyes open.

"How bad is it?" he asked.

"Don't see how it could be any worse," Savala replied. "You have the police chiefs of two different cities calling for your head."

"I meant my injuries."

"Oh. You'll live. That is if one of the chiefs doesn't strangle you."

More awake now, Ethan was beginning to feel uncomfortable. He tried to adjust himself. The resulting stab of pain in his chest discouraged any further attempts.

"That was a real bonehead play, Morgan. After the chiefs are done chewing your backside, I'm going to take a few bites myself. You played me. You used a department-training event as cover for unauthorized police work."

"It was personal. Team I wasn't going to pursue Corby. Someone had to. And I was right. The Outlaw T-shirt? Payback for killing his brother. He thought Sky was me."

"Tell me you recorded it. Notarized it. Something."

"He had my family's Bible in his trailer. Whoever he was selling it to, or possibly stole it for, whacked him to get it."

"The Bible?" Savala said. "All that was over the Bible?"

"To get it they shot me, killed Corby, then torched the place to cover their tracks."

"Did you get a good look at them?"

"Looked like hired guns."

Savala mulled this over. "All I can say is that you are lucky your service revolver has not been fired," he said.

"Do the Las Vegas police have any idea who did it?"

"That's none of our business. This isn't our city."

"Come on, Savala! I paid for that information."

Savala checked the door. It was closed. "They don't have a clue," he said.

"How'd I get out of the trailer?"

"A neighbor. Watched everything through his bedroom window. He was angry because Corby's motorcycle woke him from his nap."

Savala walked over to the chair and gathered up crumpled cracker wrappers.

"The doc says you'll be good to go in a couple of days. We head back tomorrow morning. I suspect as soon as I leave you'll have a visit from some of the locals. And you can expect an audience with your own chief when you return."

"Thanks for staying," Ethan said. "It means a lot to me."

"Actually, I did it for myself. The casinos don't do anything for me. And I don't need what they have to offer at those girlie shows."

"This is Vegas. It would be a crime to go back to your room and watch a movie."

Savala grinned. "Thought I'd head over to the Riviera. Got myself an invitation to attend that Sweet Adelines competition. Bumped into one of the finalists yesterday. A real sweet gal from Oklahoma City."

"You got a date?"

Savala smiled as though he had a secret, waved, and hurried out the door.

# NINE

F. Malory Simon leaned back in his chair, sipping a chilled bottle of water and listening to his meeting planner's summation of the conference. It'd been a good year, record numbers across the board: a hundred conferees more than the previous conference, double the number of preregistration applications for the next conference, and a 35 percent increase in back-of-the-room sales. The planner beamed while she read the report like a star student giving an oral presentation.

"Release another book between now and the next conference," she said, "and we can double these figures at next year's conference."

Libby Basinski was a shapely blonde with the instincts of a shark. Those who didn't know better believed that Simon had hired her because she looked fantastic in a pin-striped women's business suit. Those who were aware of her talents knew Simon hired her because she got things done. She focused on the larger goal and didn't bother

Simon with the details. If Ms. Basinski said they could double the figures at the next conference, that's exactly what would happen.

"Another book?" Simon said, gazing the length of the Las Vegas strip from twenty stories high. "Do you know how long it took me to write the last book?"

Ms. Basinski laughed appreciably. She was the one who interviewed and hired the ghostwriter for *Simon Says*.

"Should I start interviewing?" she asked.

Setting the water bottle on his glass desk, Simon stood as regally as any king.

The spaciousness of his office was accentuated by two walls of floor-to-ceiling windows, providing a panorama of Las Vegas and beyond. Tastefully styled, the furniture was modern. The decorations largely consisted of autographed pictures and artifacts and mementos of the National Football League, including footballs autographed by Y. A. Tittle, Joe Namath, and Roger Staubach, along with the November 12, 1892, framed contract of William "Pudge" Heffelfinger—the first pro-football player in history.

"Coordinate with Palmer for the final report and see that it's printed and distributed to all the board members," Simon finally said.

Libby Basinki's expression soured. Standing was Simon's way of dismissing her. Having her coordinate with Palmer, his accountant, was his way of telling her that there would be no new book and no next conference, which meant that she was out of a job. She was smart enough to know that and shark enough to fight.

Standing and squaring her shoulders, she began, "Mr. Simon—"

Simon cut her off. He was already at the door, holding it open.

She paused in the doorway. "The preregistrations—"

"Instruct Palmer to wait six months before making the announcement, then have them request refunds. Not everyone will. Those who do, delay repayment for three months. That will give us nine months of interest on their money."

Ms. Basinski nodded.

Simon didn't tell her good-bye. He didn't offer to write her a letter of recommendation. When something was over, it was over and Simon moved on. Explanations were unnecessary.

Simon supposed he ought to feel something knowing this was the last time he would see her. But Simon reserved his feelings for conquests, not good-byes. Ms. Basinski got what she wanted out of the deal: his name on her résumé. She had accepted the position at a grossly reduced salary, just as Simon knew she would when he hired her. That was his gift.

He got people to do things for him, sometimes for reduced pay and other times for no pay at all. The way he saw it, there was no law against deceiving someone or antagonizing someone into doing something that benefited him. They would do the dirty work. They would pay the price. He would reap the rewards.

That's how he ran his football program, the Nevada Outlaws. Simon didn't hesitate to have his head coach tell a player to take a cheap shot if it meant eliminating a quarterback, a receiver, or another key player from the game, even if it meant a career-ending injury. The results were predictable, and for Simon, money in the bank. The player would be fined and sometimes ejected from the game or suspended. But if it meant winning the game, it was worth it.

If the player took too much heat in the media as a cheap-shot artist, Simon would trade him, making it clear that he didn't want such players on his team. If the coach objected, Simon fired him, informing the media that it was the coach who ordered the player to take a cheap shot. Of course the traded players and fired coaches would make a ruckus, but it would blow over. It always did. The record books never failed to record the win. A winning team earns more revenue and attracts new and talented players. In the end, Simon always won.

Gil Getz passed Ms. Basinski in the outer office. Entering Simon's office, he took the seat that was still warm from its last occupant. He sat back and crossed his legs.

"Good conference from what I hear," Getz said, testing the waters.

"The last one," Simon replied.

Getz turned and looked at the door. "That explains the tears. Shame, really. What am I going to do now with my keys workshop?"

Simon grinned at the humor. Gil Getz's workshop, "Three Keys on Every Great Leader's Keychain," was an inside joke. The son of a locksmith, Getz had not used a key to open a door since the fourth grade. Like Simon, he had disdained his father's middle-class approach to business. In high school they teamed up to pull off a series of heists. Simon chose the business. Getz gained them entrance. There was not a lock in the world that could keep Gil Getz out if he set his mind to it.

In the keynote address Simon mentioned an incident when he realized he did not want to follow in his father's footsteps. What he didn't tell them was that this realization came following a successful robbery.

It was the summer between their junior and senior years. Simon and Getz had summer jobs with a local construction company owned by a friend of Getz's father. Bored with menial labor, Simon set his eyes on the company lockbox. He convinced Getz that it would be fun to break into the construction office at night and steal the lockbox, then arrive early the next morning to watch the fireworks when the foreman found it missing.

The heist was easy. Simon and Getz got away with several hundred dollars. It was what happened next that revolutionized their lives. While the foreman was beside himself, the owner seemed to take everything in stride. Simon overheard him telling the investigating police officers that he was relieved. The stolen cash was of no great concern. He was just happy the thieves didn't trash his files. That's when Simon realized that the contents of a business's file cabinets were more valuable than the cash in the safe.

"Tired of the spotlight?" Getz asked, referring to Simon's decision not to hold any more conferences. "Weary of all that applause and adulation?"

Getz rarely asked a direct question. He preferred broaching subjects. He knew Simon well enough to know that if Simon was going to abandon a business line it was for one reason and one reason only: perceived goals.

Despite what Simon taught at his conferences, success and money were secondary to him. Simon had an agenda. And as part of that agenda he either wanted something somebody else possessed, or he wanted to force somebody to do something he or she didn't want to do. It was the challenge, the head-to-head competition that made life worth living.

"Have you dealt with Corby?" Simon asked, ignoring Gil Getz's question.

"My boy is standing outside."

"Bring him in."

Corby was a prime example of how Simon operated. Through intermediaries, he was able to get Corby to agree to steal a Bible in exchange for giving him the necessary information and tools to avenge his brother's death. Corby botched the job.

He killed the wrong man. Then he left evidence at the scene that could link him to the murder. But his biggest mistake was learning the value of the Bible and holding it for ransom.

A stocky man wearing a suit and dark glasses entered the room. He set an oversized Bible on F. Malory Simon's glass desk.

"Corby?" Simon asked.

"Presents this book to you with his compliments. It was his dying wish."

Simon looked at the Bible with satisfaction but didn't pick it up. "Complications?"

"There was another guy with him."

"Do you know who he was?"

Simon's use of the past tense was not lost on the man wearing the dark sunglasses. "He's still alive," the man said, quick to add his reassurances. "But we followed him to the hospital and we know who he is. There is nothing to worry about. We'll take care of him once he is released."

"You know I don't like complications," Simon fumed. "Who is he? A friend of Corby's?"

The man in the dark sunglasses fidgeted. "His name is Ethan Morgan. He's a cop from—"

"Morgan! I know who he is."

"I hit him bad. He was just lucky, that's all. I swear to you, the moment he's released—"

"Get out," Simon said.

"I'll finish the job," the man insisted.

"Do you think I'm going to give you another chance to botch the job? Get out!"

The set jaw of the man with the dark sunglasses indicated he understood. Getz followed him to the door and shut him out.

Simon sat behind his desk staring at the Morgan Bible in thought. "It was the T-shirt that led him to Corby," he concluded.

"What do you want me to do about Morgan?"

Gil Getz was the one man Simon had always been able to count on. Men like Getz were not meant to be leaders. Their talent was in serving great leaders.

"Morgan must have a guardian angel," Simon said. "That's twice he should have been shot dead." He pondered Morgan's fate for a moment. "Leave him alone."

"As you wish."

Simon thought of something. He reached for the packet Ms. Basinski had left on his desk and searched a computer printout. "Well, what do you know," he said. "Morgan was one of the conferees."

"No! There's no way he could have connected us to—"

"He didn't. He was here with his department. Coincidence, nothing more. If he'd made the connection, why would he enroll in my seminar and attend with an assembly of cops? But I don't like the idea of anyone waltzing into my city on some kind of personal vendetta. There has to be some reprisal."

"What do you have in mind?"

"Make his life miserable. Contact Kravetz and have them whip up a story on Morgan in that rag of his. Something along the line of a San

Diego cop tracking down his twin brother's killer for blood vengeance. There's his headline."

Getz chuckled, getting into the spirit of scandal-sheet headlines. "How about we mention the Bible? A headline with blood vengeance and rescuing his grandmother's Bible has a ring to it, don't you think?"

Simon grinned. "I like it. Make sure the story mentions that the Bible was destroyed in the resulting fire."

Getz stood to leave.

"One more thing," Simon said, calling him back. "Keep an eye on the sale of Andrew Morgan's business. He was the dangerous one. I want those books of his to die with him."

Getz turned to leave.

"Take this with you." Simon indicated the Bible on his desk. He didn't touch it. "Get it to Sanada. The usual route. Bleach the trail."

Ethan had plenty of time to think while he was in the hospital. He felt lucky to be alive, and while he should have felt good that he'd located Sky's killer, he didn't. He found no satisfaction in Richard Corby's death. Ethan would have preferred to arrest him and let justice work itself out in the courts. Maybe it was a cop thing to have a certain satisfaction to solving a case, having a judge and jury confirm it, and seeing the verdict announced in newspapers. Corby's assassin robbed him of that satisfaction.

Of course, Ethan had another cause for his frustration. For a second time the Morgan family Bible had been taken from him, and this time it would be even harder to track. A man like Corby didn't keep records. And even if he did, the way the chief felt about him right now, Ethan would be the last person to have access to them. He still had a couple of friends on the force. He would call them, but the lead was slim at best.

Then there was the fact that someone had given Corby an alibi. Ethan wanted to know who did it and why.

It didn't look promising. Ethan couldn't shake the feeling that he would be known to all succeeding generations of Morgans as the one who lost the family's greatest treasure. Assuming, of course, there would be succeeding generations.

Ethan's despondent mulling was interrupted twice by visits. First, his parents who had cut their Phoenix trip short when they heard the news. Later that same day Meredith and her mother arrived, having driven from San Diego. They decided to stay until Ethan was released from the hospital and ferry him home.

While in Las Vegas, Meredith and Olivia lodged with Ethan's parents. His mother had insisted. If Ethan knew his father, he was hoping the women would decline and stay in a hotel. While Buck Morgan loved Meredith like a daughter, he couldn't stand to be in a room with Olivia for more than ten minutes. For good reason.

Olivia Cooper seized every opportunity, and created a few when there weren't any to seize, to pass judgment on the way Buck had raised his boys. It lacked spiritual depth in her estimation: Andrew and Ethan were not taught to appreciate fully the significance of the Morgan legacy.

For his father's sake, Ethan healed as quickly as possible, for no other reason than to get Olivia Cooper out of the house.

# TEN

Ethan returned home from his first day back to work in the middle of the afternoon. Copely Avenue was predictably clear of traffic. Children were in school and men and women were at work. Only housewives, the unemployed, and police detectives suspended from duty rode the streets at this time of day.

He checked his rearview mirror. A midnight blue Lexus had been following him since he left the police station. The driver was standing in the lot when Ethan drove away. He'd jumped into his car and had been tracking Ethan for several miles.

It was probably nothing. Nothing that warranted any action anyway. He kept an eye on the Lexus while his mind diverted to more pressing problems.

Lying on the passenger seat next to him was one of those sensational newspapers that specialized in celebrities and rumor. All of the major scandal sheets had picked up his story. This one was *Gossip!* The title read:

## COP SEEKS BLOOD VENGEANCE IN LAS VEGAS
### SHOT WHILE RESCUING HIS GRANDMOTHER'S BIBLE

A docudrama account of Ethan's encounter with Corby in the trailer park followed. Maybe 10 percent of it was true. The rest was a grossly exaggerated portrayal of a maverick cop who tracked down his brother's murderer to even the score. It erroneously reported that the Morgan family Bible had been destroyed in the resulting fire. The gunfire scene inside the trailer resembled an old Western shoot-out with Ethan wounded but still standing. The article did not mention a third gunman or that the bullets that killed Corby did not come from Ethan's gun.

However, they accurately identified Ethan as a San Diego police detective. That was enough to get him suspended.

Ethan suffered the vitriol of not one, but two enraged chiefs of police. The Las Vegas chief participated by speakerphone. Afterward Lieutenant Savala tweaked Ethan's burning ears with a few choice words of his own. Ethan's suspension was indefinite.

Ethan exited the freeway. He checked his rearview mirror. The Lexus took the same exit. It could be coincidence, but Ethan's suspicions were raised as he turned onto El Cajon Boulevard.

If being chewed out by the chief and suspended wasn't bad enough, Ethan ran into Hinkey in the parking lot. He was returning from lunch with four young officers. Hinkey had great fun at Ethan's expense, which wouldn't have bothered Ethan except for the fact that the officers thought Hinkey was uncharacteristically funny.

The midnight blue Lexus still followed him. Ethan turned right on Oregon Street, immediately pulled over to the curb, and jumped out of his car, thinking that he'd probably see the Lexus continue down El Cajon Boulevard.

But it didn't. It turned down Oregon. Seeing Ethan at the curb, the driver pulled over behind him and stopped.

"What's this all about?" Ethan demanded, approaching the driver.

The driver-side window slid down smoothly.

"You're Ethan Morgan," the man said.

"I know who I am. Who are you?"

Ethan kept an eye on the man's hands. The man noticed Ethan's attention on them. He kept his hands on the steering wheel.

"My name is David Ostrow. I'm your brother's attorney. I need to talk with you. Is this a convenient time?"

"You're Sky's attorney?"

"I'll meet you at your house."

Ethan stepped back, and the Lexus drove on down the street needing no directions.

Ever since leaving the station, Ethan had been in a funk. He'd cut his medical leave short because of extreme boredom. This morning, when he'd left for work, he was eager to get back to his normal routine, if there was such a thing for a detective. Of course, the chief had other plans. And now this. What did Sky's attorney want with him?

When Ethan arrived at his house, the Lexus sat waiting for him in his driveway. A thin man in a gray suit with wispy red hair climbed out.

"You look just like Andrew," the man said. "But of course you do."

He held out a well-manicured hand.

"David Ostrow."

Ethan shook the man's hand and invited him inside, glad the attorney had introduced himself again because Ethan had already forgotten his name.

Ostrow declined Ethan's offer of refreshment and sat on the living-room sofa. For several minutes he spoke fondly of Andrew. All the time the attorney was speaking, Ethan wondered what Ostrow would think if he knew that his feet were inches from the spot where Andrew died.

"Should Meredith be here?" Ethan asked.

"Let me explain my mission."

Opening his briefcase he retrieved a business-size envelope with his name and address in the upper left-hand corner. Ethan's name was printed in capital letters in the center of the sealed envelope.

"My instructions are to give this to you personally," Ostrow said, handing the letter to Ethan as he spoke.

"Should I open it now?"

"That is not necessary. I am aware of the contents as I am also aware of the contents of a similar letter I delivered to Andrew's wife this morning."

Ethan looked at the envelope. "Is it bad news?"

"You will have to determine that for yourself."

"And Meredith received an identical letter?"

"Similar. Not identical. That's all I can tell you."

Ethan nodded. "Why now?"

"Andrew instructed me to deliver the letters in the event of his death. His instructions were that I was to deliver them at the date of my choosing following his funeral. He wanted to give you and

Meredith sufficient time to grieve before dealing with the subject of the letter. I hope that is the case."

His mission accomplished, Ostrow closed his briefcase and stood. He shook Ethan's hand firmly, making his way to the door with one final comment about how much he enjoyed working with Andrew.

Alone, Ethan tore open the envelope and read the letter. Each sentence was a shovelful of coal and his chest was the furnace. In quick succession he crumpled the letter, threw it across the room, and pulled out his cell phone, dialing Meredith's number.

He got her answering machine.

"Oh no you don't!" he shouted.

The next minute Ethan was in his car heading down Copely Avenue toward Meredith's house.

Meredith's car was not in the driveway. The garage was closed. And there was no answer at the door when he knocked.

"Oh my, you gave me a start!"

Meredith's neighbor held a garden-gloved hand to her chest. She had appeared from the back of her house carrying a plastic bag and a pair of pruning shears. An elderly woman, small, weighing under a hundred pounds, she wore a floppy sun hat and oversized white garden gloves that made her hands look like Mickey Mouse's.

"I'm sorry if I startled you," Ethan apologized. "I'm Andrew's brother, and I—"

"I'm not stupid," the woman snapped. "I can see that you're Andrew's brother."

"I'm sorry. I didn't mean to imply that you were...." Ethan's heart pumped furiously; something it had been doing all morning. What he'd felt in the chief's office was merely a warm-up to what he was feeling now.

"Meredith's not home," the woman said, anticipating his question.

"Do you know where—"

"Not only do I know where, but I know when and for how long. That's what good neighbors do. We look after each other when one of us is away on vacation."

"Vacation?"

Meredith had said nothing to him about leaving town or taking a vacation.

"Do you know where she went?"

"I already told you I did. I'm not stupid, you know."

Ethan apologized again. "It's important I reach her."

The woman rolled back one of the Mickey Mouse gloves to look at her watch. "I don't know if that's possible," she said. "Her flight leaves in less than an hour."

"Flight?"

"Atlanta. Manchester. Exeter."

"Exeter ... is that in Ohio?"

The woman huffed. "There is no Exeter in Ohio. There is one in Pennsylvania, Massachusetts, New Hampshire—"

"Which one did Meredith go to?"

"Exeter, England."

"England! What is she doing in England?"

The woman shook her head in disgust. "You sure don't know what's going on in your own family, do you?"

Ethan thanked the woman while running to his car. Merging onto the freeway, he headed back downtown. He tried calling Meredith again and got her voicemail again. Then he tried calling Olivia who had flown home shortly after they returned from Las Vegas. She didn't answer either.

He cursed the ticket-dispensing machine at the airport parking lot for taking too long. When the railroad-crossing-type arm finally lifted, he began the search for an empty parking space. All the short-term parking stalls close to the terminal were filled. Ethan finally got lucky in the back lot as he waited for a Cadillac Escalade to back out. After locking his car, he sprinted the length of the lot, hoping that Terminal 2 was the right one. He didn't even know which airline she was flying. Choosing Terminal 2 was a guess, a hunch. If he was wrong, the resulting delay would scuttle any chance of catching Meredith before her plane departed.

Inside the terminal Ethan scanned the bank of monitors listing departures. He looked for Atlanta. Two airlines had flights leaving within the hour. This was enough to keep him from bolting to Terminal 1. He made note of the departure gates and ran toward the security check.

The line of people waiting to go through the metal detectors snaked back and forth several times before stretching across an enclosed overpass. A sign halfway down the line indicated a ten-minute wait from that point. Ethan moved as close as possible to the detectors without getting in line. He began searching for Meredith.

The three metal detectors looked like portals to other dimensions. People queued up in front of them shoeless, beltless, and hatless, their personal items stuffed into gray plastic tubs that rode a conveyor belt into a machine where they would be scrutinized electronically for weapons.

He saw her.

Meredith had passed through the first detector and was pulling her shoes from a plastic tub. Steadying herself against the conveyor belt, she slipped them on.

"Meredith!" Ethan shouted.

At the sound of her name she looked up and saw him. So did all the security guards and half the people in line. The guards wanted to know if he was going to be trouble. Ethan smiled at Meredith and waved.

She didn't wave back. Hastily gathering up her things, she turned her back on him and continued on her way.

Ethan suppressed a reflex shout commanding her to stop. He pulled out his cell phone and dialed her cell number. He watched her slow down, reach into her handbag, retrieve her phone, and check to see who was calling. With the phone still ringing, she glanced back at him, put her phone back into her purse, and disappeared around a corner.

He was so angry he nearly threw his phone at her. Instead, he reached for his badge. Then hesitated. A scene played out in his head of him flashing his badge to security. They would want to know who he was looking for and why. They would also want to accompany him. When the chief of police learned he used his badge to get through security for personal reasons, he might make Ethan's suspension permanent. He withdrew his hand.

He ran to the ticket counter where there was another line of at least fifty people waiting to check in. He went to the front of the line. No amount of pleading got him any special favors. The personnel at the counter insisted he would have to wait his turn. Facing a chorus of angry stares, Ethan made his way to the back of the line.

By the time he reached the front of the line, Meredith's flight had already left the gate.

"Would you like to take the next flight to Atlanta, sir?" the woman behind the counter asked. She spoke to him with forced civility, treating him as a hostile customer, which is what he was. He had his credit card and driver's license already on the counter to speed things up. He shuffled them back and forth impatiently.

"Actually, I need to get to Exeter, England," Ethan said.

The ticket-counter attendant, a brunette in her late twenties with hollow cheeks and broad shoulders, hammered the keyboard. "San Diego to Manchester to Exeter," she said.

"That's the one. When does it leave?"

She didn't answer immediately, studying a screen that Ethan couldn't see. "Flight 1460 for Atlanta leaves in one hour," she said.

"I'll take it," Ethan said, his hopes rising.

"However ..."

Ethan wasn't in the mood for "howevers."

Thirty seconds of silence separated her "however" from the rest of the sentence as she continued punching the keyboard. "... in Manchester, it looks like you will have a delay of eight hours and twenty-five minutes between flights."

"Eight hours!"

"Let me check something," she said without looking up, not surprised at his reaction. She tapped a while longer. "It's the same from London. Eight hours. The airplane is a De Havilland Dash 8 Turboprop and there are only two flights a day." She looked up. "That's the best I can do."

Ethan imagined himself camped out in an English airport for eight hours. The prospect wasn't attractive.

The counter attendant said, "Might I make a suggestion? I've noticed you have no luggage and that you're local." She indicated his driver's license as the source of her information. "I've also noticed that while you have a credit card and a license, there is no passport on the counter. Instead of standing around in an English airport, I could book you on a later flight to Atlanta which would give you time to go home and pack and get your passport."

A later flight would mean that Ethan wouldn't have a chance to intercept Meredith at the Atlanta airport. Had he failed to do that, however, he still planned on flying to England without anything but the clothes on his back. The absence of a passport would have made that impossible.

A calm resolve came over him. Since leaving the house, he had frantically chased after Meredith with little thought and less success. She couldn't run from him forever. He would catch up with her, and when he did, she would answer his questions.

His hands stopped waving the credit card and driver's license. When he spoke, he did so in a manner of a man who had all the time in the world. "Excellent idea," he said to the counter attendant. "Use your discretion to put together the best itinerary."

For the first time the attendant smiled.

Four hours later Ethan Morgan boarded a flight from San Diego International Airport to Atlanta.

# ELEVEN

Ethan slumped in the concourse chair at the Manchester airport terminal. While the San Diego ticket agent had redeemed some of his layover time in Manchester, she hadn't avoided all of it.

Ethan dozed. Weariness embraced him. The long transoceanic flight had combined with the emotional events of the morning to do him in. He kept one ear cocked toward an overhead speaker for any flight-change announcements.

The preformed plastic chair made it impossible for him to get comfortable. Across the concourse, signs advertised rooms with names like Comfort Zone and Oasis of Calm where he could get comfortable. There was a charge for the room, naturally, but it wasn't the charge that kept Ethan balled up on the plastic seat. It was his mood. If he got comfortable he might forget to be angry. And he wanted to remember his anger when he caught up with Meredith.

His cell phone rang. He fumbled for it. The screen indicated it was Meredith.

"Where are you?" they both asked at the same time.

"Ethan, where are you?" Meredith repeated.

The question confused Ethan. Where did she expect him to be? At work? At home? There was no way she could know he was tracking her.

"Are you in Exeter yet?" she asked.

"What?" He pulled the phone away and looked at it. How could she know? He could deny he was tracking her, but to what purpose? "I'm in Manchester," he said.

"Do you have a pen? Write this down."

"What are you playing at, Meredith?"

She ignored the question. "When you get to Exeter, rent a car and drive north on A396. Are you writing this down?"

Ethan groped for a pen in his shirt pocket. He grabbed a newspaper from the seat next to him and wrote the road number in the margin.

"Drive north approximately thirty-two kilometers," she continued. "There is a stone bridge with three arches just outside of Bickleigh. I'll meet you there. When does your plane leave?"

"Meredith, I'm not driving anywhere until you tell me—"

"You can yell at me later, Ethan. Just give me your departure time."

Ethan checked his watch, which didn't do him any good. He hadn't yet changed it from Pacific time. He found a clock at the top of the departure monitor.

"I leave for Exeter in forty-five minutes," he told her.

"Good. I'll meet you at the bridge in three hours."

She ended the call.

Ethan glared at his phone. He had forty-five minutes to waste and now was as good a time as any to get some answers. He redialed Meredith's phone. She didn't answer.

"Of all the stubborn—"

A few feet away a bank of pay telephones gave him an idea. When he called her using his cell phone she knew it was him calling. But if he used a pay phone, all she would know was that it was an unidentified caller.

Using his carrier's long-distance calling card Ethan dialed Meredith's cell-phone number. She still didn't answer. Ethan slammed down the receiver.

---

The flight from Manchester to Exeter was a sixty-minute thrill ride that would rival the world's best roller coasters. Up. Down. Sideways. The flight had it all. When Ethan disembarked, his hands and arms hurt from gripping the armrests. He had never been so glad to plant his feet on an airport tarmac in his life.

At the rental-car counter the agent (a man in his sixties at least) gave Ethan a well-worn lecture about road courtesy and driving on the left side of the road. The agent must have said, "This isn't America, mind you," at least a dozen times. After finally (with great reluctance from the agent) receiving the keys, Ethan consulted his scrap of newspaper upon which he'd written Meredith's instructions and steered north on route A396.

The road was relatively free of traffic. It was a blustery day with an ever-changing pattern of gray clouds set against a sparkling blue sky. Leaving Exeter behind, Ethan entered a green and brown patched countryside. The ancient river Exe proved to be a constant companion for the journey, occasionally veering off and hiding behind cottages or trees or bushes, but always reappearing.

He kept a close eye on the odometer. At thirty kilometers he slowed. And a little past thirty-two kilometers a three-arched stone bridge appeared.

Ethan recognized Meredith standing in the center of the bridge, looking at the river below in quiet contemplation. She had parked her car in a turnout on the south side of the bridge. Ethan pulled to a stop next to her car, parked, and got out.

She stood with her hands folded peacefully on the side of the bridge as though she'd arranged to meet him at Balboa Park on a lazy afternoon. The wind blew her red hair like a flag and whipped the hem of her simple black-and-white patterned dress.

Ethan charged toward her, his legs working as a pump to inflate his rage. A hundred questions vied for position, each one wanting to be the first out of his mouth.

"All right, Meredith," he barked. "I want to know what's going on. Why the sudden need to come to England? And why didn't you answer your phone in the airport when you knew it was me? Exactly what are you—"

"It's peaceful here, isn't it?" Meredith said softly.

"I had a lawyer at my house this morning. You owe me some answers."

"I come here once a year," she said dreamily, the bursts of sunlight from the river mirrored in her eyes. "It never fails to refresh my spirit."

She was talking like someone on tranquilizers. In all the time Sky and Meredith were married, Ethan couldn't remember one time when Meredith took a trip to England.

"Andrew thought I was visiting my mother," she said. "It wasn't really a lie, was it? I'd fly to Ohio and Mother would join me. She loves this place nearly as much as I do."

"You deceived him," Ethan said. "But then, that's not the only thing you've been lying about, is it, Meredith?"

She turned to him, showing no offense. "I'm glad you're here. I was afraid Mrs. Quigley would get it wrong and that you'd end up in Exeter, Massachusetts or New Hampshire. You would have thought I was drilling her on the multiplication table."

"You lured me here?" Ethan cried.

"Can you believe that woman charged me fifty dollars to have her stand in front of her house and wait for you to show up?"

Ethan seized Meredith by the shoulders. His patience had run out.

"Listen to me and listen good. I'm tired. I'm hungry. I'm angry. And now I learn that you have suckered me into chasing you halfway around the world. I want some answers and I want them now!"

Tears filled Meredith's eyes. "You're hurting me, Ethan," she said.

He eased up and released her. He knew he was hurting her and it scared him. It scared him because he wanted to hurt her.

"I don't blame you for being angry," she said. "You want answers. But that's why I brought you here. I couldn't tell you in California. I tried, but I couldn't find the strength or the words. I'm hoping that here my words will make sense."

"Here? Why here?"

"Because this is where it all began. This is Edenford."

Ethan looked beyond the bridge to what had once been a thriving village. All his life Ethan had heard of Edenford. In a way Meredith had brought him home.

She ambled across the bridge, brushing the tips of her fingers against the stone. "This was the road they used to escape from Bishop Laud," she said. "It was Christopher Matthews, the curate, who urged them to 'fly to the wilderness.' They did. From here to the coast where they boarded John Winthrop's ship, the *Arabella*."

There wasn't much left of the town, mostly rubble. Building foundations embedded in the soil clearly indicated the presence of a past town.

"Let me show you," Meredith said.

Despite the way he'd treated her, she took him by the arm. He could feel her come alive as they crossed the bridge into the town. Her eyes glistened. Her step was lively. She spoke with a tone of hushed reverence.

For all of his pent-up anger, Ethan couldn't help but be impressed by Meredith's undying passion for the Morgan family heritage. In America it bordered on fanaticism. Here, it breathed with life.

"The town died shortly after our ancestors fled to America," Meredith said. "There weren't enough people to produce and dye the wool, and the bone lace was largely the handiwork of Nell and Jenny Matthews."

They came to a fork in the road. To the right, Bridge Street paralleled the river. They went left on Market Street into the center of the seventeenth-century town.

She showed him where the Puritan church had once stood, where Christopher Matthews defied King James' decree in his *Book of Sports* that forbade churches from holding Sunday-evening services, the king preferring his subjects playing sports instead.

She showed him where the curate Matthews lived with his two daughters, Nell and Jenny, and where her ancestor, the cobbler David Cooper lived with his two sons, James and Thomas. They looked across fields that had once been a patchwork of drying wool serges stretched out on racks.

"From herding sheep to the spinning wheels inside of family residences to the looms and the dying vats, Edenford did it all," she said.

She led him to the place where the large dying vats had once been.

"This is where Drew Morgan saved Thomas Cooper's life," she said. "Had Thomas died, I wouldn't be here. Do you know that story?"

"Thomas Cooper fell into a vat of blue dye."

"Very good, Mr. Morgan!" Meredith said. "I'm impressed."

"That's the kind of history even a kid who hates history remembers. Of course you know what that makes you?"

"What?"

"A descendant of the original Smurf."

She laughed and squeezed his arm, glad to see his mood improved.

They continued up the hill, the town and azure ribbon of a river growing smaller as they climbed. It wasn't far until they came upon a low stone wall.

"The remnants of a Saxon castle," Meredith told him. "These ruins were ruins when Drew Morgan was here. He and Nell came up here to get away and talk." She sat on a large granite block.

Tree branches covered them with nature's canopy. Sunlight dappled the ground and lit the village below in such a way it appeared it would spring back to life at any moment.

Meredith plucked a leaf from a branch and began folding it, back and forth in zigzag fashion. She focused on the leaf as she spoke. "That phone call the night Andrew was killed?" she said. "I called my mother."

"Why so secretive about it?"

Unfolding the leaf, she set it on her leg and smoothed it back to its original shape. "I wish I could tell you that I was in shock. But that's not why I called her."

"Why then?"

She looked away as though she was ashamed of what she would say next. "My husband lay dead on the floor," she said, "and all I could think to do was to call my mother and tell her that the Bible had been stolen."

Ethan wasn't buying it. "You thought it was a replica that was stolen."

With a half smile Meredith said, "Ostrow said he was going to deliver Andrew's letter to you as soon as he left me. Can you believe that husband of mine? He beat us at our own game! Mother and I went to a lot of trouble to create and install a replica."

"That's why you kept telling me to be careful, that the Bible wasn't worth risking my life."

Meredith came to life. "And you! Almost getting yourself killed over it in Las Vegas!"

"But now it turns out it wasn't the replica in Las Vegas after all."

Meredith turned serious. "Not until Andrew's attorney delivered that letter did I know Andrew had switched them back. I've racked my brain to figure out how he discovered our plan, and how and when he made the switch on us."

"You're certain you have the replica and not the original?" Ethan asked.

Meredith nodded. "As soon as Ostrow left, I called Mother to have her check. She's beside herself."

"All this time your mother had what you thought was the original Bible? Why? Why the cloak and dagger? Why go to all the trouble to create a replica and switch it for the original without telling Andrew or me?"

Crumpling the leaf, Meredith tossed it to the ground. She took a deep breath and several moments to bring herself to the point where she could tell him.

"We didn't trust you," she said at last. "The Morgan family Bible is … is … it's not something to be taken lightly. We had to ensure its safety."

"You didn't trust me?" Ethan cried.

The idea worked on him like a burrowing beetle. The deeper it dug into his consciousness, the more upset he became.

"You didn't trust me?" he shouted, taking a swing at the tree limb. "The last time someone said that to me I was seventeen years old!"

Meredith absorbed his outburst. She must have expected he would react this way. In a way he almost pitied her. For him, little had changed. The family Bible was still gone. For her, it was a major blow. He would have pitied her if he wasn't so angry, more for Andrew than himself.

"In his letter Sky told me to ask you whose idea it was for him to write the Morgan novels, and whose idea it was to have a local school perform them."

Her eyes moist, Meredith looked up at him. "What else did he say?"

"One thing at a time. Answer the question."

She plucked another leaf and went to work folding it, back and forth, zigging then zagging.

"It was my idea," she said. "Someone has to protect and preserve your family's heritage. Andrew said it was your responsibility as the older brother and you showed no interest in it. But I could tell he wanted to do something. The novels and the play seemed a good way for him to do that without showing you up."

"You didn't love him."

It wasn't a question.

Tears fell onto the leaf-folding project. "He knew?" she asked in barely a whisper.

"He knew."

Meredith wiped tears from her cheeks. "I can't believe he never said anything."

"He loved you. Maybe he was hoping someday you'd come around."

More tears were brushed aside. "He was such a sweet man," she said. "I just never—"

"You married a man you didn't love?"

Meredith climbed down from the rock. She walked a short distance to the low stone wall overlooking the town ruins.

"Throughout history people have married for reasons other than love," she said. "It's not that unusual."

"So if not for love … why?"

Ethan knew the answer before he asked the question, but he had to hear her say it.

"The Morgan heritage. All my life I wanted to marry a Morgan. Ever since I first heard the story of Drew Morgan and Edenford."

"You were going to have a child with a man you didn't love?"

She turned to face him. She was defiant now. "A Morgan child. A dozen if necessary. I wasn't going to stop until I delivered a Morgan boy into this world. I would have worn myself out to produce a male heir to the Morgan family line."

"Is that what this is all about?" Ethan shouted. "Years of lies and deception and manipulation, for a Morgan heir?"

Her admission that she didn't love Sky ignited something inside him that started a chain reaction of fury that was mushrooming out of control. His hands clenched and unclenched. His face burned. Three quick steps and he was in front of her.

"That's what you want? A child? All right … okay … well then, let's get to it."

He pawed at the sleeves of her dress.

"Ethan! What are you doing?"

"You want a child? Let's make a child. Right here. In front of God, the angels, and all the dead residents of Edenford. It's what the Morgan clan would want."

"Ethan, don't!"

She was crying. Pushing his hands away. He kept coming after her.

"What? Now all of a sudden you're shy? Throughout history children have been born to couples who didn't love each other. It's the bloodline that counts, isn't it? Come on! Let's do it. Right here. Right now! Let's produce a Morgan!"

She slapped him. Hard. Hard enough to snap his head to one side. Hard enough to raise a welt on his cheek.

Ethan stepped away. He stood with his back to her. She had slapped the fight right out of him and all he felt now was a great weariness.

"Meredith … I'm … I'm sorry …" he said.

To his surprise, she laughed softly. "You took me by surprise," she said. "Coming here, imagining how this would all play out, I thought there was a good chance you'd strangle me. It never crossed my mind that you would—"

"I said I was sorry."

The rustle of the wind in the trees was the only sound for several minutes.

"There's one more thing I haven't told you," Meredith said. "Something that I know wasn't in Andrew's letter."

"There's more?"

"If I don't tell you now, I don't think I ever will."

Ethan folded his arms to prepare himself. He didn't know if he could take any more.

"When was the first time we met?" she asked.

It was an easy question. "On Andrew's twenty-first birthday. For months before that I'd heard about you and seen about a hundred pictures he'd drawn of you."

"That wasn't the first time," she said.

"You're wrong. I'm sure it was."

"Homecoming. Your senior year. I flew out from Ohio to watch you play football and to meet you."

"You were at homecoming? That wasn't a good game."

"After the game, along the sidelines you and some of your teammates got into it with the other team—"

"The brawl. They'd been egging us on all game, taking cheap shots and getting away with them—"

"It wasn't your proudest moment."

"No, it wasn't."

"You have to understand. For years I'd imagined what you would be like. Foolish girl fantasies. And then to see you acting like that—"

"I wasn't what you expected."

"No," she said softly.

"I wasn't Drew Morgan."

Meredith lowered her eyes. "No," she said. "You weren't."

"Well, I've got news for you, Meredith," he said. "I'm still not Drew Morgan. I never will be. Do you realize how sick that is, Meredith? You're fantasizing about a ghost!" He paced angrily. "You know what I think? I think if Drew Morgan were to appear here right now, you wouldn't like him. Do you know why? Because the Drew Morgan in your mind can do no wrong. He's perfect. Exactly what you want him to be. No man can live up to your expectations. Not even the sainted Drew Morgan."

He started to walk away. He'd had enough.

"Don't go, Ethan. Please? I … I love you."

"What?"

Meredith took a deep breath. "I have since the moment I saw you, but you scared me. You still do. So I married the safe brother."

Ethan made a slow turn and faced her. "You love me?"

She risked a smile. "Yes."

Ethan glanced down. He found it hard to think. "All this time—"

"Yes."

"What do you want me to say, Meredith? That I love you too? That I always have?" He looked heavenward in disbelief. "You lured me here under the same trees where Drew Morgan professed his love, thinking what? That his spirit would possess me and I'd do the same?"

"I don't expect—"

"Do you know how twisted this is?" Ethan cried. "You're my brother's wife!"

He was halfway down the hill before she called to him.

"Ethan, don't go. I have rooms booked for us in Bickleigh. It's just across the river."

But Ethan wasn't about to stay in Bickleigh. He wanted to drive to Exeter, fly to Manchester, wait eight hours on an uncomfortable molded plastic chair, and fly home. He cursed himself for letting himself to be lured here in the first place. However, as he walked, weariness wore heavy on his shoulders, and he didn't know if he could stay awake long enough to drive to Exeter.

# TWELVE

The next morning Ethan came down from his room for breakfast feeling almost human, and a little ashamed. He'd regretted the way he'd acted at the old Saxon castle ruins.

In the darkness of his hotel room he'd tried to rationalize his behavior to Sky, telling him he'd acted out of weariness and anger and frustration. His brother wasn't buying it. There was no excuse for boorish behavior, he'd said. Sky was right of course.

Meredith was waiting for Ethan at a quaint breakfast table next to a window overlooking the lush English countryside. She was spreading jam on a crumpet that sat next to a half-finished cup of tea.

Sensing his approach and without looking up from her jam spreading, she said, "Sleep well?"

He wanted to get this over with. Looking down at her, he said, "Meredith, I want to apologize for yesterday—"

"As well you should," she said smartly, cutting him off. She took a bite of crumpet. "Sit. Have some tea."

Her curt reply ruffled his well-combed gentlemanly demeanor. Couldn't she see he was trying to do the right thing here?

"Sit ... sit ... sit ..." she said as though the matter was settled.

With reluctance, Ethan sat.

She reached across the table. "Let me fix you a cup of tea, English style," she said, pouring him a cup from a white china teapot with cornflower blue trim. "Remind me to purchase tea before we return home. You just can't find good English tea in California. Believe me, I've tried."

"I don't like tea," Ethan said, watching her hands work with practiced rhythm.

"You'll like this," she replied, adding cream to his tea. "This isn't like anything you've tasted in the States. And try one of those swirly pastry things. I don't know what they're called, but they're heavenly. This is the only place I've ever had them."

Ethan sat stiffly. He didn't try anything. Not the tea. Not the swirly pastry things. Meredith had stirred more than his tea. She'd stirred yesterday's anger back to life. He pushed the cup of tea away and looked for a waiter. "They do have coffee in England, don't they?" he said.

"Try the tea first," Meredith insisted. "You'll like it. I know you will."

Ethan pushed his chair back. "I need to get going," he said as he stood. "I'll grab something at the airport."

"Oh ... about that ... I canceled your return flight."

"You what?"

"And your rental car. I paid a boy to return it to Exeter. Nice young man. The gardener's son. He wants to be a dentist. Isn't that odd? I've never met a young man who aspired to be a dentist."

"You ... you canceled my flight?" Ethan sputtered.

Meredith took a bite of one of the swirly pastry things. "I thought we'd drive to London," she said. "It's only a four-hour drive. Mother and I do it often." She chewed a moment. "Do you know it's impossible to get a direct flight from Exeter to London? The only way to get to London is with a stopover in Guernsey, Dublin, Glasgow, Manchester, Belfast, Aberdeen, or Leeds. Now why do you think that is? And taking into consideration the layover times, it's faster to drive to London."

"I paid for a round-trip ticket!"

"And the countryside is so beautiful."

"Meredith!"

"Oh simmer down," she said. "Sit down and drink your tea. We can get a better flight to Cincinnati out of London. Besides, this way you can see the white horse."

"Cincinnati? I'm not going to Cincinnati."

"It's just a short stop on the way home," Meredith said. "It's not like it's out of your way. Besides, what difference does it make if you return home by way of Atlanta or Cincinnati?"

"Your mother doesn't live outside of Atlanta."

Meredith conceded his point with an indulgent nod. "Trust me, the stop will be worth it."

"Trust you! Trust you?"

Meredith pursed her lips. "Why are you being so stubborn about this? I'm only thinking of you. You've never been to England in your life. Since you're here, why not spend a little time in London? And the white horse of Uffington is on the way. Sit down and drink your tea."

Ethan was so angry he couldn't look at her. An array of plans presented themselves. He could try to undo the cancellations. There would be a fee, of course, but right now he'd gladly pay it. Or he could purchase a new ticket. Even if it had a twelve-hour layover in Baghdad, it would be worth it.

He sat down. He hated himself for it, but he couldn't see himself spending hundreds of dollars just to spite Meredith.

"I'm not drinking the tea," he said.

"Suit yourself."

She'd won and she knew it, and that infuriated him even more.

"And we're not stopping to pet some silly white horse," he said.

Meredith laughed. "The white horse of Uffington is a carving in the hillside. It was made three thousand years ago and is so large, it's best seen from the air. That's the intrigue, isn't it? Why would ancients, who couldn't fly, create something to be seen from the air?"

"I have a better question. Why would someone drive four hours to see a horse carved in a hillside?"

"You're saying you don't want to stop at Uffington?"

"That's exactly what I'm saying."

"Fine. That'll give us more time in London. I thought we'd cruise by St. Paul's Cathedral and go to the Tower of London. A law-and-order guy like you will enjoy seeing the place where famous heads were chopped off."

"When is our flight?"

"Not until late tonight. We have plenty of time."

"You've arranged everything."

Meredith smiled at him sweetly as she sipped her tea.

Ethan gazed out the window. "It's hard to believe our ancestors used to live here ... to walk beside this river."

She joined him in his reverie, lost in the green countryside.

"You did all this because of family heritage," he said.

She nodded slowly. "It's important to me."

"Yes, it is," he said. "In fact, the past is more important to you than the present."

She set down her teacup. "I wouldn't go that far."

"I would, because it is." Ethan had set her up. He looked at her to drive home his point. "Yesterday was my first day back at work. You knew that, yet not once did you ask me how it went."

Flustered, Meredith said, "I ... I ... was going to call you. But then Andrew's lawyer came over and—"

"Not once have you even wondered how I found out so quickly about Sky's letter. After all, I was supposed to be at work."

"Well, I just assumed Ostrow arranged to meet you at headquarters ..."

"You assumed, did you? Meredith, you don't assume anything, at least not for things that are of concern to you. You plan every single detail, down to sightseeing stops on the road to London to view a three-thousand-year-old white horse carved in the hillside!"

He was shouting.

Meredith's eyes were wide and defensive. Her mouth open but unable to function at the moment.

"Ostrow tried to deliver the letter to headquarters, but he couldn't. And do you know why he couldn't? Because I wasn't there. I was on my way home."

"Home?" She grew concerned. "Oh, Ethan, your wounds ... and all this time traveling ... I didn't think ..."

"No, you didn't think! And I'm fine. I tire quickly, but it's not my wounds that sent me home. It was the chief of police. After verbally bludgeoning me, he suspended me."

"Suspended?"

"Indefinitely."

"But why?"

"What's this? Concern over a living Morgan?"

"Ethan, that's not fair."

It wasn't fair. He knew it wasn't. But he didn't apologize. For once he had the upper hand and it felt good.

"He suspended me because the scandal newspapers are having a heyday with the events in Las Vegas. Renegade cop goes to Vegas for blood vengeance, that sort of thing."

"Suspended ..." she said.

"Yeah ... suspended."

She gathered herself. "That means we can take our time in London. Now drink your tea before it gets cold."

"I told you, I don't like tea!" Ethan blustered.

---

After checking out of his room, Ethan wandered the grounds of Bickleigh Castle. From the brochures at the front desk he learned that it was built in the fourteenth century. Thirty acres of land boasted a garden, an outdoor play area, hiking, fishing, tennis, and golf. As he surveyed the structure from the front, he couldn't help but wonder what the ancients would think of their stronghold being turned into a cozy little bed-and-breakfast.

The trip to London was tedious and uneventful. They followed a flock of clouds that looked like sheep on their way to market all the way to the city. For four hours Meredith did the talking, mostly of her experiences in England, each occurring while Sky thought his wife was visiting her mother in Ohio. Now that he was dead, Meredith could speak of them openly. It put Ethan in a surly mood.

"I wish we had more time. There are so many places I want to show you," Meredith said as they entered the city.

Ethan glared at the stalled traffic surrounding them. The drive along Millbank Road paralleling the Thames had been pleasant, but once they approached Westminster Abbey and Big Ben, it was as though traffic had given them the equivalent of a group hug and wouldn't let them go.

"Just point out the places you want me to see," Ethan said moodily. "I'll jump out, take a tour, and catch up with you a block down the road."

Nodding at the open map on his lap, Meredith said, "You can put that away now. The Tower of London is pretty much due east from here, though the name of the street will change as we go along."

Ethan consulted the map. "Change to what?"

"Several names, really. Right now, we're on the Strand. At the next intersection it will change to Fleet Street, then Ludgate Hill, and then St. Paul's Church Yard as we pass the cathedral. After that, it will become Cannon Street, then Great Tower Street."

He followed her litany across the page of the map. She got all the names right. "I suppose every large city has it own peculiar brand of confusion," he said, folding the map closed.

Looking up, his heart leaped into his throat. It wasn't the first time. During several unguarded moments along the way he'd experienced a moment of panic when he thought Meredith was driving on the wrong side of the road.

She didn't notice this time. Traffic had eased and they were traveling at a steady clip.

"St. Paul's is straight ahead," she said.

And so it was. In front of them the massive dome was framed by twin towers. Steps the width of the building led to a colonnade entrance. With the sun to their back, the cathedral facade shimmered with light. For the first time Ethan was glad Meredith was driving so he could give his full attention to the building.

"During Hitler's bombing blitz of London, the area surrounding the cathedral was reduced to rubble, while the cathedral itself went miraculously unscathed. Photographs of the dome rising above the smoke and fire became a symbol of the country's indomitable spirit."

Ethan could understand the sentiment. Even against a patchy sky on a peaceful afternoon the dome was impressive.

Merging right, they flanked the edifice.

"The church is built in the shape of a cross," Meredith said, stealing glances as traffic permitted, "with the dome crowning the point where the arms intersect. It's one of the largest domes in—"

The next thing Ethan knew the car was lifted off the ground and moving sideways, doing a slow roll midair with the street coming into view out his side window while a screaming Meredith crested over him.

"No-no-no-no ... dear God, no!"

She didn't seem to comprehend that the wheels were no longer touching the road. Her foot pumped the brake and she turned the steering wheel as though she could reverse the roll and land them safely on the street.

She couldn't, and they came down hard. Ethan's window shattered upon impact, his head and shoulder slamming into the safety glass. Meredith slid across the seat and tumbled down on top of him, her head hammering against his jaw. The car bounced and skidded a short distance, and while Ethan was able to hold his head up, his shoulder rolled in the glass.

Everything was sideways. The concussion of the blast that had propelled them through the air had done a number on Ethan's ears. Meredith was on top of him crying in short gasps, but it sounded as though she were far away.

She let out a scream as the car shuddered when another vehicle fell out of the sky in front of them. It was followed by what seemed to be a meteor shower of stone and brick that pelted the street and cars. Some of the chunks were huge; one struck the car in front of them with what appeared to be a deathblow. Steam rose from the engine like a spirit departing a body.

Ethan covered Meredith's head with his arms to shield her from the falling debris.

"What ... what happened?" Meredith whimpered. She made a weak attempt to push herself off Ethan.

"Lie still a moment," Ethan said, then repeated it louder because he hadn't heard his own voice the first time.

He thought he heard a hum, then realized it was a vibration. The car engine was still running, and with the transmission engaged, the back wheels were spinning as though continuing merrily on their way.

The world outside the front windshield had tipped on its side, or so it appeared. Debris, rubble, and immobile cars littered the street.

"What happened?" Meredith asked again.

In answer to her question, a sight so unimaginable Ethan knew it couldn't be happening occurred in front of them. Meredith's hand flew to her mouth to stifle a scream of disbelief. Ethan stared wide-eyed at the horror.

In school he'd read about momentous events like this, black days in history that people talked about for centuries, and he'd always imagined what it would be like to be there and see it firsthand—the attack on Pearl Harbor, the explosion of the Hindenburg, 9/11, the assassinations of presidents Lincoln and Kennedy.

And here he was, watching as the dome of St. Paul's Cathedral slid sideways through the sky and crumpled on St. Paul's Church Yard Street as easily as a cellophane wrapper. As the dome disintegrated, it whipped up clouds of dust that rolled toward them with surprising speed.

"Down! Get down!" Ethan shouted, pulling Meredith's head against his chest and once again shielding her with his arms.

The cloud hit the windshield with force, pelting it with rocks and debris until it shattered. Dust engulfed them, coating every breath with grit and stinging their eyes. They coughed and gagged and fought for breathable air.

Meredith's shoulder wedged into Ethan's belly. Each cough was a prizefighter punch in the gut.

He pushed at her. "Off … get … off …" he wheezed.

She coughed into one hand while pushing with the other to climb off of him. In the attempt she pushed on his bullet wound. If the wound had been a target, she hit the bull's-eye.

Ethan let loose with a howl that ended in another coughing spasm.

"Sorry ... sorry ..." Meredith cried, trying not to hit the wound again. But there weren't many places for her to put her hands, and her efforts tore at the edges of the wound. It began to bleed.

After several more jabs, she managed to position herself so that her weight was against the back of the seat. Ethan blinked back gritty tears of pain.

"Meredith ... are you ... are you ... all right?" he managed to say.

He asked because she had a frightened animal look in her eyes as the realization of what they had witnessed began to sink in. Her chin quivered, and her lips softly mumbled something Ethan didn't hear. Confused, she tried reaching across his chest for the door handle, trying to get out.

"Meredith," he said. "Meredith, listen to me. We can't get out that way. We're going to have to climb out."

"Climb out?"

"Through your window. The one up there."

Meredith looked up at the driver's side window. Where there should have been blue sky and patchy clouds, there was a dark cloud of dust.

"Reach up there, roll down the window, and climb out," Ethan instructed her.

Meredith looked up at the window. Her eyes quickened with resolve. Grabbing the steering wheel with one hand she reached up and rolled down the window. Ethan steadied her as she climbed out.

Through the front windshield he could see her step away from the car and take in the surrounding area. Her hands flapped helplessly at her sides.

He pulled himself into a sitting position, then managed to get his feet under him. The hardest part was next. Climbing out the window required using wounded muscles. Wincing and groaning, he pulled himself up and out.

They stood in the middle of St. Paul's Church Yard Street. It looked like a war zone, as though Hitler's bombers returned for one last raid to take care of unfinished business. This time they didn't miss.

The southern wall of the church was gone. With nothing to support them on this side, the roof and dome came tumbling down. To see such a proud structure marred in this way was a black mark against humanity.

Cars and stone and bricks littered the street. People walked like zombies through streets that were so heavily coated with dust it looked like winter. Sirens blared in the distance.

"Let me get you out of here," Ethan said to Meredith.

"No. I'm fine. Let's see if anyone needs help."

She had cuts and abrasions.

"Are you sure you're all right?" Ethan asked.

"Check the cars," she replied.

The car immediately in front of them had landed on its roof and collapsed down to its frame. Meredith bent down on the passenger side.

"I can't tell if anyone …" she yelled to Ethan, "… wait a minute … here …" She got down on her knees, disappeared for a moment, then surfaced. "Passenger side's empty. How's the driver?"

"Let's move on to the next car," Ethan said. She didn't need to hear about the driver's condition. He was beyond their help.

The next car was upright, but a huge portion of the church wall had crushed its hood. Someone was kicking the driver's side window from inside. It gave way and a boot appeared.

A cry came from the direction of the church.

"Help! Somebody, help! There are children in here!"

Ethan turned to see a man standing on the edge of the ruins, shouting.

"Meredith, help this man in the car," Ethan said. "I'm going—"

Before he could finish his sentence she was agreeing with him. "Go! Go!"

Ethan did his best to sprint toward the man calling for help. Two other men appeared from nowhere.

"Ethan?"

He turned back.

"Be careful," Meredith said.

"In here," the man calling for help cried. "They're pinned under debris."

A young man, late twenties Ethan guessed, with a large forehead and sad eyes that drooped like a bloodhound guided him. His shirt was torn and bloodied.

He helped Ethan and the two other men over a low remnant of wall and led them to the trapped children. About a dozen sat in a cluster free from danger at the base of a pillar, dazed, dirty, and sniffling.

The guide enlisted the oldest of the volunteers to lead these children out of the building. It was a good move. Not only did it get the children out from underfoot, the man assigned to lead them was frail and appeared to be in his midseventies or older.

He proved to be a good shepherd with a kindly way about him. He had no trouble getting the children to follow him.

"Over here," the guide said. He led them through a dusty haze to a pile of rubble, the remains of a partially collapsed wall. "It's tricky," he said, using the larger pieces as stepping-stones.

With each step the portion of the wall still standing teetered. If the guide noticed, it didn't stop him.

"Wait ..." Ethan warned.

Two more steps and the guide bent over, pointing to the place where the children were buried.

"Don't move!" Ethan shouted. "The wall—"

But it was too late. Without further warning, the wall fell toward them. Gravity did the rest, ripping it apart as it collapsed on the guide.

Ethan and the other helper dove to get out of the way. Neither of them was successful. Three pieces of wall the size of watermelons hit Ethan in the back in quick succession. St. Paul's punches, he later described them. Had the apostle hit him in the jaw with a right hook, Ethan would have been down for the count.

The other helper wasn't as lucky. A huge piece of wall fell on the back of his leg, then for good measure bounced up and landed again, pinning the man's leg beneath it.

Ethan, flat against the cathedral floor, looked over at the man who was grimacing in pain.

*Don't struggle. I'll get that off of you.*

Ethan tried to say those words. They formed in his mind, but not his mouth. He tried to get up. That effort, too, became unrealized thought.

The pressure on his back lifted a little at a time.

"Ethan! How bad is it?"

He turned his head and recognized Meredith's shoes, then her knees, then her face as she bent low to look at him.

Ethan took stock of himself. "I don't think anything's broken," he said. "Help me get up."

With Meredith's assistance Ethan got to his feet. His head swam in circles for a moment then cleared. Like a computer running a diagnostics program, Ethan systematically checked his functioning ability—he blinked and his vision cleared, his neck swiveled, his arms rose, his hands clenched, his legs moved. He took a tentative step.

He felt stiff, and he was going to hurt in the morning, but for now he could function.

"Help me free his leg," he said to Meredith.

Together they lifted the portion of wall from the man's leg. Despite their suggestion that he take it slow, the man stood, tested the leg, and walked in a small circle. He limped and winced as he walked, but otherwise seemed to be in working order.

"Let's help those children," the man said, turning his attention to the rubble.

Under ordinary circumstances Ethan thought he and the man probably wouldn't have liked each other. The man was big with a three-day growth of beard, girlie tattoos on both forearms, and smelled of raw fish. Ethan guessed he worked at the docks. But these weren't ordinary circumstances and at times like this a man's willingness to ignore his own pain to help someone else was the best testimony he could have.

While falling walls no longer posed a threat, the collapse had withdrawn support from a portion of the roof that threatened to come down at any moment. It dropped bits of rock and wood splinters on the rescuers in way of warning.

Ethan and the dockworker unearthed the guide. He was dead. His skull crushed.

They heard the whimpering and crying of children as emergency personnel began to arrive. Shouts and orders echoed through the church, but so far none had made it to this part of the building.

Pebbles pelted the back of Ethan's neck as he lifted rocks off the pile, handing them to Meredith. A little more digging and they found a treasure greater than gold: four small children hunched over in a space no larger than the back of a station wagon.

Ethan lifted the first little girl out and handed her to the dockworker who handed her to Meredith just as a fireman arrived to take her out. Two more were plucked from the grave and handed over to Meredith and the dockworker. Ethan carried to safety the last of the children, a little girl whose legs were broken.

"Where to?" Ethan asked a fireman.

The fireman attempted to take the girl from him. Ethan refused to give her up.

The little girl stared at him with wide blue eyes. She was in shock. Ethan attempted to calm her.

"You're all right now," he said.

She looked at him strangely. "You're a Yank?" she asked.

Ethan grinned. "Yank?"

"An American."

"How can you tell?"

"You talk like in the movies."

Ethan smiled at her. "I walk funny too. You just can't see it right now."

Her smile was cut short by a grimace that nearly tore Ethan's heart out of his chest. What sort of monster would do something like this with complete disregard for innocent life?

"Do you live in Hollywood?" she asked him.

"I live in California, not too far from Hollywood."

Her eyes brightened. "Do you know Tom Cruise?"

"No, Tom lives in a different neighborhood."

"I prayed to God to send Tom Cruise to rescue us."

"Sorry. You'll have to settle for me."

She seemed to be fading. "I think Tom Cruise is hot," she said.

"What! He's a married man!"

His exclamation stirred her. She grinned. "I still think he's hot."

After handing the girl over to emergency personnel at a makeshift triage, Ethan insisted on going back into the church to assist in the rescue effort. A policeman—constable in England—blocked his way until Ethan identified himself as a detective.

"You're a bit of all right, bloke," the man said.

Meredith remained at the triage unit, wrapped in a blanket, her feet elevated.

Ethan wandered into the sanctuary looking for victims. In the middle of the church he had to shield his eyes from sunlight, something no man had done for hundreds of years while standing on this spot.

He called out to anyone who needed help. His voice roused a man who pulled himself up from between pews. The man looked like he was climbing out of a coffin. Ethan started toward him.

A dark figure appeared under an archway.

"Jason?" the figure said.

The man in the pews seemed to recognize the figure who was still a silhouette to Ethan. Using the back of a pew for a railing, the young man made his way toward the figure who pulled a gun and pumped two quick bullets into him.

"Hey!" Ethan shouted from instinct. It was also instinct that sent his hand to pull out a service revolver that wasn't there.

The gunman turned toward Ethan. One step and he was in the sunlight.

"You!" Ethan cried.

It was the same man who had shot him in Corby's trailer.

"You?" the gunman cried, equally astonished.

The gun raised. Ethan hit the floor. The back of a pew exploded with splinters.

"What's up here?" a third voice shouted. It was the dockworker. Shielding himself behind a pillar, he shouted for help.

The gunman wasn't in the mood to take any risks. He lifted the dead man onto his back and disappeared through the archway.

A moment later the dockworker was bending over Ethan. "What is this world comin' to?" he said. "Shootin' people in St. Paul's? Hasn't the day already had its share of evil?"

"It's just not safe to go to church anymore," Ethan lamented.

# THIRTEEN

The blue haze of video monitors lit F. Malory Simon's face as he stood in the center of a dark room with remote controls in both hands. The room had no windows. Air-conditioning kept a constant temperature; its processed air mingling with electrical odors gave the room a machine smell. The walls hummed with high-definition flat-screen monitors carrying different news broadcasts, including telecasts from Britain and France. Newscasters from around the globe covered the rescue efforts following the bombing of St. Paul's Cathedral. Clips of the explosion and collapse gathered from tourists' video cameras played repeatedly.

Simon watched the broadcasts with a satisfied smile, his gaze moving from monitor to monitor. He clicked remotes, alternately turning on and muting the sound of various broadcasts. All reported that the same terrorist group that bombed Notre Dame was taking credit for the attack on St. Paul's Cathedral.

This room was Simon's mission control. Here he monitored projects during crucial stages of their development. On some days that meant the screens displayed stock quotes and financial reports. On other days they displayed the faces of business partners around the world as he moderated a video conference. Today, he watched the aftermath of his most ambitious secret project.

The door opened. Gil Getz stepped into the room, taking in the monitors with a glance. He joined Simon in the center of the room.

Mission control had no chairs, only a belt-high desk with a keyboard, mouse, and a tablet PC that linked to the system of monitors. Simon preferred conducting business standing up.

Simon set the remotes on the desk and sipped from a bottle of water. "Impressive, isn't it?" he said without taking his eyes off the images of destruction.

The smoking ruins of the cathedral could be viewed from any angle—exterior shots, interior shots, even overhead shots from a helicopter, which provided a jittery view of a portion of the dome, still intact, lying on its side next to the church.

Simon stuck out his chest. "Makes me feel like a medieval knight standing over a slain dragon," he said.

Gil didn't offer a reply. He knew better than to interrupt Simon's moment of victory.

"Is that the latest?" Simon asked, indicating the manila folder Getz was holding.

"Affirmative."

Gil angled the open folder toward one of the brighter screens in order to read the report.

"All the apprentices have been accounted for. All of them save one succeeded in placing their package at the designated coordinates on time."

"And the one who failed?"

"We believe he ditched his package along the exterior of the south wall. Maybe he was coming back for it, maybe not." Gil approached the monitor with the overhead helicopter shot. "Which accounts for the dome in the street," he said, pointing to it.

The plan had been for St. Paul's to implode as is commonly done to raze buildings for new construction. Had all the packages been placed correctly the legendary dome would have sunk downward into a cloud of smoke rather than toppling onto its side.

"Who failed to place his package?" Simon asked.

"Neuman."

Simon scoffed. "The Yale grad. Figures. Blowhard Ivy Leaguer. Did he survive the blast?"

"He was neutralized and extracted."

"The body?"

"Incinerated, as per procedure."

Simon had been so pleased with himself. This glitch spoiled everything. He'd misread Neuman. The thought tormented him. What had he missed?

Gil said, "On the whole, this one went smoother than Notre Dame."

"Don't play me," Simon snapped.

Gil knew what he was doing. The comment goaded Simon out of his wallowing to course corrections for the next project.

"Theory," Simon observed. "That's all they teach those Ivy Leaguers. They don't teach them to be smart, they teach them to over-analyze. Neuman wasn't hungry like the others. Are there any Ivy Leaguers in this next batch?"

Gil thought a moment. "Klein's from Cornell."

"Dump him."

"What should I tell him?"

Simon grinned. "Tell him our background check revealed questionable moral and ethical issues."

"Did it?"

"No. It'll drive him crazy trying to figure out what we know. And on the next project I want more cameras installed in the interior. One on each target. I want to see who is placing their package and when."

"Done," Gil said, jotting down a note.

With a nod Simon turned his back, signaling Gil that he was dismissed. But his partner didn't leave.

"There's one more item to report."

Simon scowled. He hated addendums. Addendums were admissions of sloppy work.

"When Neuman was neutralized … there were witnesses."

Anger flashed in Simon's eyes. "Who was the idiot who allowed himself to be seen?"

"My son," Gil said flatly. He offered no excuses for the boy.

"How many witnesses?"

"Two."

Simon thought a moment. "No body, no murder," he concluded. "All they have is the testimony of two traumatized victims. The whole thing will get buried in the rubble of the greater tragedy."

Simon did his best to keep the anger from his voice. Leaving behind witnesses to a shooting was inexcusable.

The matter was settled. Again, Gil should have left. Again, he didn't, which meant there was more bad news.

"One of the witnesses was Ethan Morgan."

"Morgan?" Simon shouted. "What was Morgan doing in England?"

"We have no idea."

Simon began to pace. He swung around and stared hard at Gil. "The guy's a bad penny. He keeps showing up at the wrong time."

Gil agreed.

"Had your boy eliminated him in Corby's trailer this never would have happened. Loose ends, Gil. You know I don't like loose ends."

"I'll take care of Morgan."

"How?"

"We have a man in San Diego."

"Kill a cop in his own city? Don't be stupid. Nothing motivates detectives more than investigating the murder of one of their own."

"I'll make sure that—"

Simon cut him off with an upraised hand. "We're not Mafia. We're businessmen. To kill a man just because he's in your way is a waste. The key is to find a way to profit from his death. Morgan isn't a threat to us, he's an opportunity."

"As long as he's alive, he's a risk," Gil argued. "Morgan can tie the Corby hit to the cathedral bombing."

"And whose fault is that?" Simon roared.

Gil lowered his gaze.

Simon shrugged off his anger. It blinded reason, and he needed to think clearly now. He slapped Gil good-naturedly on the back, thanked him for the report, and led him to the door.

"I want you to find out what Morgan was doing in England. I'll work up a plan for him and turn your son's blunder to our advantage."

———

Ethan walked along a dirt path that paralleled the muddy Ohio River. Meredith strolled beside him. It was twilight and the air was crisp with the odor of October. Jacket weather.

Something about the enduring nature of the river invigorated Ethan. For hundreds of years it had flowed past this shoreline and would for a hundred more. Day in and day out, a tireless traveler.

Meredith felt it too. She was unusually quiet. The orange glow of the setting sun added warmth to her complexion and fiery highlights to her hair. She seemed to feed off the strength of the river and its history.

"This is where Marshall and J. D. Morgan ferried runaway slaves to safety," she said. "On the Kentucky side of the river they were slaves. Here they were free."

"And the Coopers?" Ethan asked. "Did they run slaves too?"

She looked at him oddly.

"What?" he said. "Did I say something dumb?"

"Don't you know?"

"Apparently not."

"The Coopers were Southerners. They owned slaves."

"Sorry. Didn't know."

Meredith offered no defense for her family's slave holding. She was more intent on the relationship between the Coopers and the Morgans.

"Seth Cooper and Jeremiah Morgan were best friends before the war," she explained. "Both of them were preachers."

"And during the war?" Ethan asked.

"The split came before the war. Jeremiah Morgan invited Seth Cooper to preach at his church. The whole Cooper family came. However, during their stay Marshall and J. D. were seen running slaves. Seth Cooper became furious that Jeremiah's sons would run slaves while at the same time entertaining Southern guests."

"Surely Cooper knew they were abolitionists."

"He knew. He also knew Marshall and J. D. were members of the Underground Railroad."

"Then why did he blow his top?"

"He felt the Morgan boys should have suspended their operations during his family's visit, out of respect."

"Respect?" Ethan cried. "Seth Cooper expected the slaves to stay on the Kentucky side and risk capture and whippings and chains just because he was visiting? Who did he think he was?"

"He was a Southerner," Meredith said, getting defensive. "Don't judge what you don't understand. Times were different back then."

Ethan picked up a rock and threw it into the river. "Not that different," he said. "Enslaving human beings is wrong in any century. And endangering lives to keep from offending a friend is criminal. Somebody needed to tell Seth Cooper to take a hike."

"Spoken like a true Morgan," Meredith said, smiling at him.

Ethan had expected her to rise to the Coopers' defense. After all, she was one of them. Instead, her eyes glistened warmly as she looked at him. It made him uneasy.

He said, "So what would Seth Cooper think of you walking with a Morgan? Aren't we the enemy?"

She lifted her face to the setting sun and Ethan found it difficult to tell which was more radiant. A breeze toyed with a strand of hair on her forehead.

"You really should read Andrew's novels," she said. "The Morgans and Coopers had some exciting encounters together during the Civil War. After the war, Sarah Morgan married a Cooper. She was the one who wrote the dime novels, adventures of Truly Noble and Charity Increase."

"Wait a minute ... a Morgan married a Cooper? That makes us cousins, doesn't it? Distant, yes, but ... you married your cousin?"

Meredith laughed. "I'm the fruit of a different Cooper branch. I'm afraid there's no Morgan blood in me."

She said it lightly, but with a tinge of genuine disappointment.

Meredith stopped walking. The sun had set, the shimmer had gone from her complexion, and all of a sudden she looked tired. Ethan felt it too. Once the sun went down, the air became cold and damp. It sapped his strength and made his wounds and muscles ache.

"We should get back to the house," he said.

"I won't argue with you."

Ethan took her by the arm and helped her up the embankment. Halfway up they had to stop so Meredith could catch her breath. Together they enjoyed the elevated view of the river.

He felt her warmth. It stirred something inside him. It angered him that it did, but he couldn't ignore the feeling. Ever since London he'd been looking at her differently. When the world was falling apart all around them, she was magnificent, overcoming her fear to help others. He'd never seen that side of her.

Apparently they were both remembering that day because Meredith said, "You were brave back there in London."

"Don't spoil it, Meredith."

"All I said was—"

"It's what you stopped short of saying."

"So now I anger you by what you suppose I'll say?"

"We both know what you were implying."

Meredith folded her arms. "And just what do you think I was implying?"

Ethan looked at her. It didn't need to be said. They both knew what she meant by it. She just wanted him to say it and he wasn't going to.

It became a staring contest. And when life is reduced to a staring contest, women always have the advantage.

"You meant I was brave in London …"

"Yes—"

"… just like Drew Morgan."

She smiled her victory. "See? Even you think so."

"No, I don't!" Ethan protested. "I was simply finishing your sentence. And in London I was simply lending a helping hand."

"You can't fight it, Ethan," she said, resuming her climb. "You're a Morgan. You fight for what you believe."

"Yeah? And tell me, what do I believe?"

"I'd like to hear the answer to that question myself." The reply came from atop a nearby bluff. Ethan spun around to face the voice.

Hands on hips Olivia Cooper stood tall against the sky looking down at them. The first stars of the evening twinkled behind her. Her ankle-length skirt flapped like a flag in the wind.

From this angle she looked like Scarlett O'Hara standing on a hill, vowing she would fight to her dying breath to save Tara.

"Let me give you a hand, dear," Olivia said, reaching down to help Meredith up.

She didn't offer a hand to Ethan. He was glad she didn't. If she had, he didn't know if he would have taken it.

---

The house that had once belonged to Jeremiah Morgan was now a bed-and-breakfast ten miles outside of Cincinnati. Ethan and Meredith followed Olivia up the steps to the porch and inside.

Hearty dinner odors greeted them, the meat and potatoes kind. Ethan's mouth watered appreciably if not enviously because the odors were from food he would not taste. The inn was full. Getting a room at Olivia Cooper's bed-and-breakfast meant putting your name on a two-year waiting list. Ethan and Meredith had rooms not far from the airport at the Radisson Riverfront in Covington. A short-order cook would slap together their dinner.

"Cheryl's beef stew and cornbread with homemade blueberry pie for dessert," Olivia said before Ethan asked.

Ethan had heard about Cheryl from Sky. She'd been the chef at the Heritage Bed and Breakfast for thirty years. Her meals were one reason for that two-year waiting list, and her pastries were the stuff of local legend.

"Who are tonight's guests?" Meredith asked.

"We have a soft-drink executive and his wife from Atlanta, a history professor from Michigan State, and a local pastor and his wife who are celebrating their twenty-fifth wedding anniversary. She's a sweetheart. Keeps offering to help."

They removed their coats and hung them on a rack inside the

front door. To their left a stairway to the second floor hugged the wall. Directly in front of them a hallway stretched into the kitchen. Olivia motioned them to a doorway on their right into what had once been the Morgan family's drawing room. Now it was a small museum where dark woods, display lights, and glass cases housed an extensive collection of Bibles. The centerpiece of the display area in a round mahogany case was the replica of the Morgan family Bible.

A twinge of desperation charged Ethan, refreshing his determination to recover the authentic version.

"All of the Bibles in this room belong to families who, inspired by Drew Morgan, started a similar tradition of handing a family Bible from generation to generation," Olivia explained.

Within the display cases each of the Bibles lay open. Printed on the inside of the front covers were family names and dates indicating when that particular Bible had been handed down to the succeeding generation.

Ethan read some of the family names aloud. "Howland. Sargent. Diehl. Mason. Boyle. Kramer. Graham. Price." He looked up. "Why are these Bibles no longer kept by the families?"

Olivia recited a prepared reply with the tone of a museum docent. "Additions to our collection come to us in a number of ways. Some have been found in an attic or basement by a nonfamily member and donated to the museum. Some have been entrusted to us for safekeeping by the families themselves. And still others we have purchased at antique-book auctions."

Ethan moved to the center of the room and the Morgan Bible display. The twinge of desperation hit him again. He had the uneasy feeling that time was running out.

The Bible in the display was a replica, of course, but it looked so much like the real thing it made his heart ache just to see it again. Memories of the night Sky was killed compounded the ache.

This was the Bible Meredith had attempted to swap for the authentic version. Had she been successful the Morgan Bible would be safe within this display case.

"How do you know for sure this—"

"—is the replica?" Olivia finished his sentence for him.

She pulled keys from her pocket and unlocked the case. Donning a pair of cotton gloves she removed the Bible with expert care.

"This Bible is a genuine 1611 edition that we purchased at an auction," she said, "so it has an intrinsic value of its own."

Opening the cover, she pointed to the names that had been penned on the inside, starting with Drew Morgan and ending with Ethan Morgan. The writing appeared exactly as Ethan remembered it.

"One way to determine if this is the authentic Morgan Bible would be to test the ink used to pen the names. While we replicated the penmanship of the original, the ink we used is modern. A lab test could reveal the truth. But there's an easier and quicker way."

Closing the Bible she turned it over. Like the authentic Bible there was a prominent gash in the back extending several inches deep.

"The gash cuts all the way to the Gospels," Olivia explained, "and with sufficient light you can see a name printed on the first page that wasn't marred by the shrapnel."

She handed Ethan the Bible. He positioned it so that a display light illuminated the gash. At the bottom was a single word. A name. He read it aloud.

"Judas."

Olivia nodded. "A different name can be seen at the bottom of the gash of the authentic Bible: Thomas."

"That's how Mother was able to tell so quickly when I called her from your house the night of Andrew's murder," Meredith explained. She turned to her mother. "Why hadn't you checked it before, after I made the switch?"

"Why would I? You told me everything went off without a hitch," her mother said, refusing to accept any blame.

Ethan grinned. Somewhere Sky was grinning too, having turned the tables on his mother-in-law's sneaky plan without her knowing it.

"Still, had you checked—" Meredith said.

"I shouldn't have had to check," Olivia replied.

The botched swap was obviously a sore point between them.

"When you made the replica," Ethan said, switching topics for Meredith's sake, "were the different names at the bottom of the gash by design?"

Olivia shifted her gaze to him with no loss of energy in the exchange. "Did we cut until we found Judas? No." she replied. "It was pure coincidence. The antique dealer who helped us create the replica was the first to notice Judas's name."

"The name is ironic, don't you think?" Ethan quipped.

Olivia ignored him. "Not until then did we think to examine the bottom of the gash of the original. When Meredith reported that it was Thomas, we thought it prudent to keep them as they were for identification purposes."

Ethan leveled an accusing finger at Meredith. "The time Sky borrowed the Bible when he first started writing the graphic novels … which was also your idea. It was all a setup to switch Bibles!"

"That's how it began," Meredith said, defending herself. "But Andrew wrote such wonderful stories, the publishers were eager to—"

"But Sky became wise and foiled your plans."

"And as a result, the Morgan Bible was stolen," Olivia snapped. "Had Andrew not meddled—"

"Meddled?" Ethan cried. "You're the ones who were meddling! You had no right—"

Olivia was eager for a fight. "We had every right! If you had shown just an ounce of responsibility—"

"My responsibility has nothing to do with it!" Ethan yelled.

"It has everything to do with it! You made it obvious you cared nothing for your family's heritage. Someone had to step in—"

"And what? Seduce my brother into a loveless marriage?"

"Ethan!" Meredith cried, stung by the accusation.

"It's true, isn't it?" Ethan pressed. "You didn't love him. You married him for property, and when you couldn't get what you wanted by marriage, the two of you attempted to steal it. That's grand theft!"

Meredith suppressed sobs.

"Don't be ridiculous," Olivia snapped.

"Let me make something clear to you," Ethan said to Olivia. "You are not a Morgan." Then, to Meredith, "And except for the letter of the law, neither are you. Stay out of our affairs."

Ethan had wanted to shout at someone since Sky's attorney showed up on his doorstep. It felt good to confront Olivia Cooper, the mastermind of the plan, but not as satisfying as he thought it would be to confront Meredith, even though he couldn't believe she married his brother over a Bible.

A figure darkened the doorway, drawn to the room by the shouting. "May I be of assistance?" he said.

"Thank you, Rev. Larson," Olivia said reassuringly. "I apologize for disturbing you. If you wouldn't mind, tell Cheryl to serve dinner. I'll be in shortly."

The minister glanced warily at Ethan before departing.

Ethan handed the replica back to Olivia. She made no effort to accept it.

"You keep it," she said.

"I don't want it. This isn't the Morgan Bible."

"Place it in your display case. For now at least," Olivia replied.

Ethan glared at her. She didn't believe he would recover the Morgan Bible. Slowly, he set the fake Morgan Bible on top of its display.

"I already have a replica in my display case."

"You do?" Meredith asked.

"The one from the school production."

It took a moment for Meredith to make the connection. When she did, she laughed.

"I don't understand," Olivia said.

"You know, Mother—the elementary school production." Turning to Ethan, "You put it in the display case?"

"Only until I recover the authentic Bible."

"Is it a good replica?" Olivia asked.

"It's made of construction paper," Meredith replied.

"And a laundry-detergent box," Ethan added. "With a hole in the corner. There's a pile of blue and white granules in the bottom of the case."

"Oh for heaven's sake," Olivia scoffed. "Take the replica Bible, Ethan."

"Thanks," he said, "but I like my replica better."

# FOURTEEN

It was time to get down to business.

"Meredith said you had information that would help me track down the Bible."

Olivia acted as though she hadn't heard him. She placed the Morgan Bible replica back in its display case and locked it, then stripped off the cotton gloves and walked to the far end of the room. Meredith and Ethan followed.

A partition separated a cluttered workplace from the museum display area. The space couldn't have been more than three feet wide and six feet deep. Illuminated by a desk lamp, a small woman sat hunched in front of a computer monitor. Since the only way into the room was from the entryway, she'd apparently been working the entire time and heard everything.

Every available space had something sitting on it or crammed into it. Stacks of papers and catalogs. File folders. A calendar of cats surrounded by a snowstorm of notes pinned to the walls.

Because the room was cramped, they lined up the length of the office space: Olivia, Meredith, then Ethan.

"This is Alice Culver," Olivia said in way of introduction.

"Hello, Alice," Meredith said.

The woman swiveled around in her chair but didn't get up. She filled the chair to overflowing. Rectangular frame glasses perched on the end of her nose.

"Meredith, dear, it's nice to see you. My whole prayer group has been praying for you when we heard you were at St. Paul's."

"How sweet," Meredith said. "Thank them for me, will you?"

Olivia motioned toward Ethan. "And this is—"

"I know who he is," Alice said, her mouth a thin line. She looked him up and down, and what she saw didn't seem to change her impression of him.

"Nice to—" Ethan said.

"I assembled the information you requested," Alice said to Olivia. She swiveled around to face her computer and began tapping the keys.

Ethan thought about asking Alice if her prayer group had been praying for him, too, but decided it wasn't the best idea to poke the lions in the den.

A printer sprang to life somewhere beneath the computer near Alice's feet. When it fell silent, she reached down and collected three printed sheets. Stretching in front of Olivia and Meredith, she handed them to Ethan.

"Do you recognize any of these names?" she asked him.

"What am I looking at?" Ethan asked as he began scanning the columns on the first page.

"These are some of the more prominent collectors of antique books," Olivia explained, making it clear that while Alice was supplying the documents, she was in charge of the operation. "Many of them bid at auctions, often through intermediaries. We have—well, let's just say we've called in some favors—to secure the names of some of the more discreet buyers."

Ethan glanced at her.

"It's best if you don't know the details," she said, answering his unasked question. "Because of what happened to you in Las Vegas, it was evident that Corby was working for someone when he broke into your house and stole your Bible."

She didn't say, "And murdered your brother." She didn't have to.

"The question is," Olivia continued, "who was he working for?"

Ethan continued scanning the columns. His moving gaze hit a brick wall of a name.

"F. Malory Simon," he said.

Olivia nodded. "… is one of the most active purchasers of antique books, exclusively Bibles."

"The thing is," Meredith added, "once Mr. Simon acquires a Bible, it disappears. No one ever hears of it again."

"It's not unusual for collectors of antiquities to keep private collections," Ethan said.

"Is that what you think Mr. Simon is doing?" Olivia asked. "Can you see him going home at night to enjoy his collection of Bibles?"

"No, I can't," Ethan replied. "But he could be doing any number of things with them, all of them perfectly legal if he's the legitimate owner of the Bibles. He could tear out the pages and wallpaper his bathroom with them and there's nothing anybody could do about it."

"But the Morgan Bible wasn't obtained legally," Meredith said. "And don't you find it suspicious that F. Malory Simon's business is located in Las Vegas, and that the late Mr. Corby worked at one of his shredding plants?"

*Or that the night Sky was murdered he was forced to put on an Outlaw T-shirt, the football team owned by Simon,* Ethan thought.

"There's more," Alice said. She grabbed a sheet of paper from a stack on her desk and handed it to Ethan.

Olivia explained. "We did a little research into Shiva Enterprises," she said, "the company that attempted to purchase Andrew's graphic-novel business. Guess who owns it?"

The paper in Ethan's hand listed Shiva Enterprises as one of F. Malory Simon's holdings.

Meredith added, "One of the nonnegotiable clauses in the offer was that the Morgan Bible would be loaned to the company for a nation-wide tour to promote the books."

Ethan looked at the evidence in his hand. While it didn't constitute a smoking gun, there were too many connections to F. Malory Simon to ignore.

"I think I'll have a talk with Mr. Simon," Ethan said. "I'll fly to Las Vegas in the morning."

"I'll go with you," Meredith said.

"No. I'm going alone."

"But Ethan—"

"You're not going with me."

Meredith's eyes blazed. "And how do you think you're going to—"

Olivia placed a restraining hand on her daughter's arm. "Stay here with me, dear," she said. "Let me nurse you back to health. I think London was harder on you than you think."

"Mother, I feel fine. Really. I want to go—"

"But he doesn't want you," Olivia said.

Meredith recoiled visibly. It took her a moment to recover. "All right. I'll stay."

Ethan thanked Alice for the information.

"Just doing my job," Alice replied.

"Are you ready to drive back to the hotel?" Ethan said to Meredith.

"You go on ahead, Ethan," Olivia said. "I'll drive her back later."

Ethan looked to Meredith who confirmed her mother's plan with a nod. He said his good-byes and turned to leave.

Standing at the front door and pulling on his jacket, he suddenly felt alone. For reasons he couldn't explain, it felt wrong to leave Meredith behind. The thought of eating dinner alone at the hotel only increased the feeling.

He considered changing his mind and inviting Meredith to fly with him to Las Vegas. But then he stepped out into the night and closed the door behind him.

---

Meredith sat next to her mother on a love seat in the hallway.

"He was brave in London, Mother," Meredith said, her hand clutching a well-used tissue. "You should have seen him. Total disregard for himself. Chaos everywhere and by the way he was acting you would have thought this kind of thing happened every day. All my life

I've read about how the Morgan men rise to the occasion in time of crisis. In London, I saw it firsthand. I couldn't take my eyes off of him. Had he been riding a white stallion and brandishing a sword I couldn't have been more impressed."

Olivia Cooper listened intently. "And at Edenford?" she asked.

"We walked up the hill to the ruins." Meredith began weeping softly again. "And I told him how I felt. How I've always felt."

"And?"

The tears flowed freely now. "He doesn't love me, Mother. Dear God, what am I going to do? He doesn't love me."

---

"All I need is a moment of his time."

Ethan pleaded his case to a woman who was paid to shield F. Malory Simon from people like him. Painfully thin, pristine, and proper, she sat straight-backed in her chair, her hands folded, clenched, on top of a phone and message diary. She looked up at him with an unyielding gaze from behind her name plaque: Ms. Weidenkeller.

"If you will leave your business card, I will see to it that Mr. Simon is made aware of your attempt to reach him," she said.

"Nah ... I'd rather not do that."

She shifted in her chair. "Then if you will give me your name and a number where we can reach you ..." Head down, pen in hand, she prepared to write it down.

"He is available, right?" Ethan said. "Time is of the essence. Please tell me you'll be able to get a message to him today."

She looked up at him with pursed lips. "I will be seeing Mr. Simon this afternoon. Now, if you'll just give me your name …"

Ethan motioned to a couple of chairs nearby with a small table between them along with the requisite outdated magazines. "If I were to sit over here and wait, what would you say my chances would be of catching him before quitting time?"

He sat in one of the chairs. She did not appear to be pleased at the prospect of babysitting him all day.

"Where are you staying while in Las Vegas?" she asked.

"Right here at the Hilton."

She seized that bit of information with joy. "I'm sure you'll be more comfortable waiting in another part of the hotel. Should Mr. Simon be able to see you today, I could have you paged."

"You know, on second thought," Ethan said, "maybe I'll arrange to meet Mr. Simon some other time when he's not so busy."

With a little wave, he turned and walked away. Behind him he heard the receptionist slap down her pen in frustration.

He didn't walk far, just around the corner where he stood in front of a bank of elevators. The receptionist had given him the information he needed.

During his flight from Cincinnati, Ethan had formulated his plan to confront F. Malory Simon. There were obstacles to meeting with a man of his wealth. Normally, Ethan overcame those obstacles by flashing his badge.

Instead of his badge, he'd considered using his business card. It identified him as a detective on the San Diego police force and was almost as good as a badge. But if Simon was involved in his brother's murder and the missing Morgan Bible, announcing himself would only give Simon time to cover his tracks. That's why he didn't give the receptionist his card or his name.

Chances of walking through the front door into Simon's office were slim. So Ethan had to figure out a different way of connecting with Simon. The creative wrangling paid off.

Ms. Weidenkeller had done her part to give him the information he needed. From their brief exchange he learned that Simon was in Las Vegas *and* in the building. Now all Ethan had to do was find him.

He could wait in the lobby for Simon to leave. He could try to slip in through a delivery entrance. Or he could haunt the elevators and hope an opportunity presented itself.

The meager bit of information he'd given Ms. Weidenkeller was the kernel of his plan. He needed only a moment of Simon's time.

As it turned out, he didn't have to haunt the elevators for long. Two of the three elevators arrived on the floor within a second of each other, announced by the customary elevator ding.

The doors opened and a flock of future executives strolled onto the floor. Twentysomething, impeccably groomed, dressed to impress, and shrouded in self-importance, they departed the elevator cars without so much as a glance at Ethan.

"I've been on the floor of the exchange," the smallest of the males said to anyone who would listen. "Imagine a cockfight without feathers and you have a pretty good idea what goes on there."

A perky brunette had a following of her own. "Rolling hills as far as the eye can see with the mist hugging the grass," she said. "Perfect for an early morning ride. And polo season! Don't even get me started about polo season at Langdon Stables."

There were seven of them. Instead of turning toward the front door and Ms. Weidenkeller, they exited down a side hallway that led to a windowless locked door. Ethan knew it was locked because he'd already tried it.

He waited to see if they would be let in or if they would let themselves in. A blond fellow took the lead. He reached into his pocket.

"A key," Ethan said beneath his breath. "Perfect."

The blond opened the door and let them in. Ethan hurried down the hallway toward them, reaching for his own set of keys. He caught the door just as it was closing. The last young woman through the door, a plain-looking girl with intelligent eyes looked at him questioningly as he followed her in.

"Thank you," he told her, holding up his keys. "Saves me the trouble."

She blinked and turned to catch up with the others.

Ethan was inside.

He waited until the plain-looking yuppie disappeared around a corner. They hadn't gone far. He could still hear them.

He walked the opposite direction down a hallway with doors on both sides. They were all locked but had panel windows allowing him to see inside. They appeared to be meeting rooms, each with a long table encircled by chairs. They were empty. At the end of the hallway was another door. This one had no window. It was locked. He put his ear to the door but heard nothing.

Ethan retraced his steps. Reaching the door through which he'd entered, he could hear the wannabe execs again. Chatting. Laughing. Scoffing. Challenging. Making enough noise to cover his steps.

Two hallways branched off to the left with nothing but wall on the right. Ethan approached the first hallway, the one the plain girl had used. Cautiously, he peered around the corner.

It wasn't a hallway at all but a tunnel beneath stadium-style seats that opened into an amphitheater. The voices of the young execs grew louder. A male voice announced his goal of becoming the general manager of the Nevada Outlaws. A female voice gave directions to a manicure shop on the Strip. And another woman's voice entertained them with anecdotes of her cheap boyfriend. "For our one-year anniversary he said he'd take me out for dinner. Do you know where we went? To the mini-mart where he ordered two chili dogs for ninety-nine cents!"

Ethan slipped down the hallway to the second opening. It was a second tunnel into the amphitheater.

Ethan had two choices. Go out the door he came in and hope for another opportunity to present itself, or go down the tunnel into the amphitheater. In all probability there was an exit behind the stage. He could walk past them like he knew where he was going, or he could pretend he was lost and ask directions to Simon's office.

"There's only one way to find out," he mumbled.

Halfway down the tunnel, he heard a new voice. Louder. Bolder. Authoritative. Familiar.

F. Malory Simon had entered the room.

The young execs fell silent.

Ethan backed away. He wanted to get a feel for the environment before charging into it.

"I trust you all had a productive morning with Scott Deveaux," Simon said. "He's the most brilliant advertising executive this side of the Mississippi."

From his vantage point, Ethan could see only empty seats and a portion of the platform. It sounded like all the players were to the right, probably center stage. He couldn't see Simon, and Simon couldn't see him, but after watching one of Simon's performances, Ethan had enough to visualize what was happening.

"One way to make a lot of money," Simon lectured, "is to form partnerships with people who are the best in their field. Scott Deveaux is the best. That's why he does all of my advertising and promotion for the Outlaws. You're going to be working with him for your next project, and he's going to report back to me. You will each have one shot to impress him.

"A second way to make money is not to spend it in the first place. As you undoubtedly know, I don't pay salaries. I don't believe in salaries. Promise a man a steady paycheck and he'll sit around fiddling with his day planner waiting for lunch. That's why I don't pay. I motivate. Promise that same man something he desperately wants and he'll work desperately to get it. With the proper motivation, you can get a man to do anything—even work for you for free.

"I have thousands of people who work for me. I don't pay any of them. They arrange for their own salaries, either through commission or donations. Not everyone is motivated by money. Find out what motivates your employees and you own them."

Ethan heard a noise down the hallway. A door opening and closing. Now was the time.

*All I need is a moment …*

While Simon proceeded with his lecture, Ethan eased down the tunnel passageway. With each step, more of the amphitheater's stage and seating came into view. With each step, Simon's voice grew louder.

Ethan paused. He'd reached the end of tunnel where the wall was still high enough to conceal him. One more step and he was inside the amphitheater. He prepared himself to be seen. He didn't have the privilege of distraction.

He entered the amphitheater.

His movement caught the attention of several of the young execs ... and Simon.

A swell of satisfaction swept through Ethan. His plan had worked.

He continued making his way into the theater and took a front-row seat next to the aisle. His entrance had disrupted the lecture but only for a moment. Simon picked up where he left off. While talking, he moved toward a woman in a business suit sitting on the front row. She wasn't one of the young execs. Simon whispered something to her, then continued his lecture as though Ethan wasn't there.

The woman glanced at Ethan, made a quick evaluation, then got up and left the room. A few moments later she reappeared, entering the amphitheater through the same tunnel Ethan had used. Two security guards accompanied her. The larger of the two, an African American with a neck the size of a redwood, whispered in Ethan's ear with a bass voice that would make James Earl Jones weep.

"Please come with me, sir."

Ethan nodded and stood. His work here was done.

Simon didn't glance his direction as Ethan was led out of the amphitheater between two towering guards, but his lecturing voice had a definite edge to it.

Ethan sat in one of the meeting rooms he'd seen earlier. One of the security guards stood at the door, his back blocking the window. The other guard stood between him and the door.

Ethan's wallet, driver's license, badge, and gun had turned the conference table into an evidence table. The only things missing were identification tags.

Neither guard spoke. They had helped themselves to his personal effects.

Ethan sat patiently. He got what he'd come for. Now all he had to do was get out of here alive. There were a lot of unmarked desert graves between Las Vegas and Los Angeles.

The door opened, and F. Malory Simon entered the room. He stood at the opposite end of the table.

"Who are you?" Simon demanded.

Ethan grinned. "Cut the act, Simon. You know who I am. You recognized me the moment I entered the amphitheater. Your expression gave you away."

Simon reached for the driver's license and studied it. "You're that cop, aren't you? The one who shot and killed my wrestler."

"Ancient history."

"Maybe to you, but after you took down Deathblow the first time in the stadium parking lot—by luck, I might add—I couldn't get him a fight with a Girl Scout, let alone a contender. You drove him over the edge."

"I drove him over the edge? Or did you motivate him to do something reckless, something that would get him arrested, possibly even a little jail time? Seems to me that would go a long way in restoring his image as a crazed maniac. Only he went overboard and got himself killed."

Eyes as hard as rock studied Ethan. "What did you come here for, Morgan?" he asked.

"I want my family's Bible."

A moment of incredulous silence was followed by erupting laughter. Even the guards joined in.

"Does this look like a Sunday-school class to you?" Simon roared. "I think you left your Bible at some other church on the Strip."

One of the guards laughed so hard he wiped a tear from his eye.

"I know you're an active collector of Bibles. I know you spend a lot of money at antique-book auctions," Ethan countered.

This didn't set well with Simon. It soured his cup of joy considerably.

"I also know that you own Shiva Enterprises in Dallas, Texas," Ethan pressed, "a corporation that attempted to buy out my brother's business *and* gain control of my family's Bible."

Simon was no longer laughing.

"I also know that it was Roger 'Deathblow' Corby's little brother who broke into my house, stole the Bible, and killed my brother. Let me guess. You motivated him. In return for helping him revenge his brother's death by killing the cop who shot him, he was to steal the Bible and deliver it to you. But you forgot to tell him I had a twin brother, and he shot the wrong Morgan, but not before leaving a calling card, something to indicate it was a revenge killing and not just a robbery gone bad. Before Corby shot my brother he had him put on an Outlaws T-shirt. Had that been me, nobody would have thought twice about it. But my brother would never wear an Outlaws T-shirt.

Corby really botched the job, didn't he? Because he didn't kill the one person who could piece together his message."

"You've got quite an imagination, Morgan."

"Then Corby made another blunder. Somehow he discovered the value of the Bible and either decided to hold it for ransom or renegotiate your deal. You chose to renegotiate by having him killed. Only you didn't know I'd tracked Corby down and witnessed the whole thing."

Simon stood motionless, staring at him.

"Maybe you should rethink this whole motivation scheme of yours," Ethan said. "You'd probably get better quality workers if you paid them."

Ethan touched a nerve. Gone was the charismatic self-confident motivator of millions. The man standing over him was stiff with rage.

"Anything else you wish to accuse me of?" he seethed. "The high price of gasoline perhaps?"

"Just tell me where I can find my family's Bible."

Simon did an about-face. As he marched out the door, he said to the security guards, "Call the police. Tell them we're holding a trespasser."

─────────────

F. Malory Simon was leaning against the workstation desk in mission control when he heard a soft knock on the door. The monitors were dark, as though he'd closed the curtains on the windows to the outside world.

"Enter," he said.

Gil Getz ventured into the room and took note of the absence of visual images. "Everything all right?" he asked. "You dismissed the apprentices early."

"Guess who I just had a conversation with?" Simon said. He didn't wait for Gil to guess. "Morgan."

"Morgan? Why? Did he call?"

"He didn't. He interrupted my session."

"Morgan's here?" Gil said. "What's he doing here?"

"I had him arrested for trespassing."

"What did he want?"

Simon launched himself from the desk with no destination in mind. He paced and thought aloud.

"He's got a pretty good grasp of how things have played out with Corby and the Bible," Simon said, fuming. "Largely because of what that dimwit pulled with the Outlaws T-shirt. I'm tempted to dig him up so I can have him shot again."

"Did Morgan threaten you?"

"He says he wants his family's Bible back."

"What did you tell him?"

"I don't give out information to trespassers. What have you found out?"

Gil opened an unmarked file folder and shuffled pages and print-outs before starting. "It appears he and his brother's widow flew to England on the same day."

"Together?"

"No. That's what's odd about it. They flew separately. She went first; he followed. He caught up with her at Bickleigh where they spent the night. Separate rooms."

"What's at Bickleigh?"

"Nothing. An old castle. Tourist stuff."

"Do you think there's something going on between them?"

"G-rated from all appearances. They stayed the day, had dinner and breakfast the next morning. Walked the grounds."

Simon sighed. "Continue," he said.

"From Bickleigh they drove to London. They were supposed to be on a flight out of Heathrow the day of the bombing. They were scheduled to return a rental car. As far as I can tell when the bombs went off they were sightseeing in London."

"Sightseeing!" Simon shouted. "You're telling me Morgan just happened to be at St. Paul's on the day of the bombing? What are the odds of that?"

Gil shrugged. "There's no information to indicate otherwise. If they stopped anywhere between Bickleigh and London, they left no record of it. And they made no purchases or charges in London until after the bombing."

"They had to be there for a reason."

"From London they flew to Cincinnati."

"What's in Cincinnati?"

"Her mother. She owns a bed-and-breakfast. But here's where it gets good. The bed-and-breakfast has a museum of antique Bibles."

That got Simon's attention.

"The centerpiece of the collection?" Gil said, allowing the question to dangle unanswered for a moment. "A replica of the Morgan Bible."

He handed Simon a brochure of the inn and museum. Unfolding the promotional piece, Simon studied it carefully. The centerpiece of the Bible collection, the Morgan Bible, was described as "the Bible that started the heritage movement."

"You're certain it's a replica."

"It has to be. We have the real one."

"Do we?"

Gil knew better than to venture a guess.

Simon's eyes moved back and forth in thought. A plan was formulating. "I think we just found the key to motivating Morgan. Not just the Bible, but the Bible and the girl. What's her name?"

"Meredith."

"Go to Cincinnati. Do whatever it takes to find out if the Bible in that museum is indeed a replica. I also want you to find out everything you can about the girl."

"When do you want me to leave?"

"Immediately. We need this information before Boston."

"The bed-and-breakfast has a two-year waiting list for reservations."

"Arrange a cancellation."

Gil nodded. "On my way," he said, turning to leave.

"And send Ms. Weidenkeller in."

Gil left Simon in mission control holding the brochure of the Heritage Museum. A minute later Ms. Weidenkeller arrived, pen and pad in hand.

"Get me Brad Pitzer on the phone." He dug a slip of paper out of his pocket and handed it to her. "Here's the number."

She accepted the information dutifully.

"Transfer the call in here. Use a secure line."

While he waited for Ms. Weidenkeller to make the connection, Simon pulled together everything he knew of Ethan Morgan, trusting the same instincts that had made him a millionaire to formulate a plan that would dispose of Morgan and the Morgan Bible at the same time,

Ms. Weidenkeller's voice came over the speaker phone. "I have Mr. Pitzer on line three."

"I have a job for you," Simon said without introduction. "Arrange for two seats on a flight to Cincinnati for Saturday. False IDs. You can pick up the details of your assignment tomorrow at the usual drop. One thing more. Don't say anything to Gil about this. When you get the assignment you'll understand why."

# FIFTEEN

Exhausted from the eight-hour drive across the desert and an unplanned side trip to San Diego police headquarters, Ethan steered the car into Meredith's driveway. Cincinnati seemed like a month ago. It had been only three days.

"Come in and I'll fix you something to eat," Meredith said from the passenger seat.

"Thanks, but I'm going home to crash."

"You have to eat."

"I smell like a Las Vegas holding cell. Thanks anyway, but I'll grab a burger on the way home."

"Nonsense," Meredith insisted. "You can shower while I cook."

"I don't have any fresh clothes. I packed for a couple of days in England. I didn't anticipate trips to Cincinnati and Las Vegas."

"I have a closet full of clothes that will fit you."

Sky's clothes. She was suggesting he wear his dead brother's clothes? Apparently his face telegraphed his thoughts.

"There are some new shirts Andrew never wore," Meredith said. "Please? Just for a while. I don't want to be alone."

Like a horse heading toward the barn, Ethan's desires had been for his own house. His own shower. His own food. His own recliner and undisputed control of the TV remote.

"Please? You owe me one," Meredith said. "I drove all the way across the desert to bail you out of jail."

"Owe you one? I flew all the way to England for no good reason, and then got blown up."

Meredith lowered her gaze. He'd hurt her.

She looked away and fumbled for the door latch. "You're right," she said with a shaky voice.

"Meredith—" he said.

She climbed out of the car.

"Meredith—"

He got out himself and caught up with her.

"I'm sorry," he said.

She smiled weakly and sniffed as she dug into her purse, finding first a needed tissue and then her house keys.

"This isn't some scheme to empty your refrigerator of leftovers, is it?" he said.

Meredith grinned. "I can do better than leftovers."

While Ethan showered in the guest bathroom and Meredith stirred sumptuous odors in the kitchen, images of the past twenty-four hours flashed in Ethan's mind.

F. Malory Simon's security had held him until the local police arrived, after which he was transported to Las Vegas headquarters, fingerprinted, photographed, and placed in a holding cell along with the drunks and pimps.

He'd called Meredith who had flown home to San Diego. She arranged bail and offered to drive to Las Vegas to pick him up. He suggested she use his car.

While waiting for her, Ethan was summoned to the chief's office where the top officer unleashed a fresh fury upon him accompanied by a carefully worded, but unmistakable, threat to stay out of Las Vegas and away from F. Malory Simon.

When Meredith finally sprung him and drove him to his hotel room, he found his bags packed and waiting at the concierge's office. Simon had thoughtfully arranged to have him checked out of his room, but not before emptying the honor bar (probably the motivation to get someone to throw Ethan's clothes into his bags), which left Ethan with a grossly inflated bill.

The ride home with Meredith was peaceful enough until they hit Barstow. Ethan was telling her the tale of his exploits to see Simon when his cell phone rang. It was Lieutenant Savala.

"Where are you?"

"Just outside of Barstow."

"The chief wants to talk to you."

"Let me guess. He got a call from Las Vegas."

"This isn't funny, Morgan."

"Yeah ... okay ... um ... let me stop by the house first and freshen—"

"Negative. Do not stop. Do not pass Go, Morgan. Go directly to the chief's office. And don't expect a Get Out of Jail Free card this time."

Savala may have told Ethan "this isn't funny," but he was doing a pretty good job at being witty. Ethan didn't mention this. He simply agreed to drive straight to the department.

The San Diego police chief's tirade was a variation on what was becoming a familiar theme, "Have you lost your mind?"

F. Malory Simon's publicist might as well have written the chief's script. The chief did everything but canonize the man.

"He's a celebrity, a millionaire, and a national guru rolled into one!" the chief wailed. "We just paid premium prices to send two dozen of our people to Las Vegas to sit at the man's feet and learn from him. And you have the nerve to break into his office and attack him? While you're on suspension? Why, Morgan, why?"

"I believe he has my family's Bible, the one stolen from my house the night my brother was killed."

"And your evidence?"

Ethan told him about Simon being an antique-book buyer specializing in Bibles, but he didn't tell him how he obtained this information since it had been obtained somewhat questionably, and to his relief, the chief didn't ask.

"All I wanted to do was gauge his reaction when he saw me," he explained. "He recognized me. He knows who I am."

"Of course he knows you," the chief said. "You killed his wrestler in the parking lot of his football-team franchise. Your picture was on the news and in the papers."

Somehow Ethan managed to leave the meeting with his badge. Since he was already suspended, he expected to be fired. For some reason the chief didn't fire him, but he threatened to fire him. Repeatedly.

"If I so much as hear you're listening to F. Malory Simon's motivational tapes, I'll have your badge! Understand? If you hear Simon is going to San Francisco, I want you in New York."

Ethan offered the required "Yes, sirs" and counted himself lucky.

The dressing down did have its consequences. It ruled out the possibility of using the department's resources to track down further information on Simon.

"Ethan? I put some shirts and pants on the bed."

Meredith's voice came through the bathroom door, bringing him back to the present.

"Um ... thanks."

He felt uncomfortable having even a brief conversation with Meredith while standing in the shower without a stitch of clothing on. But not nearly as uncomfortable as he felt when Meredith caught her breath when she saw him walking down the stairs. She had to steady herself against the counter.

"Oh ... Ethan ... I'm ... I'm ... sorry," she managed to say.

Ethan stopped halfway down. "Maybe this wasn't such a good idea," he said.

It didn't matter that the shirt had never been worn and the pants looked good as new. They were still his brother's clothes and he was in his brother's house being served dinner by his brother's wife.

"I'll just ..." He motioned upstairs to where he'd left his own clothes in a heap.

Meredith reached out to him. "No ... Ethan, please ... stay. The steaks are ready. The table's set. You just caught me in an unguarded moment, that's all. My mind wandered and when I looked up ..."

When she looked up, she saw her dead husband coming down the stairs.

Ethan wanted to leave. For Meredith's sake he set his discomfort aside and took his place at the table. She had set it for two, sharing a corner with her seat closer to the kitchen.

"This way we can both watch the sunset." She pulled the cord on the curtains of a sliding glass door, revealing the patio and an impressively large, manicured lawn.

She placed a plate in front of him, detailing the night's menu. "Top sirloin, medium. Boiled new potatoes with parsley. And steamed zucchini."

"I told you I could do better than leftovers," she said, taking her seat.

"Much better," he said, looking it over. "It's almost better than a burger."

His comment drew a protest as he'd intended.

"Medium," he commented. "Is that the way Sky liked his steaks?"

She didn't answer immediately. "No. It's the way you like your steaks. Andrew liked his well done. This isn't the first time we've eaten steak together, Ethan."

Ethan nodded, accepting her gentle chastising. They were both going to have to be patient. It was going to take some time for them work past all the uncomfortable moments.

For a time they ate in silence as the sky grew orange then crimson then black.

They were just finishing the meal when Meredith's cell phone rang. She jumped up from the table.

"It's my mother. Do you mind?"

Ethan waved for her to answer it.

"There's fresh coffee on the counter," she said, reaching for her phone. "Pour yourself a cup and take it into the den. I won't be long."

Flipping open the phone, Meredith fended off questions with non-responsive answers while she hurried down the hallway and shut herself behind the bedroom door.

Ethan found a coffee cup with a montage of superheroes on it and poured himself a cup. He took a sip. It was dark, rich, bold, and black, just like he liked it. Had Meredith been there, he probably would have stuck his foot in his mouth again and asked if that's the way Sky liked his coffee.

He wondered how long it would take for him to get on with life, especially around Meredith. It surprised him he didn't know how his brother liked his coffee. Is that the sort of thing brothers know about brothers, or was he just a bad brother?

He carried his cup into the den, a dark-paneled room that felt warm and manly. Neither he nor Sky smoked, but he could easily envision the two of them sitting in this room puffing on pipes discussing world affairs.

Sky's graphic novels were arrayed on a mahogany table, the complete story of the Morgans from the time of the Puritans to the sixties and Vietnam War. The white panels of *The Adventures of Sky Walker*, inked drawings ready to be colored, were also stacked on the table.

Ethan felt his ire rising. This wasn't a casual display. Meredith set these out for him. She'd ambushed him. Lured him into the house with food for bait.

*"Pour yourself a cup of coffee and go into the den," she'd said. Was that what her mother had called about? "Has he gone into the den yet? Did he*

*fall for the trap? Have you finally convinced him to start acting like Drew Morgan?"*

"Mother says hello," Meredith said, entering the den with her own cup of coffee.

"I'll bet she does," Ethan snapped.

Meredith frowned. "Are you all right?"

"What's this?" he asked, directing her attention to the mahogany table.

"I thought it might help you," she said defensively.

"Help me? Help me to do what? Magically transform into a super-hero? Or maybe into the legendary Drew Morgan?"

"Ethan, don't be like that. I'm only trying to help."

"How am I supposed to be? You and your mother just won't let up. Was this your idea or hers? Is that why she called, to see if I had some kind of conversion experience?"

Meredith started to say something, then pursed her lips. She walked slowly across the room and took a seat, setting her coffee on an end table.

"Have you read Andrew's novels?" she asked, her voice steady and calm.

"Why would I?" Ethan replied. "I heard the stories the same time he did."

"Your brother was a good storyteller and an excellent graphic artist. He turned down offers from several major publishers. He could have made a lot of money drawing for Marvel and DC comics. His super-heroes. Spider-Man. Batman. Superman. The Fantastic Four. He chose this instead."

*Saint Andrew,* Ethan thought but didn't say it because it would come out wrong. He admired his brother's talent and dedication to his art over money.

Ethan picked up the white boards of *The Adventures of Sky Walker*. He wished Sky were here so that he could ask him what his thinking was behind the creation of the work. Was it a family joke, or did he intend to market it?

"When did he draw it?"

"After he finished the American Family Portrait series," Meredith said. "If you ask me, it's the next book in that series. You and your brother taking the Morgans into the next generation."

The first panel portrayed a muscular, handsome hero flying across the city, his arm thrust dramatically forward, his cape flapping in the wind. He was racing to rescue the beautiful Kassia Kirk from the clutches of a seven-headed red dragon perched on the highest building in a metropolis.

Ethan held up the panel as evidence of what he was about to say. "See? This is the difference between my brother and me. He lives in a fantasy world. I live in a world filled with people who want everything and who want it now … who will elbow and shove and trample each other to get it, like Christmas shoppers at Wal-Mart the day after Thanksgiving."

"I think you're missing the point of your brother's art," Meredith said.

"Am I? This is a comic. What's the point?"

Meredith slid forward on her chair. "Kassia Kirk," she said, pointing to a panel. "*Kirk* is the word for 'church.' *Kassia* means 'pure.' Andrew's heroine portrays the church in danger."

"Of a dragon?"

"A red dragon with seven heads." Meredith looked around the room, saw what she wanted, rose and pulled a book from a bookshelf. "When was the last time you went to Bible study?" she asked.

She opened the Bible toward the back and began flipping pages until she found the page she was looking for. "Revelation 12:3–4. 'Then another sign appeared in heaven: an enormous red dragon with seven heads.… His tail swept a third of the stars out of the sky and flung them to the earth.' The dragon is Satan, evil incarnate."

"Clever," Ethan said. "All right, so Sky was writing a story about the Devil attacking the church. But even though I haven't been to Bible study for a while, last time I *was* there, they weren't handing out super-hero capes."

Meredith smiled patiently. "It takes courage to stand for something, Ethan. To live what you say you believe. Given the world as you describe it, maybe today it takes more courage than it once did."

Ethan looked at the cartoon panels with new eyes. The determination of Sky Walker. The fear on Kassia Kirk's face. The sinister evil of the seven-headed red dragon. His brother drew this. His brother believed this.

Ethan set the panels down and reached for the first of the graphic novels, the one that depicted Drew Morgan risking his life to help the church at Edenford escape the clutches of Bishop Laud.

Ethan grinned at the realization that it was Sky Walker, Kassia Kirk, and the red dragon in a different age.

He flipped through the pages with admiration. Sky had brought the townspeople of Edenford to life. The bridge with three arches, the vat of blue dye where Drew Morgan saved the Cooper boy. The old Saxon ruins where Drew and Nell Matthews went to be alone and where Meredith had ... Ethan flipped past that page quickly, then stopped abruptly, having seen something in passing that caught his attention. He flipped back to the page with such urgency it made Meredith ask what he'd seen.

"Just a second," Ethan said.

He found it again. The panel was a close-up of a piece of parchment. A hand holding a quill pen was writing a message in secret code. The last line of the code read (41/3/18/2).

"The code," Ethan said, pointing to the panel. "The code Drew Morgan used to communicate with Bishop Laud."

"What of it?"

"Do you know how it works?"

Meredith nodded. "The Bible is the key."

"Exactly," Ethan said. "In sequence, the numbers correspond to a book, chapter, verse, and word in the Bible. Which makes (41/3/18/2) say what? Sky didn't translate it."

"No, he never did," Meredith said. "That way the novels were interactive. Andrew liked the idea that people would use their Bibles to translate the messages for themselves."

"So this one says ... what?"

"It has to be a King James Version of the Bible," Meredith said. "That's the one the bishop and Drew would have used."

"Do you have one?"

"In Andrew's study. I'll get it."

While she was gone, Ethan reached into his back pocket and retrieved his wallet. From the wallet he extracted a piece of paper folded over several times.

"What was the code again?" Meredith said, returning with the Bible.

It took her a moment to determine that the numeral forty-one was the book of Mark. The index didn't number the books.

"Mark, chapter three, the eighteenth verse, the second word," she said, tracking it down. She grinned. "It was his signature. The word is *Andrew*. Why the sudden interest?"

Ethan lay the unfolded scrap of paper on top of the panel with the code.

"This was the number on Sky's cell phone the night he died. Maybe it wasn't a phone number at all. Maybe ..."

"... he was sending a coded message!" Meredith exclaimed. "Let me see!"

Ethan showed her the number.

431-1617

"The phone inserted the hyphen automatically," he observed.

Meredith studied it. "Fourth book, thirty-first chapter, verses sixteen and seventeen?" she said.

"Look it up."

"Numbers is the fourth book of the Bible," she said. "Genesis. Exodus. Leviticus. Numbers."

"Show off. I'll bet you were teacher's pet in Sunday school."

She ignored him. "Wait, a minute. Would Andrew use the King James Version, or would he use the version he was familiar with?"

"He may have associated the code with the older version, the one Drew Morgan used," Ethan suggested.

"But he was lying on your living-room floor," Meredith replied. "He didn't have a King James Version to consult."

"So the verse had to be familiar to him."

"Agreed." Meredith exchanged Bibles. "Let's try Andrew's Bible and if it doesn't make sense, we'll try the King James Version."

She found the passage in Andrew's Bible. "Numbers thirty-one, verses sixteen and seventeen," she said.

Before reading it, she exchanged glances, then smiles with Ethan. The thought that they had unraveled the mystery of Andrew's last phone call energized them both. What had he wanted them to know as he was dying?

Meredith read: "'They were the ones who followed Balaam's advice and were the means of turning the Israelites away from the Lord in what happened at Peor, so that a plague struck the Lord's people. Now kill all the boys. And kill every woman who has slept with a man.'"

She looked up.

"That's it? That's the message?" Ethan exclaimed. "That doesn't make sense. Are you sure you got the coordinates correct?"

Meredith double-checked. "Four, thirty-one, sixteen through seventeen," she repeated. "Those are the right verses."

The two of them stared at each other, trying to make sense of the verses.

Ethan burst into laughter. "The plague at Peor? Kill all the boys? Hardly the inspirational message from beyond the grave I was hoping for."

Meredith was laughing now too.

"Well, it was a shot," Ethan said. "Maybe it was a phone call after all and he—"

The mental image of Sky lying on the floor, shot in the chest and bleeding while trying to live long enough to dial his cell phone for help caught Ethan by surprise. With the image came revisited pain over his brother's death.

Meredith recognized it. Maybe she felt it too, because she put a comforting hand on his arm.

"Unless …" Ethan said.

He looked at the number again.

"What if the ones aren't ones?" he said. "At least not all of them. What if they're slashes, like in the code?"

With renewed hope, Meredith bent over the numbers with him.

"You could be right!" she cried. "And if that's the case—"

"4311617—Forty-third book, slash, sixteenth chapter, slash, seventh verse. Is there such a coordinate in the Bible?"

Meredith went to work. "Forty-third book … the gospel of John. Chapter sixteen, verse—I have it!"

"It doesn't say anything about killing boys, does it?"

"Oh my …" Meredith said, her eyes fixed on the verse. Tears came. She reached a hand to her mouth.

"What?" Ethan cried. "What does it say?"

Meredith read, "'But I tell you the truth: It is for your good that I am going away. Unless I go away, the Counselor will not come to you; but if I go, I will send him to you.'"

Ethan felt his face drain of color. He stood, though he didn't know why he was standing.

Her palm pressed against the open page, Meredith said in a soft voice, "He knew he was dying."

"He knew more than that," Ethan replied and began pacing.

"What do you mean?"

"I think you're right about these drawings," he said, tapping the picture of the hero. "This ... this is Sky ... Andrew and me merged into a single being."

"You got that from the coded message?"

Ethan let out a long, slow breath. "Yeah ..."

He had to give Meredith credit this time. She didn't press him. She sat beside him patiently, giving him the time he needed to find the words.

"I was never going to tell anyone," he began. "You hear about things like this and you wonder about the sanity of the people telling you."

"Experiencing what? Ethan, what are you talking about?"

"What was on Sky's mind when he punched those numbers into his cell phone?"

Meredith thought about it a moment, then said, "He knew he was dying. He knew you'd take it hard, that you'd blame yourself. Do you?"

"Of course I blame myself. The only reason Sky was at the house was because I was too much of a coward to face an auditorium of kids."

"Ethan, there's no way you could have known—"

"Sky knew that. So why this verse?"

"He wanted to encourage you. Remind you that you're not alone, that God's Spirit is a source of strength and comfort in time of trouble."

"Yeah, but I think there's more to it than that."

Ethan took a deep breath.

"Something happened later that night," he said, "after I visited you in the hospital. Back in the hotel room—" He laughed self-consciously. "This is harder than I thought it would be."

"Take your time. You know you can tell me anything."

"I think he was telling me that if he died, his spirit would continue to live in me."

Meredith's expression was hard to read. Her eyes were unblinking. She sat motionless. She picked up the Bible and read.

"'It is for your good that I am going away … if I go I will send my spirit to you.' I changed a few words at the end, but that's what you think Andrew was saying?"

"Something like that. Does that sound weird?"

"What happened in the hotel room?"

He'd come this far, he might as well go all the way. "I sort of heard him. His voice in my head."

"You heard his voice?" she asked.

"Not audibly."

She was listening and not laughing. Ethan took that as a good sign.

"It's like when we were kids," Ethan explained. "At night when we were lying in our beds in the dark. We would talk. We told each other things we never would have said in the daylight. It's the only time I felt close to him until we became adults."

"And in the hotel room—"

"It was like when we were kids again. I talked." He turned and looked at her. "And I heard Sky's voice answer me in my head."

Meredith had a distant, thoughtful look in her eyes. "A twin thing. It's a twin thing."

"That's what I'm thinking. But we never had any kind of connection like that when he was alive."

"It is good that I go away …" she said.

"Yeah! How did he know that? Tell me, how did he know that? And here …" Ethan lifted a panel of *The Adventures of Sky Walker*. "He knew when he drew this. Maybe he didn't know when, but he knew someday."

Meredith took the panel from him and studied it as though she was seeing it for the first time. "That's strange. That's really strange."

"Tell me about it."

"Ethan?"

"Yeah?"

"Promise me you won't start wearing tights and a cape," Meredith said, her eyes giddy.

# SIXTEEN

Mike and Sue Mitchell's vacation was ruined when their house burned down five days before they were to leave. It was supposed to be the holiday of their dreams for the Salt Lake City couple: a night at the legendary Heritage Bed and Breakfast Inn at Point Providence followed by a Mississippi River cruise aboard the *American Queen*, a "floating Victorian palace of fretwork and fluted stacks."

According to the fire inspectors, the blaze started in the kitchen as a result of a faulty appliance. Mike Mitchell thought it odd that a blender from their in-laws—a Christmas present less than a year old—could have been the culprit. The fact was, the house was reduced to rubble and Mike could only grab a shovel and start clearing the charred remains when he should have been packing for the cruise. But there was nothing left to pack.

"You're in luck," Olivia Cooper informed him when he called to inquire about reservations. "We just had a cancellation."

"An answer to my prayers," Gil had replied. "I hope the cancellation isn't the result of anyone's misfortune."

Olivia thanked him for his thoughtfulness and booked the room.

Friday, at twilight, Gil Getz drove up the hill into the parking lot at the Heritage Bed and Breakfast Inn. He traveled light with only an overnight bag and a shopping list of information to collect. The list consisted of three items:

Confirm that the Morgan Bible on display was indeed a replica. Simon had been emphatic about this.

Get a listing of the Bibles in the museum and learn how they were obtained.

Get an e-mail address if they had one. None was listed in the brochure.

Gil made his way across the macadam parking lot. A woman stepped onto the porch and watched him approach.

"Welcome to the Heritage Bed and Breakfast," she said, greeting him at the top step. "May I take your bag?"

The woman was striking in her appearance, not anything like the matronly hostess Gil had expected. Middle-aged, with short red hair, she had a commanding presence about her, but not unapproachable. She came across as intelligent, confident, and warm.

"I'm Olivia Cooper," she said, reaching for his bag.

"Gil Getz," he replied, "and I'm afraid I can't hand you my bag."

"Even if I promise to take good care of it?"

"It is not a matter of trust."

"Oh?"

"Chivalry, ma'am. I'm afraid I'm a throwback to the past. I believe in men being men and ladies being ladies. Men open doors and ladies never, ever carry their bags."

Ms. Cooper smiled sweetly. "A gentleman! Well then, if you won't let me take your bag, may I offer you my arm?"

Gil smiled. She was quick on her feet and easy on the eyes. Taking her arm, she escorted him to the door. He opened it for her. She bowed her thanks and preceded him into the house.

As Gil followed, he stepped into her trailing perfume. It embraced him, feminine but not overpowering. It suited her perfectly.

"I can see we're going to have a grand time together," she turned, her eyes sparkling.

"I've not been here five minutes and already I'm glad I came," Gil replied.

He followed her upstairs to his room, and she showed him where to find towels and extra blankets.

She informed him dinner was at six o'clock. Chicken and dumplings. He would be dining with two couples, a banker and his wife from Tulsa, Oklahoma, and a novelist and his wife from the high desert in Southern California, a little town called Phelon. The author wrote suspense fiction.

Gil unpacked. This was going to be easier than he thought, and pleasurable. Women like Olivia Cooper were, to use a cliché, open books. He had no doubt she would tell him everything he needed to know.

He could smell the chicken and dumplings, and something sweet, chocolate—undoubtedly dessert. With an hour to kill before dinner, he stretched out on the bed and took a nap.

---

At the dinner table, the conversation was lively, laughter was plentiful, the food was beyond delicious, and everyone seemed to be having a great time, including Gil.

Olivia Cooper was marvelous, the perfect hostess. In less than ten minutes, after everyone had been seated, she had coaxed five strangers into sharing stories like they were family. At first the Tulsa banker was a bit of a stuffed shirt, but by the time the staff served dessert, he was wiping tears of laughter from his eyes.

The author from Phelon needed little coaxing. He welcomed an audience. By dinner's end, they'd learned he'd been a fireman, worked at a radio station, worked as an architect, planted a church, taught seminary, toured the USS *Salt Lake City* nuclear submarine, driven in President Gerald Ford's motorcade, and written twenty books. His wife, bless her heart, laughed at his jokes and listened to his stories as though she was hearing them for the first time.

Gil mostly listened. When prompted, he gave his cover story, that he was a locksmith from Huntington, West Virginia, a widower, and an amateur historian. He said he had always wanted to stay at Heritage Inn because he was interested in the house's history and museum.

As he spoke, Olivia Cooper gave him her full attention, at times gazing at him with an openness that made him self-conscious. He couldn't remember the last time a woman's gaze made him feel that way, and he found himself smiling and looking down a lot and trying to think of something clever to say to make her laugh.

While the food was superb and the conversation entertaining, the seating arrangement excited Gil the most. The banker and his wife. The author and his wife. And Gil and Olivia. Three *couples*. It had been a long time since Gil had felt feelings like this for a woman. It surprised him how much he'd missed it.

After dinner, Olivia gave everyone a tour of the house and the Bible museum, answering questions about its history and former occupants. The tour was followed by a dessert buffet and coffee from a cart wheeled into the museum. The guests stood around and snacked, sipped, and chatted. Like a lovesick boy Gil took every opportunity to stand next to Olivia. He drank in her laughter and savored her perfume.

After a time, the banker and his wife excused themselves and went upstairs. Their departure signaled to Gil that it was time to get to work. While Olivia said good night to the author and his wife, Gil walked to a display case and feigned interest in its contents. He used the time to shrug off the spell Olivia Cooper had cast over him.

She came up behind him, hooking her arm in his.

"May I get you some more coffee?" she asked.

"Thank you, no," Gil said, cup and saucer in hand.

"Would you mind if we sat?"

She indicated a love seat beneath a window, hugged by identical mahogany end tables and lamps. They sat. Gil handed his empty cup and saucer to a girl who had come to get the dessert cart. A moment later they were alone.

"What part of Huntington?" Olivia asked.

"Walnut Hills. Are you familiar with it?"

"I'm afraid I've spent only one Sunday afternoon in Huntington. I've been to the Riverfront Park and Pullman Square. The tourist spots. Have you lived there long?"

"Twenty years," Gil said.

The lie came easily. He'd been lying for so many years it was second nature. This lie, however, surprised him. The instant he told it, he felt bad. Gil Getz couldn't remember the last time he'd regretted telling a lie.

"Um … how about you?" he said, changing the subject. "How long have you run a bed-and-breakfast?"

She laughed softly. "I don't think I want to answer that question," she said.

"Why not?"

"It's been so long, it would give away my age. Some days I feel like I'm the oldest antique in the room. Any day now they're going to stand me in a corner and rope me off with one of the red velvet cords and make me part of the tour."

"I'd pay just for a chance to look at you," Gil said.

Olivia Cooper blushed. "Not only a gentleman, but a gentleman with a silver tongue."

He meant what he said. Seated this close, Gil couldn't take his eyes off her. All he wanted to do was spend the next few hours looking at her. They didn't even have to talk.

But he had a job to do.

"I'd love just to sit and chat," he said, "but I only have the one night. Would you mind if I asked you some questions about the museum, Ms. Cooper?"

"Of course not," she replied. "There's nothing I love more than to talk about our collection of Bibles. And, please, call me Olivia."

"The pleasure would be mine, Olivia," he said.

Flattery was one of Gil's stock tools. But tonight he was finding it hard to distinguish between the tool and a heartfelt admission.

"Let's start with the Morgan Bible," he said, standing.

They walked to the center of the room where the Morgan Bible was displayed. Looking down at it, he could see her reflection in the display's glass.

"The brochure says that this is the Bible that started it all," he said.

"How much do you know about the Heritage Churches of America?" she asked.

"Only that as part of their doctrine they teach families to pass a Bible from generation to generation."

Olivia told him about Drew Morgan's adventures that led him from England to America and how he began the practice of holding a ceremony that passed the Bible to the oldest son and how other families, her own Cooper line included, took up the practice.

"So there's a Cooper Bible here in the museum? But that would be your husband's line, wouldn't it?"

Olivia shook her head sadly. "The Cooper family Bible was lost in a house fire not long after the Civil War. As for my bloodline, I am a Cooper. My husband abandoned me and our daughter two months before she was born. He said he was having second thoughts about children. Come to find out, he was also having second thoughts about fidelity. I wanted to give my daughter a name she could be proud of, so before she was born I changed my name back to my maiden name."

"I'm sorry," Gil said. "I can't imagine any man wanting to give you up."

"Again with the flattery, Mr. Getz," she said. "Please don't stop. It's like chocolate to my soul."

"Gil. Please call me Gil."

"Would you like to hold the Morgan Bible, Gil?"

"Could I? That would be wonderful!"

Olivia excused herself. She disappeared behind a partition and returned moments later with a key to the display. She unlocked it, lifted the display lid, and handed Gil the Bible.

"Oh my," he said, looking at it carefully.

Very carefully. While he hadn't spent a great deal of time with the Morgan Bible that had been stolen out of Ethan Morgan's house, he knew enough to know that this was an exemplary copy. Or was the stolen one the copy?

"I can't believe I'm holding the original Morgan family Bible!" he cried. "To think of all the history it has seen. And that Drew Morgan himself—"

"It's a replica," Olivia said.

"No! It couldn't be! It looks so authentic!"

"It is an authentic 1611 version of the Bible," she said. "However, it's not the Morgan Bible." While he held it, she opened the front cover. "The printing of the Morgan names has been duplicated. And …" She turned it over in his hands. "This gash in the back was made to resemble the one in the original."

"That's incredible," he said. "Not having seen the original—" Another lie. This one twanged his conscious just as before. "—I still imagine it would be difficult for anyone but an expert to tell the difference between them."

Olivia smiled. "Can I tell you a little secret? This isn't something normally included on the tour."

She showed him how to tell the difference between the original and the replica.

Gil smiled appreciatively. "And now I know one of the museum's closely guarded secrets. Madam, I will take your secret to the grave with me."

"We call it the Judas Bible," Olivia said, placing it back in the display case. "Fewer than two hundred of the original 1611 copies are known to exist."

"It seems to me I remember one printing—probably not a 1611 copy—that left out a word in the Ten Commandments?" Gil said. "A three-letter word, if I'm not mistaken."

Olivia smiled broadly. "It was a 1631 version," she said. "And the word was *not*."

"You know of it!"

"The printers were fined three hundred pounds sterling for printing, 'Thou shalt commit adultery.'"

"They called it the Wicked Bible."

"We have one."

"You don't!"

She led him across the room and opened another display. "This is the Weston family Bible." She opened it to the offending passage. "The Westons unknowingly passed this Bible on for three generations before Charles Weston learned he had the unfortunate printing. He continued the tradition but replaced the Bible. His heirs donated this one to us not long after the museum opened."

For the next hour she led him from one Bible to the next telling him about the version and the family who owned it.

"Your recall is phenomenal," Gil said. "I'm afraid I won't be able to remember but a small portion of what you've told me. Is there a list of the Bibles you have in the museum?"

"We don't normally give out that information," she said. "But I can print you out a list. The Bible. The family. The date it was donated or purchased."

"You actively purchase Bibles?"

"Oh yes. Sometimes our funds limit what we can bid, but whenever there is an antique-book auction, we're there either in person or online. And if we don't get the Bible we want at the auction, we do everything we can to know who bought it, so that we might possibly get it later in an estate sale. Sometimes we can convince the owner to will it to us after they die."

"A list would be more than I could have hoped for," Gil said.

"Back here," she said.

He followed her behind the partition. She opened a door and tossed the key ring in, then closed it. Then she sat down in front of a computer—a toy compared to the computers Gil worked with—and a minute later a list of Bibles was printing.

"This is the computer you use to bid at the auctions?" he asked.

"It's an antique in computer terms," she said. "Sometimes it's a little slow and we start biting our nails that a bid isn't going to get in on time."

"So you're online. I didn't see a Web address or an e-mail address on the brochure."

"Mr. Getz!" Olivia cried. "Are you asking me for my e-mail address?"

Her mock offense knocked him off balance for an instant.

She laughed. "You should see your face," she cried. "It's priceless."

She reached for a card and wrote on the back, not only an e-mail address, but—

"My cell-phone number," she said. "It would be best if you weren't too forward in the e-mails.... Alice, my coworker, checks our e-mails every morning."

"I'll keep that in mind."

"We don't advertise that we have e-mail. It takes away from our old-time bed-and-breakfast atmosphere. That's why we don't provide Internet access in the rooms either. People like to come here to get away from such things."

Gil's work was finished. He had everything he'd come for. But he didn't want the night to end.

"Hot cocoa on the porch?" Olivia said.

"Hot cocoa," Gil said, grinning and shaking his head.

"You don't like hot cocoa? I can make coffee."

"No, it's not that. It's just that, I haven't had hot cocoa for ... I can't remember the last time I had hot cocoa."

"Then prepare to get a chocolate rush that will knock your socks off," Olivia said. "I make it extra strong."

Gil pulled on a coat and waited for her on the porch. The black sky glistened with thousands more stars than could be seen through the haze in Las Vegas. The air was chilly and moist off the river, not the dry cold of the desert.

Everything here was different. It was as if he'd rocketed to a different planet, or traveled to a different, simpler, friendlier time. He felt like an intruder. No, an invader, because he brought with him the corrupting influence of his world.

He eyed his car in the parking lot. If he had any decency, he'd climb in it and drive away. Right now. The longer he stayed the more he contaminated Olivia's world.

The door creaked and Olivia elbowed her way onto the porch carrying two mugs of steaming hot chocolate. Gil hurried to assist her with the door.

"Careful, it's hot," she said, handing him a mug.

Gil took it and grinned at what he saw. "Miniature marshmallows."

"Wouldn't be hot cocoa without marshmallows," Olivia replied.

They stood by the railing, gazing into the darkness, past the road to the river that sparkled with moonlight.

"Hot cocoa is so much better when you drink it outside," Olivia said. "I love the way the smells of chocolate and fresh air waltz together. Each is better in the company of the other."

"Like friends," Gil said.

She turned to him with the most angelic smile he had ever seen. Her eyes danced beneath the rim of her hat. "Like friends," she said, offering her mug in a toast.

The mugs clinked.

"Did you know my daughter married one of the Morgan boys?" she said.

She meant the comment as a conversation starter, picking up the thread of a previous discussion. She probably wanted to tell him a little more of herself, as new friends do. How could she know that she was forcing him to lie to her?

"No," he said. "I didn't know."

"He was killed tragically about a month ago."

"I'm so sorry. Did they have children? Someone to inherit the family Bible?"

"No children," she said. "But the Bible is another story. Meredith's husband was a twin, the younger twin, so his brother inherited the Bible."

She didn't say any more about Ethan and the Bible. Her thoughts were on her daughter.

"I've tried to talk Meredith into moving back here, to help me manage the place, take it over someday."

Gil rested his mug on the railing. "How old is she?"

"Twenty-eight."

"Too young to be a widow," Gil said. "Too young to know what's important in life."

"No ... it's not that.... Meredith feels strongly about family and heritage, too strongly at times. Just a few days ago she was in England visiting Edenford—well, it's ruins. The residents of Edenford inspired Drew Morgan to start the family-heritage practice of passing on a Bible. Meredith's trip—by the way—landed her in London the day St. Paul's was bombed."

"She saw it?"

"She was driving past it when the bombs went off."

"Was she hurt?"

"A concussion. Scrapes and bruises."

After a moment of silence Olivia's eyes sparkled with tears as she relived the memory of her child in danger. Her feelings for her grown daughter touched Gil. For years now the only feelings he'd had for his son were anger.

It had been that way since the boy was a teenager. The last warm feeling Gil could remember having for him was when the boy was eight after he'd been bitten by a neighbor's dog. Gil rushed him to the emergency room. There were deep gashes on his arm that required stitches. Gil knew what was coming next—injections to anesthetize the wound before stitching it up. His son had always been terrified of needles. But in the emergency room, the boy fought back his fear. He didn't whimper. He didn't cry. He didn't even look away. He took the injection like a man. The doctor made a big deal of his courage. Gil didn't say anything to his son. He wished he had.

"The death of her husband. A terrorist explosion. Your daughter's been through a lot," Gil said. "How's she doing?"

"Meredith is a Cooper," Olivia said. "We're a stern breed with red hair and a stubborn streak that stretches back for centuries."

"Stubborn? I don't see it. You're the most gracious woman I've ever met."

"You've only just met me," Olivia replied. "How about you? Do you have children?"

"A son. We work together, but we're not close."

"Your choice or his?"

Gil thought about that for a moment. "I don't think it was a choice. We just let it happen. Does that make sense?"

"Like weeds in a garden," Olivia said. "Nobody chooses weeds. They come from neglect. Same is true for any relationship. All you have to do to make a mess of one is to neglect it."

They fell to silence for a time. In the distance the historic Ohio River flowed as it had for thousands of years. Gil wondered how many conversations it overheard through the centuries.

"Oh my! Look at the time!" Olivia cried. "It's past one o'clock in the morning!"

With a heavy heart Gil picked up his mug. He wished it didn't have to end, that they would continue talking and that morning would never come. There was healing here. But it was over now, and the sooner he put it behind him, the better. He'd get up early and leave before breakfast.

"Please stay," Olivia said, putting a hand on his forearm.

Had she read his mind?

"Stay another night, until after Sunday brunch," she pleaded. "The Mitchells reserved the room for two nights. I'd like to get to know you better."

"I've enjoyed our time together," Gil said.

"So you'll stay?"

He wanted to stay. "I can't," he said. "I'm sorry."

"Well," Olivia removed her hand and putting on a brave face said, "I give you fair warning. In the morning I'm not going to let you go until you've made another reservation."

"I'll have you know, I can be pretty stubborn," he replied. "I may hold out through lunch."

Already he was back to lying. He told her exactly what she wanted to hear. He'd be gone before sunrise. How easy he found it to slip back into old practices.

They said good night and parted ways at the top of the stairs, Olivia putting out the lights along the way. Like a gentleman Gil waited for her to close her bedroom door before continuing to his room.

Once inside, he went straight to work, opening his laptop and establishing an Internet connection via satellite. He typed his report to Simon, including all the information he'd requested. Simon would want it first thing in the morning. Attaching the report to an e-mail, Gil wrote that he'd be in his office by Saturday afternoon.

He positioned the cursor arrow over the Send button, but didn't click on it. For more than a minute the arrow hovered with indecision.

Gil erased the last sentence of the e-mail, the one about his being in his office Saturday afternoon. He clicked Send.

As the e-mail bolted its way to Las Vegas, Gil Getz ventured into the dark hallway of the Heritage Bed and Breakfast. He knocked softly on Olivia's door.

Her hushed voice came from the other side of the closed door.

"Yes? Do you need something?"

"It's me."

"Gil?"

Her voice changed when she said his name. Softer. Less hostesslike.

"Can I change my mind?" he said. "I'd like to stay."

# SEVENTEEN

"I just had the strangest conversation with my mother," Meredith said, carrying a tray of coffee and snacks into the den. "She was positively giddy."

"I can't imagine your mother giddy," Ethan replied.

He was stretched out on the sofa with a book open on his lap, deep in thought. He and Meredith had taken to spending evenings together. Having a regular schedule was one of the advantages of being suspended.

They'd rented a movie on this Saturday night. While Meredith cleaned up after dinner and called her mother—a Saturday-night ritual—Ethan read. Meredith had come out of her room earlier than expected, the phone call to her mother surprisingly short.

"What prompted your mother's mood?"

"She wouldn't say. Said she'd tell me later, giggled, then hung up."

Meredith set the tray down. Ethan slid his feet off the sofa so she could sit down. His head remained in the book.

"I'm glad to see it, though," Meredith said, pouring a cup of coffee. "Earlier this week she was moody. A couple had canceled. Their house burned to the ground. They lost everything."

"That's tough," Ethan said, still reading.

"Did you put the movie in?"

Ethan didn't answer. Meredith reached for the DVD case. The disc was still inside.

"I thought you said you were going to put the movie in," she said, walking the disc across the room and inserting it into the player.

She sat back down, pointed the remote control, and readied the movie for playing.

"Are you going to read or watch the movie?" she asked.

"Just a minute."

"What are you reading?"

He lifted the book so she could see the cover. It was F. Malory Simon's best seller, *Simon Says*.

"I thought you tore your copy up," she said.

"I bought a new one."

"Why?"

"Just a sec."

He continued reading.

When he looked up, he said, "I think I know why Simon collects Bibles."

That got her attention. She set down the remote.

"It's a matter of power," Ethan explained. "In this chapter Simon describes the dynamics behind a violent transfer of power and property.

He says that history proves power is transferred not with weapons, but with ideas."

"Ideas?"

"Ideas promoted through symbols. Think about it. Revolutions start with an idea. That idea energizes a person, a group, and then a nation. Symbols are used as a visual representation of the idea. Are you with me?"

"Go on."

"For example, what was the idea that sparked the American Revolution?"

"Freedom and liberty."

"Exactly. And the symbols that represented freedom and liberty?"

"Well, there were several, weren't there? The Liberty Bell. The Declaration of Independence. Oh yeah, and the flag. Thirteen stripes, thirteen stars."

"Flags are powerful symbols. Desecrate another country's flag and you're sure to get an emotional response."

"So you're saying Simon is collecting antique Bibles because they're symbols of Christianity? But that doesn't make sense. He'd have to collect all the Bibles in the world."

Ethan inched to the edge of the sofa. "Simon said something at the seminar. He made a big deal about how in order to become his own man he had to make a break from his father. Simon revolutionized himself with the idea that he could be something his father was not."

"A personal makeover," Meredith said.

"Exactly. But what was interesting was how he said he did it. He had a slogan to describe it: 'Cut the root and the flower dies.'"

"Catchy."

"So it's not just any Bibles he wants. He wants Bibles—"

"—that have deep roots to the past! He's cutting the root!"

"Exactly."

"That also explains Simon's interest in Andrew's business. Andrew wrote his novels to remind Americans of their spiritual roots! But does it really work that way? Can he really destroy Christianity simply by taking away our symbols?"

"I don't know. What if we no longer flew the American flag or pledged allegiance to it? Or taught American history in schools?"

The question hung between them uncomfortably.

"Um, you're not going to like what I'm about to say," Meredith said.

Ethan stared at her warily. "Go ahead. Say it."

"The question you just posed." She hesitated. "Isn't it like asking, what if we didn't teach our children about their spiritual roots? Not only Bible stories, but the stories of the great martyrs of the faith, or of the men and women who gave their lives so that we could read the Bible in English."

"People died?"

"Anne Askew and Joan Bocher were burned at the stake because they were caught reading the Bible in English. There are others, of course. Hundreds of other Christians who lived courageous lives."

"Like Drew Morgan."

"I told you you wouldn't like it."

Ethan looked at the woman next to him. Could it be that she and her mother had been right all along? Was it possible that women of strong faith like them kept the F. Mallory Simons of the world from taking over?

The coffee was cold. Meredith took the tray into the kitchen to warm it up, returning minutes later. The movie remained forgotten.

"I've been doing a little detective work on Simon," Ethan said, sorting through copies of newspaper and magazine articles.

Meredith poured him a hot cup of coffee. "What did you find out?"

"He made his first million from his industrial shredding company. You know, shredding sensitive documents for businesses and banks. What with increasing government regulations and the high cost of storing documents beyond their retention period, it's become a huge business. Very lucrative. Simon was the first to provide on-site services using vans equipped with shredders so employers could watch the shredding take place.

"As computers became prominent, he expanded his business to electronic shredding, developing software for businesses to shred their own files and heavy-duty shredders that destroy computer disks and hard drives.

"Expanding his business one more time …" Ethan shuffled papers, "according to an article in *Newsweek*, Simon's business tactics came to the forefront, and major companies hired him not to shred their documents, but to shred their competition. He became a hired gun for the Wall Street crowd."

"What kind of man would build a career on destroying things?" Meredith asked. "Don't you think it would take a toll on him after awhile?"

"It's made him a celebrity," Ethan replied. "I've been telling Sky for years that we live in a world where destruction has become entertainment. Movies. Games. Video clips on the Internet. Let some terrorist group post a video of a beheading, and the site will get millions of hits and spread like wildfire through e-mail."

"That's sick."

"That's the world of F. Malory Simon. Here's one more bit of information about Mr. Simon you'll find interesting. He's very active in efforts to remove crosses and nativity scenes from public view."

"Symbols again. F. Malory Simon has declared war on Christian symbols."

"We should warn your mother," Ethan said.

Meredith's hand flew to her mouth. "I hadn't thought of that! You're right! Does Simon know about the museum? We don't know that he does, do we?"

"No."

Meredith reached for her cell phone. "No ... wait ..." She set it down. "I'll call her Monday. She's so happy right now. I don't want to spoil it."

———

Gil Getz drove into the setting sun on Kellogg Road, State 52. He wore a smile, the same smile he'd discovered Friday night. He wore it again Saturday, Saturday night, and all day Sunday. He liked the way it felt.

Olivia asked him to stay through Sunday brunch, so Gil changed his flight to Sunday afternoon. After brunch he changed it again to Sunday evening. The rescheduling charges more than doubled the cost of the flight. Gil didn't care. It had been worth it.

His stay at Point Providence was beyond therapeutic. Over the last few days he had been introduced to a life he never knew existed. Olivia was his guide and the slice of life she served him was richer than any of the desserts Chef Cheryl had whipped up.

Point Providence had no pretenses, no hidden agendas, no power plays, no watching your back, no glitter, no glamour, no bright lights to distract and dazzle. There, the coffee was strong, the conversation genuine, the walks in the woods relaxing, and the companionship heartfelt. Olivia was the most incredible woman he'd ever met, which made leaving hard.

A sign indicated his turnoff two miles ahead, Interstate 275 south. By taking the loop he would cross the river and avoid the city.

The sun was in his eyes. He lowered the visor and just as he did, a car passed him going the opposite direction. The man seated on the passenger side looked like his son, but it couldn't have been, could it?

He tracked the car in his rearview mirror as it pulled away. A late-model black Chrysler. No … it couldn't have been his son.

Olivia talked a lot of family. Especially Meredith. The mother and daughter had a bond between them that Gil didn't know was possible. Olivia spoke of her daughter with respect and admiration. Gil had never known a parent who so openly admired her child. It created a desire in him to want to get closer to his son.

That's probably why the guy in the car looked like him. Gil had been thinking a lot about his son. In fact …

Pulling out his cell phone, he pushed the speed-dial number for his son. Maybe they could get together for dinner tonight.

After four rings, he got a recorded message.

"Hey," he said. "I'm catching a flight out of Cincinnati. How about dinner when I get in? On me. Give me a call."

He flipped the phone closed. It was a start.

He merged onto Interstate 275 south and couldn't get his son out

of his mind. It couldn't have been him in the car. What reason would
he have for being in Cincinnati?

At the airport he returned his rental car, waded through security,
and found himself outside his departure gate with thirty minutes to
spare. He bought a cup of coffee to pass the time.

Opening his laptop, he established a satellite uplink and checked
his e-mail. Business-related stuff mixed with advertisements and spam.
Nothing from Simon or his son.

He tried the phone and got the answering machine again.

It couldn't have been him.

But the fleeting image kept nagging him and wouldn't let up. Gil
closed his laptop and made his way back through the terminal to the
rental-car counter.

Night had fallen by the time Gil Getz made it back to Point
Providence. Nearly back anyway. He'd pulled off the road a half mile
from the inn and approached the building on foot. He couldn't just
pull into the driveway. Olivia would see the headlights and ask him
questions he couldn't answer.

She didn't know what kind of business his son was in. What kind
of business they both were in, which was the pin that burst the romantic bubble of this past weekend. Olivia could never know who he really
was. She would never understand and she would certainly never
approve.

She lived in a world beyond his reach, a princess in a fairy-tale kingdom. His world was cutthroat, glitzy, hard, and unforgiving.

Gil watched the house through the trees from a distance. Warm lights in the windows glowed invitingly. It pained him to know that she was inside, so close. He wanted to climb the steps of the porch and surprise her. He could come up with a story. He was good at lying.

He circled around back. All was still. Peaceful. He felt like a fool. He'd missed his flight for no reason.

Continuing the circling maneuver, he moved to the north side of the building with the parking lot between himself and the house. All was as it should be. Just one or two cars in the lot. They didn't have guests on Sunday nights. The inn was closed on Monday and Tuesday.

Gil watched the windows hoping for a glimpse of Olivia. The front door opened. Olivia appeared, cup in hand. His heart seized at first sight of her, then skipped like a schoolboy. He told himself he was being foolish. He was too old for these feelings.

He hid in the shadows mooning over a woman he couldn't have. She stood serenely at the porch railing, her gaze distant and unfocused. Was she thinking of him? How would she react if he walked out of the woods? He wanted to.

A hundred objections rose up to stop him. Chief among them— how does a grown man explain hiding in the woods and spying on her? Followed closely by— It's over. Don't start something you know you can't finish.

A voice came from inside the house. Olivia turned to it. And all too quickly she was gone. The door thumped shut with an awful finality.

A chill settled over him. He knew he would walk away from here and never see her again. He also knew it was best this way.

For her sake, he would not call her. For her sake, he would leave and never return.

The first step was the hardest. He made his way down the slope toward the road. He would follow it back to his car and drive back to the airport where he'd book another flight to Las Vegas and try to forget Point Providence and Olivia Cooper.

A hundred yards from the road the trees thinned to reveal a small clearing, a pull-out. Gil spotted a car, parked among the trees, shielded from the road. A black Chrysler. Identical to the one with the man he thought was his son.

The hair on the back of Gil's neck prickled.

The car was unoccupied. The doors were locked.

Gil scampered up the hillside back to the house. He took up a position where he could see anyone approaching the front or the back.

The inn looked as it had every time he'd seen it, in a perpetual state of peace. But all was not right. He could sense it. Darkness surrounded the house like an approaching thunderstorm.

Gil settled in. He would wait. All night if necessary.

A few minutes after ten the interior lights went off one room at a time. The house became dark. The night swallowed it.

Gil waited, every sense on high alert.

The crack of a limb was the first alarm, followed by the rustling of feet through the fallen leaves. A solitary figure approached the house from the rear, moving cautiously from tree to tree.

The dark figure skulked across the clearing between house and forest. Even in the darkness Gil recognized him. He'd seen those same movements when, as a boy, his son played army with his neighborhood buddies; and more recently when working together, doing Simon's dirty work.

Gil didn't need to see any more. Nor did he take the time to skirt the edge of the parking lot and approach the house under the cover of trees. Leaving his post, he strode directly across the parking lot toward the back of the house.

He lost sight of his son as the boy reached the back door. Gil heard the ripping of wood as the boy jimmied it with a metal blade. Quick. Sharp. Then silent. It might have been a branch splitting off a trunk.

No lights came on. If anyone heard it, they'd ignored it.

Gil picked up his pace.

When he reached the back door, it stood open. He looked around. There had been two men in the car. Gil saw nothing but forest stretching into darkness.

He entered the house, stepping into the kitchen. All was still. His hand flexed. It wanted a gun. Gil hadn't brought one. And if he had? Would he shoot his own son? Would he shoot his son if Olivia's life was in danger?

In answer to his own question, Gil crossed the kitchen to a cutting block and gripped a hefty butcher's knife.

He made his way to the darkened hallway just in time to see a fluttering of white disappear into the museum looking like some sort of apparition.

The museum light switched on.

"Who are you? What are you doing here?"

The tone of Olivia's voice tore at him. She was afraid and something rose up inside of him, some ancient human instinct that responded to the tone with ferocity and he knew he would do anything … anything … to protect her and calm her fears.

Gil stepped into the doorway linking the museum and the hall. It took only an instant for him to size up the situation.

Olivia stood with the center display, the one with the Morgan Bible, separating her from the intruder. In her hand she held her cell phone as though it was a weapon, a futuristic light phaser.

The intruder stood frozen on the far side of the room, facing her, holding a nylon backpack by the straps. By the stretch of the straps, the contents of the pack were heavy.

Gil knew exactly what the pack contained. He'd assembled dozens of them for Simon. Inside the backpack was an incendiary bomb with a remote trigger.

His son saw him first. The boy's face went from anger at being caught to bewilderment.

Olivia swung around to see what he was looking at. An array of expressions crossed her face in an instant—from surprised to perplexed to relieved.

In that instant, for the first time in his life, Gil felt complete. Her eyes told him she knew he was there to save her, not harm her. At that moment Gil Getz found his mission in life, to protect and love and cherish this woman to his dying breath.

"Gil? What are you doing here?" his son demanded. The boy hadn't called him Dad since he was ten years old.

"Gil? Do you know this man?" Olivia said.

"Go up to your room, Olivia," he said. "Everything is all right. I'll take care of—"

The blast hurled Gil backward, out of the doorway, slamming him against the railing of the stairs. At first, everything went black. Then, he heard moaning. His. Only it sounded distant. Muffled.

His head lolled side to side. His face felt the heat of fire, sending an alarm to his brain, but his body was unable to respond. He breathed in smoke and started to choke. His eyes flickered, then squinted against the light of the flames.

*Olivia!*

Gil willed himself to move, to push himself into a sitting position, his back against the side of the stairs. Flames leaped and twirled around him in an ancient tribal dance. He tried to get up and something sent an electrical shock through his nerves. He tried again and managed to get to his knees, then his feet.

He stumbled toward the museum room and had to place a palm on the doorjamb to keep from falling. It was hot. He jerked it back.

The room was wallpapered with flame. Displays that lined the walls were troughs of fire. The center display had been knocked over, its glass case shattered, the replica Bible having spilled out onto the floor.

Olivia lay beside it.

Gil fell to his knees beside her. He shouted her name though he could barely hear it with the noise of the fire and whatever had been stuffed into his ears. She didn't respond.

He shouted again, cupping her cheek in his hand. Her skin was satiny smooth just as he'd imagined it would be. He felt her neck for a pulse. He thought he could feel one, but he wasn't sure.

He had to get her out of here.

With an arm under her shoulders and another cradling her legs, he lifted her up and found enough strength to carry her the length of the hallway and through the kitchen and down the steps to the back of the house.

Gently, he laid her on the ground.

"Olivia! Can you hear me?"

He cradled her face in his hands.

"Olivia, please ... please ... don't go. I just found you!"

Her eyes moved beneath the lids. Her lips parted with breath. Then she looked up at him.

"It's all right," he assured her. "You're out. You're safe."

"Gil?"

"Yes. I'm here. Everything will be all right."

Sirens sounded in the distance.

"Safe?" she mumbled.

"Yes. You're safe now."

"Bible ... safe?"

Gil looked back at the house. "No. The Bibles are gone."

"No ... no ..." She became agitated. "Must get ... Bible ..." She struggled to get up. A weak attempt.

"Lie still. There's nothing we can do."

"Morgan ... Bible ... must ... must ..."

"Please, Olivia. Lie still. It's a replica."

"Gil ... please, Gil ... get ..."

Tears tracked down her temples. She began to cough. Gil clutched her tight against his chest.

"Please ... please ... please ..." she said between coughs.

"All right," he said. "All right."

"Give ... Meredith," Olivia said.

Gil looked at the house, now an inferno.

Anything. He would do anything.

"Stars ..." she said. "You ... me ... stars."

They had walked together under the stars Saturday night. It had been the most perfect night in Gil's life.

He draped his jacket over his head and charged back into the burning house. Inside, the walls were fire, the ceiling thick black smoke. Bending low he pulled a handkerchief from his pocket and covered his mouth.

The kitchen was an inferno. The hallway was a corridor in hell. Gil knew he wouldn't last long. He ran the length of the hall and turned into the museum. To one side of the center lay the replica of the Morgan Bible. Untouched by flame.

He couldn't believe what he was seeing. What was it about the Morgan Bible that even its replica was protected by the hand of God?

Scooping it up, he turned to leave, but not without first glancing where his son had been standing when the bomb went off. He wished he hadn't.

A skull, separated from its body burned on the floor.

Why had he done this? Why?

Overhead, a wooden beam gave a mighty crack, then gave way. Gil leaped out of its way, rolling on the floor, clutching the Bible to his chest with the thought that if God was protecting this Bible, by staying close to it, God would have to protect him, too.

In the hallway he didn't think he was going to make it. His lungs were on fire. He coughed so hard he couldn't see where he was going, and he was afraid he was going to stumble into the burning wall.

All he could do was put one foot in front of the other and hope that with blind luck he would hit the doorway.

Step after step he thought there must only be one or two more steps to go, but he kept taking one step then another and another and there was no end to walls of flame.

To his right the wall fell on top of him, knocking him to his knees. He tried to get up, but couldn't. There were no steps left in him.

With one final lunge forward, he broke through a wall of fire and tumbled down the steps into the open. He rolled onto his back and saw stars.

He lay there for a time, curling up convulsively like a sow bug; each cough felt like his lungs were trying to jump out through his mouth.

Somehow he got on his knees. He had to check on Olivia, to show her that he got the Bible, to hold her until help arrived.

He slumped to the ground beside her and held up his prize for her to see.

But her eyes no longer saw. They were open, but the person behind them was gone. The last things she saw were the stars.

---

Ethan careened into Meredith's driveway, killed the ignition and was out the door before the car came to a complete stop. Oblivious to the pink glow that lit the eastern sky, he raced toward the door shuffling the keys on his key ring to find the front-door key.

"Meredith?"

He charged inside the house. The rooms were dark except for a light coming from the end of the hall.

"Meredith?"

The door to her bedroom was open, but the light was coming from the bathroom.

"Meredith …"

Twenty minutes ago he was in bed, asleep. Her call woke him with a start. He knew it was her from the ring tone. At first all she could do was weep. Her sobs let loose a flood of panic inside of him that had yet to subside.

"Meredith?"

A sliver of light spilled onto the hallway carpet from the bathroom. Ethan pushed the door open slowly.

She was sitting on the floor in a white robe, her back against the cabinet. Her head was tilted back, her eyes closed. The cell phone lay in her open hand. Her chin quivered.

Ethan wanted to say something soothing, but the words that came to mind were empty containers. There was no healing balm in them.

When she'd called she was barely able to get the words out. There had been a fire. The Heritage Bed and Breakfast had burned to the ground. Her mother—

She had choked on the next word and for several agonizing moments Ethan could only guess her mother's condition. Meredith finally formed the words, and Ethan's worst suspicions were confirmed. Olivia Cooper was dead.

Standing over Meredith, Ethan was struck by how vulnerable she looked sitting on the bathroom floor.

"Can I get you anything?" he asked. "Something to drink?"

He was in rescue mode, his blood racing. Adrenaline surged in his limbs. He wanted to do something to help—anything. A simple nod would launch him on a mission to find a glass and fill it with water and bring it to her.

But she said nothing. She hadn't even acknowledged his arrival.

Ethan lowered himself beside her, his back against the cabinet with hers. He didn't do anything. He didn't say anything. He just sat beside her and stared at the wall.

After a moment she slumped against him. Her cheek on his shoulder. Her eyes open, unfocused but dry now. He could feel the heat of her face through his shirtsleeve. For several minutes they sat like that, neither of them moving.

Then, in a whisper, Meredith said, "Thank you for coming."

# EIGHTEEN

Gil shoved the door to the office open with force. It didn't slow him, slamming against the wall, announcing his presence. Tucked inside his arm he carried the replica of the Morgan Bible like a football.

"Why?" Gil shouted as he approached. "Why did you do it?"

The suddenness of Gil's entrance startled Simon. Once he saw who it was, Simon relaxed as though he was expecting the intrusion.

"Can you be more specific?" he said, calmly setting the morning newspaper aside.

Gil had done the unforgivable. He'd interrupted a morning routine that hadn't changed since Simon moved into the Las Vegas offices—perusing the business dailies; followed by status reports, both verbal and printed (Gil spied the printout of his report on the top of a stack of reports on Simon's desk); an update from the Outlaws' general manager; and a morning swim and rubdown at an exclusive health spa.

Everyone who worked for Simon knew the routine. It was sacred. Secretaries had been terminated for interrupting it, project managers fired. Gil didn't care.

"You sent my boy to Point Providence to destroy the Heritage museum," Gil shouted. "I want to know why."

"I don't know what you're talking about."

"Who did you send with him? The nitwit set off the explosives prematurely. My boy's dead."

Gil had decided to refrain from mentioning Olivia, though it was her death that fueled his anger above his own brush with eternity.

"Your son was killed?" Simon rose from behind his desk in an expression of sympathy. Gil wasn't buying it.

"Why did you bypass me on this?" he demanded.

Simon spread his arms wide with open palms. "I had nothing to do with it," he said. "Your son must have been freelancing."

"He works exclusively for you."

"Worked. Past tense," Simon said. "I fired him. His employment was terminated at the end of the day Friday. Didn't he tell you?"

Gil recognized the old Simon two-step shuffle around the truth. But he had no evidence, only suspicions.

"I was in the room when the bomb went off," Gil said.

Even now it sounded as though cotton was stuffed in his ears, his skin was hypersensitive to heat, and he couldn't take a deep breath without setting off a coughing spasm.

"You were there?" Simon came around from behind the desk. "In the room? Incredible. But what were you still doing there? Weren't you supposed to return Saturday?"

"I stayed over."

Simon's eyebrows rose with interest. "Really? At an inn for antique Bibles? For what possible reason would you … oh! I take it the service at the bed-and-breakfast was to your liking."

It was all Gil could do to keep from launching into Simon. His simmering anger had been close to the boiling point since the explosion. Frustration over a lack of evidence and answers only made it worse.

"I saw two men," he said. "One was my son. I want to know who the other man was."

"His new partner for all I know," Simon replied. "Or a trainee. Maybe he was going into business for himself. Like I said, I know nothing about this."

There was nothing else to say. But Simon's answers had not appeased him. Not in the slightest.

"I recovered this from the fire," Gil said, dropping the Morgan Bible on Simon's desk.

Simon looked it over. "Amazing," he said. "And you're certain it's a replica and not the original?"

"It's in my report. It's a replica."

"I see."

Simon lifted the cover and silently read the names written inside. Then he turned the book over.

"If you look in the gash," Gil said, "you'll see a name on the page—Judas."

Simon peered into the gash. He grinned.

"In the original you can see a different name: Thomas."

"Good work," Simon said.

"If you don't mind, I'd like to have the Bible."

This amused Simon. "For what purpose?"

"Personal reasons."

Simon thought about this a moment. "No," he said. "We can use it to our advantage."

Gil started to object. Simon cut him off.

"The woman who owned the museum," Simon said. "She has a daughter, does she not?"

"She does."

"This is the woman who was married to Ethan Morgan's twin brother and was with him in England?"

"Correct."

Simon handed the Bible to Gil. "See to it that the Bible is delivered to her."

Some men might have been pleased with their good fortune. But Gil knew that if F. Malory Simon was the source of the good fortune, it was most assuredly wrapped in high-priced self-interest. For the moment, he had no choice but to accept it.

"Consider it done," he said.

Simon returned to the power side of his desk. Gil turned to leave.

"My condolences on the loss of your son," Simon said. "If there's anything I can do …"

Gil gritted his teeth. Simon's heart was too cold to spawn condolences. The sympathetic comment was a taunt. Simon was dancing on his son's grave and both of them knew Gil couldn't do anything about it.

Twenty minutes after Gil Getz left Simon's office, Brad Pitzer stood straight as a toy soldier in front of Simon's desk.

"Report," Simon said.

No preliminaries. No chitchat. Pitzer was a pawn, not a person.

"Mission accomplished," Pitzer said. "The target and its contents were destroyed. There were three fatalities. One died instantly in the explosion as planned. The other two—the owner and an employee—died from injuries. As per reconnaissance, all other staff had the night off."

"Three. You've accounted for everyone?"

"Yes, sir. Just as it was drawn up."

"But there were four in the building, weren't there? There was another man."

Pitzer's face registered surprise. He recovered quickly.

"An unknown," he said. "I barely got a glimpse of him. He carried the woman out and then ran back into the building. He didn't come out again."

"He died in the fire?"

"No one could have survived going back into that building, sir."

"And what if I told you that man was here in my office not thirty minutes ago, and he had one of the Bibles from the museum with him?"

Surprise struck Pitzer a second time. He didn't recover as quickly this time.

"Impossible, sir," he said with an uncertain voice.

"You nearly killed both father and son, Pitzer. Your unaccounted man was Gil Getz."

"Getz? But ... he was only staying the one night. He shouldn't have—"

"But he did."

Simon glared at Pitzer. Why was it so difficult to find quality help? Gil Getz had spoiled him. He was the only man Simon could trust to get things done. Simon had hoped the thoroughness of the father would carry over to the son and had been disappointed. And now Pitzer was disappointing him.

"Sir, I followed the plan to perfection. If Getz deviated from the scheduled—"

"Excuses, Pitzer?"

Clamping his mouth shut, Pitzer's military training kicked into gear. "No, sir," he said sharply.

Simon's instincts were to dismiss him. But it was too late to train a replacement for Pitzer. So he let the man stand ankle deep in his failure for a time before proceeding to the next project.

"What's the status of the cameras at the project site?" Simon asked eventually.

"Locations targeted. Equipment ready to install. Technicians trained. Cameras will be online by 0500 Thursday as per schedule."

"And the studio?"

"Broadcast capabilities online. Web site online. We're good to go."

Simon scanned Gil's printed report as Pitzer was put through his paces. Tearing off a portion of the report, Simon handed it to him.

"See that this e-mail address is added to the promotional database."

"Yes, sir."

"Dismissed."

"Yes, sir."

Pitzer turned sharply and exited the office, but not before Simon caught a glimpse of his eyes. They were fired with determination. Fueled, no doubt, by his less-than-satisfactory performance at Point Providence.

Simon smiled. There was no better motivation for military types than failure. Pitzer wouldn't let him down again.

———

Five days after the fire, Gil Getz, dressed in black and holding a single rose, watched Olivia Cooper's funeral from a distance. The turnout surprised him. He wasn't the only one who had been caught in her charismatic spell. Upward of two hundred mourners encircled the casket under a clear sky.

The number of mourners stood in contrast to Gil's son's memorial service two days prior. Only a handful attended. F. Malory Simon didn't come. He didn't send flowers.

Two of the attendees had pressed the officiating minister—a local pastor who made himself available to families who didn't have a church—into mentioning in the eulogy that his deceased son held the record for the number of tacos eaten in a minute at a local bar.

Gil wasn't happy that his son's dying legacy was that he could stuff tacos into his face. But what other legacy could hired muscle claim? Number of broken bones? Number of hits? Square footage of buildings destroyed?

Such a different legacy for a woman who made everyone feel special.

Gil didn't dare join the mourners. He couldn't take the chance that one of the staff from the bed-and-breakfast might recognize him or offer to introduce him to Olivia's daughter, nor could he take the chance that Ethan Morgan would remember him from Simon's seminar, or identify him in the scheduled events of the next few weeks.

A schedule Morgan was unaware of.

The minister walked to the head of the casket and began the service. Meredith sat in the front row, dressed in black, a white handkerchief in her hand. Morgan sat beside her.

After a few preliminaries and a prayer, the minister motioned to an assistant who handed him a large family Bible. The Morgan replica. Gil had it messengered to the minister with instructions that it was Olivia Cooper's wish that the Bible be presented to her daughter at the funeral.

Gil added the part about where it was to be delivered.

Meredith's hand flew to her mouth when she saw the Bible. She exchanged words Gil couldn't hear with Morgan. The minister spoke at length while holding the Bible, then gave it to Meredith who tried to hand it to Morgan. He handed it back to her, and she placed it on her lap for the remainder of the service.

Following the final prayer, the mourners dispersed, some to their cars, others into clusters to talk, many to express their condolences to Meredith.

A pang of grief hurt Gil as he watched her. She tilted her head to one side just like her mother when she greeted people and tossed her head in similar fashion when she laughed. She was definitely Olivia's daughter.

Gil Getz may have stood apart from those who attended Olivia Cooper's funeral, but he was no less a mourner. His grief was real, and it was deep.

# NINETEEN

The first night home since Olivia's funeral couldn't have come quickly enough for Ethan. The trip had been four days of nonstop talking, mostly with people he didn't know. Being cordial and feigning interest put a strain on him that Meredith didn't understand. She and her mother were energized in a roomful of people. It drained him. Ethan desperately needed some alone time.

But Meredith had invited him for dinner and coffee, and since it was her first night home following her mother's death, he came for her.

Somewhere during the evening, after-dinner coffee turned to talk of cocoa. While Ethan browsed the DVD rack for a suitable movie, Meredith prepared cocoa in the kitchen.

"It's my mother's recipe," she called to him. "Guests used to rave about it. The only thing they rated higher on their feedback cards was hospitality."

Action movies were out, Ethan thought as his fingers brushed the titles. Guns and bullets and blood just didn't seem like a good idea.

"They always asked for the recipe. Mother never gave it out."

Maybe a romantic comedy? Ethan shook his head. Sky liked them. He and Meredith were forever quoting lines from romantic comedies.

"She talked about putting together a book of Heritage Bed and Breakfast recipes. Maybe even including one as part of the weekend package, something the guests could take home."

Andrew's DVDs: Superman, Batman, Spider-Man, Fantastic Four, Star Wars, Star Trek.

"The secret to her cocoa was vanilla extract. That, and the process itself. It's not only the ingredients that make a great cocoa, but the temperature and steps used to make it."

*Something lighthearted*, Ethan thought. A movie about someone who doesn't take life seriously. Danny Kaye. Both he and Sky were huge Danny Kaye fans.

Meredith's cell phone rang. With one hand she stirred the simmering cocoa, and with the other she answered her phone.

"Alice!" she said in greeting.

The stirring stopped. Meredith's brow furrowed. Ethan looked up. A phone call that could stop cocoa stirring was serious.

Meredith motioned to him with the cocoa hand. She pointed down the hallway and with a half voice said, "Turn on the computer."

Ethan abandoned Danny Kaye and hurried down the hallway to Sky's office while Meredith pulled the cocoa from the stove and turned off the burner.

"I'm heading back there now," she said to Alice.

Ethan flipped on the office light. Little had been done to Sky's office. It looked as if he could have worked in it this afternoon. Perhaps a little neater.

The computer was situated under a window. Ethan turned it on. The hard drive and fan whirred as the software booted up, playing the familiar operating-system tune.

Meredith appeared behind him. "Ethan's booting it up now, dear," she said, still on the phone.

Meredith motioned Ethan into the chair.

"Log on to the Internet," she instructed him.

Ethan clicked the Internet icon.

"All right, dear. What was that address again?" Meredith asked Alice.

She repeated the Internet address for Ethan. He typed it in. A second later a Web site popped up, one Ethan had heard of but not yet visited.

The site hosted user-generated videos. People all over the world posted video clips online. Viewers could rate the videos. The average rating appeared beneath a picture of the video clip along with the number of times the video had been viewed. If viewers liked a clip, they could send an e-mail to a friend with a link taking him or her directly to the video.

There were vlogs—video logs—of lonely girls using cameras in lieu of diaries, mock commercials, clips from television shows and movies, skits and demonstrations of all kinds, Japanese animation, soft-drink geysers spouting in dominolike fashion, and people just being downright silly.

"The top-ten list," Meredith instructed.

Ethan clicked it.

"Thank you, Alice. I see it. Thank you. Yeah. I'll let you know." Meredith closed her phone. "Click on number one."

She pointed to the most watched video of the day. There was a one-word title. *Imagine*. According to the counter, 248,603 people had already viewed it.

Ethan clicked on it.

John Lennon's song by the same name played over the speakers, imagining a world where there was no heaven, or hell, or religion, but only the sky above.

The image was that of an antique book. The camera pulled back. It was held by a pale man with shoulder-length jet-black hair and black lipstick. He was dressed in black. The fingernails of the thin, boney hands holding the book were painted black.

The camera stopped at a half shot from the waist up. There was no introduction.

He said, "This is a 1480 Latin Vulgate Illuminated Bible." He opened it. The pages were beautifully accented with a rainbow of ink colors. "A truly stunning book. One of the oldest and most impressive Bibles in existence."

"Is Alice shopping for Bibles?" Ethan asked. "Do you really think she'll rebuild the museum?"

"Just watch," Meredith replied.

The camera pulled back farther to reveal a huge red machine. *Imagine* was printed in fanciful letters on its side. The camera continued to pull back.

"Oh no!" Ethan cried when he'd seen enough to recognize the machine.

This wasn't an auction they were watching.

With a shudder the red machine whirred to life.

"At a recent auction," the gothically dressed host shouted over the machine's thundering sound, "this Latin Vulgate Bible was purchased for $65,000."

"He wouldn't, would he?"

"Just watch," Meredith said.

Her eyes were fixed on the screen. She knew what was going to happen. Alice told her.

The host flipped the five-hundred-year-old book into the machine's large red mouth. With a horrendous roar the industrial chipper made short work of the book, chewing it into mulch and spitting it out the other end.

The host was positively giddy.

Another book was handed to him. This one was larger than the first.

"A 1539 Great Bible, called great because of its size," he said. Looking the Bible over, he quipped, "You don't look so great to me."

Ethan noticed the category under which this video clip was featured. The "Entertainment" category.

"This Bible was purchased recently for $195,000," the host said.

Then, with an "Oops!" he flipped the Bible into the chipper and it was destroyed.

"This is just what I've been talking about!" Ethan shouted. "We live in a world that is so sick it has turned to destruction for entertainment!"

The host was handed another Bible. He did a little dance of excitement.

"I can't believe I'm going to do this!" he screamed, sounding like a teenage girl. "A 1410 Wycliffe Bible! Look! Hand-lettered!"

He held up a page to the camera.

"Guess how much this is worth! Come on, guess!"

His black eyebrows rose.

"A hundred thousand dollars?"

He shook his head.

"A half-million dollars?"

He giggled.

"You're getting warm! A m-m-m-m-million dollars?"

Closing his eyes with glee, he twirled around in a complete circle.

He held up the book and shouted, "This baby is worth two … point … seven … five … *million dollars!*"

Ethan and Meredith stared at the screen in disbelief as the host approached the chipper. He rested the book on the lip of the chute.

"I can't believe I'm going to do this!" he mugged to the camera.

He tipped the book. It slid downward. He caught it and pulled it back, embracing it in his arms.

"No … no … nearly three million dollars? No. I can't do it."

Still cradling the book, he turned his back to the chipper and started to walk away. He stopped. Grinned wickedly, then swung back around.

"Oh yes, I can!"

The Bible flew into the chipper. Moments later, it was confetti.

"And we're just getting started!" the host shouted.

The camera followed him to a table stacked with Bibles.

"Next!" he shouted to them.

He picked one up.

"That's my Bible!" Ethan shouted.

The chair flew backward when he stood.

"That's my Bible!"

He turned to Meredith who was hugging herself, swaying side to side, and weeping.

"He doesn't, does he?" Ethan shouted.

Meredith was too overcome to respond.

"Oh my, look at this one!" the host was saying. "It's in awful shape! Soot marks. A huge cut in the back. This one's a mercy killing."

He swung the Bible toward the chipper, but didn't throw it in.

"On second thought ... why not save it for the next show? A *live* podcast! This Bible might prove to be more special than it looks!"

"He didn't destroy it," Ethan said.

"No," Meredith said. She was shaking.

The video concluded with the host stepping so close to the camera his face appeared to be squeezed by the screen. "I leave you to ponder this riddle: How many Bibles could a Bible-chipper chip, if a Bible-chipper could chip Bibles?" He snickered and waved good-bye. "Until next time. For those who have the courage to ... imagine.

The clip ended.

A window popped up on the screen asking Ethan if he wanted to rate the video.

---

"That guy gives me the creeps," F. Malory Simon said, pointing a remote at the screen. The image blinked out.

"He appeals to the Internet demographics," Gil replied. "Our guys tell me they should hit a half million by the end of the day, a million within a couple of days."

"How does that compare to the videos of Notre Dame and St. Paul's?"

"These clips are faster out of the gate. The entertainment factor is higher for this sort of show, while the clips of the churches resemble footage from a newscast."

"And a live broadcast?"

"We could double or triple the numbers."

Simon was pleased with the numbers.

Gil turned to leave. "I'm headed out to Boston tonight."

His voice was flat. Gil had never been a demonstrative man, but something had gone out of him since the death of his son. Maybe the Boston project would reenergize him. If not, Simon would have to replace him.

"Want to know what I have in store for the second show?" Simon asked.

Gil turned back at the door. He didn't appear to be overly interested.

"A little test of my motivational abilities," Simon said. "What would you say if I told you that I could get Ethan Morgan not only to appear on camera, but to toss his family Bible into the chipper?"

Gil's interest was piqued. That pleased Simon.

"Care to make a wager?" he said.

"Me? Bet against F. Malory Simon?" Gil said. "I know you too well to do that."

Right answer. Simon grinned.

"Sometimes I surprise myself," he said.

"How did you get this number?" Ethan barked into his cell phone.

The caller was using a restricted-access number.

"That's not important," the caller said. "I want to give you a chance to save your Bible."

Ethan recognized the voice. "You're the guy on the video clip."

"So you've seen it."

"I've seen it."

The voice on the other end laughed. "Had you going there for a moment, didn't I? Tell the truth. Did your heart stop when I pretended to throw it in the chipper?"

"Who are you?"

There was a pause. The caller was cautious. "You can call me Sanada."

Ethan had just walked in the door when his phone rang. It took several hours to calm Meredith. The video clip had disturbed her. She likened it to living in pagan times and being forced to watch a child sacrificed to the gods. Ethan sat on the floor beside her bed until she fell asleep.

"Sanada? Sounds like the name of a Vegas showgirl," Ethan said, writing the name down.

"Don't be impudent," Sanada snapped. "I could feed your family Bible to the chipper right now."

"And disappoint five hundred thousand viewers? Not likely."

Sanada's tone lightened. "The numbers are impressive, aren't they? Highest I've had so far."

Ethan made note of that: *Has posted other videos.*

"Exactly what are you offering?" he asked.

"Weren't you listening? A chance to save your Bible."

"How much do you want?"

"Pish-posh! Don't be crude—you couldn't possibly … how much are you offering?"

*"Pish-posh"? What sort of person says "pish-posh"?* Ethan wrote it down.

"Now look what you've done!" Sanada complained. "You've gone and dragged me down in the ishy gutter of monetary sludge. I'm going to have to wash myself all over once this conversation is concluded."

*Pish-posh and now ishy. This guy's a piece of work.*

"If you don't want money, what do you want?" Ethan asked.

"I want you to come onto my show."

"Forget it."

"It will be my first *live* broadcast and I'm so jazzed about it! I will make Internet history."

Ethan made note that the caller's Goth appearance was probably an act. *He may dress like one, but he doesn't talk like one,* Ethan thought. *Goths have names like Ravyn or Spyder and talk like Edgar Allen Poe hoping to scare the mundanes into respecting them. Sanada's probably an actor, and not a very good one.*

"Listen to me, son," Ethan said, using his no-nonsense cop voice. "That Bible is stolen property. You're going to make arrangements to turn it over to me and surrender yourself to the police. If you cooperate and tell them who put you up to this, they might cut you deal that will keep you out of jail. Do you understand me?"

Sanada fell silent.

The next thing Ethan heard was the sound of the chipper starting up, followed by the horrible sound of metal teeth tearing into paper.

Ethan cringed. He'd gone too far.

The machine powered down and Sanada's voice came back on the line. "Doesn't look like stolen property to me," he said. "It looks like a pile of shredded paper. Chew on that, Mr. Policeman."

Sanada called him Mr. Policeman. The boy knew who he was dealing with.

"You didn't—" Ethan said.

"Yes, I did," Sanada replied. "I made confetti out of the phone book, and I'll do the same thing to your Bible unless you follow my instructions."

"I'm listening," Ethan said.

---

"Boston?" Meredith cried.

"He said the real reality shows were being broadcast from people's bedrooms."

Meredith scoffed. "He doesn't have a wood chipper in his bedroom."

"He was speaking artistically. Several times he referred to the location as the studio, but given the fact that anyone can broadcast live worldwide using a laptop computer and a Web cam, the studio could be anywhere."

Ethan sat across a small dinette in an alcove overlooking Meredith's backyard. It was a perfect place for a morning cup of coffee.

"I'm to fly out there tomorrow. I'll be met at the airport and transported to the studio. Blindfolded."

"Blindfolded?"

"Precaution. He is a criminal after all."

"What is it he wants you to do?"

Ethan sighed. He took a sip of coffee. Meredith's coffee always tasted so much better than his.

"He said I'll be given fifteen minutes to plea for the Bible's life, so to speak. Viewers will be given a chance to vote over the Internet. Simple majority rules. If I can convince 50 percent plus one of the voters to vote to save the Bible, I can walk out with it. If I fail—"

"What do you think your chances—"

"Less than zero. People don't watch those shows to see a happy ending. They watch to see something destroyed."

"And if the Bible is destroyed? What happens to you?"

"He didn't say."

"Oh, Ethan … I don't like this. You're not going to do it, are you?"

"Of course I'm going to do it. My brother was killed because of that Bible. Every Morgan stretching back to Drew Morgan has protected that Bible with his life. If a man wearing black lipstick is willing to show me where the Bible is, I'm going to do what he says."

"And then?"

"I'll figure something out."

Meredith shook her head. "No … no … I don't like it. It's too risky."

Ethan smiled at her.

"What?" she asked.

"You're choosing me over the Morgan Bible? Who would have thought."

"Don't make sport of this, Ethan. Please."

"It wasn't long ago you accused me of not being Morgan-enough."

"Things change. People change." Tears welled in her eyes.

Ethan set down his cup. He reached across the table and took her hand. "I have to do it," he said in a whisper.

She sniffed. "I know. It's just that—"

"What?"

"It's just that the choices are more clear-cut when you're reading about them."

"When it's Drew Morgan," he said.

"Yeah," she said softly.

Her chair scraped as she stood. She excused herself to get a tissue.

Even before he'd finished his phone call, Ethan knew he would take the faux Goth up on his offer, if for no other reason than to narrow the search for the Bible. He knew now it was in the Boston vicinity.

Sanada also offered to reunite him with the Bible. What else or who else would be in that room—other than a chipper, a camera, and a Goth—he didn't know. He'd have to formulate a plan once he got there.

It was made clear that he would be searched at the airport and that his badge and gun would be taken from him if he brought them. He was warned that any police presence, real or suspected, would mean he would never see the Bible again.

Ethan wondered if they knew he couldn't involve the police even if he wanted to. The minute he contacted them, they would contact the San Diego department. F. Malory Simon's name would inevitably come up and not only would Ethan be told they wouldn't assist him, he also would be ordered to stay away. Boston police would take a report, but the thought of any major police department assigning significant resources to the recovery of a family Bible was laughable.

Which meant Ethan was on his own.

That wasn't quite true. He had Sky with him.

Ethan sipped his coffee and looked out at the lawn that was still green even though winter was just around the corner. He mused that this would be Sky Walker's first adventure. Two Morgans morphed into one; his body animated by his brother's prevailing spirit.

Ethan chuckled. Sky would like the way he was thinking.

Meredith returned. She set the Morgan Bible replica on the table. "I have a plan," she said.

"You're not going with me to Boston."

She thrust out a hip defiantly. "I didn't say I was going."

"Are you?"

"Yes. And you can't stop me."

"Meredith—"

She put both hands up to stop him. "Just listen to me, all right? If you think the plan won't work, just tell me."

"And you'll back off?"

"No—" she said. "We'll just have to come up with another plan."

"Meredith—"

He stood up and went to her, taking her by the shoulders. He looked into her eyes and said, "I love you for doing this, but—"

"You love me?"

"—for doing this."

"You said you loved me."

"I said I love you—"

"There! You said it again!"

He did. And he meant it, though he couldn't believe he'd said it out loud.

"I'm sorry," Meredith said. "It's mean to tease you like that."

He wanted to tell her, but she stepped back and the moment was gone.

"I was thinking of Jacob and Esau Morgan," Meredith said, "the only other twins in the Morgan line."

"One was an American patriot who fought for freedom," Ethan said, "the other was a loyal Englishman."

Meredith smiled, proud of him for knowing that.

"There was a switch. Even though they had feuded all their lives, when one brother was captured, his twin switched places with him to free him."

Meredith picked up the replica. "We have twin Bibles. I propose we make a similar switch."

---

Simon stood alone in mission control. A single screen commanded his attention. In a conference room just down the hallway, Gil was giving final instructions to the four remaining apprentices, three men and one woman.

"This is the final test," Gil told them. "Mr. Simon has only one apprentice position open at this time."

The apprentices refrained from looking at each other, focusing instead on every word that came out of Gil Getz's mouth. The camera providing the video feed allowed Simon to study the apprentices' facial expressions and body language. Out of over two hundred applicants, these were the hungriest, the most motivated.

"Each of you will be given a task. You must complete it within a given a time. Failure to complete the task within the time period will result in your immediate dismissal."

Simon watched their reactions. All four remained cool and determined. Good. To get to this point they had already undergone a series of timed tests. They knew what was expected of them.

"This is a test of character," Gil told them. "Mr. Simon has reviewed your university transcripts and your résumés. To get to this point you have had to prove you have the business skills to succeed. Now he wants you to prove that you want the job more than anyone else in this room."

Now they looked at each other, challenging each other with a glance or a smirk. For eight weeks they had lived with each other and gone head-to-head in competition. Simon leaned forward, looking for any sign of reticence. Two apprentices that had not survived the previous cut had been held in reserve should any of these finalists show the slightest fear. Simon didn't want a repeat of the failure at St. Paul's.

"Are you ready for this?" Gil asked them.

"I was born ready," one of the guys quipped.

The others laughed.

Simon zeroed in on the joker. The smallest in stature. The cockiest. Simon picked up a phone.

"Get Hamilton out of there. Send him home. Tell Quigley he's back in."

A moment later Simon watched as the door to the conference room opened. His man approached Hamilton from behind and whispered in his ear. Seconds later he was gone and Quigley was seated in his place.

Quigley had fire in his eyes. He was determined to make the most of his reprieve. The other three candidates sobered instantly at what had just happened.

"Tonight," Gil continued, "you will be flown to an undisclosed city. At that point you will be separated. For this final test, Mr. Simon has chosen to go back to Business 101. You will be asked to deliver a package. You must deliver it on time to the correct address, to the exact spot specified in the instructions. Failure to do so will result in your immediate dismissal. Your progress will be monitored at all times. Do you understand the task?"

Heads nodded. No jokes were made.

"You will encounter obstacles along the way. Some of them physical. Some merely well-meaning people who are just doing their minimum-wage job. Security personnel, for example. Give them a badge and they think they're God. Executive secretaries are even worse. Your resourcefulness will primarily determine whether or not Mr. Simon chooses you to work for him."

Gil paused. He looked them in the eyes. He'd done his job. They were motivated. It was time to seal the deal with the personal touch.

"Let me give you a piece of advice, from someone who has worked side by side with Mr. Simon for years. You don't become a millionaire by obeying the rules."

The chuckles were obligatory, not out of nervousness. In mission control F. Malory Simon nodded, confident he had the right apprentices for the job.

"Don't be fooled by the simplicity of the task," Gil concluded. "Sometimes the simplest tasks are the most challenging. But if you can't deliver your product on time, you won't stay in business. And if you can't deliver Mr. Simon's package on time, you won't be working for him."

The woman, a brunette, said, "This is our Blue Vase test."

"Exactly," Gil replied.

Each successful applicant for the apprentice program was sent a motivational tape upon his or her acceptance. The tape was titled *The Blue Vase*. It was a dramatized story of a man, a lowly employee, who went to every length to deliver a blue vase to a wealthy customer. He woke up people in the middle of the night to get a key, he traveled a great distance at personal expense, he broke a few windows. But he delivered the vase as promised. The millionaire purchaser of the vase was so impressed with his tenacity, he hired him on the spot to run his business.

Simon's team was prepped and motivated. But the packages they would deliver did not contain blue vases.

"Pack your bags," Gil said. "We leave in three hours."

---

"Ethan, don't you see?" Meredith pleaded. "Pastor Clayton told me that it was Mother's dying wish that the replica be delivered to me! It's as though she knew we would need it."

Ethan shook his head. It wasn't that he didn't like the plan. It was the only plan they had.

"It gives us the edge we need," she argued. "They don't know there's a replica."

"You have to promise me that at the hint of danger, you'll back off, even if it means abandoning the replica."

"I promise!" Meredith said all too happily.

"Even if it means abandoning me," Ethan pressed.

This comment sobered her.

"Don't ask me to promise that."

"It's a deal breaker, Meredith. Otherwise I'll walk away from the whole thing right now."

Meredith grimaced. "What sort of danger?"

"I don't know! That's what scares me."

"But what if I can—"

"You run away and you get help. Promise me."

"Ethan, how can I promise if I don't know—"

"Promise me."

"All right! I promise!"

Ethan tried to read her face to see if she was telling the truth. He was trained to do this. But every time he looked at Meredith his attention was diverted by how different she looked to him now.

Attractive. In a ... in a physical way ... a romantic way. But it still felt weird. It was too soon. Or would it always feel weird? He'd never known anyone to fall in love with his brother's widow.

"You can go," he said.

Meredith scowled. "That wasn't the issue. You couldn't stop me from going."

"You know what I mean," Ethan said. "We'll do it your way."

Meredith beamed. "Now I liked the way that sounded."

---

Engulfed in darkness, Ethan lay in his bed and stared at a ceiling he couldn't see. He talked to Sky.

"We're going in blind," Ethan said. "That's what scares me. We have no idea what we're up against."

*Then you'll just have to proceed by faith.*

Ethan grimaced. "You've been up there too long. You're starting to sound spiritual."

*Or maybe you're becoming more spiritual.*

Ethan laughed. "What are the chances of that, huh?"

His mind drifted to Meredith's plan. The part that bothered him most was that should anything go wrong, he might not be close enough to help her. He might not even know she was in trouble.

"Here's an idea," Ethan said. "How about if you stick with Meredith and should anything happen, you can come and get me."

*You know it doesn't work like that.*

"Can you see into the future? Do you know what's going to happen?"

*Now you're just being silly.*

Ethan folded his arms. "What good is having a dead brother if he won't do a simple thing like pop into tomorrow and tell you what he sees?"

Sky didn't answer him.

"Fair enough," Ethan said. "But I'll tell you this, and don't take this the wrong way. I'm hoping that neither Meredith or I see you tomorrow."

Again, no answer.

"Which reminds me. Have you seen Olivia? How's she doing? Meredith will want to know."

*Get some sleep, Ethan.*

# TWENTY

Game day. In a Boston hotel conference room Gil Getz reviewed the scripted plan with the intensity of a football coach. From his coat pocket he pulled a couple of index cards with a few plays of his own. He clipped these to the game plan.

The three male apprentices entered the room. They were dressed in the uniforms of three different delivery services. Three sealed packages of identical size, each labeled with the company's corresponding shipping label, waited for them on the conference table.

The men were not permitted to see the address on the labels yet, which were identical.

"Your blue vases," Gil said, motioning to the packages.

The brunette who had compared their final task to the motivational tape was not in the room. At the last minute and without explanation Simon had cut her from the team. She had not made the trip with them.

"As you know," Gil began, "your final task will be to deliver your package within the designated time. Should you fail to deliver your package, you will be eliminated from the competition. Gentlemen, this is your Super Bowl. Now is not the time to hold anything back."

The three men stood shoulder to shoulder. Tense. Ready to get on with it.

"Your first obstacle will be to get your bearings. In a business the size of Mr. Simon's, there will be times when you will be called upon to navigate unfamiliar territory. For all you know, outside that door, the people of this city don't even speak English."

It was true. They didn't know. The aircraft windows were closed when they flew in last night. The windows of the limo that transported them to the hotel had been blacked out. The room they stayed in had been stripped of all identification, the shades were drawn, the telephone removed, and they were chaperoned.

"In front of each package there is a ski mask with the eyes sewn shut and a portable music player with earphones, its volume set on high. At the appropriate time you will put on the earphones and the ski mask. You will then be escorted to your individual starting places. Once there, the ski mask and earphones will be removed, you will be handed your package, at which time the clock will start ticking. Do you understand?"

"Yes, sir," said three voices in unison.

"While you are strongly encouraged to do whatever it takes to deliver your package, I warn you to restrain your creativity until you are handed the package. In other words, gentlemen, any attempt to see anything or hear anything before the clock starts will result in immediate disqualification."

The middle candidate flinched. Apparently Gil had just shot down his strategy.

"And do not try to bribe the limo driver," Gil said. "You'll only be wasting precious time. Trust me, he can't be bought."

The middle candidate flinched again.

"In order to test your abilities, your delivery target may not be an office or a person. Each target is clearly marked with a blank, corresponding shipping receipt and a phone number. You will find a disposable cell phone at that location. Call the number to receive further instructions to complete your task. Do you have any questions?"

The candidates shook their heads.

Gil smiled. "The losers will go home. The winner will fly back to Las Vegas on Mr. Simon's private jet, during which time his executive salary and benefits package will be explained over a glass of champagne."

Three men. Three smiles. One vision: flying at 30,000 feet sipping champagne on a luxury jet.

"Gentlemen. I wish each of you the best of luck. And I look forward to working with one of you. If you will, put on the headphones and the ski masks now."

Three limo drivers appeared. They picked up the contestant's packages and led the men out the door.

Gil stood alone. He didn't feel the same way he'd felt in Paris and London. The thrill was gone. He no longer felt the passion he and Simon had shared over the years to force America to turn its back on the past and look to the future.

Something happened to him at that bed-and-breakfast in Point Providence. The past put on a smile and sparkle that made his heart ache every time he thought of her.

So he wouldn't think of her.

Gil gathered his things and left the room. He had a game plan to coordinate.

---

Two floors above Gil, F. Malory Simon briefed the lone female contestant, the brunette, whom he had pulled aside the night before. He told Gil she'd been eliminated. It was the first time Simon had ever kept part of the game-day plan from Gil Getz. Simon no longer trusted him.

"Your final task is different from the others'," he told her.

The brunette stood across the breakfast table next to a window overlooking Boston harbor. Keeping their destination from her wasn't necessary. She had flown with Simon in his private jet while Gil and the boys took a chartered flight.

"The reason your task is different is because you are the leading candidate, Miss Seger," Simon said.

She beamed despite herself. He'd already informed her of her front-runner status during the flight to Boston but made a point of mentioning it again. According to her profile, Miss Seger was the kind of person who lapped up praise and kept coming back for more.

"Put this on," Simon said.

He handed her a lapel pin and briefed her on its significance. She started to say something. He stopped her with an upraised finger. She also had a tendency to talk when she should be listening.

"Business is people, Miss Seger," Simon said. "Like product, a wise businessman learns how to move people from place to place efficiently and with a minimum of fuss. That's where you come in. Like the male contestants, you will deliver a package, only your package has a mind of its own."

"Yes, sir," she said, the pin in place on her lapel.

"Now, there are several obstacles you will have to overcome, the least of which is the package itself. Regardless of what she says or does, who she's with, what they say or do, you are to get her to the designated location within the allotted time and keep her there until I arrive."

"Just tell me where and when, sir."

"Do you watch football, Miss Seger?"

"A big fan of the Outlaws, sir."

She was good. Simon couldn't tell if she was telling him the truth or kissing up to him. He handed her an earphone attached to a radio receiver.

"Our quarterbacks have headphones in their helmets," Simon said, "so that the coach can call the play from the sidelines. That's what I'll be doing with you. I'll be monitoring the situation. When your package arrives, I'll notify you. At that time, I'll instruct you where to deliver the package and at what time."

She took the earphone and receiver from him and began to put them on.

"By whatever means, Miss Seger," Simon emphasized.

"Yes, sir."

"If you accomplish this task, regardless of how the men do, you will fly back with me back to Las Vegas as my apprentice, during which time you will be presented the salary and benefits package as one of my executive officers."

She was all smiles.

"While sipping champagne, of course."

"Of course," she replied.

Simon stole that last line from Gil. It worked perfectly on Miss Seger. She was purring like a cat. Unprofessional, but oddly arousing.

"I won't disappoint you, sir."

He stood. She offered her hand. He shook it.

"I look forward to working with you, Miss Seger," he said.

———

Carrying an overnight bag, Ethan followed the flow of traffic through Logan International Airport to baggage claim and ground transportation.

He spotted a large man in a dark suit standing next to an exit and holding a makeshift sign with E. MORGAN printed with ballpoint pen.

Ethan pretended not to see it at first. He bent down to tie a shoe that didn't need to be tied to give Meredith a chance to catch up with him if necessary.

A flash of neon pink caught his eye. Meredith didn't need time to catch up. She was already at the baggage carousel. The pink book bag was her idea. Printed on the outside:

*I CANNOT LIVE WITHOUT BOOKS.* —*THOMAS JEFFERSON*

Inside the bag was another bag, this one a canvas book bag. Unmarked. Meredith argued that the double bagging gave them flexibility. High profile if necessary, low profile if discretion was needed.

Ethan preferred things simple. But since Meredith was the one carrying the replica, he let her call the shots. At the moment, he was grateful for the pink. He'd spied her easily in the crowded baggage-claim area.

"I'm Ethan Morgan," he said to the man with the sign.

The tall man looked down at him and sniffed as though he was expecting someone—what? More imposing? More threatening? More handsome?

"What's with the bag?"

Ethan hefted it. "Thought I'd spend the night. Take in the sights."

The man grabbed the bag, walked over to a moving carousel, and tossed it in with the bags from Flight 289 arriving from Orlando, Florida.

"Let's go," the man said.

Losing the overnight bag wasn't a setback. It really did carry a change of clothes. There was nothing in it that would have threatened Sanada.

Ethan followed his escort to a black limousine parked in the loading zone. The man stood at the back door but didn't open it.

"Open your coat."

Ethan obliged. He unbuttoned his coat. Like cloth wings, he spread open the coat so the driver could check for weapons.

"Pull up your pant legs."

Ethan did, earning him stares from a passing elderly couple pulling wheeled luggage.

"Turn around."

The man poked Ethan in the back at the waistline. He wasn't very good at this.

After examining the contents of Ethan's pockets and billfold, the man opened the back door of the limo and motioned for Ethan to get in.

Ethan risked a glance for Meredith. The amateur frisking had bought her enough time to hail a cab. From the backseat she spoke to the driver. The driver pointed at the limo and nodded.

For Ethan, Boston disappeared when the limo door shut. All the windows and the partition separating him from the driver were black. Ethan's world was reduced to the backseat, a stained and sticky and gritty world at that. He wondered what punk-rock group had used the limo last. There were no door handles. It reminded him of the back of a police patrol car.

A lurch threw Ethan against the seat. A sudden jerk to the left sent him sideways. With no visual warning, Ethan braced. One hand forward for stops, one hand gripping the armrest to keep from toppling sideways.

All he could do now was wait.

———————

"I have absolutely no idea where they are going, so please don't lose them," Meredith said, sitting forward on the edge of the cab seat.

She held the pink bag against her chest, preparing for a wild ride. What she got was the safest cab ride in the history of cabs. Gentle acceleration. Cautious lane changes. The driver checked and rechecked and checked a third time before turning right or left.

Through the front windshield, Meredith watched as the black limo carrying Ethan began to pull away.

"Don't lose them!" she shouted.

The limo merged onto the turnpike. The cab driver began his mirror-checking procedure. He was a swarthy, middle-aged man from some Mediterranean country. He removed a hand from the steering wheel long enough to waggle a finger at Meredith.

"Life is too short to bruise the broth," he said.

"What?"

The driver offered no explanation.

*Great*, Meredith thought. She had to catch a ride with the world's only safe cab driver-philosopher.

The turnpike took them under the harbor and into the heart of Boston.

They caught up with the limo. With a toothy grin, the cabby said, "See, Ms. Lady? You must ask yourself, are today's weeds worth tomorrow's supper?"

Clearing the tunnel, the limo merged right toward Atlantic Avenue. Meredith lost sight of it amid the traffic. When she picked it up again—

"Right lane! Right lane!" she shouted.

The cabby nodded calmly. He checked the side mirror. Turned on his signal. Checked his side mirror again. Then the rearview mirror. Then he turned to check his blind spot. Turning back to the front, he flipped off the turn signal.

"You must sit back," he said to her, still in the middle lane. "I cannot see if it is clear."

Meredith rolled her eyes. Strangling her bag instead of the cab driver's throat, she slumped back against the seat.

The driver began his turning procedure again, checking his side mirror—

By some miracle, the cabby made it into the right lane in time to merge onto Atlantic Avenue. They were skirting the bay.

With frantic eyes Meredith looked through the windshield for a black limo. It was turning left onto Broad Street. The cabby was three cars back in the same lane.

"See?" the driver gloated. "Good things come to those who brush with Crest."

From here the limo did a little jig through city streets—Broad Street to Milk Street, left on India to State Street, left again to Congress Street, then back around to Atlantic Avenue where they emerged from the tunnel. Despite all the mirror checking, the cabby managed to stay with the limo as it headed into historic Boston.

From Hanover Street the limo turned left and then made another quick left into a parking lot. The cabby flipped on his turn signal to follow.

"No, no! Go straight!" Meredith shouted.

With exaggerated patience the cabby flipped off the signal and eased the cab forward. "Next time please make up my mind sooner," he said.

She instructed him to circle the block.

Salem Street was a one-way street. They turned right, then right again down Tileston, right on Hanover, past Bennett and right on Prince Street She pointed to the curb under some trees.

From here she could see across a basketball court to the parking lot. The limo had pulled up to the doorway of an old redbrick tenement building, five stories tall.

The driver had left the limo.

Clutching her bag, Meredith climbed out of the cab. She paid the driver.

"See? All worked out," he boasted. "Never forget: Slow and steady gets the worm."

Meredith's heels clicked as she walked across the basketball court toward the redbrick building. Just as she reached center court, the limo driver came out the door and climbed into the limo. The engine roared to life. Putting the vehicle into gear, the driver looked up. Meredith was right in his line of sight, standing in the middle of a basketball court holding a hot pink bag with nowhere to hide.

With a squeal of tires the limo came toward her, then swerved around the court.

Meredith did the only thing she could do. She turned her back to it, shielded the bag with her body, and hoped he didn't recognize her from the airport. She scrunched her shoulders and squeezed her eyes shut.

The limo roared by. With tiny baby shuffles she rotated, keeping her back to it. Tires screeched as it pulled into the street. A moment later it was gone.

Meredith's hunched shoulders slumped. Her heart was pounding so hard she was certain it had bruised her ribs. This undercover business was harder on the nerves than she'd imagined.

Not until she opened her eyes did she see two little boys on the edge of the court, one of them sitting on a basketball. They stared wide-eyed at the lady with the hot pink bag cringing at center court.

Meredith smiled at them, shrugged, and made her way to the red-brick building.

# TWENTY—ONE

Before Ethan was allowed out of the limo, his captors required him to pull a ski mask over his head. The eyes had been sewn shut.

The driver grabbed him just above his elbow and yanked him out of the car. Another yank up a single step and through a door. The air inside was musty and old. They crossed a tile floor. The room was large enough to echo their footsteps. Then they walked down a narrow cement stairway, an awkward passage given the size of the driver.

The mask was pulled off Ethan's head unceremoniously, and he found himself in a basement lit with studio lights. One item in the room caught his immediate attention.

On the far side of a stage stood the big red wood chipper. The word *Imagine* was printed on its side. A pile of shredded-book remains lay behind it on the floor.

A dark purple curtain separated the stage from the rest of the basement.

Between the steps and the stage were two long tables. One table was laden with electronic equipment. Cables snaked to and from black boxes with rows of dials. The second table held stacks of Bibles.

One Bible caught Ethan's eye. He hadn't seen it since the night of the elementary school play when he walked out his front door, purposely leaving it behind.

The curtains parted. Sanada made an entrance. He looking uglier in real life than he did on camera. Anorexic. His white skin and black makeup were heavily layered.

"Ah, the guest of honor," he said.

He looked Ethan over, cringing at what he saw as though Ethan was the oddly dressed of the two.

"Totally and unequivocally mundane," Sanada concluded.

He turned suddenly, clapping his hands. "We're going to have so much fun today, people!" Turning back to the driver, "He has been properly neutered, hasn't he?"

"No badge. No gun. If that's what you mean," the driver replied. The big guy was obviously not a fan. "Am I done?"

The driver disappeared up the steps. Ethan looked around to see who Sanada had been talking to when he made his announcement, but at the moment it was only him and the Goth.

Ethan liked his chances. All that stood between him and rescuing the Morgan family Bible was an anorexic host and a cement stairway.

Sanada grinned. He knew what Ethan was thinking.

The curtains parted again. A man whose photo could be used in Webster's dictionary to define "muscle" walked toward them. Ethan didn't know which was more formidable about him, his massive arms and neck or the holstered gun strapped to his chest.

"This is Frank," Sanada said to Ethan. "Think of him as a playground monitor. As long as you play nice, you won't get into trouble. He's also a door monitor, and he will let you leave only after one of two things happen. Either you convince our viewers to save your Bible from the chipper—did I tell you you'd have fifteen minutes to do that? If I didn't, I'm telling you now. You have fifteen minutes—or you toss your Bible into the chipper. Once either of those things happens, Frank will step aside and you will be free to leave."

Frank reinforced the rules with a glare, then stationed himself at the foot of the steps.

Sanada continued, "You and I are going to make Internet history today. We are going to put all the reality TV shows to shame!"

Sanada was genuinely enthused about the possible ratings with no regard to what he was doing to get them. The Bibles on the table were a means to an end—to make Sanada famous.

The Goth continued. "There's no phone number to dial. All that those who watch our little program have to do is position their computer mouse over a button on the screen and—Click! Their vote is instantly registered and recorded and tabulated! We'll know in real time exactly what the vote count is!"

He clapped his hands.

"Simon Cowell—eat your heart out!" he crowed.

Ethan didn't celebrate. He walked over and picked up the Morgan Bible.

To the Goth, he said, "You know I'm going to bust you for grand theft, don't you?"

The comment stunned the Goth. Hurt him. "What are you trying to do?" he cried, his voice quivering. "That's just cruel! You don't say things like that to the talent just before a big show!"

His hands flopped in a flustered fashion.

"It's just … It's just …"

Tears marred his makeup.

"I can't be here right now," he whined. "I need to compose myself." He started to go, then turned back, "I can't believe you said that! That was just … just … mean!"

He disappeared behind the curtain.

Sanada was by far the most flamboyant Goth Ethan had ever encountered, and Ethan was certain he wasn't the mastermind behind the show.

First things first, Ethan told himself. Rescue the Bible, then go after Simon.

He gazed at the Bible in his hand, the symbol of his family's spiritual heritage. For all of his boasting to Olivia and Meredith that he'd get it back, a part of him feared he'd never see it again.

"Sometimes it takes losing something to realize how valuable it is to you," he muttered. "A brother. A Bible."

A thought came to him and brought a smile with it.

Standing here in Boston, the Morgans and this Bible had come full circle. Somewhere nearby, Drew Morgan once stood holding the Morgan family Bible. Now, more than 350 years later, after surviving a Revolutionary War, a Civil War, World War I, World War II, trips back to England and over the flak-filled skies of Germany, after traveling the breadth of America and back again, this same Bible was back where its American journey first began, in the hands of a direct descendant of Drew Morgan.

Ethan's heart swelled with family pride.

He made a vow.

Someday ... someday ... he would take this symbol of his family's spiritual heritage back to Edenford where it all began and in the Morgan family tradition, he would pass it on to his son and tell him the story of Drew Morgan and the courageous adventures of the Morgans who had gone before them.

---

Five floors above the basement studio F. Malory Simon and Gil Getz were seated in a room that resembled a television-station control booth with flat-screen monitors, laptop computers, sound equipment, headphones, cell phones, and binoculars. From here they could monitor the entire operation: the approach of the three contestants with their packages, the studio where Sanada and Ethan Morgan would make Internet history, and the destruction of their third historic church—Boston's famed Old North Church where the signal "one if by land, two if by sea" was given, launching Paul Revere on his midnight ride.

Microcameras had been installed at strategic places within the church so Simon could follow the progress of each of the deliveries and ensure that the bombs were in place before detonation. From their fifth-story perch they could see the roof and steeple of the church.

Simon had his game face on, the one he used when pacing the sidelines of every Outlaws football game, ready to exert his authority if at any time he didn't like the play calling. He had watched the previous two demolitions from mission control in Las Vegas. Not satisfied with the way Gil had called the game on those two occasions, he was stepping in.

"They're off and running," Gil reported.

The three apprentice contestants had been transported to different locations in the city equidistant from the church. At the designated time their blindfolds were removed, and they were handed their sealed packages and a delivery address:

```
193 Salem Street
```

None knew they were all three converging on the same location. Upon reaching the address, however, their instructions varied. One would place his package on the ground floor, east wall stairwell; another on the first floor, west wall closet; and another on the second floor, steeple storage closet. Simon had paid a demolitions expert well to select these locations.

Simon didn't just want to bring down the building, he wanted to make the destruction of the steeple spectacular. Memorable.

Simon studied it through his binoculars. How many generations had looked at this steeple and heard its bells? How many people couldn't imagine Boston without them? Today that part of Boston would be erased forever. People would mourn for a time. But with the church no longer there to draw their attention to the past, they would grow accustomed to looking to the future for their salvation.

*Cut the root and the flower dies.*

Simon set down the binoculars. It was going to be a good day.

"What's she doing here?" Gil said, pointing to a monitor.

A perky brunette was arranging things atop a desk inside the doorway to the building downstairs.

"Miss Seger? Sad story, really," Simon said. "The poor girl was in tears when I told her she didn't make the final round. She begged. You know how they are, determined to prove you wrong."

Gil glared at the monitor. He didn't like that Simon was messing with the game plan. The coaches on the sidelines never liked it either.

On the monitor, the door opened. Miss Seger greeted a female visitor who was carrying a pink book bag.

"Meredith Morgan?" Gil cried.

"She's right on time," Simon said. He flipped a switch and spoke into a microphone. "It's her."

---

"Excuse me," Meredith said, entering the building. "Maybe you could help me."

The brunette behind the desk appeared friendly enough. Meredith had envisioned having to talk her way past steely-eyed men with guns.

"What do you need?"

"Well ... it's my understanding that there is some kind of broadcast taking place here ... it's just that ... um, this place doesn't exactly look like a television studio."

The receptionist smiled.

"I'm afraid you're living in the past," she said. "Today, you don't need huge soundstage buildings and rooms of equipment to broadcast a show."

"So there is a show?"

The receptionist nodded. "And you are …"

"Meredith."

She held out her hand. As they exchanged greetings, she noticed the receptionist's lapel pin.

"The show," Meredith said. "It has something to do with Bibles?"

"An auction, actually. We auction off antique Bibles over the Internet. We get bids from all over the world!"

"An auction? Oh … well … then … maybe I'm in the right place. You see, I have this antique Bible." She pulled it from the pink bag, then the canvas bag. "A 1611 King James Version. It's quite valuable. I'd like to arrange to have them auction it off for me."

The receptionist looked the Bible over. She wrinkled her nose. "This isn't the way we—"

"Of course, I'd pay whatever commission you charge."

The receptionist turned the Bible over. She recoiled at the gash in the back. "It's not in very good condition, is it?" she said.

"That's one way to look at it, I suppose. But this Bible has a thrilling story behind it. That gash saved the owner's life!"

"I don't know— We don't just take Bibles from walk-ins without documentation." She handed the Bible back to Meredith. "I think you need to talk to our producer. Let me give you his card. You can call him. Maybe we can auction your Bible at the next show."

The receptionist reached into a drawer.

"No, I really don't think I can do that," Meredith said. "I'm quite desperate, you see."

The receptionist frowned. She was suspicious.

Meredith dropped the act. "Look, Miss …"

"Seger."

"I couldn't help but notice your lapel pin."

In way of acknowledgement Miss Seger touched the pin.

"It's the symbol for the Heritage Churches of America. Are you a member?"

"All my life."

"Your family. They have a Bible that is passed down from generation to generation?"

"We do."

"How many generations?"

"Five," she said proudly. "It was presented to my older brother last Christmas."

"Have you heard of the Morgans and their Bible?"

Miss Seger beamed. "Of course. Drew Morgan is the founder of the tradition."

Meredith opened the replica Bible so that Miss Seger could see the names printed on the inside flap. She pointed to the first name—

"Drew Morgan!" Miss Seger shouted, covering her mouth.

Trembling, she brushed the ink with her index finger.

"This is really the Morgan family Bible?" she whispered.

Meredith hesitated. But only for a moment. She had to risk the truth.

"It's a replica."

Miss Seger frowned. A defensive wall went up.

"Please hear me out," Meredith said. "I don't know what they told you is happening in there. But it's not an auction. They are destroying Bibles."

"I'm afraid you'll have to leave," Miss Seger insisted. "The people I work for wouldn't do that."

"Right now, Ethan Morgan is in that studio. If he is unable to convince viewers to save the Morgan family Bible, they will destroy it by throwing it into a wood chipper."

"No ... no ... they wouldn't do that!"

"Have you been in the studio?"

Miss Seger shook her head. She hadn't.

"The authentic Morgan Bible is in that studio right now. Ethan and I are trying to save it and you are our only hope."

"The real Morgan Bible is downstairs?"

Meredith slipped the replica into the canvas bag, and it into the pink bag. "Our plan is to switch Bibles so they destroy the replica instead. Help me get it into the studio. Ethan will do the rest."

"I don't believe you. The people I know ... they wouldn't throw any Bible into a chipper, let alone an antique Bible."

"You've been deceived."

Miss Seger shook her head stubbornly.

Meredith walked around to the working side of the desk. Alarmed, Miss Seger backed away until she was against a wall and could go no farther.

"Don't make me call security," she cried.

Meredith took the woman's hand and placed the handle of the book bag into it, then backed away.

"Go downstairs," she said. "Look into the studio. You will see a big red wood chipper with the word *Imagine* printed on the side."

The receptionist studied her warily.

"If the chipper is there, set the bag down and walk out. If I'm wrong, I'll leave quietly. But I'm telling you, the fate of the Morgan Bible rests in your hands. Literally."

For several moments Miss Seger stood motionless with indecision. Then, taking the bag with the replica Bible, she walked down the stairs.

Meredith slumped against the edge of the desk.

---

"Why don't we have sound?" Gil asked.

He and Simon had followed the exchange between Meredith and Miss Seger on the monitor.

"Isn't it obvious what took place? I alerted Miss Seger someone might attempt a switch. She handled it."

Gil stared at the image of Meredith sitting on the edge of the desk. She was slimmer than her mother, but alike in so many other ways.

A cell phone rang. Progress reports were coming in from the spotters in the field as the contestants neared the church. Simon took the call.

Turning his back to his boss, Gil opened his own cell phone. He tapped in a text message. Recipient: Marcus. The message read—

        4 Olivia

---

Activity in the studio had increased considerably. Besides Sanada there were sound and light men and several other backstage technicians.

"Marcus, secure those cables," the sound tech said.

With the Morgan Bible on his lap Ethan watched as a beefy boy dropped to his knees. Ripping off three-foot lengths of duct tape, he secured the cables to the floor.

His pocket beeped.

The boy flipped open his phone, glanced at the screen, then got up and walked away.

"We're not done here," the sound tech shouted at him.

Marcus kept walking, leaving the sound tech to mutter curses about minimum-wage help.

Ethan was anxious for the show to start. He'd never been good at waiting. One of the perks of being promoted from patrolman to detective was that he no longer had to sit around waiting for tow trucks, or janitors to arrive with keys, or paperwork to be processed on prisoners.

Sanada clapped his hands and told everyone to get to their places. Just then, Ethan caught a flash of pink out of the corner of his eye. He saw a brunette descend the stairs carrying Meredith's book bag!

Without being obvious about it, Ethan tracked her. She walked toward the table with the Bibles.

Ethan felt a surge of emotion. Meredith had done it!

He took in the table and the surrounding area. He was running out of time. He had to figure out a way to get to the table without being conspicuous. He could make the swap and stash the authentic Bible among the boxes of electrical cords. He could do it. All he needed was a minute.

Ethan didn't have a minute. The next second everything changed. Marcus intercepted the brunette at the Bible table. He said something Ethan couldn't hear. She handed him the pink bag. He reached in, pulled out the canvas bag, checked the contents and disappeared back-stage with it.

Ethan's heart stopped.

Still carrying the empty pink bag the brunette retraced her steps and went upstairs.

Ethan got up. As casually as he could, he started to follow Marcus.

On stage Sanada was clapping louder. "Let's go, people, let's go! Where's the guest? Where's Morgan?"

Sanada spotted him. Churning his arm, he motioned Ethan into the lights.

Ethan had run out of time.

His hand on the curtain, he took a quick look. He saw Marcus backstage, kneeling on the floor, the Bible in front of him. He had a knife.

Ethan watched as the boy lifted the front cover of the replica and plunged the knife into its pages. He ripped and plunged again, work-ing quickly and with feverish intensity.

"Come, come, come!" Sanada called to Ethan. "And bring your Bible."

Ethan had failed.

Authentic Morgan Bible in hand, he stepped into the spotlight with Sanada and the big red wood chipper.

---

"Good news," an empty-handed Miss Seger said.

Meredith leaped forward, pushing off the receptionist's desk with pent-up anxiety.

"And bad news. First, the bad news." Miss Seger leaned close to Meredith. "Can you believe it? There really is a chipper down there just like you said! Why would auctioneers need a chipper?"

"They're not auctioning anything," Meredith said.

"I know … I know …" Miss Seger said, apparently struggling to accept the fact that whoever hired her had lied. "All my life I've been taught to cherish the Bible and now …" She struggled with her emotions. "… now I find that I've been part of …"

She shook her head, unable to say the words.

"You left the bag downstairs," Meredith said, coaxing her.

Miss Seger wiped away tears. "That's the good news."

Meredith was dying a hundred deaths inside wanting to hear what happened.

Finally, Miss Seger said, "I recognized one of the men down there. He …" Her eyes lit up suggestively. "… he has this thing for me … anyway, I gave him the bag."

"You trust him?"

Miss Seger smiled. "Believe me. He'd dress like a gorilla and do a King Kong imitation from the top of the Empire State Building if he thought it would impress me."

Meredith grinned.

"There was a table down there with stacks of Bibles. He put the bag under the table."

"Under?" Meredith panicked. "It can still be seen, can't it? If it's hidden, Ethan won't be able to—"

"I said I had good news."

Meredith pursed her lips to stop the flow of words.

Miss Seger's eyes flashed excitedly. "Mr. Morgan saw him!"

"So he knows the replica is there!"

Miss Seger nodded. "Better than that. My friend shielded him while the exchange was made."

Meredith was so happy to hear this news an involuntary squeal of joy bubbled up from within. In her excitement she grabbed Miss Seger's arm.

"How can I ever thank you?" she cried.

"It gets better."

"Better? I don't think that's possible."

"Mr. Morgan asked Marcus to hide the bag with the authentic Bible backstage. After the show he'll get it and rendezvous with us. I'm so anxious to meet him! I mean, he's one of *the* Morgans!"

Meredith could no longer contain her joy. It erupted in tears and hugs.

"Did he say where?" Meredith asked.

"He wanted someplace public. Safe."

Meredith nodded, searching for a tissue.

"The Old North Church is right around the corner," Miss Seger said. "Mr. Morgan said he'd rendezvous with us there."

Miss Seger led the way.

As Meredith passed the desk, a thought occurred. "What about your job?"

Miss Seger scoffed, "Do you think I'm going to work for people who lie to my face and mulch Bibles?"

---

"Well played, Miss Seger," Simon said from his post four stories above them. He pulled an earphone from one ear.

While Gil heard none of the conversation, Simon heard every word. He had to admit Miss Seger was impressive. He almost regretted that she would die today. She had a Machiavellian quality about her that made her very attractive.

"You knew they'd attempt a switch," Gil said to him.

"I knew they'd try something. By returning the replica Bible, I steered their course down the obvious road. Disappointing, really. It was too easy. I was hoping they'd show a little more creativity."

Gil checked the basement monitor. Ethan had just completed a sound check. One of the stage crew ushered him to a waiting area. The show would start in two minutes.

"Report," Simon said.

"All three deliveries appear to be on time. They're minutes away from the church."

"Excellent," Simon said. "It's time to motivate Mr. Morgan."

# TWENTY — TWO

Ethan sat backstage with the Morgan Bible on his lap. The boy with the replica had left.

From the moment Ethan picked up the authentic Morgan Bible, he hadn't let it out of his possession. A monitor and a headset, his link to the show on the other side of the curtain, sat on a table in front of him. The man guarding him had taken up a new position nearby.

Ethan ignored the monitor. He'd put the headset aside. He needed time alone.

"Sorry, Sky, but I don't think we're going to win this one," he said softly.

Ethan hated being right. Sky was unrealistic to think that miracles still happened. That superheroes swept in at the last moment to save the day. Those days were gone. This was the world of F. Malory Simon now, where men climbed to the top over the carcasses of their competition. This was the world of Sanada where people entertained themselves with death and destruction.

Ethan hated this world.

He hated that people reveled in cheap glory. It's easy to criticize and destroy. Creating is hard work. Building something worthwhile takes imagination and determination and perseverance and sweat. America's lost values.

Why couldn't people see that the glorification of destruction was ultimately self-defeating? Soon there would be nothing left to destroy. And if somehow dreamers did survive, why would they build when hoards of people were waiting to dance around the burning rubble of their creation?

Ethan stroked the cover of the Bible. He envied Drew Morgan for living in an age when people joined forces to carve a nation out of a wilderness, when people risked their lives to create a new country on dreams of freedom.

He opened the Bible for one last look at the names printed on the inside cover, a congress of American dreamers. Reverent fingertips brushed across the name at the top of the list: Drew Morgan, 1630, Zechariah 4:6. Beneath that, his son Christopher Morgan, 1654, Matthew 28:19. And on down the list—Philip, Jared, and the other Morgan twins in the family—Jacob Morgan, Esau's brother, 1786, 1 John 2:10.

Each name, a story of courage and faith, a portrait of American history from 1630 to the present, with his name the last on the list—Ethan Morgan, 2000, Hebrews 8:10.

His father had waited to present the Bible to him until the year 2000. He wanted Ethan to be the first Morgan listed in the new millennium.

Ethan stared as someone on the other side of the curtain fired up the chipper, then turned it off, testing it to make sure it was working.

The guard gave him a warning glance just in case he was thinking ideas about trying something heroic. He didn't know Ethan's ideas had gone from heroic to desperate and crazy.

He envisioned getting a chokehold on Sanada. He could threaten to kill the host, hold him over the chipper. But it would be an empty threat and everyone knew it.

Ethan's only chance was to convince a destruction-crazed Internet audience. He would tell the story of the Morgans and hope that he could do it convincingly enough to influence a favorable vote.

He read down the list of names again, remembering what each of them had done. He wished Sky was here. Sky was the storyteller, not him.

———————————

Three sharp raps, a pause, then two more sounded on the door. Simon jumped.

"Rest easy," Gil said. "It's my man."

Gil unlocked the door. Standing in the dark hallway was Marcus. He handed Gil an oversized book. The two men locked eyes. Marcus nodded slightly.

"What's that?" Simon snapped.

The sharp tone reminded Gil how much Simon hated surprises on game day.

"I thought you'd want to see this," Gil said.

He handed Simon the Morgan Bible. Simon looked at it, didn't take it. Gil turned it over.

"It's the replica," he said, offering Simon a look inside the gash. "Would you like to check for yourself?"

Simon glared at Gil.

"I'm just being thorough," Gil insisted. "It's obvious you no longer trust me."

"I don't have time for this," Simon said.

He turned his attention back to the monitor showing Ethan sitting backstage. He flipped a switch and barked an order.

---

The sound tech came up behind Ethan and tapped him on the shoulder. Ethan turned.

"Put the headphones on," the tech said.

The monitor in front of Ethan showed Sanada center stage. A countdown clock in the corner of the screen indicated that the show would start in two minutes.

Ethan slipped the headphones on. But the voice he heard was not Sanada.

"Welcome to Boston, Mr. Morgan."

It was F. Malory Simon.

"What do you want?" Ethan said.

"To tell you how much I'm looking forward to your show. Just like all the other viewers, I have a vote. Do you think you can convince me?"

"Cut the comedy, Simon."

"If my comedy is not to your taste, maybe I can entertain you with a little drama."

The monitor flickered to a different scene. No longer did it show the stage on the other side of the curtain; it showed the interior of a church, row after row of pew boxes. Walking down the aisle was—

"Meredith!" Ethan cried.

She was empty-handed and not alone.

Simon said, "Just wanted to encourage you to give this show your best effort. Anything less and—well, you're a cop. You know how those missing-person cases go. You hope for a happy ending, but ... hey, this is real life, not the movies."

Ethan couldn't keep his eyes off Meredith. She was smiling. Carefree. Completely unaware that her life was in danger. Ethan recognized the girl with her. The polo girl. He'd seen her coming out of the elevator at the hotel.

"Simon, if you so much as—"

On the monitor something caught the girls' attention. A delivery boy dressed in brown appeared behind them on the far side of the pew boxes. He was out of breath. He stopped, shifted his package under his arm while he read from a slip of paper. His eyes frantically assessed his surroundings, oblivious to the girls. He removed his cap, wiped his forehead and was off and running again.

"No time for threats, Morgan," Simon said over the headset. "It's showtime."

The monitor flickered and once again Ethan saw Sanada center stage. The clock in the corner showed thirty seconds until the show started.

"You didn't tell me Meredith was going to be inside the church," Gil shouted.

"You didn't need to know."

Gil was on his feet, staring at the monitor that showed Meredith and Miss Seger. He was fuming.

"Sit down, Gil," Simon said. "Do your job. And watch a master at work."

---

Ethan's chest swelled with fury. His hands clenched so tight they hurt. He was so angry he couldn't think.

He fought to regain a measure of control.

Fifteen seconds to showtime.

He thought again of all the Morgans who had gone before him. They were mostly men who had seen combat experience, gone behind enemy lines, fought on the ground and in the sky.

This was Ethan's time. This was Ethan's war.

*Think! Think!*

He thought of the Scripture passage next to his name, Hebrews 8:10. The verse his father had chosen for him.

Ten seconds to showtime.

Ethan pushed back his chair with such force the guard jumped, preparing to stop Ethan from getting to the stairs.

But Ethan went the other direction.

He skirted the edge of the curtain just as a stage tech was saying, "Five seconds to show ... four ..."

Ethan flipped the switch to the chipper.

It rumbled to life.

"… three seconds to show … two …"

Ethan tossed the Morgan family Bible into the blades.

"… one …"

The show started with host Sanada gasping at the chipper as it spewed out bits of Morgan Bible. From the floor speakers came music. John Lennon's song "Imagine."

Ethan raced across the stage and shoved past the astonished host.

The guard stopped him.

"Get out of my way," Ethan shouted. "I've fulfilled one of the two conditions."

The bewildered guard looked to Sanada. The host stood in the lights, his hands flapping helplessly at a loss for words.

Ethan pushed his way past the guard who made no attempt to stop him. He bounded up the stairs, stepping on a crumpled pink book bag with the words *I cannot live without books …*

# TWENTY—THREE

Simon shouted into a microphone.

"What's going on?"

When the sound tech confirmed that Ethan had indeed destroyed the Bible moments before the show started, Simon ripped off the headset.

He quickly recovered.

"That was unfortunate," he said calmly.

Simon watched from the window as Ethan Morgan emerged from the building, ran into the middle of the street and turned in circles, looking … looking …

"Who would have thought the cop would give in so quickly?" Simon said. He turned to Gil. "But didn't I tell you? I told you I could get Ethan Morgan to destroy his own family's Bible. And now—"

He turned toward the window.

Ethan was crossing the street into the park.

"And now he will rush into the church just like he did at St. Paul's, only this time— If there's one thing I've learned about the Morgans, it's that they all think they're heroes. I knew if I put the girl inside the church he'd go after her. Heroes are so predictable." His hands went to his hips. "You have to be a villain to defeat a villain."

He turned to Gil for accolades.

"Morgan has thrown the whole timetable off," Gil said. "The packages aren't in place."

Simon looked out the window just in time to see Ethan take off in a beeline toward the church.

"Get them in place!" Simon shouted, donning his headset, his full attention on the monitors.

---

Ethan bolted into the street with no idea where he was in Boston. He looked every direction for a church and saw nothing. Trees and buildings blocked his view. Unless they had whisked her away in a vehicle, Meredith couldn't be far.

He ran to an open space in a park and saw a steeple rising above the trees. Down an alley, between buildings, he ran, spilling out into a main street.

A sign across the way marked it as Salem Street.

He turned and saw the steeple, and the instant he did, he knew the situation was worse than he'd thought.

The Old North Church stood proudly as it had since 1723, the oldest standing church building in the city.

Ethan broke toward the entrance at a dead run. He wasn't going to let F. Malory Simon do to it what he had done to Notre Dame and St. Paul's.

---

"The first package is in place," Simon said.

He needn't have bothered. Gil could see it as clearly as Simon on the monitor.

Crouched in a corner beneath a stairwell, the blond contestant ripped the matching invoice off the bottom of a step and compared it to his. Satisfied the shipping numbers were identical to the numbers on his package, he looked around for the disposable phone and dialed the number indicated.

Simon took the call.

"Good job, Barrington," he said. "You are the first to reach the target."

On the monitor, Barrington beamed. He was still out of breath.

"But the task isn't complete," Simon said.

Barrington's smile faded.

Simon said, "The package is mine. Not until you hand it to me have you won the competition. You must stay at your post and regardless of what anyone says or does, you must not surrender that package until I arrive, do you understand?"

"Yes, sir."

"Only the tenacious are good enough to work for me, Barrington, those who are not easily distracted from their goals, those who refuse to be deceived."

"I'll not let you down, sir."

"I know you won't, son. I'm looking forward to working with you."

On the screen Barrington punched a button to end the call. His face showed the obstinacy of a bulldog.

"The first package is secure," Simon said. "Where are the other two?"

---

Ethan burst into the Old North Church.

"Clear the building!" he shouted. "There's a bomb!"

That got the attention of the personnel in the lobby and two security guards. Following the bombing of Notre Dame and St. Paul's, high-profile churches around the world had increased security. Ethan was hoping the Old North Church was one of them.

The guards were on him in an instant.

Ethan identified himself. "I'm a San Diego police detective. The same terrorists who bombed Notre Dame and St. Paul's have targeted this facility."

He reached for his badge. It wasn't there. Neither was his gun. His pockets were empty.

"Sir, I'm afraid we're going to need to see—"

"We don't have time for this!" Ethan shouted. "Get these people out of here! You can arrest me later."

Already people in the lobby were screaming and running toward the exits.

"Clear the building!" Ethan shouted. "Go! Go!"

The two guards looked at each other, neither wanting to make the decision. Ethan took advantage of their indecision and bolted for the sanctuary.

One of the guards lunged for him, missed, then decided to let him go. He started barking orders for people to evacuate the building while the other guard shouted orders into his radio.

Ethan called as he ran. "Meredith! Meredith!"

He found her and the brunette standing at the front of the church. Their reactions to his sudden appearance were polar opposites. Meredith was overjoyed. The brunette was ticked.

Ethan yelled to the dozen or so other people in the sanctuary.

"Evacuate the building! There's been a bomb threat!"

It took a moment for the warning to register. When it did, people started running toward the exits.

"Ethan?" Meredith cried, starting toward him.

The brunette caught her by the arm. "Don't listen to him," she said.

"Meredith, you have to get out here."

"What's going on? Where's the Bible?"

Ethan sized up the brunette. He didn't know what she had told Meredith to lure her to the church. Whatever it was, Ethan's presence was punching holes in it.

"No time for that right now," Ethan said to Meredith. "You have to get out here."

"Oh no—" the brunette cried. "She's not going anywhere. She's staying here with me. I've come too far to lose this competition now."

"Competition?" Ethan shouted. "That's what you think this is?"

The brunette clung to Meredith's arm like a drowning woman to a tree limb. "All I have to do is keep her here until Mr. Simon arrives and the position is mine."

"If you stay here, the only position you'll be filling is a drawer at the morgue!"

The brunette didn't yield. Ethan was tempted to break the woman's grip and get Meredith to safety. He had another thought. This woman had information.

"How many are there?" he asked her.

The brunette looked at him suspiciously.

"How many?" he shouted.

Proudly, she said, "I've beat out hundreds. Maybe thousands for this position."

"I mean today. How many today?"

"Finalists?"

"I saw one a short time ago. He was holding a package, dressed as a delivery boy."

The brunette appeared perplexed that he knew about the competition. "There are three other finalists," she said hesitantly.

"All three of them have packages?"

"Yes, but my task was more difficult. I had to deliver a live package."

"Do you know what's in those packages?" Ethan said. "Bombs. Your competition is planting bombs in this church. Simon intends to blow up the building and you along with it."

"Oh, Ethan!" Meredith cried.

"I don't believe you," the brunette said.

---

"How close are the other two?" Simon shouted.

Gil shook his head. "They're in the building. That's all we know."

Simon slammed the flat of his hand on the table. The equipment and the Morgan Bible replica jumped.

"Come on, find the targets, it's not that difficult!" Simon shouted at the monitors.

On one monitor, Barrington crouched in front of his package, ready to defend his position.

The sound of running feet could be heard coming from Barrington's monitor. Then, a voice.

"Evacuate the building! There has been a bomb threat! Evacuate the building!"

Barrington eased back into the recesses of the stairwell. The voice passed him by.

The monitors for the other two target areas showed no movement.

The monitor displaying the main sanctuary showed Miss Seger in animated discussion with Ethan and Meredith.

"We can't wait. We have to blow it now," Gil said.

He reached for the trigger.

Simon smacked his hand away.

"Is that what you did in London? You panicked?" Simon moved the trigger closer to him. "I'll decide when to blow the building. That steeple is coming down."

---

They were running out of time.

Ethan grabbed Meredith by the arm. The brunette stubbornly held on to Meredith's other arm.

"Let go," Ethan shouted. "I'm a cop, and you're holding this woman against her will."

Meredith turned to the brunette. "You lied to me! You lied to get me here. You lied about the Bible and your friend, too, didn't you?"

The brunette offered no defense other than to strengthen her grip.

Meredith shook free from Ethan and rammed the flat of her hand into the brunette's face. The grip broke, and the brunette stumbled backward and fell on her backside.

She touched a finger to her bloodied nose. "That's going too far. Job or no job. I'm suing!"

Ethan grabbed Meredith. He fought the urge to put his arms around her and hold her tight. But he couldn't shield her from a bomb blast. To save her, he had to let her go.

"Run," he told her. "I'm going to try to find the bombs."

With one last longing glance, he turned to go. She pulled him back.

"There's three of them," Meredith said. "One of them went through that door. I'll go after him."

"No," Ethan cried. "Find a security guard. Tell him. And then get out of here."

Meredith shook her head. "I can do it."

"I can't let you do it."

Meredith looked him in the eye. "When are you going to get it through that thick head of yours—we're Morgans. This is what we do."

---

"Ha! Did you see that punch!" Gil exclaimed. "That'll give your Miss Seger a fat lip for a month!"

Simon scowled. "I fail to see the humor in this."

Ethan and Meredith had parted ways, leaving the brunette on the floor to nurse her bloodied nose.

Two target monitors still showed no activity.

"What's keeping them?" Simon shouted.

He was standing now. Pacing.

On the stairwell monitor, the blond reacted to the sound of someone approaching.

"Delivery guy!"

It was a female's voice. Meredith's.

"I know you're here somewhere."

Simon focused on the stairwell monitor. "Stay where you are," he coached.

"Delivery guy! Come on, where are you?"

"Stay where you are."

"Mr. Simon sent me," Meredith said.

The blond cocked his head in thought.

"Stay where you are," Simon said to the monitor.

The blond crawled out from beneath the stairwell. He was no longer on camera, but the microphone picked up voices.

Simon slapped the table again. "Can't anybody follow instructions?" he shouted.

"The package is still in place," Gil said.

"But for how long?"

There was movement on one of the other two monitors.

"We have another delivery," Gil said. "West wall closet."

The back of one of the contestant's head could be seen on camera. Then, a hand reaching for the delivery slip to compare shipping numbers.

Simon was nodding.

"Two out of three packages in place," Gil said. "Let's count ourselves lucky. Push the button."

"No," Simon said.

The arrival of the second package pacified him for the moment. He took his seat.

"I want the steeple."

"What good is the steeple if Morgan and the girl survive? They can connect us to the bombing. I say blow it now!"

Simon shook his head. "That's the difference between you and me, Gil. Always has been. I play in the pros. You've always stood on the sidelines and watched. I want that steeple."

# TWENTY-FOUR

Meredith nearly walked past him. She had a foot on the stairs. His appearance from under the stairwell startled her.

"I was sent to get you," she told him.

He grinned at her. "Nice try. Won't work."

"I'm serious. Get your package and let's get out of here."

He made an unconscious glance in the direction of the stairwell.

"The only person I'll hand that package to is Mr. Simon."

Meredith stood directly in front of him. If this got physical, he had the advantage. Somehow, she had to convince him.

"Look, delivery guy," she said, "I know what's in that package, and believe me, I'd love to see you hand it to F. Malory Simon, but that's not going to happen."

"Trust me, it is going to happen."

"Haven't you heard people yelling?" Meredith cried. "This church is being evacuated! Haven't you been watching the news? Churches are being bombed and this one's next!"

The blond chuckled. "There is nothing that is going to move me from this spot."

The next thing Meredith knew she'd been grabbed from behind, her arms pinned to her sides.

Miss Seger's mouth was right next to Meredith's ear. "You're coming back with me," she said.

"Seger! What are you doing here?" the blond shouted.

"Winning this competition, Barrington. Now stay out of my way!"

Miss Seger was stronger than she looked. Meredith tried to break the hold on her but couldn't.

She appealed to the blond. "Do you know what's in your package? A bomb!"

The sudden appearance of Miss Seger rattled the delivery guy. He wasn't as certain about things as he had been a second ago.

"You have to believe me!" Meredith shouted.

Miss Seger was dragging her backward. Meredith's heels scraped the wooden floor. She had no traction and lost all leverage.

"Delivery guy!" Meredith shouted. "If Seger gets me back to the front of the sanctuary, she wins the competition!"

That he understood.

With a roar, the blond plowed into both of them, sending all three crashing to the floor. The delivery guy used his strength to pin Miss Seger down. Meredith was free.

She scrambled beneath the stairwell for the package, reaching at the same time into her pocket for her nail clippers. It was all she had to open it.

It was Ethan's guess that the bombs were some kind of plastic explosive. In the other churches the explosions were simultaneous, so they were probably detonated off site, not by timers. And with the delivery guys jostling them, they had to be fairly stable.

He told her what to look for. If she saw any sign of a wire on the outside of the package, near a seal or bulging under tape, she was to walk away. It was booby-trapped. But if she saw no wires, she could open the package. Wires would connect a battery to a detonator cap in the explosive. She was to clip the wires and then get out.

While Miss Seger and the delivery guy wrestled on the ground, Meredith crawled under the stairwell. She saw the package.

---

"Trouble," Gil said.

Meredith could be seen reaching for the package. At the same time, on the wall-closet monitor the entire image shook as Ethan Morgan tackled the other contestant as he was reaching for the disposable cell phone.

The two men wrestled. It was over before it began. With a punch to the jaw, Ethan knocked the contestant unconscious.

"Time's up," Gil said. "Now, you have no choice."

Simon stared at the monitors. He said nothing.

"Time's up!" Gil shouted. "Push the button!"

Simon's focus bounced back and forth from one monitor to the other. The third target monitor, the steeple, showed no activity.

Simon gripped the trigger. His thumb hovered over the button.

"Come on, come on …" he said, sounding like he was urging on a horse at the racetrack. "Anything. Give me anything. A shadow. Anything!"

With surprising speed, Ethan ripped open the package and disconnected the wires to the explosive.

---

The package was within reach, and just when Meredith thought she had it, someone grabbed her by the ankles and pulled her back.

The blond delivery guy. His face was red with rage.

"No!" she pleaded. "Don't do this!"

He wasn't listening. He was dragging her backward out of the stairwell.

"I'm sorry," Meredith said to him. "But you're giving me no choice."

Yanking one foot free, she kicked him hard. The sound of his nose breaking was sickening. He let go.

While he howled in pain, Meredith grabbed the package.

In the dim light she looked it over carefully. Too carefully, she feared. She expected it to blow up in her face at any second. But if it did, she wanted it to be Simon's doing, not hers.

When she saw no wires, she slit the packing tape on one end of the box. Pulling down the cardboard flap, she saw two wires. She clipped them.

Nothing happened. The wires dangled harmlessly. She'd done it. It was over.

Meredith closed her eyes and cried.

She showed the bomb inside the box to Miss Seger and the blond delivery guy—both of them covered with their own blood.

Their eyes grew wide with alarm. They clawed at each other to get out of the church.

Meredith placed the package on the stairs and followed them, praying that Ethan was having similar success.

------

The stairwell monitor and the wall closet monitor showed no activity. The packages had been removed, possibly disarmed.

"They may still be active," Gil argued. "Push the button, let's see what happens."

Simon removed his hand from the trigger and sat back.

"You don't get it, do you?" he sneered. "It's not the building, it's the symbol. It doesn't do us any good just to blow a hole in the back of a church."

Simon's anger welled. He violently stood up. His face was redder than Gil had ever seen it.

"We have to bring the steeple down!" Simon bellowed.

He stared at the floor, reining in his emotions. When he spoke again, his tone was civil.

"Of the three packages, the steeple closet is the most vital. We'll wait. The moment it's delivered, I'll push the button."

"And if it's not delivered?"

Apparently, Simon had already given this some thought. His answer was immediate. "We back away and come after it again later."

"The contestants?"

"Contact your spotters. Implement the backup. I want them dead before they can talk to anyone."

Gil nodded. His spotters served a double purpose. Not only were they to report on the progress of the contestants in the field, but should any of the contestants exhibit unacceptable behavior—such as attempting to open one of the packages—the spotter was to take him out of the game. Permanently.

Gil walked to a corner to make the call so as not to distract Simon. Pressing his cell phone to his ear, he gave the order for the spotters to find the three contestants and take them out.

Gil Getz spoke into a dead phone. He'd dialed the number, but he'd never pressed the Send button.

He closed his cell phone and turned back into the room.

"What about Morgan and the girl?" he asked.

Simon nodded. "I'll take care of them." He pulled out his cell phone and opened it. He dialed a number and as he was lifting it to his ear, Gil snatched the phone out of Simon's hand.

"I can't let you do that," Gil said.

———

Ethan had to trust that Meredith disabled the blond guy's bomb and that she was out of the building. He wanted to check on her to make sure. But there wasn't time. He had to go after the third bomb.

But where?

These guys weren't just walking into a church randomly. They were given specific instructions for strategic placements.

Meredith had gone to the east side of the building. Ethan had found the second bomb on the west side of the building. That left—

"North and south," Ethan said to himself, "or possibly a central wall, or the basement, or—yes! That's it!"

Ethan ran toward the steeple.

---

"What are you doing?" Simon shouted. "Give me back my phone."

Gil closed it and tossed it across the room.

Simon eyed him knowingly. "The Cooper woman. It wasn't like you to stay a couple of extra days."

"It's over, Simon," Gil said.

Movement on the steeple monitor caught their attention. The door to the closet opened. The third contestant fell against the wall and slumped to the floor, his chest heaving from the climb up the stairway.

Simon grinned.

A voice was heard on the monitor.

Ethan Morgan.

"Son, hand me that package."

Simon's grin widened. He would get Morgan after all.

"You have to trust your instincts, Gil," Simon said with an air of superiority. He reached for the trigger. "The same instincts that told me I could get Morgan to throw his family's Bible into a chipper told me that I could lure him to the church. Instincts separate winners from losers, Gil. Instincts."

JACK CAVANAUGH

"I lost him," the guard said. "I don't like it. Why would a delivery driver run?"

"Where did you lose him?" a second guard asked.

"Visitor Services."

"Okay. Work your way toward the offices. I'll double back to the entrance."

They were going the wrong way. Ethan didn't have time to correct them. He sprinted toward the steeple stairs.

Just as they came in sight he caught a glimpse of shoes disappearing up the stairway. He yelled and gave chase.

The first floor was clear. As was the second. On the third floor, halfway down a hallway Ethan saw a breathless delivery boy with a package under his arm open a closet door and lunge inside.

Ethan reached the door just as it was being closed. He grabbed the handle, jerked it open, and stood over a startled delivery boy.

He said, "Son, hand me that package."

———————————

Gil Getz slugged his boss before Simon could press the button.

Simon tumbled out of his chair to the floor.

"Game's over, Simon."

Looking up from the floor, Simon rubbed his jaw. "What did that Cooper woman do to you?" he said.

"It's what you did to her."

Simon shook his head slowly. "I told you, I had nothing to do with that."

"I don't believe you."

Simon shrugged. "So it's come to this, has it?"

"Yeah, I guess it has."

"All right. But there's something you need to know."

He kicked the chair into Gil, knocking him backward.

"It's not over until I say it's over."

———————

"Do you know what's going on here, son?" Ethan said.

"Yeah. I'm proving that I'm good enough to work with the best."

"The only thing you're proving is that you're a fool."

The boy didn't like that.

"You've been duped, son. F. Malory Simon has demolished two churches and he's using you to destroy the third. Think! Why would anyone have you deliver a package to a hall closet? That's a bomb you're carrying. Now, hand it over!"

———————

Gil struggled to get to his feet.

Simon was faster. He picked up the chair, hefted it over his head, and threw it at Gil.

The caster slammed the floor inches from Gil's head. He rolled to escape the blow. But a second caster jabbed him in the kidneys. Nothing fatal, but enough to give Simon time to get to the trigger. He checked the monitor before pushing the button.

The back of Ethan Morgan's head blocked his view.

———————

With one hand the boy clutched the package to his chest, with the other he attempted to push himself off the floor.

"Don't say I didn't ask," Ethan said.

He grabbed a mop from the corner. With one motion, he swept the boy's feet from under him. With another, he twirled the handle around and jabbed it into the hollow of the boy's throat, enough to make it difficult for him to breathe.

Apparently, the boy understood the situation now. He held the package up to Ethan.

Tossing the mop aside, Ethan sliced the end of the package open.

Wrong end.

There were no wires at this end.

He turned it over. The packing tape was double thick on this side.

---

His eyes fixed on the steeple of the Old North Church, F. Malory Simon pushed the button.

Nothing happened.

He pushed it again.

Still nothing.

From the floor Gil closed his eyes and smiled.

Simon threw the trigger device against the monitor, as onscreen, Ethan Morgan shifted the package under his arm and helped the boy up. The end of the package was open. Cut wires hung uselessly in the direction of the camera.

Gil righted the chair and sat in it.

"I hold you responsible for this," Simon said.

"It doesn't matter. Nothing matters anymore."

"You've changed," Simon said.

"Yeah. I guess I have. You're still predictable."

Simon took exception to that.

"You don't believe me?" Gil said. "I knew if I told you to blow the building, you wouldn't do it. I knew the harder I pressed, the more you would resist. You always think you know better. You always have to do things your way. So if anyone's to blame for today, it's you. I outwitted you."

Simon walked to the Morgan Bible. He placed a hand on it. "I suppose you switched Bibles, too. Is this the authentic one?"

Gil smiled. "Look for yourself."

Simon turned the Bible over. He stared into the gash and read aloud what he saw, "Judas."

Turning it over, a strange expression came over him. He lifted the front cover to see explosives nestled among the pages.

Gil held a triggering device in his hand.

"Say good night, Simon."

With a roar Simon threw the Bible-bomb at Gil, knocking the trigger from his hand. It skittered across the hardwood floor. Both men lunged for it.

# TWENTY—FIVE

"I think that's all of them," Ethan said, handing the package with the explosives to a member of the Boston demolitions team.

A lieutenant approached him. "You're going to have to come with us to headquarters, Detective," he said.

Ethan nodded. It was a familiar tune.

He stepped outside the Old North Church to see that a perimeter had been set up. A crowd five- and six-people deep stood behind the barricades looking anxiously at the historic church.

"They don't realize how close they came to losing her today," the lieutenant said.

On the street, patrolmen loaded the three delivery guys and Miss Seger into a couple of squad cars. They were squawking like a quartet of frightened chickens.

Ethan had informed the lieutenant about the studio and Sanada.

The lieutenant said he'd send a patrol car over to investigate.

Ethan spotted Meredith standing behind the barricades.

"Lieutenant, can you give me a minute?"

Even from a distance he could see her face was tearstained.

"Everything's all right. They're taking me downtown," Ethan told her from midstreet.

"I'll follow you," she said.

He continued toward her, moving the barrier aside; he didn't stop until he had his arms around her. He buried his head against her neck.

"I thought I was going to lose you today," he said.

He didn't want to let go. He never wanted to let go.

"It's about time you came to your senses," she said.

For several timeless moments there was no crowd, no church, no Boston. Just the two of them.

When Ethan finally found the strength to step back, he didn't go far. With his arm around her, they took in the sight of the Old North Church.

"We were Morgans today," Meredith said.

"Yeah, we were, weren't we?" Ethan said. He laughed. "I pity our great-grandchildren."

"Why is that?"

"It's going to be hard to live up to our story."

Meredith grinned. "You and Drew Morgan, huh?"

"Something like that."

"Wait a minute. *Our* great-grandchildren?"

Ethan kissed her. Then kissed her again. He didn't care that people were watching. Ooooing. Clapping.

She pulled away. "Ethan, what about the Morgan Bible?"

An enormous blast punctuated her sentence. People screamed. Ducked. Shielded their faces.

But the blast was a block away. What had once been the fifth floor of a long redbrick building was nothing but a gaping hole.

# EPILOGUE

"I was wrong," Ethan said.

He stood before twenty of their closest friends, gathered to celebrate his birthday in their backyard. Meredith's idea.

They'd been married nearly a year now. Meredith sat in a lawn chair, radiant in the summer sun, her arm draped across her abdomen. Her pregnancy evident to all.

Ethan chose this day to put into words what had been on his mind ever since that day in Boston when he shredded the Morgan family Bible.

"I had always thought that carrying the family spiritual heritage was a burden. It took my brother and Meredith to make me realize that it's a privilege."

He lifted his glass of punch in salute to his wife.

"As I sat in that basement with my family's Bible in my lap, and as

I read down the list of names, I felt like such a failure. It wasn't a new feeling. All my life I've struggled to live up to the example of my younger brother, Sky.

"But on that day I was certain I had failed. One by one, I read their names, the dates, and the Scripture references, coming to the last one on the list: my name. The date—the year 2000—testified against me. My father had such high expectations that I would carry the Morgan standard into a new millennium.

"Then I read the Scripture reference. Hebrews 8:10. I remembered what it said. And everything changed."

Emotion born of memory necessitated a pause. When Ethan was able to speak again, he quoted the passage.

"'I will put my laws in their minds and write them on their hearts. I will be their God, and they will be my people.'

"At that moment the error under which I had been laboring all my life was lifted. For the first time I understood that my family's heritage did not reside in a printed book, no matter how old it was, or how illustrious. What had been passed down from generation to generation was here—"

Ethan placed a hand against his chest.

"And here—"

He placed a hand on Meredith's heart.

"And here—"

He placed a hand on her swollen stomach.

"A family's true spiritual heritage is not printed on a page but written on their hearts. And when I saw Meredith on the monitor, I realized that the spiritual future of the Morgans was in her, not the book on my lap."

Ethan walked over to a table of birthday gifts. He took from it a present he himself had wrapped. He handed it to Meredith.

"For me? But it's *your* birthday," she said.

"It's for us. Open it."

She did. It was a new family Bible. She lifted the cover and printed inside was a list of the Morgans going all the way back to Drew Morgan.

"A worthy successor," she said.

After embracing his wife, Ethan Morgan stood in front of his guests and said, "It is customary when the Bible is handed to the next generation for someone to recite the history of the Morgan clan. And someday, I hope to do that with my son in Edenford, England. But for today, to christen the new Morgan Bible, I'm going to practice on you."

Ethan Morgan stood before his wife, unborn child, and friends, mindful that he was the only surviving Morgan male directly descended from its founder. The thought no longer frightened him. He was proud to be a Morgan. The roots to his past gave him strength.

He began—

"The story of Drew Morgan begins at Windsor Castle," he said, "on the day he met Bishop Laud. For it was on that day his life began its downward direction …"

That night Ethan and Meredith Morgan lay in bed talking into the early hours of the morning, neither wanting the day to end.

"If I don't get some sleep I'm going to be worthless tomorrow," Meredith said.

"Yeah. But it's been a good day, hasn't it?"

She snuggled close to him and kissed his cheek. "A very good day. Good night, dear."

"Good night."

Meredith turned over and pulled the covers to her chin. She turned back to the ceiling, she said, "Good night, Andrew!"

"That's not funny," Ethan said.

But it got them both to giggling and another hour passed before they finally fell asleep.

## ... a little more ...

When a delightful concert comes to an end,

the orchestra might offer an encore.

When a fine meal comes to an end,

it's always nice to savor a bit of dessert.

When a great story comes to an end,

we think you may want to linger.

And so, we offer ...

**AfterWords**—just a little something more after you

have finished a David C. Cook novel.

We invite you to stay awhile in the story.

Thanks for reading!


Turn the page for ...


- **Discussion Questions**
- **An American Family Portrait**
- **Author Interview**

# Discussion Questions

Gather some friends together after reading *The Guardians* to talk about the themes and characters in the book. Use these questions to spark a lively discussion.

What's your initial reaction to the main characters in the story? What did you like about them? What did you dislike?

What intrigued you most about the scenes depicted in the grade school play? (The play is based on books in the American Family Portrait series. Read on for more information about these novels.)

Why didn't Andrew tell the attacker he wasn't Ethan? What would you have done in a similar circumstance?

What did you learn about Ethan from the way he interacted with the other police officers?

How did Ethan's relationship with Meredith shift over the course of the story? What prompted that change?

What were some of Ethan's greatest areas of personal growth? Meredith's?

How was Ethan affected by his confrontation with Corby years earlier? How did that confrontation impact the way he did his job in the current-time storyline?

Respond to this quote from Ethan: "We're no longer a race of builders. We're destroyers."

What surprised you most about Meredith? Why?

Describe your first thoughts about F. Malory Simon. How did those first impressions change over the course of the novel?

What frightened you most about Simon and his plans?

What are examples in real life of the sort of power wielded by Simon and his team?

Describe at least two examples of redemption in this novel.

What role does faith play in the lives of the main characters? In what ways do faith and family intersect in *The Guardians*?

What story element made you most uncomfortable? What made you want to stand up and cheer?

Which character had the most dramatic change over the course of the story? The least? How is their growth like change in real life?

Describe acts of heroism in the story. Acts of cowardice.

What kind of sacrifices did the main characters have to make in this story? What does that tell you about their character?

Which character did you relate to most? Least?

What does this story (and the series that precedes this novel) say about the importance of our spiritual heritage?

# An American Family Portrait

The rich history of the Morgan Bible is chronicled in the book series An American Family Portrait. Though a stand-alone book, *The Guardians* does reference story elements in a number of these earlier books. Here's a brief summary of those direct connections.

Chapter 1 of *The Guardians* introduces the Morgan family story through the school play. The prelude to the telling of the Morgan family history appears in the final chapter of all eight books in the American Family Portrait series during a ceremony in which the Morgan family Bible is presented to the succeeding generation. Of course, the Morgan family Bible itself appears several times in each book.

Chapter 2 of *The Guardians* includes a number of references to the other books. The story about Drew Morgan and the medieval suits of armor at Windsor Castle comes from chapter 1 of *The Puritans*. The cornfield scene featuring the colonist (Philip Morgan) and the Indian maid (Weetamoo) comes from chapter 16 of *The Colonists*. And the gash in the Morgan Bible made by flak over Germany comes from chapter 15 of *The Victors*.

In chapter 3 of *The Guardians*, the scene featuring the Revolutionary War prison cell, colonial Jacob and British sympathizer Esau come from chapter 26 of *The Patriots*.

The scene where Drew Morgan enters Edenford, England—which becomes the setting for a portion of *The Guardians* (beginning in chapter 11)—comes from chapters 17 and 21 of *The Puritans*.

And in chapter 15 of *The Guardians*, the referenced code Andrew used on his cell phone comes directly from chapter 7 and on through the end of *The Puritans*.

---

*Want more adventures of the Morgan Bible? Be sure to check out all of the books in An American Family Portrait. To whet your appetite, here's a sample chapter from* The Victors.

### Excerpt from *The Victors* by Jack Cavanaugh

# 15

German Focke-Wulfs swarmed. No longer gnats. The *California Angel* was in the middle of a hornet's nest.

Overlaying shouts and whoops and warnings jammed the intercom.

Walt had been told it would be impossible to maintain intercom discipline during an attack. An understatement.

The best he could do was sort out any messages directed at him.

"This is Geller. We're over the Friesian Isles."

"Roger that."

Walt glanced at his copilot who was looking down for a visual confirmation. Keating's distinctively thin mustache twitched to an allegro tempo.

*Combat will be nothing like training.*

Another understatement. Walt wondered how many more understatements he would discover today.

The noise alone was chaotic. Intercom shouts. Roaring engines. Whining interceptors. Bursts of gunfire. Squadron radio traffic. Crew reports.

Walt's job was to keep the aircraft in tight. Maintaining the formation was their best defense. Stragglers were easily picked off as enemy fighters converged on them for the kill.

In front of them and above a plane was hit in the wing. First one engine caught fire. Then the second. The wing buckled and the plane did a slow starboard roll as it fell out of formation, directly into the *California Angel's* flight path!

Walt hit the rudder and banked hard to avoid hitting it.

Everything played out in front of him like it does on the movie screen. A plane going down trailing black smoke. Men appearing in the hatches and jumping. Falling with the plane. Some of their chutes opened. Some didn't.

It was hard to believe it was real.

But reality returned soon enough. By evading the crippled aircraft, the *California Angel* had been pulled out of formation. There was open airspace all around them.

They were a sitting duck for the German interceptors.

"Get us back up there!" Keating shouted. His voice was a high-pitched squeal.

Above them the squadron droned in a relentless line toward the target as though nothing unusual had happened. They were on their own. No one would come to rescue them.

"Get us back! Get us back!" Keating shouted.

Three enemy interceptors swooped toward them, positioning themselves for a pass. Two approached from nine o'clock high, the other from twelve o'clock high.

They were trying to keep the *California Angel* from rejoining the pack, to force Walt to bank right and low. Instead, he gave the engines full throttle and pulled up, left.

"What are you doing?" shouted Keating. "You're taking us right into their line of fire!"

Ahead of them white flashes appeared on the wings of the Focke-Wulf. The gunner was firing.

"We're hit! We're hit!" Northrop shouted.

"We're hit!" Keating echoed.

"I heard him!" Walt shouted, straining to pull the nose up.

"The two on this side are breaking off!" Jankowski shouted.

The interceptor in front of them likewise pulled up and away to avoid a collision. Walt eased the aircraft back into position in the formation.

Whoops of congratulations and relief sounded over the intercom.

"Attaboy, Lieutenant!"

"And how!"

"Well, if that don't take the cake!"

"Swell flyin', Lieutenant."

"We're not outta this yet," Walt said. "We've still got a job to do. What's the damage back there?"

"Some hits in the rear fuselage," Jankowski said. "Nothin' major."

"Any injuries?"

None were reported.

"Sabala. Are you still with us?"

No response.

"Jankowski!" Walt shouted. "See if Sabala's hit!"

A mousy voice replied, "I'm not hit, Lieutenant."

"You answer up sooner, do you hear me, son?"

"Yes, sir."

"You had me worried."

Silence.

"I know you've had a rough time of it, son, but we're going to make it through this if we stick together. We need you. As far as I'm concerned, you're the only real veteran we have onboard."

"This is my first combat mission, sir."

"Sabala, as far as I'm concerned, anyone who's gone through what you've gone through and is still man enough to stick it out, qualifies as a veteran in my book."

A pause and then a very weak, "Thank you, sir."

"Sabala," Jankowski said. "What did you go through?"

"Dummy up, Jankowski," Walt said. "This isn't the time. You keep your mind on keeping those Focke-Wulfs off our side."

"Yes, sir." Muffled, Walt heard him say, "Otis, do you know what Sabala's done?"

A black cloud loomed directly in their path. It looked like a storm cloud. It wasn't. Walt would have welcomed a black storm cloud over this.

Flak.

A storm cloud with teeth. A half mile deep. Directly over the target.

In training Walt had learned that once the enemy fighters break off their attack, he could expect to encounter flak resistance.

The enemy fighters must have missed that briefing. As the *California Angel* entered the field of flak, the fighters followed them in.

They really don't want us doing this, Walt muttered to himself.

The turbulence increased remarkably, tossing the craft about like a cork at sea. The smoke from the flak was so thick it darkened the sun.

"How are we doing, Upchurch?" Walt shouted.

The bay doors swung open.

"Coming up on the target," the bombardier replied.

Another B-17 went down. Blasted clean out of the sky. Direct hit. One moment it was flying along, the next it was a fiery comet streaking to earth.

There was nothing the pilot could have done. So much depended upon luck, or lack of it. And Walt knew there was nothing he could do to escape a similar fate. No amount of skill or intelligence could save him. All he could do was keep his plane on course. And trust God.

They were directly over the target.

"You're on, Upchurch! Let's make this little trip count for something."

All around them bombers began releasing their payloads. It looked like each aircraft was trailing a deadly string of pearls.

Beneath them plumes of fire and smoke appeared, covering what had been a pattern of streets and buildings.

"Yeeeehaawwww!" Upchurch shouted.

"Is that your official report?" Walt asked, grinning.

"Yes, sir!" Upchurch shouted. "We got it! We nailed 'em!"

"Then let's get out of here!"

An explosion beneath them lifted the plane nearly into the formation above them. Walt felt like he'd been kicked in the backside with a huge metal boot. It lifted him out of his seat with such force that his seat belts felt like they were cutting into him.

Dazed, he increased the distance between them and the plane above.

"You all right?" Walt asked his copilot who was rolling his head about.

"That was close," Keating said woozily.

"Everyone all right?" Walt said into the intercom.

"You gotta watch out for those big bumps in the road, Lieutenant," Jankowski said. "Otis hit his head. A pretty nasty cut, but he's all right."

"Sabala?"

"Here, sir. I'm fine."

"Good boy. We're heading home. You protect our rear, understand?"

"Yes, sir."

Walt brought the plane around to the heading Geller had given him.

He was relieved when the skies cleared and they left the flak behind. But the Focke-Wulf fighters refused to leave them alone.

"Owwwwww!"

The howl that came over the intercom sounded like a wounded dog.

"Who is that? Who's hit?" Walt yelled.

"Jankowski?"

"Not us, Lieutenant."

"Fargo?"

"I'm swimming in casings, but otherwise fine, sir."

"Sabala?"

"It was me, sir!" Sabala cried. "I got one! I got myself a Boche!"

"There's one goin' down, that's for sure," Northrop said.

"Well, I'll be! Attaboy, Sabala!" Jankowski added.

"Congratulations, Sergeant," Walt said. "But we're not out of the woods yet."

"Yes, sir," Sabala said. The men could hear that he was beaming by the sound of his voice.

"And Sabala?"

"Sir?"

"Don't scare me like that again."

---

The green fields of England, which had become monotonous landscape during training, never looked so inviting as the formation's shadow crossed over them.

One by one, the B-17s landed at Bassingbourn, to the cheers and hat-waving of the assembled officers manning the two-story control tower.

Even the postflight checklist was a pleasure to perform. It was a procedure reserved for the survivors. Walt ran through the list with Keating, who was somewhat reserved. Keating read the list, Walt performed the check.

"Hydraulic pressure."

"OK."

"Cowl flaps."

"Open and locked."

"Turbos."

"Off."

"Booster pumps."

"Off."

"Wing flaps."

"Up."

"Tailwheel."

"Unlocked."

"Generators."

"Off."

Keating tossed the list aside.

"Well, we made it," Walt said. "There's one down at least."

With a grunt, Keating unstrapped and climbed out of the plane.

Walt unstrapped himself and urged weary limbs to support his weight. As he turned to leave, he spotted the leather pouch on his seat. Through all the action, he'd forgotten about it.

When he grabbed it, the pouch acted as though it was glued to the seat. He pulled. It wouldn't give.

What in the world?

With two hands he pulled at the pouch, this time straining. He heard a ripping sound, so he stopped. Exploring with his hands around the edges of the pouch, he discovered that whatever was holding it down was in the middle.

After a time he managed to work the pouch free. He turned it over. What he saw sent a jagged chill through his heart.

The rest of the crew was surveying the damage to the plane when Walt emerged from the hatch.

"We took a few in the fuselage," Jankowski said, pointing to the holes. "And a few in the wing."

"Lieutenant Morgan, is something wrong?"

It was Sabala who noticed that Walt seemed a bit unsteady. The boy was cradling his can again.

"Lieutenant?"

Walt managed a smile. He realized he was clutching the leather pouch with cold, trembling fingers.

Everyone gathered around him. Walt thought he must look more shaken than he felt.

"Remember the Bible I took onboard?"

"The one you was sittin' on?" Jankowski asked.

"It's in here." Walt held up the pouch. Then, he turned it over.

Eyes widened as big as saucers. Mouths gaped.

The object of their fascination was a six-inch piece of flak that had embedded itself in the Bible. Had the Bible not been where it was, the flak would have passed through Walt Morgan.

"I thought he was a holy man," Sabala said. "Now I know it for sure. God saved him with his Word."

After everyone had a chance to look at the flak-impaled Bible, Jankowski noticed again the can the tail gunner was carrying.

"You gonna tell us what's in that can?" he asked.

A boyish grin formed on Sabala's face. "I was saving it for our cele- bration," he said. "For when we got back from our first mission."

It was the first time Walt had seen Sabala smile. The kid had a grin that was infectious.

"I didn't realize we'd have so much to celebrate, what with God sav- ing the lieutenant's life and all."

"And your kill!" Jankowski said.

The grin grew even wider.

"So what's in the can?" Northrop asked.

"Here, you'll need these." Digging in his pockets, Sabala pulled out spoons and handed them to each of his fellow crew members. With a sheepish shrug he looked at Walt. "I swiped them from the mess tent. But I'll return them as soon as we're done."

"Done with what?" Jankowski cried.

Sabala pried open the can lid with everyone crowding around to get a look inside.

"Ice cream?" Fargo shouted.

Sabala beamed. "I got to thinking about how rough the ride was in the tail and how cold it got. I thought that riding in the tail had to be good for something. So I put the mixin's in the can and added some strawberries. After all we've been through today, it should just about be ready."

Walt gave the boy a thumbs-up sign. "Pretty ingenious, Sabala. Pretty ingenious."

That night while the various crews rode into Cambridge to celebrate, Walt chose instead to spend a quiet evening in his room.

It wasn't that he wasn't in a celebratory mood, he just preferred being alone for a while. He especially enjoyed the quiet.

He wrote a letter to his parents about the Bible, apologizing for taking it with him in the first place. He had never really taken into consideration that the Bible could be destroyed, that if his plane had gone down, the Morgan family heritage would have gone down with it.

After finishing the letter, he carefully removed the jagged piece of metal from the back of the Bible. For a long time he looked at it. Then, laying it aside, he opened the Bible and read.

It wasn't until the early morning hours that he found what he was looking for. He underlined the passage in the Bible. Then, he took a piece of paper. He wanted to write down the passage so he could carry it with him.

Copying word for word, he wrote:

"He shall cover thee with his feathers, and under his wings shalt thou trust: his truth shall be thy shield" (Psalm 91:4).

# Author Interview

**What was the original inspiration for *The Guardians*?**

The desire to bring the Morgan family into the present day. I thought it would be an interesting challenge to write about two brothers who had to live in the shadow of a legendary spiritual ancestor. Would they be proud to be the descendants of Drew Morgan, or would his 380-year-old legend intimidate them?

**Though *The Guardians* is a stand-alone book, it features familiar characters from your American Family Portrait series. What has intrigued you most about this family over the years?**

That while customs and technology change, spiritual challenges remain the same. It intrigues me when modern-day believers are of the opinion that present-day spiritual challenges are unique. We can learn a great deal from those who have gone before us.

**What sort of research did you do as you wrote this novel?**

Even though this story is set in the present day, I did as much research for it as I do for my historical novels. I researched settings, businesses, careers, and of course did extensive character studies so that the story and characters would ring true.

**How do you approach the writing of a novel? Do you map out the story first, or do you follow an idea and see where it takes you, or some combination of the two?**

I do a lot of prewriting—thinking through the structure of the story, examining the roles of each of the characters, and general background reading of the professions and places. Then I pull it all together on a storyboard. Once I'm satisfied I have a story worth telling, I start writing scenes, usually starting at the beginning, but there have been times I've written the climax scene first.

**As *The Guardians* took shape, what surprised you most about the characters or storyline?**

I'd give away too much of the story if I answered this question. So I'll simply reply by saying that a writer's characters are constantly surprising him by what they do. I know that sounds strange, but anyone who has written fiction knows it to be true.

**How would you describe the role of faith in *The Guardians*? The role of family?**

As in the American Family Portrait series, family and faith are the hub around which the story conflict turns. I believe that in every person's